ROBERT A. WRIGHT

Robert A. Wright

Printed by CreateSpace, an Amazon.com Company

Robert A. Wright
www.robert-wright-books.com

ISBN: 1456563432
ISBN-13: 9781456563431
Library of Congress Control Number: 2011901129

This book is dedicated to the thousands of courageous individuals throughout the world, especially in Europe and the Americas, who during the period 1914–1945 not only lived through perhaps the worst man-made cataclysm ever experienced but dared to question authority and tried to shape the outcomes of their smaller world to avoid the larger tragedies.

Although this is a work of fiction, I hope I have portrayed how exceptional individuals could have survived two world wars and the Spanish Civil War, while in some way contributing to the future global framework under which we live today, in an era before the jet airplane and the Internet.

Introduction and Acknowledgements

* * *

I have always been intrigued by history and who might have really driven key historical events. By writing and reading historical fiction, we are able to speculate on such matters and in some way contribute to the dialogue and revelations about past events—and perhaps offer some insights into current events and challenges.

As my first foray into historical fiction, Beyond Ultra covers a familiar period, 1915–1945, yet explores decidedly less familiar venues and events. German colonies in Africa are certainly a historical footnote for most of us and the Spanish Civil War may be also, unless of course you are a Spaniard. Similarly, other events that I have used to tell this story may have slipped into the dustbin of real history, yet at the time they influenced larger events and outcomes.

The research I conducted to support the writing of this novel was mostly through passive means and through extensive review of various electronic and paper publications. I am indebted, however, to Stanley G. Payne, professor emeritus, University of Wisconsin-Madison, for meeting with me to discuss various aspects of the Spanish Civil War and the Franco regime. As one of the world's foremost authorities on this subject, he enlightened me on the complexities regarding this period, and this allowed me to present my fictional material in a more accurate historical context than the previous conventional wisdom would allow.

I would not have been able to get this far without professional support and encouragement from friends and family. I would like to thank CreateSpace and Amazon.com for providing the means to publish this work. My early manuscript version was vastly improved, thanks to editorial support from a very skilled local writer and friend, Nancy Canyon. I also thank "first reader" Annie Crabtree, since it must have been painful to read that unpolished effort. I also am grateful to Mary Lynne and Don Derrington for reading a later and hopefully more readable version of the manuscript. I also was encouraged by discussions with neighbors Jack Kurtz and Herman Schweizer. Our "bull" sessions and oral rewriting of history enabled me to think outside the box and question the conventional wisdom. In Jack's honor, I bestowed his name on one of my leading characters. Similarly, good friend and former aviation colleague Ken McNamara encouraged me to look beyond the conventional story we are usually spoon-fed and seek a greater truth.

Most of all, I would like to acknowledge the support, love, and encouragement of my wife, Marcia Corey. She patiently and willingly encouraged my dream and urged me to find my inner creativity that did not otherwise assert itself in a lifelong career in aviation. Marci, I thank you from the bottom of my heart.

Bellingham, Washington
January 2011

Book One

* * *

A New World

Part I

* * *

Escape

1915–1920

1915 ~ The world in flames

* * *

By late 1915, the world had been at war for more than a year. The cherished illusions regarding "civilized" warfare had been shattered by technology and trench warfare in Western Europe, by the submarine at sea, and by the airplane. Millions had already died and millions more would die in the widening conflagration over the next three years.

Amid the carnage and death, the nature of civilization in Europe would change forever by the end of the war. Four empires would fall, in Germany, Russia, Austria-Hungary, and Turkey. The military establishments and hierarchy supporting these empires would be crushed. Millions of people formerly ruled by these empires would end up living in new nations or under radically different governments in the old empires.

Other elements of early twentieth-century Europe, however, would survive this disaster, at least temporarily. The great estates and manors of an earlier time would continue in parts of Central and Eastern Europe, although the conditions of ownership would change in some cases. These large agricultural estates operated under a near feudal system, with wealthy landowners presiding over vast lands supported by a working class of peasants. In many cases, noble titles would continue to be passed to the next generation, along with title to the lands.

The cumulative effect of these changes would only set the stage for the even greater upheavals to come. Following World War I, Europe would continue to experience economic deprivation, civil war, the rise of totalitarian governments, and other events that would lead the world into an even greater catastrophe.

Amid all of the horror in 1915, and events yet to come, the war had spawned battles and events in the most unlikely places. In Africa, Germany fought rear-guard actions to defend its four colonies, acquired in the last part of the nineteenth century. The colonies of Togo and German South West Africa quickly fell, while a determined German garrison hung on in German East Africa (later Tanganyika and Tanzania) until the end of the war, the last German troops to surrender. In the fourth colony, Kamerun, in West Africa, the end came in between, after an amazing resistance and retreat by the German garrison against far superior British, French, and Belgian forces.

Against the backdrop of these global events, the lives of millions of individuals played out, intertwined by history and the forces shaping this new world. Two families, the Hoffmans of

Germany and the Ortegas of Spain, distantly related by nobility and the land, became united as a result. Their union and involvement in the events of the twentieth century would lead to their discovery of secrets hidden from the allied code-breaking efforts, known as Ultra, in World War II. These secrets threatened to affect all of humanity and nearly tear the families apart, as a desperate Nazi regime sought to hide and preserve them.

As is often the case, the initiation of this chain of events began with the actions of a single individual at a particular time and place.

1.

Kamerun German West Africa
December 14, 1915

* * *

Leutnant Karl Otto von Hoffman grimaced as he took in the discouraging view through his Zeiss binoculars. He removed his pith helmet, crouched lower in order to prop himself between two rock outcroppings, and adjusted the focus. With the sun at his back, it was unlikely he'd be spotted.

His target came into focus. Yes, it was the same British column that had dogged his small team for weeks as they retreated south through the rugged terrain and tropical rain forest in southern Kamerun, also called Cameroon. The British were about fifteen hundred meters away, down in the valley below his position. He estimated they were still about fifty strong, or platoon size, a smaller part of a much larger British force. His group of seven, on the other hand, was separated from the larger body of the *Schutztruppe* weeks ago. The *Schutztruppe*, or "protection force," consisted of German commissioned and noncommissioned officers, or NCO, and native soldiers, or *askari*, who comprised the defense forces in all of Germany's African colonies.

Karl lowered his binoculars, looked around at his jungle surroundings, and thought briefly about how he had used his wits and cunning over the last sixteen months, since the World War had begun, to fight a guerilla-like battle, delaying the allied occupation of Kamerun while avoiding capture. That thought was satisfying to Karl, since it was symbolic of his burning desire to escape his rigid Prussian heritage, symbolized by the life and background of his own father, *Generaloberst* Wilhelm Otto von Hoffman, a senior officer on the German General Staff. Karl knew his father would not understand this type of warfare, since it emphasized the individual as much as the military organization and conformity to traditional tactics.

Although Karl was pleased to have achieved his goal of escaping his fate and the stifling Prussian culture by volunteering for duty in Kamerun before the war began, he now pondered a more daring idea. He had become enchanted with his new tropical environment, with its beauty, isolation, dangers—and its possibilities. Karl even dared to imagine how he could create a life in Africa—with Pilar—after the war ended. The wonderful irony of his situation was that his beautiful and enchanting Pilar was probably less than two hundred kilometers away, with her father, Pedro Ortega, in the adjacent neutral colony of Spanish Guinea as they established a new cocoa plantation. Karl wistfully remembered the day after the war began, when he was dispatched to the small coastal town of Victoria, at the base of Cameroon Mountain, to deliver a message to the garrison there. Just before returning to his unit, he looked across the Bight of Biafra, and only forty kilometers away he could see the mountainous island of Fernando Po, which was part of Spanish Guinea. Karl remembered being torn between his duty and his desire to bridge that gulf and make his escape final.

His thoughts back to that day were interrupted when the deep rumble of distant thunder ended his reverie, as if to remind Karl that such dreams would have to wait until he and his men could escape their present danger. Karl had a plan in mind that could achieve both goals if his team could continue to evade their British pursuers.

Karl tried to take his mind off Pilar as he turned and took in the rest of the view around his team. From their promontory, unending tropical rain forest surrounded them, holding a fascinating combination of flora and fauna, from beautiful pastel orchids to poisonous bush vipers and an array of mammals, including leopards and gorillas, which would make any zoo in the world famous. Karl surveyed the dense jungle and the humid sky with billowing cumulus, which provided a never-ending series of tropical rain showers in between periods of blazing sunshine. Although the rainy season had ended the prior month, the ever-present humidity was their constant companion.

Karl turned back toward the valley below and raised his binoculars again, as he thought about the two-month chase he had led his British pursuers on, smiling as he recalled the little clues and traps he had left to lead them astray. Karl and his team had used deception to delay the British and protect the bulk of the *Schutztruppe* that was some distance to the east of his small unit. Mostly, however, Karl and his six comrades were determined to avoid capture and were using their progressive retreat as a stage for a game of cat and mouse with their pursuers. Karl smiled again as he thought about what he had up his sleeve.

"*Herr Leutnant* finds the view amusing?" *Feldwebel* Anton Schulz's voice was laced with sarcasm. Schulz, originally from Bavaria, was lead sergeant and the only other German on Karl's team. He was short and stocky, almost portly, with a ruddy complexion. Sarcasm was Schulz's trademark, yet Karl valued his years of experience in Kamerun. He thought about that as he turned slightly toward Schulz and replied.

"Yes, Schulz, I find it amusing that our enemy persists in following us, since we aren't a threat to them, but it's more amusing that they don't have a clue about our intentions."

The pained look on Schulz's face revealed that Hoffman's comment had the desired effect of putting Schulz on the defensive. Clearly Schulz himself had no clue as to their intentions, since Karl had not yet shared his developing plan with his team. Schulz knew better than to question Hoffman's remark, but Karl couldn't postpone sharing his plan any longer. He looked at Schulz and then the expectant expressions on the faces of his five *askari* soldiers. They looked gaunt, with tattered uniforms and a variety of minor injuries from months of jungle warfare. He at least owed them an explanation and some hope.

He took a final look at his pursuers. One soldier, clearly an officer, was looking toward the hill east of him. Karl sensed that this was the man intent on hunting him down. It was clear that the British wanted to reach the high ground as well so they could have a better observation position. Given the thick vegetation on the slope, Karl estimated it would take them at least an hour to reach his current position. Karl focused again on the British officer. *You may try, but you won't catch me. I have other plans.*

It was time. Karl sat up and faced his team.

"Schulz, what is our current ration and ammunition state?"

"*Herr Leutnant,* our food rations ran out this morning, as you know. The five *askari* and I have a total of thirty-four rounds remaining."

Karl sighed. That was barely enough ammunition to fill the five-round magazines of the six Mauser rifles that his team carried. He also knew that at least one *askari* had no ammunition remaining, since Schulz held a few rounds in reserve. Karl unconsciously gripped his own holstered Luger P08 pistol. He had only five rounds left, not enough even to fill the eight-round magazine. Karl remembered that he had used the Luger in close quarters to kill several British soldiers during previous battles. He quickly erased that thought, composed what he would say, and turned again to face Schulz.

"Thank you, Schulz." He paused, moving closer to his NCO. "It seems that we're now at a crossroads. We can't put up much of a fight but have nowhere else to go, eh?"

Karl paused again, waiting for Schulz's reaction. Schulz usually kept his thoughts to himself, but this time he replied immediately.

"*Herr Leutnant*, we have already led the British column far astray of our main force. Perhaps it is time to examine our options."

Of course Schulz would not dare to suggest what their options might be, yet he leaned forward expectantly, as if to challenge his commander. The rumble of distant thunder again accentuated the tension in the air as Karl's teammates waited for his reply to Schulz. Karl then turned to face his lead *askari*.

"*Gefreiter* Wekesa, you will translate as I speak." Wekesa was a Bantu and tall and lean, with piercing brown eyes. He was also intelligent, having received a promotion to corporal, a rare honor for an *askari*. Hoffman relied on Wekesa for advice, as a conduit to the other *askari*, and as a way to counterbalance Schulz's influence. Wekesa spoke excellent German, as well as several Bantu dialects.

Karl continued, "We are in a tight situation. The British column greatly outnumbers us, and we are nearly out of ammunition. The nearest reinforcements are at least one hundred kilometers from us. Our ability to outrun the enemy is hampered by terrain. It will be impossible for us to successfully engage the enemy, even if we could again achieve surprise."

There was a pause. The *askari* looked at each other and then back to Karl. Schulz then replied, "*Herr Leutnant*, with all respect, if we have no prospects for engaging or outrunning the enemy, then we must consider surrender."

Hoffman had no intention of engaging—or surrendering to—the British.

* * *

As the British soldiers, including their own *askari* group, began marching again, Captain Colin Higgins wiped the sweat from his forehead and spoke to his other officer.

"Those bloody Germans must be close. I can almost feel their presence. This time, we won't be made fools of."

Higgins looked toward his deputy, Sub-Lieutenant Michael Horsley, who nodded but did not speak.

Higgins sighed, realizing that it made no sense to rehash their embarrassment of a week ago when they thought they had successfully surprised the German encampment. They had entered the site with guns blazing, only to discover that the Germans had cleverly disguised some large tree stumps with parts of uniforms and created a camp scene indicating their presence. Not only that, the Germans had created a false trail that led the British column in the wrong direction. It took a couple of days before the British *askari* scouts could again pick up the real trail and close the distance on the Germans.

Before giving orders for his column to resume its march, Higgins pulled out his map of southern Kamerun and placed it on a flat tree stump. He examined the map, sizing up the likely escape path for the German unit.

"I believe they'll either try to break to the east, to rejoin the German column as it retreats from Yaounde, or they'll head west for the coast." Yaounde was the last major German stronghold in Kamerun and the combined allied force attacking from the north had forced the Germans to give up the city and begin retreating southwest, away from the central plateau and toward the rain forest.

"I agree, sir; those are their options. Heading for the coast is probably their best option, but at least they can't head south." Horsley put his finger on the map to emphasize the barrier to southern escape.

"Yes, Horsley, you're right. I think we finally have the buggers boxed in."

* * *

Hoffman pulled out his map and pointed to key locations as he spoke. "Wekesa, you and the other *askari* will slip through the British lines and attempt to reach our main force to the east. They've probably been forced to abandon Yaounde by now so you should try to intercept them about here." Karl pointed north of the town of Ebolowa on his map, about one hundred kilometers south of Yaounde. He then pulled an envelope from his rucksack, handing it to Wekesa. He couldn't be sure who was leading the remaining German forces so he had put his plan in writing with all the necessary detail.

Karl continued, looking straight at Wekesa, "This document must reach the governor and the commander of our column."

As Wekesa nodded, Karl issued his final instruction. "This document must not fall into enemy hands. If you face capture, you must destroy it." Wekesa nodded again. Karl knew he could rely on the *askari*. He then turned to Schulz.

"*Feldwebel*, you will turn all remaining ammunition over to the *askari*, except for three rounds."

Schulz looked up uncomprehending. Hoffman glared at him.

"*Jawohl, Herr Leutnant!*"

Even if he rarely showed initiative or ambition, Karl could always count on Schulz to follow orders. Karl wanted to give the *askari* a fighting chance if they were ambushed by the British. He wanted Schulz to retain three rounds, not for the enemy, but as protection against animals. They were unlikely to be attacked by a leopard in daylight, but Karl wanted to have options.

As the *askari* soldiers prepared to depart, Karl realized he had to level with Schulz about the rest of his plan.

"Schulz, while the *askari* attempt to elude the British to the east, you and I will proceed south to this point."

Schulz looked at the map, shocked. Finally, he replied, "*Herr Leutnant*, if we cross that river, we'll no longer be able to resist the allied invasion of Kamerun. Do you propose that our entire force join us there?"

"Yes, Schulz, that is exactly what I propose."

As Karl spoke, his mind raced back to his actions of the last three years, the strange sequence of events that brought him to this location, and the even more unlikely events that would now have to unfold for him to realize his real goal. Karl was determined to escape his British pursuers and, if possible, extricate his comrades from such a fate. However, he had another goal in mind that was unrelated to the current situation in Kamerun.

Karl was determined to follow through with his dream to begin a new life in Africa, with Pilar Ortega at his side.

2.

Eseka, Kamerun
December 20, 1915

* * *

"With all due respect, Colonel Haywood, I've concluded that the small German unit that I was trailing has now linked up with the main German force and they are now trying to make their way to Rio Muni—in neutral Spanish Guinea." Captain Colin Higgins hesitated on the word "neutral" to emphasize his point.

Higgins closely watched the facial expression of Lieutenant Colonel Austin Haywood, his immediate superior, to see if he was winning him over. Higgins watched Haywood ponder his statement, probably putting himself in the shoes of his opposite number in the *Schutztruppe,* and then deciding what he would do in the same circumstances. Higgins watched Haywood briefly glance outside through the glassless window of the small hut as another brief tropical rain shower ended. Finally, he turned to Higgins.

"I suppose you're right, Higgins. If I were commanding the *Schutztruppe* now, and facing being captured, I would probably conclude that I've done my duty to the fatherland after fifteen months of war and try to save my men by seeking internment in neutral territory."

Higgins, quickly realizing that his view had been accepted, moved on to his next point. "That being the case, sir, it's likely they will be crossing the Nyong River east of us. I suggest that we immediately march east with a sufficient force, cut off their retreat, and complete their encirclement—that is, if we're not too late." The last point rankled Higgins since it was his own obstinacy that had kept him thinking the Germans would head for the coast or stay in Yaounde. Maybe it wasn't too late, he thought.

* * *

One hundred and sixty kilometers to the southwest, Hoffman and Schulz struggled through the jungle of extreme southern Kamerun. The two men looked like an odd couple. Karl had just turned twenty-three, was tall and slim, with steel blue eyes and sandy hair, his fair complexion bronzed from over two years of service in the tropics. His gait was easy, and although Karl was not particularly athletic, he adapted easily to the physical rigor of both his previous training in officer school and the conditions in his current setting.

Schulz, on the other hand, was struggling. He was twenty years older than Karl, and although he had been in Kamerun much longer than Karl and was fully adjusted to the climate, years of quiet garrison duty in Kamerun, with all the real work done by Africans rather than their German masters, had made Schulz soft. He dared not complain about their pace, knowing that Hoffman was in a hurry, but Karl sensed that Schulz was near the breaking point. Yet Karl had wanted Schulz with him rather than with the *askari* soldiers, where his corrupting influence was dangerous to the team's goal.

Karl pondered all this as he and Schulz labored up a small rise that Karl could see was leading to a clearing at the top. As the two men crested the rise and looked down the other side, they stopped suddenly. There before them was the fast-flowing Rio Campo and the footbridge they were looking for. Karl was relieved.

"Well, Schulz, Wekesa knew what he was talking about. That's where we'll cross." Karl pointed to the bridge, looked at Schulz—and sensed something building.

"Yes, *Herr Leutnant*, we're here as promised, and across that bridge is Spanish Guinea. It seems to me that by crossing that bridge we're removing ourselves from danger by seeking internment. Yet, with all due respect, how then can we be loyal to the *Schutztruppe* when we are interned and they are still in Kamerun?"

Karl, momentarily shocked as Schulz put him on the spot, quickly responded with what he thought was obvious. "Schulz, it may not have occurred to you, but it's my intension to obtain assistance from the Spanish officials in Guinea and then return to Kamerun to lead the *Schutztruppe* to safety."

Schulz was stunned. "You mean you plan for us to return to Kamerun... after we have escaped? How can you propose that, after what we have experienced—to have come this far and then retrace our steps and risk capture!"

Karl was not surprised by Schulz's rapid change of heart. "Do not worry, Schulz; I intend to return alone. You may remain with the Spaniards until I return with the rest of our men." Schulz, indignant at Karl's remark, replied immediately.

"You think I'm a coward? Is that what you think? I deserve better than that!" Schulz moved toward Karl, momentarily forgetting both his rank and his place.

Karl held his ground. "Schulz, I know you're not a coward; I've seen you in battle. I don't, however, expect you to consider more strategic issues or to be responsible for such decisions. That is my responsibility and mine alone." Karl paused, trying to break the tension between the two men, "Schulz, I accept that these matters trouble you. You may follow me over that bridge," Karl pointed to the bridge for emphasis, "or you may remain in Kamerun. The decision is yours." Karl turned and began walking toward the bridge. Halfway to the bridge he turned and saw that Schulz was following, his head bowed.

3

On a road near Anguma, Rio Muni, Spanish Guinea
December 22, 1915

* * *

Hoffman and Schulz continued their pace after crossing the Rio Campo, hoping their British pursuers wouldn't enter neutral Spanish territory in pursuit. They continued south along narrow dirt roads surrounded by dense jungle. From his conversations two years ago with Pedro Ortega and letters from Pilar, Karl knew the approximate location of the Ortega cocoa plantation and thought it was near. He needed to find Pedro Ortega soon, before it was too late to follow through on his plan.

He and Schulz had been fortunate and had obtained some food in a nearby village. Karl had learned a few words of Fang, the local dialect, from Wekesa and was able to reach out to some villagers for assistance and to determine where they were. Earlier in the morning, by using a few words of Fang and by drawing a map on the ground with a stick, Karl had obtained some directions from a villager tending his garden. He and Schulz, although tired and hungry, pressed on as they continued south, deeper into Rio Muni, past the village of Anguma and toward the presumed location of the Ortega plantation.

As the two men continued their journey into the late morning, Karl thought back more than two and a half years to his last visit to the Ortega hacienda and bodega in Alabos, Spain. Karl remembered how much Pilar had changed since his previous visit three years before that. Between ages fourteen and seventeen, Pilar had changed from a prepubescent teenager into a stunning beauty. Karl wondered what she looked like now, at almost age twenty. Their relationship had been a special one, as they saw each other about every two years as they grew up. Karl's father, Wilhelm, and Pilar's father, Pedro, had a friendship dating back to 1888, as both men were involved in vineyards and wine making and their shared interest in viticulture became a lasting bond between them. In fact, Wilhelm had invested heavily in the Ortega wine business, since his own vineyards in the Mosel valley in Germany were small by comparison. Wilhelm may have been an officer on the German General Staff, but one of his passions was the land and especially the vine.

Karl remembered his final meeting and conversation with Pilar, when she had revealed that she and her father would be traveling to Spanish Guinea to start a cocoa plantation, based on a land grant Pedro received from the Spanish government. When Karl finally returned to Germany to enter active duty in the army, he hatched his plan to volunteer for duty in Kamerun, to escape his dreary fate as a German officer in Europe but more importantly to be nearer to Pilar. They had discussed their future, but Karl was determined to act on his vision of their future together, regardless of the current world war and any other obstacles that might get in his way.

These thoughts swirled in Karl's mind as he and Schulz rounded a bend in the road at around noon. Karl looked up, spotting three men approaching in a horse-drawn wagon; two blacks and...a white man. Karl squinted, hesitated, and then finally recognized the man with the distinguished face, salt-and-pepper hair, and bushy mustache.

"Pedro Ortega!" Karl couldn't believe his luck as he waved both arms in the air to get Pedro's attention.

Karl noticed Pedro looking toward them, squinting and struggling to recognize the two strangers in their dirty uniforms, one of them with a rifle slung over his arm. Karl shouted Pedro's name again as he and Schulz approached. Suddenly Pedro's quizzical look changed to one of shock, and then...amazement.

"Karl...Karl Hoffman!" Pedro jumped off the wagon and raced over to embrace Karl, and for several minutes both men were overcome.

Finally, Pedro spoke. "Karl, what are you doing here? We last heard that you were under attack in Kamerun and..." Pedro's voice trailed off as he began to comprehend what was happening. He expectantly looked at Karl and his companion to complete his sentence. Karl obliged.

"We were cut off from our unit in southern Kamerun. They've probably retreated south from Yaounde, toward the Rio Muni border. Pedro, I need your help. I sent a plan to my comrades telling them to try to reach the Rio Campo west of the falls by early January." The two men then walked away from Schulz and the wagon as Karl continued laying out his plan.

"If you can intercede with the governor in Santa Isabel, I want to enable my comrades to cross the river, escape the allied forces, and to…to be interned in neutral Spanish territory. They have no alternative other than surrender."

They continued talking as they got on the wagon and continued on to the Ortega plantation, a few kilometers to the south. There, Karl and Schulz ate, relaxed, cleaned their uniforms, and rested. The plantation's unfinished hacienda stood on top of a plateau above the south bank of the Rio Benito River and had a commanding view of the surrounding countryside. On the way there, Pedro described his ambitious plans. The hacienda would be completed, but the rest of the initial project involved only surveying the land and planning for future cocoa cultivation. Conditions in Rio Muni, the mainland portion of Spanish Guinea, were so primitive that more intense development might have to wait a few years until roads and other infrastructure could be developed. Meanwhile, Pedro was ready to close a deal for existing cocoa plantations on Fernando Po, the island part of the colony, where the land was more suitable for cocoa cultivation and the infrastructure was better.

Karl was imagining some exciting possibilities when Pedro approached him on the hacienda's west-facing veranda and pulled up a chair.

"We will leave at daybreak tomorrow. We can reach Bata by evening and the next morning we will take the weekly boat to Santa Isabel." Bata was the main city in Rio Muni and Santa Isabel was the colony's capital on Fernando Po.

Pedro continued, "I'm scheduled to have Christmas Eve dinner with the governor and his family. Pilar will be there and you will join us. Before or during dinner, we will find an opportunity for you to present your plan to the governor."

"Thank you, Pedro. I can hardly wait to see the expression on Pilar's face."

"She'll be at the dock to meet me when we arrive. It will be fun to watch her reaction to your arrival."

Karl paused before replying, "Pedro, I admire what you are doing here under challenging circumstances. I can visualize being a part of it myself."

"Perhaps you will, Karl—sooner than you think. Come on; let's have a glass of sherry before we retire."

The next morning as they prepared to depart, Karl pulled Pedro aside and asked him an important question about his relationship with Pilar. The smile on Pedro Ortega's face immediately provided Karl with the answer he wanted. On the way to Bata, the two men maintained a continuous animated conversation about future possibilities.

4.

Santa Isabel, Fernando Po, Spanish Guinea
December 24, 1915

* * *

"Pilar, it's me, Karl!" He ran toward her, his heart racing, as he saw her approach the boat after it docked. He knew she was expecting to see her father, but not him.

Pilar looked up, blinking incomprehensively as she focused on the man in uniform, finally realizing it was not a mirage, and then shouting out, "Karl, my Karl, is it really you?" She raced to meet him and they met halfway on the dock, immediately locking in a passionate embrace. For the longest time they held each other, Pilar sobbing gently. Finally, she looked up.

"Karl, I knew you were nearby in Kamerun—I...I could feel your presence. But what are you doing here in Guinea? We have heard about the battles in Kamerun with the British. Are these battles over? Is the war in Africa over? Please tell me that it's over now!"

Karl pulled back at arm's length, holding her hands and looking at her standing tall and stunning in a lacy dress with a ribbon in her long sandy hair, her fair complexion aglow in the sunlight. He had never seen her so beautiful. He smiled weakly.

"Pilar, I'm so happy to be here with you right now, I almost could forget the war. No, it's not over, I'm afraid. We will talk about that later. Right now, I just want to revel in our reunion." Pilar smiled as Karl continued. "We have many things to discuss, but I need to meet with the governor. Your father has arranged for me to meet with him before dinner tonight. We'll have more time to talk after that."

Pilar merely nodded as they walked down the dock hand in hand, followed by a smiling Pedro Ortega.

* * *

The meeting with the governor had gone well. He quickly agreed to implement Karl's plan to provide safe passage for the *Schutztruppe* into Spanish Guinea—and internment. It didn't hurt that the governor counted Pedro Ortega as a trusted advisor; in fact, Karl had counted on that relationship. The governor actually didn't need much prodding to agree to Karl's plan. Spain maintained strict neutrality during the war, but the governor was sympathetic to the Germans' plight in Kamerun. Both Germany and Spain were late to develop colonies in Africa and settled for the scraps of territory remaining after the British, French, Italians, Belgians, and Portuguese had carved up most of the continent. Now, all five of those countries were at war with Germany. Spain was the only colonial power in Africa that was neutral. It seemed natural for Spain to support Germany in Africa, without actually entering the war.

The governor decided to send a company of soldiers with Karl on the return trip to the mainland. They would march to the footbridge west of the Rio Campo rapids and falls, where Karl and Schulz had earlier crossed into Spanish Guinea. Karl could only hope that Wekesa and his team had succeeded in reaching the main German force, had convinced the German commander to follow Karl's plan by extricating themselves from encirclement, and then retreated south and west to the border, avoiding further battle with their British, French, and Belgian pursuers. To ensure that, Karl realized he would have to return to Kamerun and personally lead his comrades to safety, since the Spanish troops would not be able to enter Kamerun to help. Karl had just one more matter on his mind that he needed to address—his relationship with Pilar.

* * *

Following early dinner with the governor's family on Christmas Eve, Karl asked Pilar to join him on the balcony outside the governor's mansion dining room, which stood on a hill overlooking the city and harbor. It was a gorgeous tropical evening, with a refreshing breeze off the water and a lush and brilliant sunset, with pastel colors radiating from the deep red sun as it slid toward the ocean on the western horizon. A full moon rose in the east. Karl thought the time and setting were perfect. He and Pilar chatted quietly and intimately for a while as they looked out over the water. During a gap in their conversation Karl sensed it was time. He turned to Pilar.

"What a stunning sunset. I'm so entranced by all the beauty around us in Guinea. Our presence here seems like an omen, a symbol of new possibilities."

Pilar smiled, turning to him. "Karl, you're still the incurable romantic, but you're right about Guinea. Even though it's primitive, I find that it's just what I was hoping for too, a chance to break away into an adventurous new life." She paused, gently reaching over to touch his hand. "Somehow, I think that there is more on your mind tonight than the sunset. What is it, Karl?"

Karl looked away from her, torn by what he wanted to say and a fear that, for Pilar, the time had not yet come. He looked at the western sky as the sun slipped beneath the waves and turned back to Pilar. She looked at him expectantly. *She is so beautiful tonight. But what does she feel?* Karl gazed at the elegant full-length turquoise dress she wore, with matching beautiful earrings. He breathed in the aroma of fresh flowers on the veranda as he gently touched her arm, running his fingers down to take her hand.

Karl struggled to gain his voice, to find a way to express himself, finally speaking softly to Pilar. "It seems we're both entranced by this place and what it could mean to our future. I'm fortunate that I was able to escape, to be here now, and to...to be able to express my dream. I told you that I need to return to Kamerun, but I know what I want to happen when I return." He paused and took Pilar's other hand.

Pilar pulled closer to Karl, accepting his embrace. She looked intently at him and spoke. "Karl, it is always best to say what it is you want most." She squeezed him gently.

Karl continued his embrace, looked into Pilar's eyes, and asked the question that was burning in his heart. "Pilar, I can't wait any longer. I love you and I want to share my life with you. I don't care about the war or the timing. Sometimes we must ignore such events and follow our hearts. Will you marry me?"

Karl looked passionately into Pilar's eyes, sensing she was looking deeply into his heart. At that moment he knew.

Pilar finally answered, "Of course I will marry you, Karl. I can think of nothing that would make me happier."

Karl smiled as they embraced again, holding each other for the longest time; the only sounds were their gentle breathing and the rustle of the tropical breeze.

"I hope we won't have to wait too long," she said.

"Pilar, if things work out in the next few days, we won't have to wait long at all." Karl released his embrace, took her hands again, and gently squeezed them as Pilar answered.

"We must ask my father right away." Pilar looked expectantly across the patio to the open door of the dining room, where her father and the governor were likely still sitting. They could hear the subdued sound of a Spanish guitar as a musician played in the dining room. She looked back at Karl. "I'm sure he will give his permission."

Karl smiled. "I already asked him; he can hardly wait to hear the wedding plans."

Pilar smiled, obviously admiring Karl's thoroughness, and replied, "When shall we marry?"

"If I succeed in my plan to save my comrades in the *Schutztruppe*, we will likely be sent to Spain itself for internment until the war is over. We should plan to marry as soon as possible following our transfer there."

Pilar's smile changed to a frown. Karl sensed that she knew full well the danger that he would be exposing himself to by returning to the mainland. She must also know that he must first complete his duty. Karl could only hope that his meticulous planning would again be successful.

5.

The banks of the Nyong River, South Central Kamerun
January 8, 1916

* * *

"Go, Wekesa! Get them across now." Karl Hoffman was shouting to his men as they reached the north bank of the river and prepared to cross in the small boat.

"Join us, *Herr Leutnant.* We won't leave without you!" Wekesa replied.

Several shots hit their boat as the sporadic fire from their British pursuers increased. Karl had only a second to act and quickly pushed the boat off, leaping inside as Wekesa and the other *askari* soldiers returned the British fire.

As they paddled the boat, Karl felt several rounds hit. Their luck held out, and miraculously neither Karl nor his men were hit in the two-minute journey across the river. As they approached the south bank, the other *Schutztruppe* soldiers pulled their boat ashore and began a steady return fire. They hit several British soldiers as they emerged from the brush and forced the remaining soldiers to seek cover. Karl and his comrades were safe—for the moment.

"Wekesa, get everybody ready to move right away. They'll find a way to cross soon." Wekesa nodded and complied with Karl's order.

Karl looked back across the river, satisfied that this final skirmish would be sufficient. He had volunteered to be part of this rear guard unit, realizing that it would buy time for the main *Schutztruppe* force to accelerate their retreat to the south and west toward the southern rain forest—and Spanish Guinea. He realized it was risky, but he felt he must go in harm's way, since it was his plan for the escape that was now unfolding. Now if only they could stay ahead of the British forces coming from the north, west, and east, until the remnants of the *Schutztruppe* could reach safety. He realized that it was a risky bet, but it was essential to make the British force think that the main body of the *Schutztruppe* was much farther north than it actually was.

* * *

"Horsley, we're right on their tail now. We might have them trapped if we can cut off their retreat and surround them." Captain Colin Higgins looked across the river as he spoke, realizing that the Germans had again, for the moment, eluded him.

"Yes, sir, I hope our main units arriving from the east and west will allow us to surround them," Lieutenant Michael Horsley replied, in a not too convincing voice, to his commander's assessment. Horsley paused before adding his own cautious assessment.

"Sir, while I hope that's the case, it is possible that the unit that just escaped across the river is only a rear guard and that their main force may be...much farther to the south."

Higgins looked back at Horsley, his facial expression changing slowly from a scowl to a more thoughtful reflection as he realized that Horsley could be right. Finally, he turned his gaze back across the river and slowly nodded.

"Horsley, you're right, of course. Let's head back to the west to rejoin Colonel Haywood's main force. He might have some intelligence information on the location of the main German forces."

Higgins quickly issued orders to the rest of the platoon and they began marching west. Higgins was determined to catch up with the enemy and prevent their escape, yet he had an uneasy feeling that the German officer responsible for their unfolding strategy was cleverer than Higgins had given him credit for.

* * *

Major Karl Zimmerman, the commander of the *Schutztruppe* in Kamerun, beamed as he addressed his subordinate. "I must commend you, *Oberleutnant* Hoffman, for your bravery and ingenuity in delaying and deflecting the British from our route of retreat. Governor Ebermaier and I are especially impressed with the plan you devised for getting us safely to Spanish Guinea. Given your exceptional record in Kamerun, I am not surprised. Your father will be proud when he learns of your success."

"Thank you, *Herr* Major; I am grateful for your confidence in my unit and in me." Hoffman paused as the first part of Zimmerman's statement finally registered. "Excuse me, *Herr* Major, but did you say *Oberleutnant?*"

Zimmerman smiled. "That's correct, I said *Oberleutnant*. Your promotion just took effect and is very richly deserved."

"Thank you again, *Herr* Major, but I suggest that we must still expedite our march to the Rio Campo. The British will not be fooled for long and we need to stay well ahead of them. They'll close the distance since our civilian contingent is slowing us down, yet we owe it to our men to see that their families can safely evacuate also."

"That's true, Hoffman. The *askari* soldiers have been very loyal to us and we owe it to them in return. Let's get the force moving right away."

As the brief meeting with his commander ended, Hoffman came to attention, saluted, and excused himself, quickly leaving the tent and heading back to his men. He knew that the most dangerous part of their plan was still ahead of them.

Colonel Austin Haywood frowned as he delivered the bad news. "I'm sorry, Higgins, but your worst-case scenario is playing out. The main body of the *Schutztruppe* has at least a seventy-kilometer advantage on us. It seems they have outfoxed us again."

"I'm sorry, sir, but I respectfully disagree. If we press hard, we can catch them in three or four days, before they reach neutral Spanish territory. We can't let them escape at this point." Higgins clenched his teeth as he tried to restrain his frustration, but he could see that he had made his point with his commander—Haywood's look was changing from one of indifference to one of determination as he realized that Higgins was right. The honor of British arms was at stake if they couldn't run down and subdue a German force greatly inferior in numbers and nearly out of supplies and ammunition.

Finally, he looked up and replied, "All right, Higgins, we'll put a maximum effort into this and see if we can beat them to the Spanish Guinea border. I'm sending you and a reinforced company ahead of us to see if you can't intercept them and slow them down until my main force arrives. Let's take a look at the map and see if we can guess where they will try to cross."

The two men walked over to the table to examine the map of southern Kamerun. Higgins thought that, with a little ingenuity and luck, they might yet turn the tables on their elusive quarry.

6

Approaching the Rio Campo
River, Kamerun-Rio Muni border
January 12, 1916

* * *

Karl Hoffman was leading the rear guard again with a small group of *askari* when he heard a familiar voice. Corporal Wekesa quickly appeared out of the underbrush behind his team, coming from the north. Karl could see that Wekesa was in a hurry as he approached Karl and got right to the point.

"*Herr Oberleutnant*, the British are only three kilometers away. After guiding the main body of the *Schutztruppe* to the footbridge, I doubled back behind us to determine how close they are. We must hurry; we don't have the means to engage them again."

"You're right about that, Wekesa." Karl was painfully aware that they were virtually out of ammunition as he peppered Wekesa with three quick questions. "Is the Spanish army unit at the bridge? How many of our men have made it across? How far away are we from the bridge?"

"The Spanish company is there, as promised. About two-thirds of our force and civilians are across. We are only two kilometers from the bridge."

Karl noticed Wekesa pausing in his report. "Is there something else, Wekesa?"

"Yes, I met the Spanish commander, Comandante Perez, halfway across the bridge. He wanted me to remind you that his orders are explicit. He cannot cross the bridge to help us and he will not fire across the bridge into Kamerun unless he is fired upon."

Karl pondered that for only a second. "All right, Wekesa, we need to move, fast!"

In less than an hour, Karl's team penetrated the rest of the dense jungle leading to the same footbridge he had crossed nearly three weeks earlier. They caught up to the last unit of ragged *Schutztruppe* as they reached the bridge and began filing across. As the soldiers and civilians reached the southern bank, they were greeted by the Spanish soldiers, disarmed, and led to a camp nearby where they would be fed and receive medical attention.

The amazing migration had been underway for hours until nearly fifteen hundred individuals had made it across the bridge to safety—and internment. Karl and his unit finally approached the bridge themselves. They would be the last to cross.

At that moment a shot rang out, followed by more intermittent rifle fire. The group approaching the bridge moved faster, starting across. Karl could see that he would be the last man to cross. The gunfire increased. Karl looked across the river and could see Perez shouting orders as the Spanish unit quickly took their positions.

Karl stepped up his pace as the last couple of *askari* ahead of him started running down the bridge. He pulled out his Luger pistol, knowing he only had three rounds left, and starting jogging rapidly. At that moment Perez shouted Karl's name from across the river. Karl instinctively ducked. Karl could feel the wind as the round flew by him. He turned.

The British soldier emerged from the brush and engaged the bolt action on his Lee Enfield rifle to chamber the next round, just fifteen meters from Karl. Karl quickly turned and raised his Luger and fired three times. The last two were unnecessary. The British soldier crumpled.

Karl wheeled around and raced across the bridge, which was clear down its twenty-meter length. Rifle fire started again, but Karl's surprise sprint had caught the British off guard. Karl reached the midpoint of the bridge, running like the wind, when Perez shouted again, and this time about fifty Spanish soldiers on the south bank rose in unison and raised their Mauser rifles. Two more shots rang out, one striking the bridge, and as Karl ducked a second time, the other shot grazed his forehead. He was stunned but continued running, finally reaching the south bank. There he collapsed into Wekesa's arms as the shooting stopped amid shouting on the north bank.

* * *

"Cease fire, you damn fool! Cease fire! Stop the shooting!" It was Captain Colin Higgins of the British army, screaming at the top of his lungs at his soldiers. Finally, the shooting stopped. Higgins turned back to look at the bridge, furious that the enemy he had been stalking for months may have finally eluded him. He looked across the river at the large group of regular soldiers and knew who they were and where he was. He had come very close to creating an international incident. He had not come this far to be either skewered by his superiors for starting a war with Spain or to see his quarry escape after months of pursuit. He shouted at his lead NCO.

"Bring me a post with a white flag, RIGHT NOW!" The NCO raced to find a suitable flag of truce.

Higgins looked back across the river at the large number of Spanish soldiers. Where the blazes had they come from? He couldn't believe that so many soldiers could have been stationed at such an obscure bridge.

* * *

On the other side of the river, Perez's medic was attending to Karl's wound, which was not serious. Perez spoke first. "You are very lucky, my friend. But now that I see you're all right, I don't want you to miss the drama that must now ensue."

Karl sat up and looked in the direction that Perez was pointing. He could see the British officer approaching the north end of the bridge followed by a soldier displaying a white flag. Perez smiled as he got up to go meet the officer.

"You must watch as we make our British friend eat a little humble pie," he said.

* * *

Perez and Higgins crossed the bridge simultaneously, meeting appropriately at the middle. Higgins saluted and Perez returned his salute. Higgins spoke first.

"*Sprechen sie Deutsch?*"

"Yes, Captain, I do speak German, but I also speak reasonable English. How may I help you today?"

Higgins glared at him but continued, "I demand that you return to my custody those criminals who just crossed the river. They're guilty of war crimes and I demand that you surrender them."

"Captain, I do not believe that any of the soldiers you speak of were ever in your custody to begin with. In any case, I have identified them as soldiers of a belligerent power who have entered neutral territory along with a number of civilian refugees. I have disarmed them, and they will be interned for the duration of this conflict. They are no longer a threat to your force."

Higgins's face reddened. He opened his mouth to reply to Perez's insult but realized he was powerless. He glared and spoke formally. "I intend to have my superiors contact London and lodge a protest with your ambassador!"

"Captain, you may make whatever protest you wish, as that is your privilege. Meanwhile, I have some work to do, so you must excuse me."

With that comment, Perez saluted, wheeled around, and headed back to the south bank. He could see Karl Hoffman standing and grinning broadly, knowing his plan had worked.

7.

On a train from Zaragoza to Haro, Spain
June 1916

* * *

As the train headed west, Karl's attention constantly shifted between the ever-changing terrain outside the slow-moving train and the recent events in his life, anticipating what would soon happen. He admired the stark scenery unfolding as the train followed the course of the Ebro River between Zaragoza and his intermediate destination, Haro. He always looked forward to the sunshine, brown hills, and other topographic features along the Ebro. *Very unlike West Prussia in Germany,* he thought.

Karl first thought about the events since his internment. Following their harrowing escape from the allied forces pursuing them, thanks to Karl's daring plan the interned *Schutztruppe* contingent was transported from Rio Muni to a hastily built compound on the island of Fernando Po. After negotiations between Spain and the Allies, the African soldiers were repatriated back to their homes in Kamerun. Karl interceded with the ex-governor of Kamerun to ensure that the Africans were honorably discharged from the *Schutztruppe* and paid the salaries due them. He made Wekesa promise that he would visit the Ortega plantation in Rio Muni after the war.

The 832 German soldiers and civilians in the contingent were finally transported to an internment camp in Spain in April 1916, where they joined a small number of their countrymen who were similarly interned for the duration of the war. It had taken two months to arrange, but because of Karl's "special status" and Pedro Ortega's political connections, Karl was finally designated as the liaison between the interned Germans, the German embassy in Madrid, and their Spanish guardians. As part of the arrangement, Karl was relatively free to travel throughout Spain on his "liaison" duties. He had finally obtained leave and was traveling from the internment camp near Madrid to Alabos, in Northern Spain, to visit the Ortega family.

When news of the *Schutztruppe*, and especially Karl's exploits and his role in their escape, reached Germany he became an instant hero. His bravery during four battles with the British and French, the incident at the Rio Campo Bridge, and his being wounded three times ensured that the army would decorate him upon his return to Germany. His father was justifiably proud of Karl as his first letter to Karl expressed this pride and the relief that Karl had escaped with only minor wounds. Unfortunately, they could not be united until the war was over.

Karl's actions weren't the only source of pride for Wilhelm von Hoffman. Karl's only other sibling, Walter, was two years older and took a slightly different path. For a Prussian military family, its members often exhibited a nonconformist streak. Walter wanted to see more of the world, joining the German navy in 1908 as an officer cadet. Karl still remembered the family battle that occurred over his brother's decision, although Wilhelm finally relented and allowed Walter to join the navy. Walter later compounded his rebellion by joining the new submarine arm in 1910, after his mandatory first two years on surface ships. During this period, submarines were an obscure new weapon, usually more dangerous to the sailors on them than to any potential enemy vessel. Walter, however, wanted an early opportunity to rise through the ranks, and the submarine service provided that opportunity. Naturally, that meant that Karl had no choice and was expected to enter the army to carry on the family tradition.

During the war, Walter had distinguished himself in submarines—or U-boats as they had come to be known by the allied powers and Germany. Walter was a junior officer on the U-9 when it sank three British cruisers in September 1914, creating a sensation in naval circles as the submarine demonstrated its potential to sink large naval ships. Walter was now a hero also and quickly moved up the ranks to executive officer on another boat and would soon get his own command.

Unfortunately, the U-boats had since acquired a different reputation. The sinking of unarmed merchant ships, and especially the passenger liner *Lusitania* in May 1915, heralded a new era in warfare, as Germany struggled to break the allied blockade that was slowly strangling the country. The letters Karl received from Wilhelm and Walter contained increasingly grimmer news as the devastating trench warfare on the western front decimated a generation of young European men.

Karl's thoughts quickly turned to more pleasant matters as he contemplated his upcoming marriage to Pilar. They had chosen a wedding date for

November 1916, recognizing that Karl's father and brother would be unable to attend. Nevertheless, Karl and Pilar didn't want to wait, and Wilhelm had given his blessing to the early wedding, overjoyed that he and his good friend Pedro Ortega would now be even more closely knit. This thought caused Karl to reflect on the deep connections between the two families.

The immediate connection between the Hoffman and Ortega families dated back twenty-eight years, but was really centuries old. In 1888, Wilhelm began a year of inactive duty from the German army. He was already on a track for higher command but, unlike in modern armies, there could be chronological gaps in an officer's career during extended periods of peace. Wilhelm used the year to travel through Europe to expand his knowledge of wine making and the entire viticulture process. While in Spain he met Ortega, who was eight years his junior. To both men's amazement, they discovered in their conversations that they were distantly related to nobility tracing all the way back to the 1580s, when Spain ruled what is now the Netherlands.

As was typical in the ancestry of royal families of that earlier period, many had intermarried. The Ortega ancestors had stayed on in the Netherlands for some time and their descendants adopted the Protestant faith, since the Dutch had rebelled against the harsh Catholic rule to achieve independence. It was during this period that the Hoffman ancestors married into the Ortega clan. Eventually the Ortega family returned to its ancestral lands in Rioja. In doing so, they had to keep a very low profile. Although the Spanish Inquisition began in the 1500s, it did not formally end until 1834. In 1868, things finally loosened up, and for the next sixty-five or so years, there was relative religious freedom in Spain.

The friendship that developed between Hoffman and Ortega endured. Both men married shortly after their 1888 meeting and each had two children during the 1890s. Ortega married another Protestant, Maria Castillo Rivera, in 1890, the year after Wilhelm married Ursula. Ortega had a son, Ernesto Ortega Castillo, born in 1892 within months of Karl, and a daughter born in 1896, Pilar Maria Ortega Castillo. About every two years, beginning in 1894, the two families would gather, usually in Spain but occasionally in Germany. They celebrated their friendship, common heritage, and increasing involvement in wine. Both Walter and Karl enjoyed their time with Ernesto and Pilar, and Karl and Ernesto had become fast friends. It was during Karl's last visit before the war that his interest in Pilar had become markedly different.

The impending union between Karl and Pilar signified even more than Karl's good fortune. Wilhelm had invested heavily in Pedro Ortega's wine and other enterprises just before war broke out. Wilhelm's investment was paying off handsomely as Spain's neutrality in the war resulted in greater prosperity from the wine trade, since wine production in the warring countries was down severely and Spain's increased exports satisfied demand, which had not dropped.

Wilhelm had made other important financial decisions prior to the breakout of war, reflecting his conservative investment approach and his reading of world events. Sensing that political conditions were about to change, he sold off more than half of his huge agricultural holdings in West Prussia for millions of marks in 1913, when the lands were at the peak of their value. He invested a small portion of this in the Ortega enterprises but wisely and quietly moved the rest of the proceeds into Swiss marks deposited in Zurich banks. This later proved to be a wise move.

Karl wondered whether his father would ultimately accept his plans for his new life, given Wilhelm's status and their family heritage. Wilhelm was, after all, a senior officer on the German General Staff, having entered the Prussian army in 1870 as an officer cadet, as had his father and grandfather before him. Wilhelm had distinguished himself in the Franco-Prussian war of 1870–1871, in which the French army was humiliated and after which the unified German Empire was created.

Despite his background, Wilhelm had two sides to his personality. Although he was a strict disciplinarian, he also encouraged independent thinking. He found his nurturing side also, since his wife Ursula died giving birth to Karl, meaning Wilhelm then had to be both father and mother to the two boys.

That thought brought Karl back to the view out the train window. The banks of the Ebro were now rising, and Karl saw the agricultural landscape evolve as the train continued west. The slopes began to include vineyards and olive trees. Karl was fascinated by the art and science of wine making, another family tradition. In the late nineteenth century, the family expanded their prime vineyard holdings in the Mosel valley and later in the provinces of

Alsace and Lorraine, after France ceded these territories to Germany following the 1870–1871 war. Karl knew that Romans had planted those ancient regions in vines two thousand years ago, as they had the hillsides in Spain outside his window.

Karl realized that the train would soon arrive in Haro and headed to the dining car for a quick bite. As he reached the dining car, sat down, and ordered, he began thinking about his role in the Hoffman estates. Since Wilhelm was a senior officer on active duty, he normally resided in Berlin. Normally managers who had been working for the Hoffman clan for decades and were considered extended "family" by Wilhelm and his two sons oversaw the agricultural holdings in West Prussia, the Mosel, and Alsace-Lorraine. The West Prussian estates even included some Poles in the lower management ranks, and they and the Hoffman family had excellent relations.

Non-land-owning workers performed all of the menial work on the estates, a form of "sharecropping." Nevertheless, Wilhelm, Walter, and Karl had all grown up getting their hands dirty for a brief period in their childhood, a rite of passage of sorts. Now, however, they could best be described as gentlemen farmers.

Karl had an indifferent interest in the agricultural activities in West Prussia but was fascinated by the cycle of activity in the Mosel vineyards. After all, grapes and wine were more interesting than cattle, pigs, potatoes, and beets. Even then, Karl was less interested in the planting, cultivating, and harvesting than he was in the wine making process itself. The Hoffman estates were noted for producing some of the finest Rieslings in the Mosel Valley. They produced exclusively high-end wines, without added sugar during the fermentation process. Karl fondly remembered the 1893 *Trockenbeerenauslese* from their estate that they had enjoyed the night before he left Germany for Kamerun more than three years before.

As this fleeting but pleasant thought passed through his mind, Karl was jarred back to the present by the lurching train as it began its ascent up the Ebro Valley and the train blew its whistle at a grade crossing. Karl leaned over and looked out the window of the dining car, noticing a donkey cart waiting at the crossing, its peasant driver staring at the old, slow-moving steam-driven train as if it were an apparition. As the cart faded from view, Karl looked back to the northwest, toward a high plateau on the north side of the valley, on which were located the best wine-producing areas in Spain. His destination was on that plateau, in the Rioja Alta region near the small village of Alabos. It was there that he would finally be reunited with the family of Pedro Ortega Cruz de Alabos.

Karl's reverie ended as he noticed the train slowing down and the conductor came through the dining car, announcing their impending arrival at Haro. Karl quickly paid his bill, returned to his coach, pulled his two bags down from the overhead bin, and exited the train onto the station platform. Karl walked down the crowed station platform and, in the waning afternoon sunlight, looked expectantly for the Ortega family.

* * *

"Karl, I'm over here!"

Karl turned toward the voice, quickly maneuvered through the crowd, dropped his bags, and embraced and then shook hands with his distant cousin and future brother-in-law.

"Ernesto, you look great! I can't believe I finally got here." He paused. "Where's Pilar?"

"She was impatient to see you but thought it was better to avoid the dusty drive so she would be at her most beautiful when you arrive at the hacienda."

They both laughed as Karl replied. "As if I cared whether she had a little dust on her!"

Ernesto Ortega was not quite as tall as Karl, standing about six feet. He was of medium build, with a handsome, square-jawed face and slightly curly reddish-brown hair and an infectious smile. He was dressed casually, with brown slacks and white shirt open at the top. Ernesto was outgoing and engaging and immediately got the discussion going, inquiring about Karl's trip.

Karl easily transitioned into Spanish. He felt fortunate to have begun learning Spanish at age two. Ernesto also spoke German passably, although both he and Karl preferred the easier cadence and idioms of Spanish for normal conversation. They jabbered for several minutes before Ernesto grabbed one of Karl's bags and motioned for him to follow.

"So you are now a German officer and a hero as well. And I suppose a *caballero* too?"

Karl liked Ernesto so much because he enjoyed kidding around and poking fun at things that he considered too formal. "So you think I'm a gentleman? We both know that's not going to happen!"

They both laughed at that one. When growing up, both boys could occasionally be hellions, but they had reached a different level of maturity now. Karl had experienced the horror of war and killing and Ernesto was actively involved in the family wine business.

"I've been looking forward to getting here for weeks. I didn't think they would ever let me leave the internment camp. How have you been, Ernesto? Tell me about Ana and little Alberto." Ernesto had married in late 1914, while Karl was in Africa, and their first son was born the following year.

"You will get to meet Ana and my son later on tonight." Ernesto raised his hand to his heart as he spoke Ana's name and then continued, "What do you hear from Germany? I understand Walter's doing well in the navy. How's your father doing? Is he still on the move?"

"He's fine and still very much in charge in both the manors and in the army. I'm afraid the war news is rather grim. Thankfully Spain seems to be weathering it pretty well." Karl paused as they continued to walk down the station platform. "Is everyone in the family all right?"

Ernesto nodded as they walked together briskly off the platform toward the rear of the train station. There was a brief pause before Karl continued.

"And how is Pilar, apart from her concern about getting dusty?"

Ernesto looked over with a mischievous look, his brows arching up and a wry smile forming. It was almost as if he read Karl's mind. "She is eagerly awaiting your arrival—and the chance to complete the wedding plans."

At that moment, Karl stopped in his tracks. There in front of him was a nearly new automobile, a 1914 Mercedes Town Car.

"Well, what do you think?" Ernesto put Karl's bags in the rear seat and opened the passenger door for Karl, who immediately noticed the aroma of the fine leather seats. "We got it just before the war started. Hop in, let's get going!"

The automobile age had reached rural Rioja. As they bounced down the primitive dusty road toward Alabos, Karl and Ernesto kept chattering away.

During gaps in the conversation, Karl could hardly contain his impatience, wanting to see Pilar. Now that his meticulous but risky plan had succeeded, he wanted to get on with planning their future together. Most importantly, he wanted to be sure that Pilar was still comfortable with Karl's dream of a life in Africa.

After the one-hour drive over bumpy country roads through endless vineyards and rolling hills, Karl happily recognized the Ortega hacienda as they drove up the driveway to the residence. It sat at the top of a small rise, with commanding views in all directions, including hills to the north and the Ebro Valley to the south. The west side of the hacienda was adjacent to a large flower garden, whose colors stood out in the last rays of the setting sun.

As they came to a halt, he saw Pedro and Maria approach the car with broad smiles on their faces. He quickly got out, embraced them both, and they happily chatted for several minutes as Ernesto unloaded the bags. Karl was then interrupted by a familiar voice.

"Karl, do you remember me too?"

Karl turned around and immediately stopped talking. Pilar was stunning, wearing a low-cut embroidered blouse and a full-length dress that revealed her shapely, very feminine figure. He quickly averted his eyes from her breasts. Three years ago he had first noticed how puberty had changed his childhood sweetheart, but as Karl had noticed during their brief reunion in Spanish Guinea, she was now completely transformed.

"Well, are you just going to stare or have you lost your tongue?" Her voice was soft and sultry as she reached out her arms to embrace him.

Everybody laughed at that, including Karl, whose face turned red. He finally got his voice back and embraced Pilar, providing the mandatory peck on each cheek.

"I'm so glad to see you, my love. It's been a long three months." They both smiled as they drew back, holding each other's hands. Karl smiled at Pedro and Maria and gave nearby Ernesto a sheepish look.

The Ortega clan and Karl quickly adjourned to the west veranda, where they continued to laugh and reminisce as servants brought them wine from the Ortega proprietary bodega and later served them a fine dinner.

* * *

Later, after dinner, Karl and Pilar were able to catch up privately. Karl noticed that Pilar seemed anxious to express her own dreams of their future together. As a young Spanish woman coming of age during that era, Pilar was trying to break out from the normal boundaries of her culture, which tended to discourage if not absolutely prohibit any kind of independent behavior and thinking by young women. Pilar's parents were more liberal in this regard, and Karl was also extremely encouraging of Pilar's efforts to expand her horizons.

Karl and Pilar were seated on the west veranda in comfortable wicker chairs on a warm late spring evening with the sky full of stars. They sat side by side with a small table with several lit candles in front of them. Karl turned toward Pilar and began the conversation.

"Pilar, I'm so ecstatic to be here finally." Karl looked around the veranda, then at the beautiful night sky, and back to Pilar. "I've been thinking about this moment for months. It sustained me through the months in Kamerun, as time seemed to drag and I wondered if I could ever escape. Alabos seems like such a central place to me."

Pilar's eyes arched up as she looked at him. "So what's so special about Alabos? You must have many friends back in Germany…men and women… why isn't Germany the center of your universe?"

"Honestly, Pilar, my life there is completely unlike life here in Spain. It's like living in a detached world, where everything is scripted, even relationships, and you have to conform to expectations. I want my life to be less encumbered and I feel energized around you and your family. Your father tries to establish his own destiny and I see that in you also. You dare to be different." He paused briefly. "I also see an even bigger future in Africa, one of the few places left where you can see the results of your own efforts—a place where we can create our own identity."

"It's true, Karl, my father sees amazing possibilities there…and I want to be a part of that adventure…and of your dream as well as his. Perhaps in Guinea I'll be able to participate in creating that dream, since here in Spain it's hard for a woman to establish her own identity, much less her own dream. My father encourages me, yet my mother always reminds me of the boundaries that exist."

"Pilar, you know it won't be an easy path. There will be challenges. It's primitive in Africa, and isolated. Yet there will be few boundaries, as you call them. Are you sure you are willing to take the chance with me?" Karl paused, shifted in his chair toward her, and noticed her sigh gently, her face lit by the candlelight.

"Karl, you are a dreamer…and a romantic." She leaned, looked straight into his eyes, and gently took his hand. "That's what I like most about you. Of course I will take a chance with you."

Holding her hand made Karl's heart quicken, but he had one other thought he needed to share. "I still need to get the war behind me. Even though we are planning our wedding for November, I am still an interned German soldier. When the war ends, I will need to return to Germany, at least briefly."

"Will your father and brother support our decision to move to Africa?"

Karl paused briefly, looking into the night sky before turning to Pilar. "I think he will be heartbroken. I also think that my brother will disapprove." He squeezed Pilar's hand and finished his thought. "When that time comes, I will need all the courage I can muster…and your support and love."

Pilar looked at Karl, smiled, and leaned over the table and gently kissed him on the cheek.

8.

Madrid, Spain
July 1916

* * *

Karl was finishing his second glass of *fino* sherry at a small outdoor café after having completed his official business at the German embassy relating to the interned Germans he was responsible for. He needed to return to the internment camp outside the city the next morning, but for now, he was content to relax and recount his several pleasant weeks in Alabos. His reunion with Pilar had been fabulous, as they had planned their wedding and future together, and that made up for the several months of transit and waiting in the internment camp after leaving Spanish Guinea. Karl also recalled his many hours of discussions with Pedro Ortega regarding Karl's potential future role in the family enterprises. He and Pedro had not finalized plans or agreements because of the uncertainty generated by the war and Karl's unique status as an interned German soldier.

As Karl reviewed these events, he did not notice the person approaching his table from the other direction, and he was startled as he was addressed, first in German and then in nearly perfect Spanish.

"Excuse me, *Oberleutnant* Hoffman; may I join you for a glass of sherry?"

Karl quickly turned and saw a tall, distinguished-looking man who appeared to be only a few years older than him. Karl studied the man and finally replied, in German,

"Excuse me? I don't believe we've met."

"That's correct, we haven't, but I know of your unique situation. May I sit down?" The stranger, speaking Spanish again, looked at the empty chair next to Karl.

Karl motioned for the man to sit down, noticing that he looked carefully around him as he did so. Karl motioned for a waiter and ordered two sherries.

"Forgive my rudeness, but I was taken aback by your perfect pronunciation in both languages." Karl also replied in Spanish.

"Yes, I have worked very hard at it so let's stay in Spanish since that's not our native tongue." The man paused as he looked around him again. "Forgive my rudeness also; let me introduce myself. I'm *Kapitänleutnant* Wilhelm Canaris, and I have a special assignment here in Spain also, so I suppose that makes both of us unique."

Karl waited to reply while the waiter delivered their drinks. "*Kapitänleutnant*, it seems we are both separated from the main theatres of war. How is it that you know who I am?"

The man smiled and then leaned closer to Karl so he could lower his voice. "Please call me Wilhelm. That's a good name, since both the kaiser and your father also bear it."

"You seem to know a lot about me…Wilhelm. Perhaps you could answer my question."

"Of course; although we are removed from the main theatre of war, we both have served…serve…Germany any way we can. I am in intelligence work and I naturally thought I could approach you because of your unique duties, to see if we might collaborate."

"What kind of intelligence work are you engaged in?"

"I'm involved in naval intelligence matters involving U-boats and enemy merchant ship traffic. In fact, I met your brother Walter before I left Germany. He's a very capable and intelligent officer."

"I would certainly agree with that, but what do you want with me?"

Canaris took a long sip from his drink, looked around once more, and replied, "You have access to, and knowledge of, hundreds of German military personnel in the internment camp. I thought you could recommend to me the names of several reliable men who could assist me in intelligence gathering. Or perhaps even you may wish to assist me."

Karl looked at Canaris thoughtfully, took a sip of sherry, and carefully considered the request before finally replying, "Wilhelm, please don't mistake my response for either disloyalty or fear, because neither of those emotions govern my actions here. I am in a very sensitive position involving the trust of a neutral government, one that accommodated the *Schutztruppe* when our only alternative was surrender to the Allies and imprisonment. Since I am interned rather than incarcerated in a prisoner of war camp, my usual duty to escape or to harass the enemy really doesn't apply here. Accordingly, it is a point of honor for me and I cannot personally assist you in espionage. In fact, I must discourage any attempt that you might make to recruit in the internment camp for the same reasons."

Canaris nodded, smiled, and downed the last of his sherry. "Knowing of your history, your family, and your personal situation here in Spain that is exactly the response I would have expected—and it's a response that I understand and respect. It's difficult to keep one's honor intact in this new era of warfare, so I bow to your decision."

"Thank you, Wilhelm. I doubt that many officers would be in full agreement with us on this point, but we need to stick to our beliefs."

Canaris nodded but did not immediately reply. Karl decided to add a thought.

"You know, Wilhelm, the issue of loyalty is very complex. For most of us, it involves weighing numerous elements in our lives and our experience. We all have dreams that may conflict with traditional forms of loyalty based on blind patriotism or dogma. Do you think that this war may cause many people to question their beliefs, to question their loyalty to the state or to their country?"

"Karl, that has always been the case, but you're right that this war may upset traditional notions of loyalty. I agree with your assessment of the complexity of the issue. I know that you are to be married here in Spain in a few months. I don't hold it against you for believing that your first loyalty must be to your new family. Given your heroism in Africa, I don't believe that any other rational human would criticize you for weighing the balance as you have. But I would caution you in one respect. The world is changing, and it is becoming harder for individuals to set themselves apart. There will, in fact, be risks associated with taking such a course. You may not experience them right away in your case, but please consider the need for caution as your life unfolds."

As Canaris stood up to leave, Karl quickly rose, accepting his extended hand.

"It's been a pleasant discussion, Karl. I wish you the best as you fulfill your dreams."

Canaris turned and walked away. Karl stood there for several minutes, realizing that Canaris has precisely described the challenges that he and Pilar would face.

9.

Begur, Aiguablava, Spain
November 1916

* * *

Karl sat peacefully in his wicker chair on a balcony of their hotel suite overlooking the Mediterranean Sea, gazing at the horizon. He and Pilar had decided to honeymoon in this beautiful place sitting high on a cliff with stunning views of sea, sky, and coastline.

Their wedding two weeks earlier had been perfect. Their plans had come together nicely; everyone who attended was impressed with the ceremony and extravagant reception—and how stunning the bride looked. The guest list read like a who's who of Castilian and Rioja society. It also included the German ambassador, the former governor of Kamerun, the commander of the Kamerun *Schutztruppe*, the latter interned like Karl, and many Spanish dignitaries, including several members of the royal family. The only minor controversy occurred when Karl contemplated wearing formal civilian attire rather than his officer's dress uniform. He was politely reminded by his former commander that he was still a German officer on active duty, interned or not, and protocol demanded that he wear the uniform. Karl had accepted his advice.

The last few days at Aiguablava with Pilar had been pure nirvana. They both felt suspended in time as they discovered each other and began their life together. As if on cue, her soft voice interrupted that thought.

"Would you like some special wine, my darling?"

Karl turned to see Pilar pouring a reserve bottling from the Ortega bodega. They had just finished a sumptuous lunch served in their room by the expert hotel staff, who then discreetly withdrew from their suite.

"That would be wonderful, especially to be served by someone so beautiful and so well attired for the occasion." Actually, Pilar was hardly attired at all, but Karl didn't mind. For the last two weeks, they had hardly bothered to dress to explore their surroundings or even to leave the room.

Pilar returned his comment with a sultry smile, poured the wine, and then strode several feet to the edge of the balcony, briefly gazing out to sea before turning to him.

"Don't you wish we could stay here forever?"

Karl sensed her comment was more rhetorical than an actual request, but he knew what she was thinking. "Yes, I do. This will always be a special place for us. I believe we'll create many more special places and occasions, wherever we are, once I am free of the past."

Pilar walked to him, placed her hand on his shoulder, and then sat in the other chair before speaking quietly. "Do you think the war will continue much longer?"

"I'm afraid it will, and until it's over I will remain in limbo."

Karl had already determined that few prisoner exchanges had occurred among the warring powers, and Spain's scrupulous neutrality policy ruled out the release of any interned soldiers of any army until the war ended and peace treaties were signed. Karl had also discreetly determined that the German army was not discharging any soldiers who were interned by neutral powers.

"Karl, we can make the best of the situation if you can begin working more closely with my father and Ernesto—and allow us to begin a family."

Karl smiled and became more upbeat. "You're reading my mind. That is exactly what we will do." He turned to her and continued. "I've decided to accept your father's offer to become more involved in day-to-day activities in the business. Our life will continue and we will begin it together as if there was no war."

They both knew that was not exactly true, but for now it would have to suffice. They both smiled as they finished their wine. As Pilar moved in the chair to turn to him, her sheer nightgown slipped back, exposing her thighs. They exchanged glances as Karl placed his hand gently on her exposed thigh.

The world could wait and the war didn't matter—for now.

10.

Alabos, Spain
August 1919

* * *

As Karl Hoffman packed his bags for the upcoming journey, he thought about his good fortune, but also of the necessary events that lay ahead.

The last three years had gone by rapidly, as Karl became a full business partner with Pedro and Ernesto Ortega and he and Pilar prospered. Their first son, Hans Wilhelm Hoffman-Ortega, was born on October 15, 1917, and their second son, Ernst Peter Hoffman-Ortega, was born on November 11, 1918. Their middle names honored their grandfathers, and Karl and Pilar had decided to anglicize Ernst's middle name. They also decided to drop the "von" preceding their family name, even though the hereditary title could be passed on to the next generation. They hyphenated the last names as a compromise with the Castilian convention of father's family name followed by mother's family name.

Ernst's birth was both happy and bittersweet, since on that day Germany asked for an armistice to end the war. Throughout 1916 and 1917, the slaughter on the battlefield had continued. America entered the war in April 1917, largely because of unrestricted U-boat attacks on shipping. As America's presence began to be felt by early 1918, Germany began a final assault on the western front. Russia was knocked out of the war and the effect of fresh German troops moved from the eastern to the western front resulted in some initial German success. However, fresh American troops and America's relatively unlimited resources turned the tide, and by September 1918, the German army was in full, but orderly, retreat. By late October, Germany's three allies, Austria-Hungary, Turkey, and Bulgaria were knocked out of the war, and Germany itself was nearly in revolution, as communists, anarchists, and mutinous soldiers and sailors slowly brought the government and monarchy down. Finally, on November 9, Kaiser Wilhelm II abdicated and fled to Holland. Two days later, the interim government requested an armistice to forestall a general military collapse and bring an end to the suffering and near starvation of Germany's civilian population.

After the armistice, there was a long seven-month interval before the peace treaty was signed. During this period, and throughout their internment, the Germans in Spain became impatient and rebellious themselves. Recognizing that Germany had lost the war, they only wanted to return home, yet they couldn't be released until the peace treaty was approved. Between 1916 and 1919, Karl, as the designated emissary for the interned *Schutztruppe*, made many trips between the internment camp, the German embassy, and Spanish army headquarters trying to keep the peace until they could be free. Between these duties and his work on the Ortega enterprises he was extremely busy, spending less time with Pilar and his two young sons than he wanted to.

The Treaty of Versailles, signed in June 1919, was devastating for Germany. Their army would need to shrink from nearly five million men to only one hundred thousand, and the general staff, on which Wilhelm von Hoffman served, was abolished. The navy was reduced to only a few ships, fifteen thousand men, and no submarines. Most importantly, Germany was responsible for huge reparations for years to come and had to give up considerable land, including most of West Prussia to Poland, and the provinces of Alsace and Lorraine, which it had seized from France in 1871. Germany also lost all of its colonies, including the four in Africa.

At last, in July 1919, the German internees in Spain heard that they would be repatriated to Germany. There was another frustrating four weeks as they waited for available shipping for the voyage home; both France and Italy had refused land or rail passage through their territory.

As Karl Hoffman continued to pack for his return journey home, he paused to reflect on these events. He hadn't been to Germany in six years. What would he find there? How would he react to seeing his father and brother again? Walter did not write often, but in his last letter he said he was engaged. What was she like? All of these questions weighed on him as he realized the path of his life had completely changed. A knock on the door interrupted his thoughts, and Pedro Ortega entered.

"Am I intruding?"

"No, Pedro. Please come in, I'm nearly finished."

"I wanted to see you again before you left. In addition to giving my best to your father and Walter, I have one more request. I want to invite them both to visit us when they are able, for as long as they wish. Will you tell them that?"

"Of course, Pedro, I'll encourage both of them to do so, although I don't know when that might be. My father's last letter said that he had much to do with regard to his properties." Karl's voice trailed off.

"I also want you to give him this envelope, with a complete accounting of the results of his investment in our wine enterprises. As you know, thanks to that investment and your participation, we have prospered during the last five years. As a result, you and your father now have a large share of our enterprise." Pedro did not elaborate, but Karl knew that the excess profits had been deposited in the Hoffman family accounts in Switzerland.

"Thank you, Pedro. I know he'll appreciate that. I'll be returning here as soon as I can wrap up my affairs in Germany."

"Good luck to you, Karl. I'll see that Pilar and the children are fine." Pedro turned and left the room. As he did, Pilar entered, walked over, and gently touched Karl's shoulder.

"I was dreading this moment, but I know that you must make this trip." She paused, and Karl noticed the fear in her eyes. "Are you ready, my dear?"

"Yes." Karl closed his suitcase. It was time.

11.

Hoffman estate, Bernkastel, Germany
December 31, 1919

* * *

Karl Hoffman stood in his father's study nursing his brandy and looking out the window at the cold, grey, blustery day and at the Mosel River in the valley below, as the afternoon gave way to dusk. He was waiting for his father and brother to arrive from a late afternoon New Year's Eve event that Karl had declined to attend. His mood matched the weather as he reflected on the last four months since arriving back in Germany.

When he departed Alabos in August he had traveled by rail to the northern port of San Sebastian, where he had joined the other internees. After a three-day voyage they arrived in Bremerhaven. The port and city were in turmoil with rioting and vandalism rampant. Karl was shocked, but it was even worse when he got to Berlin. The rioting was more severe there and the army had to intervene to maintain any semblance of order. In the chaos, Karl found that he had some last duties to perform, to assist in mustering out his comrades from the army. Finally, he was granted three weeks leave around Christmas and traveled to Bernkastel to be with his father, Walter, and Walter's fiancée.

This particular Christmas was depressing, although the Hoffman clan tried to make the best of it, especially with a new family member. Erica was the first woman in the house in many years and was a great addition, with a personality that complemented Walter's. They had planned the wedding for the second day following Christmas so that Karl could be Walter's best man.

The wedding was really the only good news that year since the end of the war was a disaster for the Hoffmans' land holdings. Their entire West Prussian estate was ceded to new owners, since it was now in Polish territory, in the so-called Polish Corridor that now separated East Prussia from the rest of Germany. The Hoffmans only received a tiny fraction of its value. Wilhelm's actions to sell most of the estate before the war began proved to be the silver lining in that cloud. On the other hand, the French seized their holdings in

Alsace-Lorraine without any compensation. Only the much smaller estate in Bernkastel remained. The French would partially occupy even that area of Germany for a number of years, since it was west of the Rhine River. At least it was still in Germany and in family hands.

Walter's wedding was a beautiful event, although much smaller than Karl's. The week before the wedding, Wilhelm completely briefed both sons on the family's financial situation, which was an exceptionally good one, thanks to Wilhelm's prewar actions. Walter's war record as a U-boat commander was outstanding and he was to be retained in the small postwar surface navy. With the chaotic situation in Germany, Karl thought this was probably a wise decision. Wilhelm, as a general staff member, was scheduled to be retired from the German army in February, after fifty years of service, on the same day as Karl's pending discharge. Wilhelm intended to be more active in managing the Mosel vineyards. He did not even bother trying to talk Karl into staying in the army, even though Karl's war record and his father's status could have ensured that outcome.

Earlier in the day, Karl finally told his father about his decision to return to Spain. Wilhelm was crushed by the revelation but told Karl he would speak with him later about it. Karl had not told Walter but he was sure that by now Wilhelm had informed him. Karl dreaded the meeting that was about to take place as he heard the door to the study open. Wilhelm and Walter entered, and Karl knew from the glum expressions on their faces that this would not be a casual family meeting.

"So how was the celebration in the village?" Karl knew that his feeble attempt at small talk would fall flat.

"It was subdued, like most every other 'celebration' this month," Wilhelm replied.

Karl watched as the two men poured themselves a stiff brandy from the decanter on the liquor cabinet and then walked over to the window where he stood. The three men cut an imposing presence. All were tall, over six feet. Wilhelm had closely cropped grey hair, a square jaw, and a trim mustache with steely blue eyes likes Karl's and looked much younger than his sixty-seven years. Walter, on the other hand, had wavy black hair, a rounder face with brown eyes, inherited from his mother, and was clean shaven. Both men were dressed in business attire rather than their uniforms. Walter wasted no time in voicing his opinion as their father looked down at his brandy snifter.

"Karl, needless to say, we think you're making a big mistake in not bringing your family back here to live in Germany."

"Why is that, Walter? What's here for them now? Our lands in the east are gone, Germany is in turmoil, and Pilar and the children would not find happiness here."

"But this is your home, Karl, and you cannot say that the future will be any worse here than in Spain or in, God forbid, Africa." Walter's condescending tone immediately elicited a sharp rebuke from Karl.

"Oh, so a future where we can create our own destiny and build something new is worse than what we would face here. By what right do you also dictate where our home should be? I shall always treasure my heritage, but I will not let it dictate the future of my family."

Karl's response drew a surprised look from Wilhelm, but his father remained silent.

"Karl, it seems to me you still owe a duty to the family and to the Fatherland to support us in our hour of need and—" Walter did not get to finish as Karl interrupted.

"You think I have not done my duty? I shed blood for the Fatherland and did my best to fulfill my duty—and it will end in February! As to my family, Walter, there are newer members that I also owe a duty to."

"That will be enough, both of you." Wilhelm's intervention broke but did not relieve the tension between the two brothers as he sought to diffuse their anger. "Recriminations and accusations have no place in this household."

The three men were silent for a moment, trying to digest what they had said and to somehow reconcile the words with their feelings. Finally, Wilhelm spoke.

"Each of us feels differently about what has happened in Germany, but it cannot govern our actions as individuals. We must pursue that course which will be best for ourselves and all of our family members as we try to achieve... happiness."

Both sons looked startled as Wilhelm uttered that last word. Happiness was a word their father used sparingly, as if it were gratuitous or an alien concept.

"Thank you, Father," Karl replied as he turned to face his brother. "Walter, I wish you and Erica the very best in your lives together. I am willing to support whatever life you choose to create here since I must assume it is the course you think will make both of you happy. You must also grant me the same privilege."

Walter looked at Karl for a moment and finally replied simply, "I understand."

Karl returned Walter's flat stare and, realizing that nothing more would be forthcoming, he concluded simply, "Thank you, Walter."

After a long, awkward silence, Wilhelm sought to break the tension and end the meeting. "I would like to propose a toast to the New Year—and the new decade: *Prost!*"

The three men raised their glasses and drained the rest of the brandy, each lost in their own thoughts as to what the future held.

12.

Berlin, Germany
February 1920

* * *

Hauptmann Karl Hoffman had been sitting in the adjutant's office for a half hour, waiting for his father. Karl was in full dress uniform and was about to be decorated, the day before his discharge from the German army, with an Iron Cross First Class for bravery for his actions in Kamerun. While interned in Spain, he had been promoted to *Hauptmann* in September 1918.

Generaloberst Wilhelm von Hoffman, also in full dress uniform, finally arrived and entered the office. Both Karl and the adjutant snapped to attention and saluted. The adjutant, as senior officer, greeted the elder Hoffman.

"Good morning, *Herr Generaloberst*, the field marshal will be ready for you and *Hauptmann* Hoffman in a few minutes." Karl was to receive his decorations from none other than Field Marshal Paul von Hindenburg, the army commander and eventually president of the Weimar Republic that now held power in Germany.

Wilhelm thanked the adjutant and motioned for Karl to follow him to the other side of the office. There they had a brief conversation. Wilhelm had just returned from West Prussia, where he had bid farewell to the workers on his estate just before the ownership formally changed hands and to retrieve the family's personal possessions and heirlooms. Karl could clearly see that his father was distraught. The estate had been in the family for more than two hundred years. Karl proceeded gingerly.

"Father, I thank you for being here. Did it go all right in Prussia?"

Wilhelm was usually not sentimental, but this situation almost demanded sentimentality—and reflection.

"It's hard for me to believe that it has come to this, Karl. But it is now done. I may never see our lands in the east again. At this point in my life I could spend my time looking at the past." He paused and continued, "But I choose not to do that."

Wilhelm looked directly at his son. "It is always better to look forward. I anticipate seeing my grandchildren and spending more time with our precious vines in the Mosel. You too should look forward. You've chosen a different path than Walter and I. While I find that hard to accept, I understand it. The Germany we knew is gone now. Hopefully it will resurrect itself in some positive way. You must allow your children to see for themselves and to remember their heritage. In a few years it will be again safe to do that. Promise me that you will return with your children; perhaps not permanently, but at least to visit."

Karl made that promise. They were then called into Hindenburg's office for the ceremony. The next day, Karl was discharged in the morning and the rest of the day was spent in a gala celebration of Wilhelm von Hoffman's fifty years of service to Germany, a period coinciding almost exactly with the fifty years of Bismarck's Second Reich.

Karl said his good-byes in Berlin rather than returning to Bernkastel. He missed Pilar and the two boys desperately and wanted to get back to Spain as soon as possible. The situation in Germany was getting worse by the day. Even as order was restored, the country would fall into economic freefall over the next three years, and it would take the rest of the decade to recover. Karl felt like an alien in this new Germany. He did not yet feel like a Spaniard either. For now, Karl pushed this disturbing ambiguity aside in favor of a smaller world of peace and happiness based on his family.

The morning after his father's retirement ceremony, Karl departed for Spain.

Part 2

* * *

Prosperity

1920–1930

13.

Alabos, La Rioja, Spain
October 1920

* * *

On returning to Spain in late February 1920, Karl learned that Pedro Ortega had sailed for Rio Muni the week before, to continue the surveying and development of the embryonic cocoa plantation on the mainland part of Spanish Guinea. Pedro had also completed the purchase of a developed cocoa plantation on Fernando Po, also a part of Spanish Guinea and where the best plantations were. Growing conditions and soil weren't as good in Rio Muni, but Pedro's research and the government's desire to settle the undeveloped mainland allowed Ortega to secure the best land there.

Pedro, Ernesto, and Karl had decided to share responsibilities as "managing partners" for both the existing properties in Rioja and the new properties in Spanish Guinea. At least one of them would be attending each of the two major properties at all times. Karl would initially be the swing partner and move as necessary as the workload varied.

The wartime prosperity for Spain had abated. Although the Ortega business activities in Rioja were still operating profitably, it was time to accelerate development of the Spanish Guinea operations. Karl planned to move to Rio Muni when the rainy season ended in December, so the first real plantings could begin on the Rio Muni plantation. Karl would handle the business management end of operations there, especially finding and hiring African workers for the labor-intensive cocoa cultivation process. Pedro Ortega would be in charge of the actual agricultural activity. Karl planned on Pilar and the two children moving with him, normally staying on Fernando Po, where the governor had again offered his mansion and hacienda as temporary family quarters for Karl's family. Eventually the Ortega family planned to finish their hacienda on the Rio Muni plantation and construct another larger one in Fernando Po. Karl would also be in charge of that enterprise.

During the summer, Karl had also gotten to better know Ernesto's burgeoning family. Ernesto had married into another wealthy Rioja agricultural

61

family in 1914, while Karl was in Kamerun. The Lopez family owned extensive lands throughout Rioja, planted in nearly every crop *but* grapes. Ana Lopez was charming, loving, and upbeat, with an excellent sense of humor, perfectly matching Ernesto in most every way. By 1920, they already had three children, Alberto, Alfonso, and Anita, who enjoyed playing with cousins Hans and Ernst. Ana and Pilar got along famously and, with Pilar's mother Maria, formed an inseparable bond.

Karl was finalizing his travel plans and attending to some other paperwork one day in early October. The family would be leaving in several weeks for the nearly three-week steamship trip to Spanish Guinea. As Karl was completing this work he looked out the study window to see Ernesto approaching, bottle and two glasses in hand. Karl walked out to meet him and motioned him to the patio.

"I see you brought some afternoon refreshment. Would that be the barrel sample from the 1918 *crianza* that we have been waiting for?"

"Yes, it is, and you will be amazed when you taste it."

The family bodega produced a variety of excellent red wines, many from 100 percent *tempranillo* but some also blended with other grapes including grenache. The family was also experimenting with classic French varietals, such as cabernet sauvignon. The Ortega bodega was especially noted for its high-end wines aged in French oak. In the emerging Spanish wine classification system, these included *crianza*, *reserva*, and *gran reserva* levels of maturity, each signifying progressively more oak and bottle aging. Ernesto had poured them each a glass. They swirled the wine to release the bouquet, looked closely at the color, and took their first sip.

Karl was surprised. "This wine has incredible structure. The tannins are just right for aging, but it's already drinkable and the vanilla is just pure heaven." Karl had learned the wine business very well, from two old masters.

"I agree. I can hardly wait for the *reserva* and *gran reserva*." They had taken a chance with their 1918 vintage and it was paying off. They paused to finish their taste.

"Karl, before you leave I wanted to ask your opinion about expanding our acreage with the cabernet and other French varietals. Also, what should we do about developing new markets for export? I'm hoping that you and I can develop a strategy that will prepare us for the future and support the goals that my father has already established."

Ernesto was following up on an earlier conversation they had about business strategy. They both realized that postwar economic conditions might limit the European market for wine. The problem was where to go next. America was out—they had just enacted Prohibition. Maybe South America held possibilities. Karl finally replied.

"Ernesto, I am uncertain about the general world economic situation and how soon foreign markets will develop. It might be better to maintain the acreage we have and continue experimenting with the other varietals. There will come a time when we can make our next move in wine. Meanwhile the market for agricultural commodities such as cocoa and coffee will accelerate. Even the Americans won't give up coffee and their chocolate. Once we are established in Rio Muni, we can ask your uncle in America to intercede on our behalf."

Karl was referring to Pedro's much younger brother, Ramon, who had immigrated to Cuba in 1890 at the age of twenty. Cuba was still a Spanish colony at that time. He immigrated to America in 1896, where he eventually became established in the export-import business in New York. He became more successful and prosperous, and other than a brief period of uncertainty at the time of the short Spanish-American War of 1898, he had made his mark in the ultimate land of opportunity. Karl had met him once, in 1908, when he visited Alabos.

Ernesto immediately responded, "I agree with your assessment of the situation, and that is an excellent idea regarding Uncle Ramon. Let's toast to that."

They raised their glasses to toast a hopeful future.

14.

Santa Isabel, Fernando Po, Spanish Guinea
October 1921

* * *

Karl quickly walked up the steps to the governor's mansion in Fernando Po. He was visiting, taking the weekly boat from Bata on the Rio Muni mainland. He wanted to see Pilar and ensure she had fully recuperated.

Karl and Pilar had arrived in Rio Muni in November 1920. Although Pilar occasionally journeyed to the mainland to visit Karl and her father, the living conditions there were only slowly improving. Also, shortly after arriving, Pilar found out she was pregnant again. Although Karl urged her to stay in Santa Isabel, Pilar insisted on the visits, also bringing the children on some trips. In July, she was in Bata, the largest mainland town, with Karl, ready for the boat to Santa Isabel the next morning when she went into labor, nearly two weeks early. Karl rushed her to the Bata hospital, a far less well-equipped facility than the one in Santa Isabel. Their third son, Paul Friedrich Hoffman-Ortega, was born there on July 15, 1921. Pilar was bleeding profusely, but fortunately her doctor from Santa Isabel was also in Bata and he and other doctors were able to stop the bleeding. They broke the news to Karl and Pilar the next day that, although Pilar would swiftly recover and the baby was healthy, Pilar would have no more children.

Two weeks after Paul was born, Pilar was fully recovered from the childbirth and surgery. As Pilar and Karl prepared to leave the hospital, the lead nurse asked Karl to complete some paperwork. Karl did so and quickly completed the discharge formalities. The nurse had another routine question. What nationality should appear on Paul's birth certificate? Karl held a German passport, although he was now a legal resident of Spain. Pilar held a Spanish passport. Under both German and Spanish law, citizens could not hold dual citizenship. Hans and Ernst were registered as Germans on their birth certificates. At the time of their births, in 1917 and 1918, Karl, Pilar, and even Pedro Ortega were comfortable with that decision.

This time it was different. Karl replied without hesitation that Spanish should appear as Paul's nationality on his birth certificate.

The ambiguity about who Karl was and who his children were was beginning to weigh on him in small ways. He cared most about their closeness as a family and very little about their national heritage. Karl realized he was reacting to the aftermath of the war, in which nationalism had played an instrumental cause. Karl had no problem with duty but realized that duty was a complex idea, with many dimensions. Thinking of that, Karl remembered his conversation with Wilhelm Canaris five years previously.

15

Bernkastel, Germany
September 1926

* * *

Karl, Walter, and Wilhelm Hoffman and Pedro Ortega sat on the patio of the Hoffman estate, overlooking the Mosel and enjoying a glass of Hoffman Riesling *Kabinett*. The delicious Riesling was perfectly balanced, with just the right amount of residual sugar and acidity. Unlike many white wines, high-quality German Riesling was known for its aging potential.

Pedro Ortega and his wife were returning Wilhelm's 1924 visit to Spain, the first time he met his three grandchildren. Wilhelm's two sons reminisced about the last several years and the political and economic events that had transpired.

Karl's description of their lives made for an interesting story. For nearly six years, Karl and his family had lived in Spanish Guinea while their children and the cocoa plantation grew and matured, making only one trip to Spain in 1924. They constructed a small hacienda in Rio Muni on their mainland plantation as well as a larger one on Fernando Po on their other plantation. The Rio Muni plantation grew through land grants from the Spanish government, which started subsidizing cocoa production. The level of cocoa production on the Ortega plantations increased enormously. The price of cocoa went down initially after World War I, but the combined effect of slowly increasing prices, increased production, better efficiency, and continued government subsidies allowed the Ortega operations to generate substantial profits.

Pedro Ortega wisely invested a portion of these profits in additional land on Fernando Po, where growing conditions were better. He and Karl also experimented with coffee planting and production, which showed promise, and with exploiting the timber resources on the mainland, especially fine mahogany. The next step would be to find more export markets.

Karl and Pedro described their living conditions in Spanish Guinea. Although Rio Muni was largely lowland tropical forest, and malaria ridden, the Ortega plantation included other types of land. Their new hacienda was on the highest portion of the plantation about sixty kilometers inland from Bata, on a plateau at an elevation of about nine hundred meters. The site was on a huge underlying limestone formation. In fact, a few hundred meters from the hacienda was a large limestone cave. The upper portion of the cave had two openings, allowing the wind to blow through the entrances and keeping the cave cool and dry. The three Hoffman boys loved exploring the cave and its huge chambers, since it provided escape from the oppressive heat and humidity prevalent in Rio Muni for most of the year. Karl and Pilar imposed a standing rule that the boys always had to be in pairs and have flashlights while exploring the cave.

Walter also talked about his life in the German navy. In his eighteen years of service he had slowly risen through the officer ranks and was now assigned as the executive officer on the new cruiser *Emden*. He was about to realize his dream to see the world. The *Emden* would soon sail around the world on a good will tour to "show the flag" for the German republic and train officer cadets. On its first tour, in the Atlantic, Walter described a lengthy port visit they had made in Walvis Bay, South West Africa, the former colony that Germany had to give up after the war, along with Kamerun and the other colonies. South West Africa had the largest number of German settlers of all the former colonies, more than twenty thousand. The *Emden* and its crew received a stunning welcome from the settlers, especially in nearby Swakopmund, where the largest German community lived. Walter befriended several families and promised to stay in touch with them. Southwest Africa was now a League of Nations mandate under the protection of South Africa. Although that country had supported Britain during the war and had invaded and seized the colony, a huge portion of the white population in South Africa, the Afrikaner settlers of Dutch descent, were sympathetic to the German settlers and their plight.

The four men eventually discussed the political and economic situation in Germany and Spain and the world. Wilhelm related how Germany barely survived the economic upheavals of the early 1920s, including runaway inflation, heavy war reparations to the allied countries, and accompanying political instability, which still continued. Conditions were greatly improved in the last year or two, thanks to American loans that were provided by the Dawes Plan, named after its originator, the then vice president of the United States. Wilhelm thought that all of Western Europe now depended on America following through with this action and becoming more involved in world politics and economics. However, he thought that this was unlikely given rising American isolationism. He believed that all that would be needed was a cataclysmic economic event in America and the entire world economy would collapse.

Pedro Ortega agreed with Wilhelm's assessment. He saw what economic uncertainty and political instability was doing to Spain and it largely mirrored what had happened in Germany. In 1923, Spain became a military dictatorship, largely as a result of economic upheaval and continued poverty. The Ortegas, as with other wealthy families, were largely shielded from the effects of these conditions. The monarchy in Spain was unable to address these social and economic issues and became progressively weaker, giving rise to the military dictatorship. Also, the influence of communism became increasingly stronger throughout Europe, and this stimulated the creation of reactionary right-wing governments, such as emerged in Spain and could do so at any time in Germany.

Karl Hoffman thought about these comments, adding his own take on the situation. "I believe you're both right about the situation that's unfolding. I believe the only solution is to increase world trade and to form international alliances to reduce tensions."

Karl continued, adding how this would apply to their situation: "I believe our own future lies in developing additional foreign markets for our products. I'm planning to travel to America in a few months, to work with Pedro's brother to increase our sales of cocoa and coffee in the western hemisphere. Ramon also believes that in a few years America will cast aside its ridiculous experiment with Prohibition, and that could open up export possibilities for wine—for both families. I hope to take the whole family with me. It will be a great experience for the boys, especially, to see America and learn about its differences with the rest of the world."

Karl always thought for himself on these matters and rarely conformed to the conventional wisdom of the time. Wilhelm had told Karl earlier that it was good that he had not stayed in the army.

At this point, Maria, Pilar, and Erica joined the men on the patio. As they mingled and happily chatted about their good fortune in being together, Karl knew that his father wanted to speak with him about his sons' education. Karl remembered their earlier conversation. Wilhelm believed that the boys could receive a better education in Germany than they were currently able to obtain. Karl knew that Wilhelm was right. From the beginning, Karl and Pilar had focused on the boys' education. They were brought up in an atmosphere of tolerance and learned to respect people of all nationalities and races. Karl and Pilar emphasized this in their daily lives as the boys observed the respectful attitudes of Karl and Pedro Ortega toward the African workers on their plantation. Karl thought about how fortunate he was to find and lure Wekesa, his *Schutztruppe* comrade, to the plantation as the chief African overseer of their work force. Wekesa was invaluable in helping the plantation acquire an experienced and reliable work force. All three of Karl's sons also looked up to Wekesa.

The boys were also brought up in a bilingual family. All three were fluent in both German and Spanish. In addition, one of their servants in Rio Muni spoke excellent English and had recently spent much time with Paul, their youngest son, who was making great progress in English also. Even Karl had joined in the enterprise and was already speaking halting but understandable English. The other two boys, Hans and Ernst, started school in Bata beginning in 1923 and 1924 respectively but had shown little interest in English.

Even Pedro Ortega agreed that the boys would be better off being educated in Germany. This would be especially true if the boys could enter a gymnasium, the famous and rigorous pre-high schools and high schools that were common throughout Europe but especially rigorous in Germany. Pedro knew that the Spanish schools were not nearly as good and wanted the boys to obtain a secular education. Pedro despised the Catholic-run education system in Spain. It was one of the things he thought was holding Spain back in modernizing. He was also fearful about the political situation in Spain and thought that the situation in Germany, despite its problems, was improving.

Pilar was less enthused about the idea, but agreed that it was the best thing to do. She urged Karl to "swap" places with Ernesto, so that Ernesto could join Pedro in Spanish Guinea and Karl could return to Spain to manage the wine business for several years. That would make it easier for the boys to return to Spain or for Pilar and Karl to visit them in Germany. Ernesto was chafing for the chance to go to Africa and help with the development of the family business there and readily agreed to this idea.

Karl thought about all of this as he walked over to his father and pulled him aside to finish their earlier conversation. Wilhelm began his pitch.

"Karl, I think it is wonderful that you are planning the trip to America and taking the family with you. When you return, have you thought more about what I said about the boys' education?"

"Yes, Father, everybody is in agreement, including Pilar, Pedro, and Ernesto. Upon our return from America next summer, Hans will travel to Germany to enter school there. Ernst will follow in 1928."

At this point, Walter walked over and joined the conversation. Walter and Erica had offered to help with the boys, since they were currently childless and were thrilled with the idea of having Hans and Ernst around more often.

"Karl, you know that Erica and I would be honored to care for your children while they are here for the school year." Walter paused before making his main point. "I hope that...that it's possible for you to forgive me for my past doubts regarding your life. After hearing about your life in Africa, and seeing how your children have matured, I think I now understand what you were trying to accomplish. Erica and I would like to facilitate their education in Germany."

Karl was momentarily taken aback by Walter's sudden mellowing but quickly warmed to the offer. "Thank you, Walter, that's incredibly generous. It will be good for the boys to have family to board with while they are in school." Karl was pleased and hopeful that he and Walter might have turned a corner in their relationship.

Karl and Walter did not talk about Paul, who was several years younger and would not be eligible to enter the gymnasium until 1931, at the earliest. Karl would deal with that decision in four or five years.

As the family left the patio to have dinner, Karl began to feel comfortable about the decision to send his children to school in Germany. After all, he thought, weren't things improving in Germany finally, under the Weimar Republic?

Before their departure from Bernkastel, Karl and Pedro discussed the transition that would soon occur in the management of their enterprise. Pedro would return to Spanish Guinea. Ernesto would join him after Karl returned to Alabos from his business trip to the Americas. Karl and Pilar would manage the Rioja enterprises for several years. As they finished their conversation, Karl wondered how long Pedro would be able to continue an active role in Spanish Guinea. Although Pedro was healthy and vigorous, he had just turned sixty-six. Karl resolved to discuss the situation with Pilar and, later, Ernesto, but then thought better of it. After all, his father had turned seventy-four at the beginning of the year and he was still healthy and tending to his vineyards.

16.

New York City, America
May 1927

* * *

Karl and his family had been in New York for nearly three weeks. Their journey to the New World by rail and sea went very well and the boys enjoyed the sea voyage. That experience, however, paled in comparison to their big adventure that unfolded in America. The boys grew up in a rural environment in both Spain and Spanish Guinea, and the sights and thrills of an urban environment, especially a place as singular as New York, was a constant delight for them. Karl and Pilar also enjoyed their stay enormously.

Ramon Ortega was wealthy and owned both a large downtown apartment in Manhattan and an estate on Long Island. The family stayed in Manhattan during the week while Karl and Ramon were busy with business, and then the family spent the weekends on the island.

Karl's business activities went exceptionally well. Ramon introduced Karl to his circle of associates in the export-import business, especially those dealing with agricultural commodities such as cocoa and coffee. Karl brought samples of each with him from the plantations in Spanish Guinea, and these impressed the traders who ran the New York Cocoa Exchange, which had been established in 1925 and already had a huge influence on the cocoa market and prices. Karl negotiated incredibly favorable prices for his products and secured long-term contracts for their importation to America. Neither commodity was produced in America, yet the country loved its chocolate and coffee. The contracts would prove very timely since production on the plantations had ramped up enormously and the family needed more export markets in order to continue expansion.

By Friday, May 20, 1927, Karl concluded his business in New York, and the family was planning a major celebration of their success at Ramon's Long Island estate. They left the city very early in the morning. Karl and Ramon promised Ernst and Paul that they would swing by Roosevelt Field on Long Island to observe the activity surrounding the possible takeoff of a trans-Atlantic flight by several competing teams of aviators. One of them was an obscure air mail pilot named Charles Lindbergh, and he was planning a solo flight across the ocean. The newspapers did not rate his chances for success as very high, and the other teams were better financed.

Karl's two younger boys were fascinated with aviation and aviators. The infant aeronautical industry was beginning to generate the technology needed to create a practical air transportation system, but it was the romance, danger, and fascination with flight itself that motivated the two boys. They were only nine and six years old, but their fertile imaginations were already envisioning possibilities about their future. Karl thought often about how the boys were maturing and developing distinct personalities. Hans, at age ten, was very quiet and steady and looked out for his two younger brothers. Ernst was the adventurer, very athletic and spontaneous, yet sensitive and thoughtful. Paul was still very young, but Karl and Pilar both noticed that he was more studious and seemed to think in bigger concepts than the other two boys.

When they reached Roosevelt Field, the family found large crowds present, but they were able to get very close to Lindbergh's plane as it was rolled out for takeoff to be the first contender to try the eastbound nonstop flight to Paris. Two French aviators had recently attempted the westbound flight and had disappeared over the ocean. Despite the damp morning, Lindbergh decided to launch, and the family was thrilled as they watched the *Spirit of Saint Louis* just barely make it off the runway and clear the telephone poles and trees at the other end.

* * *

The next day, the evening papers contained the electrifying news that Lindbergh had made it safely to Paris nonstop in thirty-three hours. Ernst and Paul were beside themselves with excitement. The event astounded even Karl, but his two youngest sons were way ahead of him. Karl and Pilar had spent many hours educating the boys about geography, and Ernst led the family discussion that night before dinner, using Ramon Ortega's world globe as his prop.

"Father, look at this." Ernst had a ruler and thumb on the globe as six-year-old Paul looked on, spellbound by his brother's performance.

"If I had Lindbergh's plane, I could fly from Alabos to Spanish Guinea in only twenty-five hours, nonstop!" He continued, nearly out of breath, "I could also fly from Alabos to Bernkastel to visit Grandfather Hoffman in only seven hours!"

Karl smiled as he looked on. The boys realized that the world was shrinking. He could not then know how fast it would shrink in the next two decades—and what it would mean to the world and their families' fate and fortunes.

17.

San Francisco, California, America
July 1927

* * *

On his family's last day in San Francisco, Karl thought about their incredible journey across America. The day after their celebration in New York, he had received a letter from Ernesto replying to an earlier letter of his. Ernesto approved Karl's plan to extend their summer trip so the boys could see more of America before school started in the fall. They timed their trip to arrive in San Francisco at this time because, by an amazing coincidence, they determined that Walter would then be in the city for a port visit on the first world cruise of the *Emden*.

Karl thought about their amazing rail journey to California. The entire family was awestruck, especially by the American Southwest because of its unique geography and culture. The family also understood the irony of their presence in the Southwest. They realized that this land was once colonized by Spain, and the boys were curious about their history in this regard. How could Spain's once mighty empire have been reduced from most of the Americas to only a small presence in Spanish Guinea, a vast wasteland farther up the coast known as Spanish Sahara, and a small part of Morocco?

The family was also amazed by American attitudes and hospitality. The only thing missing in the American consciousness, noticed even by the boys, was the typical American's appalling lack of knowledge about the rest of the world. Karl considered this a serious weakness in American thought, but it seemed to be overcome by so many other attributes, including optimism about the future.

Karl remembered the *Emden's* arrival in San Francisco Bay several days ago as it steamed past Alcatraz Island on its way to dock at the Embarcadero. Later, after the cruiser docked, Walter spent some enjoyable time with Karl's family. Karl and the boys also were able to spend time on the ship, and this was especially satisfying to Hans, who was as fascinated by ships and the sea as

Ernst and Paul were about airplanes and the sky. Walter proved to be a patient tour guide and mentor for Hans. On this final day in port, onshore after dinner, Walter pulled Karl aside to say good-bye before returning to the ship.

"Karl, I'm returning to Germany in a few months and will be assigned to a staff job in Berlin, where Hans will be attending the gymnasium. I want you to know that Erica and I will look after him and treat him as we would our own son." Walter's voice cracked; he and Erica had been unable to have children.

"I know that you will, Walter. Pilar and I are thrilled that Hans will be staying with you. If you're willing, we hope that Ernst might also board with you when he enters the gymnasium next year. They're both such smart boys, and this will be a wonderful opportunity for them."

Walter nodded as they briefly embraced. As Walter walked away, Karl thought again about how he and Pilar had made the right decision. Karl thought that the 1920s were unfolding in a way that matched his earlier dreams. Perhaps their future would be even brighter as the world opened up and became smaller.

Part 3

* * *

Upheaval

1930–1939

18.

Alabos, La Rioja, Spain
June 1930

* * *

The entire Hoffman and Ortega clans had gathered at the Ortega estate for their periodic reunion. Wilhelm, Walter, and Erica Hoffman had traveled from Germany with Karl's two older boys, who had been attending school in Germany for the last three and two years, respectively. Pedro, Maria, Ernesto, and Ana Ortega had arrived a week before from Spanish Guinea with Ernesto's family. They felt able to leave the plantations for several months since they now had able management in place. Even Ramon Ortega had traveled from New York for the occasion. Karl and Pilar, with nine-year-old Paul, were hosting the event since they were still managing the properties in Alabos and had been there, for the most part, since returning from America in 1927.

On the Saturday following everyone's arrival, the two families celebrated with a gala celebration dinner. The menu and wine pairings were exceptional. The first course included a smoked trout paired with a Hoffman Riesling *kabinett*. The main course included roast suckling pigs prepared two different ways, courtesy of old Hoffman and Ortega recipes. The Hoffman version was served with a *Spätlese Trocken* from the 1921 vintage that Pedro Ortega thought was unusually full bodied and well paired with the pig. He countered with a version of the pig that he paired with his Rioja *Gran Reserva* from both the 1922 and1924 vintages. The 1924 was drinking fabulously already but would be even better in ten or fifteen years. For dessert, they served a special chocolate torte prepared from chocolate that used cocoa beans from the Rio Muni plantation. The ultimate finishing course was Hoffman *Trockenbeerenauslese* from both the 1893 and 1900 vintages, amazing dessert wines not yet at their peak at thirty-seven and thirty years old. Following this sumptuous feast, the men retreated to Pedro's study for brandy and, for Ramon Ortega, Cuban cigars.

Pedro began their discussion casually, talking about his latest real estate purchase. He had purchased a hunting lodge in Andorra, a small principality located in the Pyrenees Mountains wedged between France and Spain. This tiny little country was known as a haven for smugglers and others trying to hide out during turbulent times. Pedro maintained that they would be able to vacation there and hunt wild boar, but Karl knew that Pedro also was thinking of it as a hideaway. Hopefully, Karl thought, it would never be needed for that, but he remembered an earlier conversation in which Pedro talked about both the looming threats of Fascism and Communism and the worsening economic situation in Spain and in the world.

Pedro turned to the world economy. "We should all be grateful that our conservative investment policies and caution have insulated both of our families from the worst of the developing economic crisis in America and in the rest of the world."

Wilhelm von Hoffman agreed. "It is clear that the cycle of economic activity is changing. I am afraid that my prediction of four years ago about America is about to come true. Wisely, we've sheltered much of our profits in stable currencies and not overextended our investments or overproduced on our estates and plantations."

Everyone nodded. Wilhelm didn't need to elaborate since both families took the same action with their excess profits by converting them to Swiss marks and depositing them in Swiss banks, adding to their already large fortunes there. Wilhelm Hoffman had wisely invested the family fortune in these instruments and avoided the catastrophe brought on by the hyperinflation in Germany during 1923 and 1924, which wiped out the middle class and those wealthy Germans who had not diversified. Pedro, Ernesto, and Karl had taken similar steps.

Karl continued the discussion. "My big fear now is not inflation but a monetary crisis brought on by America's retrenchment following their stock market crash and the institution of protectionist trade policies. This could impact us, even though America has no domestic coffee and cocoa production to protect. We were fortunate to have negotiated long-term contracts for our products, which won't expire until 1935. Even though America may raise the tariffs on our products, we will still be able to market them there, as long as we anticipate several years of reduced sales."

Everyone nodded at Karl's assessment. Ernesto turned the discussion to politics.

"I wish I could be as optimistic about our situation here in Spain. The collapse of the military dictatorship and the inability of the king to address the pressing political and social issues make us vulnerable to the same forces that created revolution in Russia and nearly did so in Germany. The communists and socialists are especially strong right now. I'm afraid that the monarchy is very vulnerable."

Pedro added to Ernesto's assessment. "Although we have supported the monarchy, and even some of the reforms tried under the military dictatorship, I am afraid these actions are not enough to appease the left wing."

Wilhelm von Hoffmann nodded his agreement. "Yes, and although the situation in Germany is not yet as bad, I fear that economic conditions and lingering resentment about the war could cause similar upheaval eventually. But in Germany the threat is from the right wing."

Karl thought that this was a remarkable admission from his father, a Prussian aristocrat who had served fifty years in the German army. Karl knew that Wilhelm placed little faith in the republic that currently governed Germany but also believed that a unified Germany was needed and desired by the population—and it would likely be a unifying effort from the right wing. Karl remembered the discussion with his father about an up-and-coming politician named Hitler. Karl dismissed an uneasy feeling he had about that prospect.

In an earlier discussion with Wilhelm and Walter, Karl had learned that Hans and Ernst were doing exceptionally well in the gymnasium. They would begin the high school portion in 1931 and 1932. Both boys had spoken highly of their experience. Karl hoped that the situation would allow them to continue their high-quality education. He and Pilar had decided to enroll Paul in a special school in Madrid, since Pilar wanted Paul to remain in Spain.

Eventually the reunion came to an end and the two families returned to their responsibilities. Ramon returned to America, agreeing that Karl should return again in a few years to negotiate new contacts. Karl and Ernesto agreed to "swap" roles again in conjunction with that trip. They both agreed that by then they wanted Pedro, who was seventy, to come back to Spain. Neither Karl nor Ernesto needed to elaborate.

19.

Berlin, Germany
August 1931

* * *

Karl and Walter Hoffman sat in Walter's study catching up on family matters. The day before they had seen their father off, as Wilhelm returned to Bernkastel by train. Karl listened as Walter raved about Karl's two boys and how well they were doing.

"Hans has done exceptionally well in the gymnasium program. I think someday he may be an engineer. You've also seen how Ernst has matured. As you know from my letters, he has entered the sports league for gliding and his progress is outstanding. He will be eligible to solo when he turns fourteen next year. His performance has earned him a trip to the Wasserkuppe next year."

Ernst seemed destined for the sky. Ever since witnessing the Lindbergh flight in 1927, he was enthralled by everything to do with flying. The Wasserkuppe was a famous location for the German gliding movement. All German military aviation had been banned after the war, but civilian aviation was taking off in Germany, and the government saw to it that promising boys with the aptitude were directed toward aviation, starting with gliding activities at the age of twelve. Karl thought briefly about the connection between the heavy government promotion of aviation and what it really meant, but the thought was only momentary.

The big news for Walter and Erica was that Erica was finally pregnant, after eleven years of marriage. They were, of course, overjoyed, but assured Karl that they still wanted his two boys to live with them during the school year. As Karl absorbed this good news, he was also curious about Walter's naval career. Although Walter had been in staff jobs in Berlin since early 1928, he spent considerable time traveling to places like Finland and Holland and even Spain. Karl couldn't resist asking Walter about these activities.

"Pilar and I are overjoyed about the boys and the news about Erica." He paused. "I'm curious, however, about your extensive travel outside Germany on navy business. What could possibly be of such importance in Finland and Holland?"

Walter's sudden angry reaction to Karl's innocent question took him by surprise.

"That is none of your business, Karl. It is forbidden to discuss such matters and..." Walter stopped abruptly, suppressing his outburst. There was an awkward silence.

Karl finally replied, "Walter, I'm sorry if I raised a sensitive matter. I didn't mean—"

"That's all right, Karl; I didn't mean to raise my voice." Walter paused before continuing, his tone still edgy. "Let's go and see if Erica and Pilar have returned from the village."

Karl nodded, and Walter led them out of the study. Karl's curiosity was even stronger now, but he suppressed an urge to probe deeper.

As a result of their awkward conversation, Karl and Walter did not continue with a deeper discussion of the current economic and political situation. It was just as well, since the news was mostly grim. The world economy was now in a full depression and Germany was again in turmoil. The situation in Spain, however, was even worse. The king had abdicated earlier in the year and Spain was now a republic. Moreover, the new government was decidedly left wing and raising issues from land reform to education. Karl thought this was exceedingly risky in a conservative country like Spain, and he already saw signs of pushback from some landowners, the army, and the Catholic clergy. On the other hand, the new government had immediately created a more liberal education system and reforms involving women's rights, among other new ideas. Karl and Pilar were pleased with their earlier decision to enroll Paul in the special school in Madrid, since he would now have access to a more liberal education. Karl and Pilar were traveling to Madrid next to enroll Paul in the school.

When Karl later said his good-byes to Walter, Erica, and his two boys, he wondered what Germany would look like when he next returned.

20.

Alabos, La Rioja, Spain
August 1934

* * *

Most of the Ortega clan gathered for their annual summer rendezvous, except for Ernesto who remained on the plantation in Spanish Guinea. Pedro had returned from Spanish Guinea, and Karl and Pilar thought that he was unlikely to return, although nobody brought the subject up.

All three of their sons joined Karl and Pilar, although Wilhelm, Walter, and Erica were not able to make the trip. Walter and Erica now had a daughter, Kirsten, born in 1932, and they had elected not to travel to Spain.

Karl and especially Pilar were overjoyed that all three of their sons were with them for the first part of the summer. Both Hans and Ernst had flourished in the gymnasium environment. Ernst had achieved an outstanding record and had been advanced one year. Thus he and Hans would graduate at the same time, in June 1935. Ernst had completed extensive glider training and was now enrolled in an accelerated powered aircraft training program. As a result, he had returned to Germany in late June.

Paul had done well in the Madrid school and would complete middle school in June 1935. Pilar had at last recognized that the improvements in education in Spain were transitory at best, because of the changing political landscape and resulting turmoil in the country. The extreme left-wing government in power from 1931 to 1933 had given in to right-wing pressures, and the new government was foundering, resulting in a retraction of some of the educational reforms. It was clear to both Karl and Pilar that the next school year would be his last in Spain.

Some of the changes taking place in Germany also alarmed Karl and Pilar. In the 1932 elections, no party secured a majority. The elderly, famous president, Paul von Hindenburg, allowed the Nazi party to form a government in early 1933, with Adolf Hitler as chancellor. Hitler quickly consolidated power after Hindenburg died in early August 1934, combining the offices of president and chancellor to become führer, or leader, of Germany.

Karl and Pilar were on the patio discussing these changes when Pedro Ortega and Hans joined them after inspecting the vineyards. Karl hoped that Hans might shed some light on some of the events taking place in Germany. After some small talk, he posed a question.

"Hans, how is the public accepting the new regime in Germany?"

Hans paused before answering, clearly taken aback by the question. "The new government is supported overwhelmingly by the public. We have already begun to notice positive change throughout the country. Germany is again united."

"I see. But what about some of the violence, the burning of the Reichstag, the laws against Jews, the Night of the Long Knives, and—" Karl was immediately interrupted by Hans, who had reacted as his father referred to the popular name for the June 30, 1934, assassination of many leaders of the SA, a group of Nazi thugs known as the "Brown Shirts."

"Father, these are all reactionary elements opposed to the new Germany. Some of them are inspired by communist agitators and the Jewish—"

This time Karl interrupted his son. "Hans, do you really believe the Jews are responsible for Germany's past problems?" Hans looked at his father, dumbfounded, clearly torn between the heritage of his upbringing and the recent dose of propaganda that he had been exposed to. Pilar broke the awkward silence.

"Karl, this is clearly an uncomfortable question you pose, given the current upheavals in Germany...and Spain." Pilar paused. "Hans, could you please see if your cousins are ready to join us for dinner?"

"Of course, Mother." Hans quickly excused himself, not wanting a further confrontation with his father. This time, Pedro Ortega broke the awkward silence.

"I fear it's a difficult time to be growing up in either Germany or Spain. I sympathize with your and Pilar's concerns for your sons. Ernesto and Ana are going through similar agonies over Alberto's decision to join the Spanish navy. In the final analysis, they must all find their own way and make their own judgments regarding their world and their place in it."

Karl and Pilar nodded. Ernesto's oldest son had, like Walter Hoffman, chosen the sea as his means of expanding his world. He had entered an officer cadet program upon graduation from school last year and would soon be commissioned as an officer in the Spanish navy. Karl responded to Pedro, echoing and embellishing on his conclusion.

"It's true, Pedro. They must find their own way and make their own judgments. It's just that I fear that their allegiance and loyalties to the state will force them to make unwise choices. I don't question the need for patriotism, but what exactly should they believe, given the events taking place today in Europe?"

Pedro responded, "As you know, I have continued to support the monarchy in Spain, since it provided us with stability. That position is popular with neither left nor right wings in the current government. Similarly Hans may believe that stability in Germany is important right now."

"Do you really believe that the Nazi regime is best for Germany?" Karl replied.

Pedro Ortega's answer was to the point. "No, but I fear that both Germany and Spain will follow a similar path."

21.

Berlin, Germany
June 1935

* * *

Karl, Pilar, and Paul arrived early in June for Hans and Ernst's graduation. Following this event they planned to sail to New York, where Karl and Ramon Ortega would renegotiate their cocoa and coffee contracts and conduct other family business. Paul would accompany them. From New York the family would return briefly to Spain and then to Spanish Guinea, where their arrival would allow Ernesto to return to Spain to be with his father and mother.

The changes in Germany since Karl's last visit in 1931 shocked him. The signs of the new Nazi regime were everywhere. In addition, the political changes in the world scene surrounding Germany were stunning. Germany had renounced the military provisions of the Treaty of Versailles and had begun rearming. This included creating an air force, the *Luftwaffe*, and adding a submarine force to the navy. Karl learned that all of Walter's discreet trips to Finland, Holland, and other locations, as early as 1928, had been in support of secretly recreating the U-boat arm of the navy. Walter was promoted to command one of the new U-boat flotillas, and the first boats had already been built, commissioned, and were fitting out.

Karl was even more shocked when he found out what his sons' plans were after graduation. Hans was joining the German navy as an officer cadet and had already been accepted into the U-boat arm. He would report to submarine school upon reaching his eighteenth birthday next month. Karl was furious with Walter when he heard the news. Furthermore, Ernst was in a pretraining program for the *Luftwaffe*. He would be inducted in November upon reaching age seventeen. After one year of advanced flight and officer training, he would be commissioned as a flying officer in the *Luftwaffe* on his eighteenth birthday in November 1936. It was clear now to Karl that all of these decisions had been premeditated but not revealed to either Karl or Pilar.

Several days after the graduation, Karl waited in Walter's study for Wilhelm and Walter to arrive. There was an uneasy peace in the family, at Pilar's insistence, but Karl was determined to confront his father and brother over his sons' decisions. Finally, they arrived, and after a hasty greeting, Karl began.

"Walter, I can't believe that my sons' decisions were not somehow influenced by your encouragement. Why did you allow this to occur?"

Karl could see that his brother was visibly nervous as Walter responded quietly, "Karl, it's true that I encouraged them, but I also encouraged them to complete their schooling and saw to it that they were diligent about their studies. I believe the results speak for themselves in that area."

Karl nodded, realizing that both boys had graduated with honors. Walter continued, "As to their decision about military service, I can honestly say that they came to this decision on their own, and considered their required duty, as well as their family heritage. Karl, it could be that they view their obligation to Germany in a different way than you."

Karl reacted immediately. "What is that supposed to mean? Do you dare to question my obligation and record of service? I too served the fatherland, in uniform, but perhaps it would be better if more people would serve Germany now by questioning the path it is taking!"

"Be silent, both of you!" Wilhelm von Hoffman's booming voice could still command. "Your disrespectful remarks are shameful. Walter, you know better than to question Karl's service record." Walter bristled but lowered his head as Wilhelm turned to Karl and spoke slowly. "Karl, you are as impatient and headstrong as ever and perhaps too outspoken, but you must realize that a new generation of Germans, including your sons, is ready to perform their duty and to help in building your country."

Walter, recovering from his rebuke, interjected. "My brother, I am sorry for my comment. I honor your service to Germany. You should also be proud of your two fine sons, for what they are doing." Walter could have left it at that, but he continued, "It would also be wonderful if Paul could come to Germany to finish school and perhaps he too could then—"

Karl cut him off, fuming and barely in control of his voice. "Walter, I accept your apology, but I can guarantee you that Paul will *not* come to Germany to finish school or to enter the military!"

Karl then turned to his father, who stood erect, in silence, staring at Karl with an expressionless face. He turned back to Walter, who was speechless also. Karl composed himself one last time and concluded his statement.

"In three days, Pilar, Paul, and I will sail for America, to conduct important commercial and family business." Karl did not disclose the nature of the "family" business. "From there we will return to Spain briefly and then sail for Spanish Guinea, which will allow Ernesto to return to Spain to be with his father."

Karl paused, turned his head to look out the window, and continued, "Pilar, Paul, and I would like some time to be with Hans and Ernst before we leave..." Karl was nearly unable to finish his statement, but regained his composure and finished defiantly, facing his father and brother. "I intend to propose to them that they have other obligations and duties besides supporting a repressive dictatorship."

Karl's provocative comment got an immediate response from Walter. "Karl, you must be careful with your ill-considered remarks!" Walter paused, looking straight at Karl. "Your remarks can be very dangerous to yourself and your sons."

Karl, surprised by the remark, again responded defiantly. "What exactly does that mean, Walter? Are you such a Nazi thug that you would threaten your own family?"

"That will be quite enough, Karl!" Wilhelm intervened.

Karl paused for a long moment looking at both Walter's icy stare and the continued shocked look on his father's face as he searched for the words to conclude. "I am not sure when I will be able to return to Germany to see you. I hope that when we meet again, events and circumstances will be...different."

With that comment, Karl turned and left the room. As he walked slowly to their suite to join Pilar and the three boys for a dinner celebration, he tried to devise a way to extract his two oldest sons from their fate. He realized with a heavy heart that such a plan could be dangerous and would, in all likelihood, be rejected by Hans and Ernst.

Over dinner, the mood was subdued. As they were finishing their meal, Ernst and Paul were having an animated conversation about flying, but Hans and Karl were mostly glum and silent. Pilar, desperately seeking closure and assurances that the family would stay united, tried to break the ice.

"I am overjoyed that we were able to spend this time together, as a family. I want us all to pledge to remain in touch…after we depart…and…" Pilar could not finish her statement and began to weep. Hans, as the oldest son, immediately consoled her.

"Mother, we will always treasure our time together as a family. Although Ernst and I must fulfill our obligation to the fatherland," Hans turned and glanced briefly but respectfully at his father before continuing, "We will both look forward to our next reunion." He then turned to Paul and continued, "Although you will not be with us, Paul, Ernst and I will be looking forward to hearing from you about the next part of your schooling…wherever that might be."

Karl immediately sensed that Hans knew what he had planned for Paul and that any proposal Karl would make to Hans and Ernst about leaving Germany would fall on deaf ears. Karl finally replied, "I also have treasured our time together. Hans, I am very proud of both you and Ernst, despite what you might think." Karl paused, realizing that the conversation was over, and he finally concluded, "I will respect your decisions about your future."

Late the next afternoon, Karl was sitting alone at a small café in Berlin quietly sipping a beer after picking up the family's visas at the American embassy. He had earlier made a few inquiries and was mentally searching for some last-minute idea that would liberate his eldest sons from their fate. Karl didn't notice the approach of the uniformed man and was interrupted from his deliberations.

"*Hauptman* Hoffman, may I join you?"

Karl looked up, shocked to see the jack-booted man in the black uniform with a swastika on his arm and an arrogant look on his face. Karl replied instinctively.

"Excuse me? I am no longer in the German army, so you may address me as *Herr* Hoffman, Herr…*Sturmbahnführer*, is it? You must excuse me; I am not completely familiar with the ranks of the SS."

The SS officer smiled as he seated himself at Karl's table without an invitation. "Very well, *Herr* Hoffman, at least you correctly identified my rank; I am *Sturmbahnführer* Schellenberg. It seems you are the only member of your family that is not proud of their own rank and, perhaps, confused about your loyalties."

"I disagree with you. I no longer hold the rank and I have no confusion at all about my identity and my loyalties."

"Yes, *Herr* Hoffman, I understand. It seems you are not confused at all about your identity that is antagonistic to the new Germany and contemptuous of your sons' achievements and loyalty to the Reich."

Karl felt a chill as he sensed both the arrogance and the implied threat in the officer's reply. Yet he didn't hesitate to respond to the challenge. "*Herr* Schellenberg, I'm a Spanish citizen now, and my first loyalty is to my family and their well-being. I also find it unusual that you presume to know so much about me. How did you come about such misinformation?"

Schellenberg glared. "To be honest, *Herr* Hoffman, your brother was concerned about your sons, and since I am casually acquainted with your status, I thought I would be doing you and your family a service by warning you about the consequences of interfering in your sons' lawful service in the *Wehrmacht*."

Karl was aghast as he absorbed the meaning of that threat, as well as his brother's role in the intervention of the SS. He realized now the true nature of the Nazi regime and what he was up against. He also now recognized the need to temper his defiance for the sake of Pilar and Paul, as well as his two oldest sons.

"*Herr* Schellenberg, I can assure you that I have no intention of interfering with the lawful duty which my sons have undertaken. You must realize, however, that my wife and I live a different life, in a different place. My service to Germany ended fifteen years ago, and for the last five I have been a Spanish citizen."

Schellenberg smiled and stood up. "Yes, *Herr* Hoffman, I understand the legalities behind which you hide as you prepare to depart for America. Maybe you will realize that eventually you and everyone else in Europe will face the need to stop straddling the fence and choose sides. Perhaps one day you will realize that your sons have chosen the side that shall prevail. I advise you to consider that and remember that your failure to so choose will mean you will not be welcome again in Germany. Good day, *Herr* Hoffman." Schellenberg came to attention, clicked his heels, turned, and walked briskly away from Karl's table.

Karl sat there for several minutes, profoundly depressed by the Nazi officer's appearance and its implications for his family. Karl could now think only of getting Pilar and Paul safely out of Germany—and hope that Hans and Ernst would somehow survive the upcoming cataclysms. The next day, Karl, Pilar, and Paul traveled to Bremerhaven, and the following day they sailed for America.

22

Madrid, Spain
October 1935

* * *

Karl sat at his favorite sidewalk café on an unusually warm autumn day, trying to enjoy the ambiance but preoccupied as he recapped in his mind the activities of the last four months. As usual, the combination of stunning business successes mixed with uncertain personal and public events commanded Karl's thoughts.

On the one hand, Karl was thankful that he, Pilar, and Paul had gotten safely out of Germany in June and then traveled to America, where Karl and Ramon had achieved excellent commercial success. They renewed several hugely lucrative deals for importing cocoa and coffee to America from Spanish Guinea. America was emerging from the Great Depression, and economic conditions were improving slowly. Karl had also concluded a deal for importing a small amount of wine from the Ortega bodegas. Now that America had finally repealed Prohibition, Karl and the Ortega family thought they could gain an edge in the wine trade before American production could really ramp up after the repeal and the depression.

This success was enhanced by Paul's acceptance into the prestigious Choate School in Connecticut in September, thanks to his success as a student, fluency in English, and performance on entrance exams, not to mention Ramon's timely contribution to the school the previous year. Paul now had a visa that would enable him to remain in America for his schooling.

Their success in America was followed by equal success in Buenos Aires, Argentina, where Karl negotiated favorable cocoa and coffee import agreements. Karl and Pilar had only just returned from the grueling journey from South America and were preparing to return to Spanish Guinea. That plan was now somewhat clouded by Pilar's reluctance to return to the isolation in Guinea, where she was even more removed from her children and parents.

Karl had come to Madrid to iron out some difficulties involving permits and currency exchange. This issue hammered home to Karl the incompetency of the left-leaning governments that had generally ruled Spain for the last four years. He wanted to get these issues cleared up so he could return to Guinea.

Karl realized that there was more going on here than just incompetent bureaucrats. In elections in 1933 and 1934, the right-wing parties regained power and reversed most of the reforms enacted when the republic was created in 1931. This put them in direct confrontation with the left-wing elements who were still trying to create a popular revolution. Pedro Ortega and his family were trying to walk a middle but very dangerous course, since they still supported the deposed monarchy, which was paid lip service by the right wing but also had very little popular support. The change in government had at least resulted in resumption of subsidies for cocoa planting and other development in Spanish Guinea. This would benefit the family operations in Africa, if not the vineyard operations in Spain itself.

While in Spain, Ernesto asked Karl and Pilar to take Alfonso back to Spanish Guinea so he could begin learning that aspect of the family business. Actually, in a long conversation with Karl while in Alabos, Ernesto confessed that he was worried about conditions in Spain and had already seen his oldest son, Alberto, join the Spanish navy. He wanted to keep as many family members as possible removed from the looming conflict and saw this as an opportunity to remove eighteen-year-old Alfonso from the danger zone. While in Spanish Guinea as a working colonist he would be exempt from military service. Karl, of course, understood Ernesto's concerns immediately and readily agreed to his proposal. Alfonso, for his part, looked forward to the change in venue and the chance to assume greater responsibility in the family business.

Karl was deep in thought when he felt a presence next to his table. He looked up at the tall, silver-haired man in a suit and tie and blinked in astonishment.

"*Kapitänleutnant* Canaris…Wilhelm, I mean…is it really you?"

"Hello, Karl, it's good to see you again—and to see that you remembered me."

This seeming apparition before him still overpowered Karl, yet he could clearly see Canaris and finally overcame his momentary shock.

"Please, Wilhelm, sit down and join me for a while."

Karl summoned the waiter. "Bring us two glasses of *fino*, please." As the waiter left, Karl turned to Canaris. "Wilhelm, this is incredible; just the other day I had a déjà vu that you would appear, exactly as you just did. Also, please forgive me for addressing you by your prior rank; I'm sure that's all in your past."

"Actually it's not. Although I have advanced from that rank, I continue to serve the navy and the country the best way I can. I must say, however, that it is very easy to find you, since you favor this same café where we first met."

"Yes, perhaps I'm too predictable." Karl smiled as he looked expectantly at Canaris.

"I really wasn't trying to startle you, Karl, and I am neither trying to follow you nor trying to recruit you again, if that is your fear."

"Wilhelm, I have no such fear, but you will pardon my curiosity as to your interest in me after…how long?"

"It's been more than nineteen years, but I would say that the world has changed dramatically in that time. Yet I truly admire your perseverance in doggedly pursuing your dream—and achieving it. Nevertheless, I certainly feel obliged to offer you whatever advice I can in these perilous times."

"Perhaps you can elaborate, Wilhelm? First, maybe I can provide you with some details on what has transpired in that time."

"There's no need for that, Karl. I know generally what has happened in your life, especially recent events. You tangled with both your brother and the SS in Germany, your two oldest sons are now in the *Wehrmacht*, and you have taken your youngest son to safety in America. You also clearly sense the danger here in Spain as communism and anarchy try to gain a foothold."

Karl's attention intensified as he mulled his response. "You seem to know about everything in my life, and about Spain. Do you also now work for the SS?"

Canaris scowled. "No, of course not. They are a bunch of thugs and are repulsive. I still work for military intelligence, the *Abwehr*."

"What do you do for them? Do you have a rank?"

"I am the head of the *Abwehr*, a *konteradmiral*."

Karl was stunned but quickly retorted, "Then what are you doing here in Spain, in civilian clothes? Or am I supposed to ask such questions about your 'cloak and dagger' activities?"

"Actually very little counterintelligence, espionage, and other undercover activity take place with drama. It's actually all about relationships and impassionate observation. That is what I am here for now, to renew our relationship and to make a few observations. I am not looking for an agent or to recruit you in any way."

Karl looked at Wilhelm carefully, sensing that he was being truthful. "Then I suppose I should ask you what your observations are as they pertain to me."

Canaris took a slow sip of his sherry, looked casually around him, and replied, "Spain is at the precipice now, one step from chaos and on the brink of civil war. It's all likely to explode within a few months, and it will affect every Spaniard and probably every European, perhaps even the world. For someone as outspoken and fearless as you, this could be a time of intense danger. It is good that you are about to return to Spanish Guinea. You and your wife should go there and continue to pursue your dream."

"So I was just driven out of Germany, and now you are saying I will be driven out of Spain. Why shouldn't I stay and try to do what is right?"

"For a while it will be impossible to say what the right thing to do is. I know you to be a fearless yet rational and realistic person, who knows when and where it is possible to influence events, and when and where it is not possible. As the saying goes, it may be better to be a 'big fish in a small pond' and influence developments in Guinea, where you already have a huge stake. One more thing—at some point in the future, and I don't know when that might be, you will sense opportunities to influence larger events by leveraging your contacts and capabilities for the betterment of your country and without the use of blunt force or other trauma."

Karl was briefly silent as he searched for the right words to reply to such insights. "Wilhelm, the advice you just provided is…quite profound. Why are you making such an effort to do this for me?"

"It's really quite simple. I don't want to see a communist bastion in Western Europe, and only thinking individuals such as you, people who have a larger view of the world, will be able to prevent that. There will likely be a violent interim solution to this issue, one that could take Spain down for years, but ultimately a few individuals such as you will find ways to relieve the danger—and find a way for Spain to recover. As I said, I don't know how this will unfold, but you will sense that moment and you must then be prepared to act, most likely in subtle ways. One last item—throughout this dangerous period, there will be no place on earth where you can escape the consequences, not even in Spanish Guinea."

Karl looked at Canaris, thought about recent events, and then realized the truth in these observations. "Wilhelm, I'm grateful for these insights—and your advice. I only hope that everything you're predicting will not occur."

"I also wish for that outcome, Karl, but you and I both see what is happening in the world—and you and I will deal with it, each in our own way."

23.

Aboard the Spanish navy cruiser Canarias, El Ferrol, Spain
July 21, 1936

* * *

Teniente de Navio Alberto Ortega held his ground as the shouting mob of enlisted sailors pressed him for information. He had been assigned by the captain of the *Canarias* to stay on the main deck to try to control the mob of rebellious sailors that had gathered. As a junior officer in the navy for only two years, Alberto had already acquired a reputation for leadership and an ability to relate to enlisted men. As he stood on the deck, he briefly touched his side arm, hoping he wouldn't need to use it.

The *Canarias* was a new cruiser commissioned in the Spanish navy only last year. It was currently in El Ferrol to install its final weapons and to complete other fitting out work before its first operations. Only four days ago, the Spanish Civil War had begun, instigated by right-wing elements in the army led by Francisco Franco. Earlier on this day, the men on the cruiser had heard distant gunfire, possible emanating from the entrance to the naval base about two miles away. It had quickly died down, and everyone was wondering what had happened. The bridge staff had lost telephone contact with the base and was trying to restore the link. Meanwhile the ringleader of the enlisted group approached Alberto and spoke first.

"We want to know what is happening on the base, and more importantly, what's happening in the rest of the country!" The rest of the crowd began cheering, but Alberto immediately raised his hands and issued a loud command through his bullhorn. "You will be silent! I order you all to attention!" Alberto shouted and then raised his hand slowly as the shouting rapidly stopped and the men came to attention. Rather than raise the bullhorn again, Alberto slowly walked toward the crowd, away from his escorting detail as he entered the middle of the crowd of nervous sailors. They gave way and gathered around him. Alberto turned slowly around, looking each man in the eye as he did so. He began talking and continued to turn slowly.

"You may remain at ease." He paused as the men relaxed and then continued to talk and turn. "I don't know the full situation as it exists in the country, nor do I know what is happening on the base. We are trying to restore contact and we will inform you as soon as we know, but I am ordering you now to return to your duty stations. This kind of mob action is not authorized and is not honorable."

"*Teniente*, is it honorable for the military to attempt an overthrow of the established government? Is it honorable for us to participate in such activities?" the ringleader replied.

Alberto turned to the ringleader, thinking fast, and responded, "I believe not. But above all, we must obey the orders that we receive. It's not for you or me to decide who is doing what to whom in the political arena. Rather, we must trust the military leadership to ascertain who, in fact, the legitimate government is and then respond appropriately. If the military cannot perform that function then we have no hope."

Alberto paused to let that sink in. He was not sure himself about who the legitimate government was and wondered whether the military leadership was capable of determining that, or whether they were, in fact, the problem. Yet he had sworn an oath to serve in the military and uphold the legitimate government—whoever that was.

As Alberto saw that he was slowly winning over most of the enlisted sailors in the crowd, they all heard a gathering noise as a long column of trucks entered the dock area. Several minutes later they saw a large number of heavily armed soldiers and sailors dismount and rapidly approach the *Canarias*, mounting the gangway. Alberto, as officer of the deck, approached the leader of the group as he arrived on deck, noticing he held the rank of colonel in the Spanish army. Alberto came to attention and saluted. The colonel returned his salute and immediately stated his purpose.

"Good afternoon, *Teniente*. I am here to arrest the revolutionaries who may be attempting to take over this ship." The colonel turned to look at the faces of the sailors, some of them terrified of what might happen. They then looked at Alberto expectantly. Alberto turned to the colonel.

"*Coronel*, sir, I am pleased to report that we have no such revolutionaries on board the *Canarias*. I was just briefing the men on upcoming exercises. The officers and men of the *Canarias* stand ready to support...the government."

Alberto's pause was deliberate and possibly risky. He had no idea who or what the government had become in the last five days, but he wanted to be sure that he and his men, and the ship, would not become an instant battleground. He posed a question to their guest.

"Perhaps the *coronel* could enlighten us on developments and how we may serve? My captain is ashore trying to restore communications and I am officer of the deck."

Alberto and the men promptly got their answer. "Of course, *Teniente*, I would be happy to inform you. The army...and navy...have acted to foil a plot by revolutionaries to destroy the government and the country. This revolt, by communists and their sympathizers, is being opposed by loyal army elements led by General Francisco Franco, who has returned from his post in Spanish Morocco to save the nation. Army elements, acting with our navy comrades, have seized this base and we will soon mount operations to put down the revolutionaries. As I see that you have the situation on this ship in hand, I will provide you with some additional troops to secure the dock, and the rest of my men and I will depart."

Alberto looked around and quickly saw the relief and gratitude on his sailors' faces. The Nationalist rebels now had control of the most modern warship in the Spanish navy.

24.

Berlin, Germany
November 1936

* * *

Leutnant zur See Hans Hoffman and *Leutnant* Ernst Hoffman entered the office of *Kapitän zur See* Walter Hoffman, came to attention, and saluted their uncle. Walter stood, returned their salute, and motioned them to join him at his conference table. The family tradition called for them to resume informal family names and manners after the initial rendering of military protocol. Before they could begin, Wilhelm von Hoffman also entered the room. All three of the younger Hoffman clan instinctively rose and snapped to attention. Wilhelm motioned them to sit down with one hand. He had a bottle in the other hand. It was late, after 5:00 p.m., and office protocol was over for the day.

Wilhelm, still hale and hearty at age eighty-four, joined them at the table and began the conversation. "So we are here to honor Ernst, who's now an officer and pilot in the *Luftwaffe*. For this occasion I have brought a special bottle of *amontillado* provided for the occasion by Pedro Ortega."

It was Walter's turn. "I toast Hans's new U-boat assignment as watch officer." After that toast, the glasses were nearly empty and Wilhelm promptly filled them. Hans was next.

"I also toast my brother Ernst, not only for his new commission and graduation from pilot training in the *Luftwaffe*, but also his volunteering for the Condor Legion in Spain, to protect our Spanish family members."

Ernst was last. "I propose a toast for my uncle, on his recent selection to the staff of the U-boat force." Everybody drank to that and by this time the bottle of very expensive sherry was over half empty. Wilhelm poured them all another glass.

Indeed, three generations of military Hoffmans had much to toast. The only controversy was over Ernst volunteering for the assignment with the Condor Legion. Only just turned eighteen and right out of pilot school, his application to join had initially been rejected, but he had persisted, and his sterling flight training record finally won the day. Since the *Luftwaffe* was newly created, they did not have an experienced reservoir of pilot applicants to call on. Ernst was leaving for advanced fighter training the next day and would be sent to Spain in several months.

Germany had just formed the Condor Legion to support the new Nationalist movement in Spain led by Franco, joining with Italy to counter the support provided to the existing Spanish Republican government by the Soviet Union and other countries. By this time, the conflict had become a full-fledged civil war and the Nationalists had already achieved significant victories, although the Republicans still held Madrid, Barcelona, and territory in eastern Spain. All of the Ortega properties in Rioja and Jerez were well within the zone controlled by the Nationalists. Although the conflict had started as a civil war, it was playing out on the world stage as a test between the fascist and communist movements.

Germany had formed the Condor Legion partly as a means to test new military equipment and to rapidly season its new air force. In the end, Spain was caught in the middle. Both the Hoffman and Ortega families were in the thick of it, mostly supporting the Nationalist uprising. Although the four Hoffmans in the room were committed to this enterprise, none of them verbalized what they also knew—Pablo and Ernesto Ortega and Karl Hoffman had reservations about the Nationalists but had no choice but to support the movement, since they were in Nationalist territory.

After their toasts and lively conversation, Wilhelm, Hans, and Ernst rose and prepared to leave Walter's office. Walter was leaving in a couple of days for Wilhelmshaven to begin his assignment as senior staff officer for the U-boat force. Hans would follow after seeing his brother off for fighter training. As they were leaving the room, Walter asked Hans to remain for a few minutes. He motioned for Hans to close the door and join him at the conference table.

"Hans, I have a special assignment for you that will be important to our effort to assist Spain—and the U-boat force." He then poured the remainder of the sherry in their two glasses and outlined the assignment.

25.

Aboard U-34, off the coast of Malaga, Spain
December 1936

* * *

The skipper of the U-34 peered through his periscope to get a closer look at the submarine he had spotted cruising on the surface leaving the harbor. He adjusted the focus and confirmed his initial identification. It was the Spanish navy submarine C-3. Since all twelve Spanish submarines were in the possession of the Republican forces, the C-3 was fair game for U-34.

In November, U-boat command had sent U-34 and a sister boat secretly to Spanish waters to assist the Nationalist forces and reconnoiter ports and anchorages for future U-boat operations in the Atlantic. Walter Hoffman had planned the mission in great detail and saw to it that Hans was assigned to one of the boats, to gain experience and fast track his career. Hans was the third-ranking officer in U-34 and was working the plotting board and serving as the captain's primary assistant for this attack.

As the captain's data observations came fast and furious, Hans had to work quickly to calculate the torpedo firing solution. They would have only one chance to fire because of the distance and firing angle. Finally, the captain gave the order to shoot the single torpedo. As it left the tube and the boat shuddered, the captain retracted the periscope and quietly asked Hans for an update.

"Hoffman, what is the time to target?"

"Two minutes, fifteen seconds, *Herr Kapitän!*"

Two minutes later, the skipper asked for the periscope to be raised. He turned it to the calculated bearing and focused. Seconds later, he was rewarded with the sight of an exploding target and a huge splash where the torpedo hit. He watched as the Spanish submarine quickly sank. He called Hans to the periscope.

"Good work, Hoffman. Come over here and take a look."

Hans looked through the periscope at the rapidly sinking target. He noticed immediately that there did not appear to be any survivors. They had completely surprised the Spanish boat. Hans fleetingly thought about what it must have been like on the boat in the few seconds the crew might have had to contemplate their deaths. He quickly erased the thought from his mind. In his initial introduction to war and death, Hans shrugged off such humanitarian considerations and stuck to business.

"*Herr Kapitän*, it was an excellent hit, but I'm sure that shots at these extreme angles must be carefully plotted and executed. It may be desirable to shoot a spread of two or three torpedoes to ensure a hit in the future."

"You may be right on that, Hoffman, but this time we'll assume that our skill was complemented by a little luck."

26.

In the air, approaching Guernica, Spain
April 1937

* * *

Ernst Hoffman kept his eyes on his element leader as the two Messerschmitt Bf-109B fighters orbited several thousand feet above and behind the formation of He-111 bombers and He-51 ground attack aircraft. During fighter school it was hammered into him that he must stay close to his element leader to ensure that he could protect the leader's rear position. They were escorting the bombers on a mission to attack Republican forces near Guernica in the Basque country in Northern Spain. This was Ernst's third combat mission. The other two had been simple patrols. He had yet to see an enemy aircraft.

It was early in the morning, and the bomber formation was headed west with the Bf-109s following behind several kilometers, with the sun at their backs. As they flew toward the target, Ernst thought how lucky he was to have this assignment. The Bf-109 was a new fighter model, very advanced for 1937, and it had only recently entered *Luftwaffe* service. In fact, the bugs were still being worked out of it, and engine and landing gear problems were common. Ernst had experienced both problems and had been commended for his skill in returning the aircraft intact each time. The *Luftwaffe* used the Condor Legion as a proving ground to deal with just such issues. The early models of the Bf-109 had only been approved for combat the previous month, and Ernst was privileged to be flying one at the tender age of eighteen and a half.

All three Hoffman boys were tall, but Ernst was the shortest at five feet eleven inches and just barely fit in the Messerschmitt's cramped cockpit. He was also the most youthful looking, with an athletic build and manner, blond hair and blue eyes like his father. He was cool yet amiable, with a sense of humor and positive outlook that endeared him to his squadron mates.

Ernst's thoughts were interrupted by the quick wing waggle of his element leader. He looked at the leader's cockpit and saw him make the hand signal for enemy aircraft, pointing down and to the right. Ernst maneuvered the 109 down and back a little and quickly saw the aircraft: three

Russian-built Polikarpov I-16 fighters, known as *Rata* to the Nationalist forces. They were starting a dive to attack the bombers and probably had not spotted the two 109s. Ernst quickly maneuvered back close in to his leader's wing. The leader gave the hand single for attack. Ernst acknowledged by hand signal. The element leader then rolled off to the right and Ernst followed, staying close in and tight.

As the two 109s dove they quickly closed the gap with the I-16 formation. Ernst remembered his pre-briefing: don't attempt a dogfight with the I-16 since it is more maneuverable than the 109 at lower altitude, just dive from above to attack one and continue your dive to outrun the rest of them.

His leader rolled to aim at the last I-16 in the formation. Ernst quickly flicked the switch to arm his two machine guns as he followed the leader's moves. At the optimum range the lead 109 fired at the I-16, still unaware of the 109s behind him. Ernst watched as the tracers reached the fuel tank in the left wing of the I-16, and within two seconds it exploded and tumbled uncontrollably. The pilot did not get out.

As the two 109s blew past the other I-16s, they quickly outdistanced them and then pulled up into a zoom climb, trading airspeed for altitude in preparation for another attack. By this time, the I-16's were alerted and maneuvered toward the 109s. Ernst clung to his leader as he turned steeply and prepared for a head-on attack. The lead 109 dived steeply to a lower altitude and then pulled up to meet an I-16 with a near head-on deflection shot. The leader anticipated that the I-16 would turn in toward him and maneuvered to be in the right space for a quick shot. He fired a quick two-second burst and his aim was perfect. He hit the engine and cockpit area of the I-16. Ernst broke right to miss the I-16 as it went past them and his leader broke left. With a wispy stream of oil following it, the I-16 slowly rolled inverted and headed for the ground, its pilot dead.

The last I-16 had anticipated the head-on attack and pulled up into a steep wingover before the 109 formation flew by, to position himself for an attack as the two 109s pulled up after their attack and were slow and vulnerable. His timing was near perfect as he found himself coming up behind the lead 109 as it finished its zoom climb and had used up its precious airspeed.

Spotting the I-16 as it closed on his leader, Ernst slammed his throttle to the stop and rolled left to catch up to the I-16. He hoped he would be in time.

The 109 had a blind spot behind and below and his leader might not see the rapidly approaching I-16. Ernst rapidly closed the distance. The *Rata* started firing, and Ernst saw his leader trying to avoid the fire, but the I-16 was more maneuverable at the lower speed.

Finally, Ernst reached a good position and fired. His aim was dead-on. He anticipated a left roll off by the I-16, and when it happened, Ernst fired again and watched the rounds hit the fuselage and engine. Ernst must have hit a fuel line, as he saw vapor pouring out of the engine area toward the cockpit. The *Rata* pulled up hard and broke left; Ernst saw the pilot trying to get out of the cockpit to bail out but his harness must have jammed because he could see the pilot pounding on the mechanism. Just then, a huge fire broke out starting from the engine and then engulfing the cockpit area in flames. Ernst saw the desperate pilot struggling to get out as his clothes caught fire. Ernst pulled closer and instinctively shouted out.

"Come on, release it and get out!" He saw the pilot struggling in agony. Finally, the entire I-16 became engulfed in flames. Ernst quickly rolled off just in time as the flames reached the I-16's fuel tanks and it exploded into a fireball.

Ernst flew by, just missing the debris. He quickly scanned the skies and noticed his element leader slowing and pulling up to him. Ernst took one last look at the I-16 as it impacted the ground and disintegrated. His leader pulled up alongside and Ernst could see the grin on his face as he saluted him. He then pointed back toward the German bombers in the distance.

The two 109s closed the gap on the bombers they were escorting, having destroyed all three Republican aircraft. It was easy to spot the bombers, since there was a huge pall of smoke in the distance coming from the ground. As the two 109s raced to the scene, they slowly descended to the target area. They had orders to assist the He-51 aircraft with the ground attack mission once any enemy aircraft had been destroyed.

As they rapidly approached the target area, Ernst could see that the He-51 formation was conducting a staffing attack on the target area. As they finally closed on it, Ernst could see that it was—a village! As they flew over on their first pass, Ernst saw people on the ground running. They looked like women and children! The element leader was in position for an attack and motioned for Ernst to follow.

As the two 109s descended on their run, the element leader started firing. Ernst watched in horror as his leader's fire accurately hit several people running for cover. Ernst followed the leader closely but did not fire. Finally, they pulled up away from the village. Ernst saw the leader motion for a return to base; they were low on fuel.

Ernst contemplated the mission as they flew back. He had gone to an adrenaline-rushed action as he destroyed his first enemy aircraft but quickly lost the exhilaration as he relived the horror of the ground attack.

After landing, Ernst was uncharacteristically quiet at the evening mess. Later, his element leader, who had been in Spain three months longer than Ernst, came over to him as he was sitting quietly in the squadron briefing room.

"*Leutnant* Hoffman, I want to congratulate you on your first victory—and for saving my own hide in the process. You're an excellent wingman."

"Thank you, *Herr Hauptmann*. I'm thankful for the excellent training I received. I think the mission went well—at least the first part of it." Ernst instantly wished he hadn't qualified his statement.

The other officer paused before replying, "Look, Ernst, I think I understand how you may be feeling now. You've now killed in combat, for your country and for your loved ones. I know you have family in Spain. As for the end of the mission, it is often hard to distinguish friend from foe in the heat of battle and—"

Ernst interrupted him. "But *Herr Hauptmann*, that was a village we attacked and I saw no evidence of enemy troops or activity!"

The other officer again paused, for a longer time, before replying. He came around and looked Ernst square in the eye with a stern look on his face. "My dear Hoffman, you are young and idealistic. Those are desirable traits, but I must warn you. We're about to enter a new era of warfare, one where we may be conducting total war against our enemies. I'm afraid that will be hard for you and many others to grasp, but it will come to pass, no matter what you or I believe. Please keep that in mind." He then got up, briefly put his hand on Ernst's shoulder, and walked away.

Ernst considered what his fellow officer said and sat there awhile thinking about it. He'd followed all the rules and obeyed orders. He had a sterling record in school and in training and he must have seemed like the perfect

Luftwaffe officer to his superiors. Ernst wondered how other officers were coping with the new realities of anonymous air combat. How could that include the destruction of civilian villages and their inhabitants? Ernst had already heard a lot about atrocities committed by the Republican forces. Could it be that the Nationalists were no different? If so, then Germany would be complicit if it continued to aid the Nationalist cause.

Ernst realized he could not broach the subject with his colleagues. It would be risky and to no avail. He wished he could discuss the issue with his father. Had he not served the fatherland well in the World War? Was he not a decorated hero? Surely, he would be able to reconcile the issues here. What would Hans think? Although the brothers were close, they had talked very little about such matters. In any case, Ernst knew that Hans was very rational and calculating by nature and would approach this issue without emotion.

What about Alberto Ortega? He was serving the Nationalist cause as a naval officer. Surely he could reconcile the conflicts racing through Ernst's mind. Everyone in the Hoffman and Ortega families agreed that the communist menace was the main problem faced by Spain and that the Republican government and forces represented this menace.

Ernst finished his introspective analysis and resolved to think about it later. He could not then know the horrors he would eventually experience and the impossibility of reconciling innocent civilian deaths against any recognized rules of war.

27.

* * *

Paul Hoffman pulled the throttle back on the small Piper J-2 Cub aircraft and set up his power-off glide as he eyed the grass runway below him and to his left. He wanted to make this approach and landing perfect. He timed his turn on to base leg and then final approach perfectly. He could tell from the sound and control feel that he had the speed just right. As he approached the runway, he began his landing flare, gradually pulling the stick back into his lap as the Cub slowed and approached the precise touchdown spot that his instructor had demanded he hit. He told himself to get the stick all the way back in his gut so the Cub wouldn't bounce on touchdown. The aircraft touched down smoothly at the precise target spot and slowly rolled to a stop. As they taxied back for another takeoff, his grizzled instructor indicated that he should stop. He got out of the front seat onto the grass and faced Paul.

"All right, kid, you're ready to have a go at it yourself. I want to see three takeoffs and landings just like that one." He grinned, turned around, and walked away. On his sixteenth birthday, Paul was about to make his first solo flight.

He taxied to the end of the runway, turned into position, and opened the throttle on the anemic little 40-horsepower engine. It was a warm day, and with two people aboard, the Cub barely had enough power to climb out. As Paul knew it would, the Cub climbed better without his 180-pound instructor. Paul made three perfect takeoffs and landings, taxied back to the gas pump, and shut the engine down. He got out and his instructor came over to shake his hand, unable to miss the wide grin on Paul's face as he experienced what all newly soloed pilots have—a complete transformation as they realized they could escape the bounds of the earth.

Paul stretched his hand out to his instructor. He was the tallest of the Hoffman boys at six feet two inches and was not only five inches taller than his instructor but twenty pounds lighter. Of the three sons, Paul looked the most like his father, with light sandy hair, blue eyes, and handsome features.

He was the least athletic of the three sons, but at Choate, he had made the track team and his peers considered him a determined competitor.

During this summer session between his sophomore and junior years, Paul had enrolled in an exchange program at the Mount Hermon School in nearby Northfield, Massachusetts. He was earning credits there and advancing his academic standing. When he arrived in June, he immediately bicycled every afternoon to the nearby small airport at Turners Falls to begin flying lessons. He had planned this for some time and had a deal with his uncle Ramon that as long as the lessons didn't interfere with school, he could continue flying. Paul remembered in vivid detail Lindbergh's flight to Paris more than ten years ago and ever since, like Ernst, he had been determined to fly.

All summer, until the end of the term in late August, Paul flew nearly every day and made excellent progress. He was a good pilot, approaching it in a methodical way and absorbing all the knowledge he could from his instructor.

When Paul returned to Choate in September, he buckled down and dove into the new academic year. He kept flying on weekends at a nearby small airport but knew where his priorities lay. Like his father, Paul excelled at taking tests and realized that everything they threw at you was, in fact, a test. All of the elite prep schools considered themselves grooming places for the Ivy League, and Paul always had a sense that he was being watched.

Paul found that, as a foreigner in America, he had to work extra hard to gain respect among not only his peers but faculty also. He thought it was not as much xenophobia as it was the ignorance of the rest of the world demonstrated by most Americans. It certainly wasn't politics. Most of his fellow students never asked Paul about the civil war in Spain because they didn't really know what the issues were or even that it was taking place. This wasn't universally true, but Paul himself tried not to bring the subject up. He was more concerned with blending in as he discovered virtues in the American ethos of the melting pot. The tribalism he had experienced in Africa and the class distinctions of Europe didn't matter as much here. Again, that was not universally true—Paul had already noticed the overt racism by whites toward Negroes in America.

All of these observations and influences were slowly transforming Paul Hoffman. Without knowing it, like his father, he was developing ambivalence toward nationality. Like his brothers, he was coming of age, but outside the crucible of war.

28.

Santa Isabel, Spanish Guinea
December 1938

* * *

Karl and Pilar were guests at the governor's residence for their traditional Christmas Eve dinner. This year, they had arrived weeks earlier and stayed at their hacienda on the Fernando Po island plantation.

There was a reason for their early arrival on Fernando Po. Like his two younger sons, Karl Hoffman had discovered the sky. By arrangement with the governor, Karl had lobbied to have the government create an aero club in Santa Isabel, where a new airport had recently opened. The aero club was formed and its first aircraft was a Bücker Jungmann. This was a German-designed aircraft that had become the basic training aircraft for the *Luftwaffe*, and a number had been supplied to the Nationalists in Spain. By this time the Nationalists had firm control of all three Spanish colonies in Africa, Spanish Morocco, Spanish Sahara, and Spanish Guinea. They were anxious to create infrastructure in all the colonies and recognized the role that aviation would play in that. The governor had also authorized the construction of an airport at Bata on the Rio Muni mainland portion of Spanish Guinea.

Karl had decided to learn to fly so he could eventually have a means to travel between Rio Muni and Santa Isabel that was faster than the boat. He envisioned constructing his own airstrip on the Rio Muni plantation to save a further day of travel. He also needed a faster way to get to other places in the region to conduct plantation business. Much of this activity revolved around securing plantation labor in places like Nigeria, a British colony, and Cameroon, formerly German Kamerun and now a French protectorate. Spanish Guinea was under populated and all of the available labor pool had been exhausted. To support his vision of travel, Karl began learning to fly in October and had already soloed.

Karl and Pilar set aside New Year's Eve as their own private celebration each year to recap the events of the prior year, reminisce, and look at the year ahead. This year they had enjoyed a fine dinner complemented by an excellent

1924 Ortega *Gran Reserva* that was right at its peak. They then retired to their patio to enjoy a glass of dessert wine. The *Pedro Ximenez* from the family bodega in Jerez was exquisite, with high residual sugar but perfectly balanced acidity, making it smooth as silk rather than syrupy. They were thrilled because they had five unopened letters from their three sons, Ernesto, and Walter to read. As they eagerly opened the envelopes and began reading, Karl was first to summarize, reading from Ernesto's letter.

"Ernesto says everyone is well but the war has taken its toll on all. He says Alberto has been promoted again and took part in an important naval battle for which he will be decorated." Karl paused, knowing it meant that Spaniard was fighting Spaniard. "At least the war may be winding down. Ernesto says the Nationalist victory in the Battle of the Ebro was the turning point."

Ernesto was referring to a major victory for the Nationalists several months ago that now had the Republican forces on their knees. At this point they clung only to Madrid and Barcelona and a small amount of territory in eastern Spain. In a previous letter, Ernesto had recounted how the Ortega bodegas had been forced to deliver two-thirds of their grape crop to the Nationalist forces, without turning it into wine. At least they hadn't had to rip out their vines and replant with other crops, as some bodegas had been forced to do.

Pilar was next, smiling effusively as she read from Paul's letter. "Paul is doing exceptionally well in his last year at Choate. He had nearly perfect grades and hopes to hear soon from Columbia University." In previous letters, Paul had made clear his desire to stay in America and attend university, with Columbia as his first choice.

Pilar continued, still smiling, but less effusively. "Paul said he now has more than one hundred hours of flying time. He has convinced Uncle Ramon to invest in an aircraft so that they can more easily reach wholesalers and distributors for our products throughout America. Next summer he wants to work with Uncle Ramon in the family business prior to entering university."

Karl smiled. Like every Hoffman generation, his three sons had their own visions of their lives and how they would lead them. How could he argue with that? In fact, Karl's own determination to learn to fly in support of the company business merely reinforced what Paul planned to do.

Pilar had been reading letters from Hans and Ernst while Karl was finishing Ernesto's and Paul's letters. This time there was no smile on her face.

"Hans and Ernst are both doing well. Ernst returned to his unit in Spain while Hans continues to progress with the navy." She paused, starting to weep, but regained her composure. "Hans met a girl that he really likes and he thinks this could be serious." She handed the letter to Karl, covering her eyes with a handkerchief to dry her tears.

Karl leaned over and gently touched Pilar's hand. He read the letter and smiled again, realizing that his three young boys were now men with their own lives.

Karl opened and began Walter's letter. Their father was still doing well. At eighty-six, Wilhelm von Hoffman still tended his vines in the Mosel and looked forward to seeing his extended family again. Walter hoped it would be possible to hold another Hoffman-Ortega reunion before "events" prevented that from happening. Karl was puzzled by Walter's choice of words.

"Pilar, Walter says that Erica and Kirsten are doing fine. Kirsten is now a precocious seven and doing well in school. She sends her best." Pilar smiled again.

After they finished their letters and Pilar briefly left the room, Karl poured himself some more sherry and read the rest of Ernesto's lengthy letter. Ernesto related how the war had affected the wine business but was thankful that Karl, Pilar, and Alfonso were in Spanish Guinea and that the cocoa and coffee trade was thriving. The families had astutely decided to export directly from Spanish Guinea to both the American and South American markets, rather than through Spain. Their proactive approach, with an assist from Ramon in New York, had greatly increased the wealth of both families. However, economic conditions were changing. On the one hand, as the world came out of the Great Depression, economies and market demand for products were improving. The cocoa from Spanish Guinea in particular had become sought after as superior to that from other cocoa-producing countries. On the other hand, cocoa was turning into a commodity increasingly traded on a world market that was dominated by traders in London and New York. Ramon's contacts in New York had ensured that the family's interests would receive insider treatment there. The British were using the London market to favor British colonial cocoa interests in both the Gold Coast and Nigeria. They were collaborating with the French, who had cocoa plantations in their colonies in Ivory Coast and Cameroon. They were trying to dominate the European cocoa market to the detriment of both Spanish and Portuguese interests. Portugal had cocoa plantations in their island colony of Sao Tome and Principe, only about 450 kilometers south of Fernando Po.

Karl paused, took a sip of sherry, and considered what Ernesto had said, including his two recommendations. Ernesto wanted Karl to travel to London to try to make inroads and negotiate with the trading exchange there. Ernesto thought that by summer the war in Spain would be over and that Karl, Pilar, and Alfonso could travel to Spain for a reunion, in conjunction with the London trip. Karl paused, finished his sherry, and resolved to write back immediately to Ernesto. He agreed with both ideas and knew that Pilar would be ecstatic.

Karl went back to Walter's letter, which he had not finished. Earlier in 1938, Walter was assigned as naval attaché to the German embassy for the Nationalist government in Spain. Germany had recognized the Nationalists as the legitimate government in Spain in 1936, right after the civil war began. Walter divided his time between El Ferrol and Cadiz, the two naval bases held by the Nationalists, since the capital of Madrid was still in Republican hands. His official duties included providing advice to the Spanish navy elements controlled by the Nationalists.

Karl could not know, and Walter did not disclose, that the German naval attaché also had other duties in Spain, of a very secret nature, to establish the groundwork for future U-boat operations from Spain and to establish liaison with Nationalist intelligence services. Walter's career had evolved, and he was now considered a navy insider, working behind the scenes and out of the limelight and normal career progression. Walter was tagged by the navy high command as a key right-hand man for planning future operations and in intelligence and counterintelligence duties. It was unlikely that he would ever command a ship again or even command larger fleet elements operationally. Yet he had clearly been marked for flag rank. When he returned to Germany from his current assignment, that promotion would be the next step.

Although Karl did not know these things, he wondered how Walter's career might affect the rest of their family, especially Hans. Karl paused, sipped the last of the sherry, and decided to pose that question to Walter when they next met.

29.

Barcelona, Spain
May 1939

* * *

"Karl, Pilar, we're over here!"

Karl looked toward the familiar voice and immediately spotted his brother-in-law, Ernesto Ortega, waving at him. Karl grabbed Pilar's arm, and she also quickly spotted her brother and then his wife, Ana. Within a few seconds, the four of them were reunited and immediately started catching up.

"Was your journey all right? You both look like you're well rested," Ernesto said.

"All things considered, I'll travel by air from now on," Karl replied, as he noticed that Ernesto looked nervous and distracted.

"It's certainly more convenient than the three weeks by steamer," Pilar added.

Karl and Pilar had elected to travel by air from Spanish Guinea for the first time. It had only been in the last two years that reliable air service was reaching equatorial Africa, and Karl had booked them on Air France flights for the three-night trip to Barcelona. The first flight originated in Douala, Cameroon, with overnight stays in Abidjan, Ivory Coast; St. Louis, Senegal; and Casablanca, Morocco. It actually involved a four-night stay since Karl and Pilar had traveled from Santa Isabel to Douala by boat the day before so they would be there for the 6:15 a.m. flight departure.

"I know you're probably hungry, so we thought we might have lunch here first before we begin the drive. Ana, why don't you take Pilar over to the restaurant in the terminal? Karl and I will join you after we've attended to the baggage."

Without replying, the two women continued their nonstop conversation and began walking to the restaurant. Karl sensed that Ernesto wanted a few minutes with him—alone.

"Ernesto, it's good to see you and it's good to be back in Spain." Karl paused. "You seemed anxious to pull me aside. Is there something wrong?"

Ernesto smiled weakly. "Was it that obvious? Yes, I needed to talk with you before you do anything else while you're in Spain. You've been gone nearly four years and things are very different here now that the Civil War has ended. The last three years have been like hell, and the war has completely disrupted the economy and normal life. Our wine trade is in ruins and we lost most of the decade to economic chaos and war. The nation is still divided, even though the fighting has stopped. That's all bad enough, but that's not the worst of it."

Karl looked at Ernesto, shocked. He had a premonition about what Ernesto was implying as he replied, "I knew from your letters that times were bad and I...sensed that there were some underlying issues that you couldn't talk about. What's really going on?"

Karl watched as Ernesto nervously looked around them before replying. "I'm sorry for my preoccupation but it's possible that we are under surveillance, perhaps even as we speak."

"What are you talking about, Ernesto? Who could be watching us?"

"There are many possibilities, but the BPS is the main worry."

"What's the BPS?"

Karl noticed Ernesto's surprised look. "Forgive me, Karl, for getting ahead of myself. The BPS is the *Brigada Politico Social*, Franco's secret police force. They have increased their activity as the war ended and the recriminations began against the Republicans—or anyone suspected of supporting the Republicans."

"But how does that affect us, Ernesto? The family never supported the Republicans. We supported the monarchy, but that doesn't mean..."

"Karl, even the monarchist supporters are suspect. Only full support of Franco's Nationalists, the *Falange*, is acceptable now in Spain." Ernesto paused and his expression became even more serious. "But there is even more to be concerned about."

"What do you mean?"

"You may also be under suspicion. I haven't told you yet, but Alberto was recently assigned to intelligence duties in the navy. He served in the Civil War with distinction so his superiors quietly provided him with information obtained from the BPS. It seems you are suspected of helping Republican officials to escape in October 1936 as the Nationalists assumed power in Guinea. The governor in Guinea vouched for you and extolled your leadership in the colony's development, so for now you are not under an immediate threat."

So that was it, Karl thought. He recalled how the current governor was installed after the previous incumbent was overthrown by the Colonial Guard, or local Spanish army troops, who were loyal to Franco and the Nationalists. The guard staged their coup in September 1936, only two months after the rebellion started in Spain. Karl had recognized that the colony needed the stability and had no trouble rallying the other planters to support the change in government, despite his concerns regarding Franco. Originally the old governor's representative on the Rio Muni mainland, in Bata, had resisted the coup. Karl had convinced him to stop the resistance and to leave the colony. Karl had secretly helped him and a few other Republican loyalists escape into nearby French Cameroon. Karl's old friend Wekesa had led the group over the same bridge over the Rio Campo that Karl and Wekesa had used for the escape of the *Schutztruppe* in 1916. Karl thought of the irony in that event and how both incidents had resulted in the avoidance of greater bloodshed. But now there was a more sinister consequence for him to worry about.

"Ernesto, that event is now history. I'm sure we'll be under no further scrutiny now that the war is over."

"If that was the whole story, you might be right. But I'm almost afraid to raise one final issue that is very troubling."

"What is it?"

"Alberto also learned from his superiors that the BPS shared information with their German counterparts in the Gestapo and the SS as a result of links that Germany and the Nationalists developed during the Civil War. According to Alberto's contact, you came under suspicion in Germany in 1935, when you were trying to find a way to extract Hans and Ernst from the Nazis."

Ernesto paused, clenching his fist, but finally concluded, "I hate to suggest this, Karl, but it is possible that your brother, Walter, may also have a role in this. You may not know this, but Alberto says that Walter traveled to Spain many times during the war, and although his official function was naval attaché, his real job was intelligence gathering and sharing. I am sure that he was and is privy to BPS files—and he may have shared German information about you."

Karl closed his eyes, horrified that Ernesto's supposition could be true. Yet even though he was estranged from his brother, Karl couldn't believe that

Walter would betray him or cast doubts on Karl's real loyalties. He suddenly realized that his attempt to walk an independent path may be a dangerous one and he wondered how the balance was tipping—for or against him. He remembered Wilhelm Canaris's warning four years ago.

"Thank you, Ernesto, for your frank assessment. I'm sure it was difficult for you to suggest what might have occurred. I wonder what we can expect next."

"There is probably no immediate cause for alarm. Our sons distinguished themselves for the Nationalist cause during the Civil War. In fact, Alberto, Ernst, and Hans are to be decorated next month for their actions. Also, your influence with the governor in Guinea is viewed very positively. I might add that your successful development of our plantations and trade between Guinea and the Americas has been a godsend to our family's financial well-being. Without your efforts, Karl, our situation would be dire, yet we are now actually at least as well off as we were ten years ago, maybe more so." Ernesto paused. "My reason for raising this issue is so you can exercise caution in the future—and be prepared next week when we meet your father and brother and travel to our hunting lodge in Andorra."

"You're quite right. It could be an awkward moment, but thanks to your revelations, I'll find a way to deal with it. Perhaps now we should join Pilar and Ana in the restaurant—before they think we disappeared."

With that, the two men smiled weakly and headed off to lunch, preoccupied with the changes in their lives.

30

Andorra la Vella, Andorra, in the Pyrenees Mountains
May 1939

* * *

The older male members of the Hoffman-Ortega families sat around a table in the modest restaurant in the "capital city" of the small, independent principality of Andorra. Pedro, Ernesto, and Ramon Ortega joined Wilhelm, Walter, and Karl Hoffman. They were enjoying a special dinner of jugged wild boar and two other presentations of the highly desired wild pig. They had arrived at the Ortega hunting lodge, about five kilometers north, several days ago. The previous day, their successful hunt netted two of the succulent beasts with Wilhelm Hoffman and Ernesto Ortega securing the honors for the shots that felled them. During these several days, Karl and Walter were cool and barely civil to each other, but at Wilhelm's insistence, Karl had agreed not to raise the issue of his two sons serving in the German *Wehrmacht*.

Pedro Ortega had befriended the owner of the small dining establishment earlier in the decade, right after buying the hunting lodge in 1930. Pedro ensured that the restaurant had a steady supply of fine wines from the Ortega bodegas, even during the height of the war when the only Spanish access to Andorra was through Republican territory. However, both the Andorrans and their Spanish collaborators were experts at the art of smuggling, which was the whole basis of the Andorran economy.

The Civil War, on the other hand, had ended less than two months ago with a complete Nationalist victory. Remnants of the Republican army and many refugees had fled over the border to France, many through Andorra. The French to the north and the Spanish Nationalists to the south now closed that route. The repercussions of the Civil War were only beginning to be felt.

For tonight's special dinner, the restaurant owner had provided them with the establishment's private dining room. The restaurant was a solid structure, with high ceilings sloping down and huge, massive beams. The private room had a large stone fireplace with a single window higher on the wall. The six diners lit a fire to kill the chill of the May evening. They were seated around a massive circular wood table enjoying their dinner.

For this occasion, Wilhelm and Pedro had requested separate preparations of the boar to old family recipes paired with their wine selections. In addition, the chef offered a portion prepared in accordance with a traditional Andorran recipe for jugged boar. Although the meal had other accompaniments, the evening was mostly a salute to protein and the culinary nuances of wild game expertly prepared.

As usual, the real highlight of the meal was the wines from the Ortega bodega and the Hoffman Mosel estate. Pedro had provided *gran reserva* from each of the excellent 1920, 1922, and 1924 vintages, still drinking nicely and allowing for a vertical tasting of the traditional Ortega bodega bottling. For the more subtle Hoffman recipe, Wilhelm had shipped in bottles of outstanding *Kabinett* and *Spätlese Trocken* from the 1929 and 1934 vintages. For dessert, the real star was the *Trockenbeerenauslese*, or TBA, from the 1937 vintage. This silky, lush piece of heaven was so perfectly balanced that Wilhelm predicted it could last a hundred years, although he could produce only forty cases of this liquid gold.

After enjoying these courses, the restaurant staff cleaned the table and Pedro Ortega poured them all a fine old *oloroso dulce* from the Ortega bodega in Jerez. Although this bottle was not vintage dated, Pedro explained that it was from the first year that he had owned the bodega. It was exquisite, sweetened by adding a little Pedro Ximenez and just perfectly balanced.

As might be expected, the after-dinner conversation dwelled on business and politics, initiated by Pedro Ortega as he poured the first round of sherry.

"We're grateful for many things tonight, especially that we're all able to gather here to celebrate the end of this tragic civil war that has been so divisive." He raised his glass for the toast. "*Salud!*"

Pedro continued, "The war has weakened Spain economically and has affected everybody, including our own interests. My hope is that the new regime will quickly concentrate on rebuilding our economy—and not pursuing sides in…coming events."

Everybody understood the pause in Pedro's last sentence. Ernesto reinforced his father.

"Our wine trade has been devastated by the war. Fortunately our coffee and cocoa trade in Spanish Guinea is thriving, thanks to the steps taken by Ramon and Karl. We will now have to rebuild our wine trade and continue to expand our trade from our African plantations. How best can we do that?"

Karl promptly answered, "We should continue our direct exports to some distributors, especially in the Americas, but we must also acknowledge that these products, cocoa and coffee, are increasingly becoming commodities with world markets controlled by New York and London. Ramon's connections and influence have the New York connection covered, but I am planning to travel to London in a couple of months to try to make inroads there that will improve our distribution in Europe."

Ramon agreed. "Yes, this is an important step and I agree with Karl's plan. We should also try to expand our direct connections in America with wholesalers and distributors. I'm planning to travel throughout America periodically to accomplish this."

Wilhelm stepped into the discussion. "You all have summarized the situation well and have developed an excellent strategy to protect our investments. I believe that our conservative business practices and diversification have served us well over the years."

Karl chose this moment to up the ante. "The only unknown in the equation is whether we also need to anticipate the effects of...an outbreak of war in Europe. It would be devastating to our economy if European markets were closed."

Wilhelm glared at his youngest son. Before dinner he had asked Karl to avoid sensitive subjects during this occasion. But it was too late as Walter took the bait.

"I don't believe that war is a possibility. With the resolution of the situation in Czechoslovakia, the führer has assured the world that Germany's territorial demands are complete and that war could only result from provocation by the Poles, aided by Britain and France."

There was an awkward silence as everybody stared at Walter, trying to comprehend his statement and shocked that he had verbalized the straight Nazi party line. Even Wilhelm stared at his oldest son, his mouth agape, speechless. Finally, Pedro Ortega broke the ice.

"Let us hope that the system of alliances and more negotiation can defuse any situation before conflict develops."

Ernesto added an assist to change the subject. "Next month will be a very special occasion for our families! Alberto was granted leave, Alfonso will arrive from Guinea, and Walter assures us that Erica and Kirsten will be here. Paul will also arrive from America. We are pleased by the news that Alberto, Ernst, and Hans are to be decorated for their service to Spain during the Civil War. These are proud moments for both families. I would like to toast the next generation. *Salud!*"

Alberto had indeed been decorated for his actions as an officer on the cruiser *Canarias* during two important battles. Ernst was also receiving a special award from the Spanish government for his service in the Condor Legion. His assignment in Spain would end next month, after receiving the award, and he was granted leave to attend the family reunion. Walter had also assured everyone that Hans obtained leave for the event.

Later, after the party returned to the hunting lodge, Karl and Walter hardly spoke to each other. Karl knew that he would not get a straight answer from his brother on the role that Hans may have played in the war or what would happen next in his naval career. Karl wished he could take some action that might allow him to get his two sons back before any world calamity ensued. But he knew from his conversations with Ernesto earlier in the month that it was too risky to intervene further on his sons' behalf. He kept an optimistic front for Pilar but also knew that both boys…men…were now on an irrevocable course that neither Karl nor anybody else could control. He only hoped the course of events in Europe would spare the Hoffman family from participation in another general conflict.

Karl also decided not to risk confronting Walter about the more sinister matters raised by Ernesto when they met in Barcelona early in the month. Karl still couldn't believe that his brother would betray him. He resolved to focus on his three sons at next month's reunion. It would be a time to focus on family rather than the world around them.

31.

Alabos, Spain
June 1939

* * *

The Hoffman and Ortega family reunion was both a joyous and a somber event. On the one hand, all members of both families had managed to make their way to the Ortega hacienda from Germany, America, and Spanish Guinea. In addition the family was rejoicing that the horror of the Spanish Civil War was now over and that the family and their interests were intact. On the other hand, there was an underlying feeling in the families that their lives had been permanently changed and that the fleeting moment of stability that they now had would soon end.

Despite the mixed mood, the final arrival of Paul from America, Hans from Germany, and Alfonso from Spanish Guinea was enough to spark a family celebration that was to last for days. During this event, everyone noticed the subtle shifting that had begun as the next generation of Hoffmans and Ortegas began to assert themselves.

The most obvious theme was the camaraderie that had developed among Karl's and Ernesto's five sons. Despite the different paths they had taken, they clung together and shared the joys of the family and the beautiful summer weather. Each day they walked together into the village from the hacienda, about a kilometer away, and sat at an outside table at the single small cantina. Despite their unanimous appreciation of fine wine, the beverage of choice was beer, and during these several days, the light, hoppy, Spanish *cerveza* flowed in enormous quantities. As with all young men, the subjects of conversations were women, automobiles, motorcycles, music, and sports. They were all curious about life in America so Paul was constantly answering their questions about subjects such as swing music, American fashion, and the latest automobile models.

Even though they enjoyed these discussions and shared much laughter during those long summer days, each session inevitably resulted in the brothers unconsciously separating into two groups as the day wore on. Paul and

Alfonso huddled to discuss the family business and how they could support their fathers, Karl and Ernesto, in recovering from the war. Their conversations, while serious, tended to be positive and proactive. Hans, Ernst, and Alberto tended toward a more negative mood. They were all in the active duty military, had experienced firsthand the horrors of war and combat, and tended to accept their fate rather than challenge the status quo. In a difficult decision, Alberto had decided to remain in the Spanish navy. While this had disappointed his father and mother, Alberto saw it as a chance to make his own mark while helping to stabilize Spain.

Neither Hans nor Ernst had much control over their fate at this point. Serving in the German *Wehrmacht* was compulsory and without any apparent escape in the short term. Both Hoffman men accepted this, Hans more readily than Ernst. Ernst still remembered the horrors of Guernica and the ensuing worldwide condemnation of the Condor Legion, but he had gone on to overcome these feelings and had become a celebrity in both Germany and Spain for shooting down six Republican aircraft to become a fighter ace. Earlier in June, he had received a medal from the Nationalist government, and Alberto was recognized for his actions in battle. Their celebrity had helped protect the senior Ortegas and Karl Hoffman for their lukewarm support of the Nationalist cause.

The five sons were not the only members of the next generation who had bonded. Anita Ortega, now twenty and a stunning beauty, had taken young Kirsten Hoffman under her wing and was teaching her Spanish. Kirsten was only seven, yet took an active interest in her surroundings during her first trip outside Germany. Ana and Anita Ortega, and Pilar, Erica, and Kirsten spent many hours reveling in their friendship and family ties.

The family also felt underlying concerns not openly expressed. Pedro Ortega, at age seventy-nine, was visibly slowing down. Last month, the gathering in Andorra had energized him, but since then he had visibly declined. Ana, Anita, and Pilar were worried. After discussing this with Ernesto and Karl, they all agreed that, as respectfully as possible, they should relieve Pedro of day-to-day concerns regarding the business operations. Karl agreed that Alfonso should remain in Alabos to help Ernesto with restoring the vineyards and wine business. Karl would return to Spanish Guinea after his upcoming business trip to London and other locations in Britain and a trip to America so he and Pilar could go with Paul back to New York. Paul had been accepted to Columbia University and secured a four-year nonresident student visa to return to America.

As the several days of celebration drew to a close, the mood at the Ortega hacienda gradually grew more bittersweet as the inevitable parting loomed. Walter's term as naval attaché had ended and he was being recalled to Berlin for his next assignment—and a promotion to *Konteradmiral*. In addition, Hans and Ernst were notified that their leave was shortened and they were directed to return to Germany by "all expeditious means." Karl asked Walter what this was all about, and Walter replied, unconvincingly, that there were special exercises and maneuvers scheduled throughout Germany during July and August. Karl didn't press the matter; he was suspicious about Walter, yet both brothers were anxious to avoid a confrontation, for the sake of family unity. Karl nursed a sense of foreboding but kept it to himself.

The day of reckoning approached. Wilhelm, Erica, and Kirsten had traveled to Spain from Germany by air, on Lufthansa flights from Cologne to Barcelona. For the return, Wilhelm, Walter, Hans, and Ernst would take the return flights from Barcelona. Erica and Kirsten would follow in early August. Ernesto would drive the four Hoffman men to Barcelona. Pilar was originally going to accompany them but wisely decided to say her good-byes at the hacienda.

* * *

The evening before the departure, Pedro Ortega and Wilhelm Hoffman met on the private veranda to share some final reminiscences. They treasured their time together and their more than fifty years of friendship and business partnership. As they sat there together, each sipping a glass of *manzanilla*, Wilhelm reflected.

"My dear Pedro, I feel so fortunate that we met and shared these years together and watched our families grow. As an old man, I feel that this is our real legacy rather than our wonderful business partnership."

Pedro nodded slowly. "You're right, my dear friend, and we may both take pride that our two families have become one. It gives me so much joy to see them together. I hope that we have many such occasions in the future."

There was a pause as both men contemplated what Pedro had said, both knowing that events were sure to affect the likelihood of that happening. They also sensed that this would be their last meeting.

Finally, Wilhelm replied to Pedro in a soft, almost ethereal voice, "When I think of my fifty years in the army and the family lands we lost after the war, I could dwell on the past, but I choose not to. Rather, I think of my good fortune and smile that we have both lived to see our families flourish. To me, the future is always the most important part of life, and I would propose that we toast to our families' future."

Pedro raised his glass in reply. "*Prost*, my friend!"

Wilhelm replied, "*Salud*, to you, my dear Pedro!"

* * *

The next morning, Pedro and Wilhelm embraced, for the last time, as family members watched respectfully. Maria and Pilar wept openly. As the cars drove away and Wilhelm waved to Pedro one last time, a tear formed in Pedro's eye as he waved back.

As the car pulled out of sight, Pilar could no longer control her feelings as she watched her two eldest sons depart. She turned and ran toward the hacienda. Maria and Erica turned to be with her, but Karl motioned that he would comfort her and quickly followed her into the hacienda.

Karl reached Pilar and embraced her. She fell into his arms and continued sobbing uncontrollably as Karl tried to assuage her fears.

"Pilar, please don't worry. Our sons are men now and can watch after themselves."

Pilar would have none of it, as she replied, still sobbing, "I don't believe it, Karl. They will be caught up in horrible events to come and I'm so afraid."

Karl had every reason to agree but kept upbeat. "Pilar, they have survived the last three years, and I have every reason to believe they will be fine."

Pilar looked up at Karl, controlled her sobbing, and spoke in a steady but insistent voice. "You must promise me that when we take Paul to America, I will be allowed to stay there with him for a while. I hope you may stay also, but in any case, I want to remain there, even if you have to return to Guinea."

Karl sensed both her frustration and her defiance. He realized that Pilar had made an irrevocable decision to be near her youngest son, regardless of the potential for separation from Karl for an extended period. Karl felt disappointment rather than betrayal, realizing how Pilar must be feeling. He finally replied, still holding Pilar in his arms, "I don't want to think about the prospect of our being separated, yet…" He paused, searching for the right words, "… I truly understand the loss you feel, because I feel it also."

Pilar looked at him expectantly as Karl finally summoned the courage to make the commitment he knew he must. "I will try to make arrangements to have the three of us together for a while, in New York. We will find a way to survive our separation, in order for you to be with Paul."

Pilar looked gratefully at him and managed a faint smile. As they embraced, Karl hoped that he could, in fact, endure a long separation, realizing that his long-term dream may now have a price that he must pay.

32

London, England
AUGUST 25, 1939

* * *

Karl and Pilar's first trip to England went smoothly from a logistics and entertainment point of view. They chose to fly, from Barcelona to Geneva, where Karl conducted family banking business, and then to London. Karl was more convinced than ever that flying was the only way to travel.

In London, they arrived early for business so that they might enjoy the pleasures of the theater and the sights of London. The city was surprisingly quiet as many Londoners were on their annual holiday, hoping that war could be avoiding for at least a few more weeks. Indeed, the increasing tension between Germany and Poland looked ominous, although Karl attempted to reassure Pilar.

From a business standpoint, the stop in London provided mixed success. Karl was appalled at the negotiating and business practices of the English and saw quickly that they were determined to favor English-owned cocoa and coffee interests. Karl saw that, unlike in America, the English were not operating in a true free market capitalist system but were engaged in a version of mercantilism left over from the rapidly diminishing colonial era. Nevertheless, Karl endeavored to cut a deal. It boiled down to supplying cocoa at ordinary prices and then being allowed to import more or, alternatively, to obtain a premium price for the high-grade cocoa produced by the Ortegas in Spanish Guinea and accept a quota limiting the amount they could sell on the London market. Karl chose the latter, to keep a toehold in the commodity distribution system. That would be important later since it was becoming harder to sell agricultural commodities directly in Europe. Karl, however, secured a concession to sell a small amount of cocoa directly within the British Isles since a shortage of cocoa on the world market had developed as the Great Depression ended and demand picked up while supply lagged. Karl and Pilar were scheduled to leave London the next day and had appointments with distributors in Birmingham on the twenty-eighth and Manchester on the thirty-first.

The only disappointment had been that they were not able to accompany Paul back to America when his ship sailed in mid-August. This was partly due to the difficulty in securing timely business appointments in England, but the main reason was that Karl and Pilar had been unable to book passage on a ship. Paul had reserved his passage many months prior and had a firm ticket and sailing date, but Karl and Pilar could not get passage on the same ship because of the huge numbers of Americans, Canadians, and others suddenly trying to get out of Europe before war started.

Karl was contemplating all of this as he sat waiting for his final appointment in London. The executive he was due to meet was late for some reason. Finally, the gentleman arrived and motioned for Karl to join him in his office. They sat down, and Karl immediately found out the reason for the delayed appointment as his host began to explain.

"Mr. Hoffman, please forgive me for being late, but I rather expect you will be happy to know the reason for my tardiness." Karl looked up expectantly as his host continued,

"Knowing of your travel dilemma, my secretary made some inquiries to the shipping lines and called a few of my acquaintances. It turns out that we can book you and Mrs. Hoffman on the Donaldson liner *Athenia*; sailing from Liverpool on September 2 after it arrives from Glasgow. I am afraid it is bound for Montreal rather than New York, but you and your wife can make a convenient rail connection from there, and my secretary would be happy to set that up with the shipping company, if you like."

Karl was ecstatic and immediately accepted his host's offer. After completing his business, he returned to the hotel and gave Pilar the good news. She was overjoyed at the arrangements.

"Karl, this is wonderful. That would allow us to get to New York just before Paul starts his fall term. That's what I was hoping for. We should send word to Ramon and Paul."

"I already sent them a cable. All we have to do now is get to Liverpool and that should be easy, given that it's only about fifty kilometers from Manchester, where I have my last meetings. By a week from today, we should be aboard the *Athenia*, bound for Canada."

Pilar was relieved. "I'm so looking forward to seeing Paul. I feel the need to connect with him, especially now." Karl nodded, hoping it would all go as planned.

33.

Manchester, England
September 1, 1939

* * *

Karl could not believe his eyes. As he read the special late morning edition of the newspaper, he was stunned. Germany had invaded Poland before dawn, and England and France had issued ultimatums to Germany to withdraw. Karl placed the paper on the table, completely overcome by what this meant. At that moment, Pilar joined him at the hotel dining room table for breakfast. At once, she knew something was wrong. She glanced quickly at the headlines, dropped the paper on the table, and placed her hands over her eyes.

"Hans and Ernst will be involved! Oh, Karl, what can we do? I'm so afraid."

Karl stood up immediately to console her, gently touching one arm. "Pilar, please don't worry. Our sons are men now and will take care of themselves. We mustn't jump to conclusions. Germany may respond to the ultimatum," he lied.

As they sat down, Karl ordered tea and composed himself. Despite the truth, he must reassure Pilar. "I'll cable Walter and ask him to watch over them. Everything will be fine."

Pilar held his hand. They ignored their breakfast, lost in thought.

34.

Aboard the Athenia, Liverpool, England
September 2, 1939

* * *

As the Donaldson liner cast off its lines and it was inched slowly away from the dock by the tugs, Karl and Pilar stood on the deck watching the scene. It was pure chaos. Large numbers of people were still on the dock, most of them having tried to get on the *Athenia* at the last minute, in a panic to escape England as the war began. Fortunately, Karl's English hosts had secured firm booking on the ship, even though it was only in second class and their cabin was deep in the ship. Even with their passports and visas previously secured, they still had to rush to make the sailing because Karl had made various last-minute efforts to communicate with Germany. As they finally reached the deck, Pilar asked him what he had learned. Karl's reply was not encouraging.

"All communication lines with Germany are either overloaded or have been cut off. I was unable to send a telegram. I tried all available phone connections and was unable to get through. As a last resort, I posted a letter and told Walter to cable Ramon in New York so that we might find out about Hans and Ernst shortly after we arrive."

The anxious look on Pilar's face didn't change. Karl continued, "Pilar, we must believe in our sons and in Walter. We raised them to be self-reliant, didn't we?"

Pilar replied, with doubt in her eyes, "How can we be sure they'll be safe?"

Karl paused, sighed, and finally answered, "I am afraid that...we can't."

35.

Aboard the Athenia, near Rockall Bank, North Atlantic Ocean
September 3, 1939

* * *

Karl walked slowly in the chill night air on the upper deck of the *Athenia*, huddled against the cold but feeling grateful for the chance to clear his mind of some nagging thoughts. After dinner, Pilar had returned to their cabin many decks below saddened by the captain's announcement that Britain and France had declared war on Germany earlier in the day. World War II had begun.

Karl stopped walking and turned toward the sea, wishing he had been able to anticipate the events that had just unfolded and wondering how he could have found a way to spare his sons the agony of war. He realized that it was now too late and pondered how long it would be before he and Pilar saw Hans and Ernst again. He could only hope that Walter would listen to his plea, in the quick letter Karl had sent from Liverpool, to watch out for his sons as best he could.

As Karl stood on deck, staring at the sea, an uneasy feeling came over him. He could almost sense Hans's presence, calling out to him. It was unlike any feeling he had ever experienced. As he stood there trying to grapple with this feeling, he could only wonder what Hans, his oldest son, would be saying to him now. Was it a plea for forgiveness, an appeal for support—or was it a warning?

36.

Aboard German submarine U-30, 2,000
meters from the Athenia
1930 hours

* * *

The captain of U-30 raised the periscope again to confirm the observation. As he focused the periscope, he spoke to the officer working the plotting board.

"The identification is confirmed, Hoffman. It's a large blacked-out ship, zigzagging, and appears to have guns. It must be an armed merchant cruiser so we are authorized to attack. Stand by for final bearings!" They were under orders to observe the rules of war and let all passenger ships pass. If they could identify the ship as armed, however, it was fair game. In the fading twilight, it was difficult to distinguish the features of the ship.

Hans Hoffman had been selected to command a U-boat, but his boat was not ready on schedule and he had been assigned to U-30 for this patrol because of his experience as watch officer. He responded to the captain's order.

"Can you be sure, *Herr Kapitän*? Our orders are specific and—"

The captain cut him off. "Your objections are noted, *Leutnant!* The target is identified. Plot the final bearings!"

Hans Hoffman complied with the order. Within seconds, the two torpedoes were fired and headed toward the target.

37.

Aboard the Athenia, two minutes later

* * *

The torpedo struck the *Athenia* with a thunderous explosion. As the whole ship shuddered, Karl was thrown against the deck. He got up, dazed, but then quickly recovered. He knew instantly that it must have been a submarine.

Pilar, I must get to her! He raced down the deck as the ship quickly erupted into chaos, a kaleidoscope of smoke, flames, screams, and crew and passengers racing on deck. Karl was going the wrong way, against the crowd rushing topside, but he tried to push his way down to the lower deck where their stateroom was. He had to find her.

Karl got only as far as the third deck before two pursers stopped and then forcibly restrained him.

"I'm sorry, sir, you can't go any farther! The torpedo hit just below here and access to lower decks is cut off. Please, you must come topside with us; we are abandoning ship."

"I have to find my wife! She is on the lower deck, let me go!"

One of the pursers, a huge man, grabbed Karl hard by his arm and replied firmly, "It's no use, sir, the stairwell was destroyed by the torpedo hit and there's no other way below. Your wife may already be topside. Please come with us and we'll try to help you find her."

"But she was in our cabin when I went topside earlier. She must still be there!" Karl was trying to break away from the pursers but both men were now restraining him.

"What cabin number was she in, sir?" asked the lead purser.

As Karl replied with his cabin number, both pursers looked at each other. Finally, the larger of the two men replied, "Sir, I'm sorry, but if she was there when the torpedo hit then there is no chance she survived. You must follow us topside. It's the only way we will find out if she made it there."

Karl turned toward the stairwell shaft, a grief-stricken look on his face, but all he could see was smoke pouring from the shaft and the acrid smell of burning wood and paint. He finally realized he needed to see if Pilar had actually made it to the main deck and nodded to the two men.

As the men reached the lifeboat deck, Karl began a frantic search for Pilar amid the panic-stricken passengers, also searching for passengers whom he had met that were in adjacent cabins. Ominously, he could not find them either.

The *Athenia* finally sank, going down by the stern, fourteen hours later. For Karl, they were the longest fourteen hours of his life, his hopes for a miracle slowly crushed as the ship settled inexorably. Karl stayed on board as long as possible and was one of the last passengers to leave the dying ship, finally breaking down and sobbing as crew members ordered him into the last lifeboat.

38.

Berlin
September 18, 1939

* * *

Walter dropped Karl's letter on his desk and placed his hands over his eyes, nearly weeping. When he read that Karl and Pilar had booked passage on the *Athenia*, he was aghast. How could this have happened to them? The cruel irony and the amazing thread of fate that had enveloped the family struck him.

He resolved to hide this knowledge from Hans for as long as he could. In any case, his first task was to engineer the cover-up of the *Athenia* sinking. The Nazi propaganda machine denied that a U-boat was responsible for the sinking and claimed that a British mine was responsible. When the U-30 returned from its first war patrol, probably in about one week, the crew would be sequestered and sworn to secrecy. Fortunately, the heavy dose of Nazi propaganda already issued on the incident had probably ensured that the sub captain and crew would not be punished. To do so would risk disclosure that a U-boat was responsible for the sinking. In any case, the previous day another submarine had achieved an amazing feat by sinking the British aircraft carrier *Courageous*. They would emphasize this U-boat event and not the *Athenia* sinking.

As Walter mulled over the events surrounding the beginning of the war, he wondered how it would unfold. The navy had not planned on a war so soon. He could only hope that it would quickly conclude and that his family could properly deal with their tragedy.

39

London, England
September 20, 1939

* * *

Karl Hoffman stood his ground as the English officer continued his questioning. The officer repeated his earlier question.

"Mr. Hoffman, although I recognize that you are traveling on a valid Spanish passport, I see that you were born in Germany. Are you, in fact, a German national and where are your other family members?"

Karl composed himself before answering, sensing that his dislike for the British was going to get worse. "As I said, although I was born in Germany, I have been a permanent and legal resident of Spain since 1920 and a citizen since 1930. My family currently resides in a variety of places, including Spain, Germany, and the United States. I protest this line of questioning. My wife died on the *Athenia*, I'm distraught, and I need to return to Spain, if I am unable to get to New York. Is this the way the English treat civilian victims of war?"

That provoked his questioner. "Mr. Hoffman, we'll help you arrange alternate transportation and I'm sorry about the tragic loss of your wife. I'm merely trying to establish your purpose in traveling." The officer paused before continuing. "I'm also curious about your family members in Germany. Are they in the German military? Perhaps it was a family member who torpedoed the *Athenia*."

That comment was the last straw for Karl. "I will not take any more of this. I've cooperated with you in providing facts on this tragedy. I will not tolerate insinuations regarding our purpose in traveling since you already have a dossier on us. I demand to contact the Spanish embassy to protest this treatment."

The officer did not immediately respond to Karl. He picked up his file, made a notation, and carefully laid it to the side. He then spoke softly. "Mr. Hoffman, we'll arrange for your immediate return to Spain. I'm afraid that passage to America will be impossible for the foreseeable future. I would also urge you to consider our point of view. The government in Spain, while declaring its neutrality in this war, is openly sympathetic to Nazi Germany. This is no surprise, given what happened during your civil war. You might want to think about how we view that in light of your own linkages to Germany. While we're sympathetic to your tragedy, you are only one of many who have already suffered. This war will be a bitter one, I'm afraid, and there will be precious little room for neutrality…for anybody."

After Karl was dismissed, he returned to his hotel, thinking about what the British officer had said. He was troubled by the conversation and his own bitter feelings regarding the war, his own loyalties, the concept of nationality, and what it all meant. Karl was proud of neither Nazi Germany nor Fascist Spain. He felt that his true loyalties were to his extended family. Contemplating this, and the loss of the woman he loved, he reluctantly concluded that the British officer was right; yet he found that thought even more troubling, with a brother and two sons fighting for Germany.

As Karl sat in his hotel room, he tried suppressing his emotions but could only think about Pilar and wonder how he would carry on. As he prepared to return to Spain, and ultimately Spanish Guinea, Karl knew he must answer that question above all others before he could envision what would come next in his life.

40.

Rio Muni, Spanish Guinea
November 1939

* * *

Karl Hoffman stared westward, toward the lush tropical sunset unfolding before him.

He sat on the veranda of the plantation's hacienda, alone, sipping a sherry, yet somehow unable to appreciate the beauty or to enjoy its private pleasure. He could only dwell on the past and the demands of the present as they were now affecting him.

When Karl returned to Alabos in Spain, the Ortega family immediately brought him under their protective cocoon, feeling both his loss and their own as they realized how the war had personally reached them, even in a neutral country. Yet there was precious little time to mourn, since the family was struggling to recover from the results of the country's recent civil war and Pilar's tragic death. Pedro Ortega was ailing, and his son Ernesto and Ernesto's son Alfonso struggled to get the family's wine business back on its feet. Karl was desperately needed to manage the plantations in Guinea and he quickly realized the need to return there despite feeling the need to mourn with other family members.

Upon his return, Karl quickly reestablished control over the daily flow of plantation life, as the cocoa, coffee, and lumber harvests continued to be the economic salvation of the Ortega and Hoffman families. Despite his isolation in this particular place and at this particular moment, in one of the world's most remote places, Karl realized that the enterprise he led was a crucial element of the two families' future. Given where he was, Karl thought that it was ironic that the world had already shrunk to the point where global economic activity, and war, could reach this isolated outpost.

With that thought, Karl realized that the dream he envisioned twenty-five years ago had played out in some ways more successfully than he ever could have envisioned while in its most central way, as a dream to start a new life with the woman he loved, it was now ended forever.

Karl looked west again, marveling as the sunset changed yet again in color and intensity. Yes, the tropical environment still fascinated him as he realized that the dream he achieved had now come with a heavy price. As he was now forty-seven, Karl realized that the bulk of his life was behind him, even as the importance of what he was doing for his family was still paramount.

As Karl sipped the last of the fine *oloroso* sherry in his glass, he realized that the next generation would soon be called upon to shoulder the burdens for the two families. Ernesto Ortega was probably grappling with these same thoughts as Alberto, Alfonso, and even Anita Ortega coped with family and national events in Spain.

Karl stood up and took one final look westward at the dying sunset, wondering how his two oldest sons, Hans and Ernst, were faring in Germany as the new war paused briefly before what Karl anticipated would be an ominous new phase. He also wondered how his youngest son, Paul, was doing in America, in a completely different environment.

At that moment, Karl realized where the next influence would be felt. It was clear to him that the future rested with a new generation in the New World.

Book Two

* * *

A New Generation

Part I

* * *

Transition

1939–1941

1.

Columbia University, New York City
November 1939

* * *

As Paul Hoffman walked across the Columbia campus on this crisp late autumn afternoon, he pondered his emerging plan and his initial exposure to college life. He quickly suppressed the bitter memory of his mother's recent death, realizing that his mourning must now end and he must move forward with his plan. Paul was determined to pursue his vision as he walked to class on this brisk afternoon. *I must find a way*, he thought, *to turn this privileged interlude into an opportunity to accelerate my family's recovery from our recent tragedy and our economic recovery from the Civil War.*

He had already proposed the outline of his plan to Ramon Ortega and tonight he planned to discuss the remaining details with Ramon. Paul's bold vision involved a completely new approach to managing the family's shipping, export-import, and commodity business with the merging realities of the new World War. Paul smiled, satisfied that these final thoughts pulled together all the elements he envisioned.

Although Paul first visited New York more than twelve years ago during his family's first trip to America, this was the first time he had lived in the city full time. He had decided to major in business and economics, with a minor in history. He was only just getting used to the entire campus scene, including the rigors of academic life at Columbia.

In most ways, Paul was far more mature and knowledgeable than the average Columbia freshman, and the mixture of culture and politics in the city and on campus was intoxicating. He dived into the music scene and was fond of visiting the Savoy Ballroom, uptown in Harlem, to hear the famous swing bands of the era compete in the "battle of the bands." He enjoyed watching celebrities such as Benny Goodman and Count Basie lead their orchestras against hometown favorites such as Chick Webb's band. Webb himself had passed away in June, leaving a young singer named Ella Fitzgerald to lead that band. When Paul wasn't taking in the music scene, he used the rest of his precious little free time to visit the haunts of lower and mid-Manhattan, especially the bohemian nightclubs in Greenwich Village. The Village and its inhabitants could always be counted on to entertain. Paul often thought about the incredible contrast between his current life in New York and his early life in Spanish Guinea and Spain.

The politics of campus life were another matter. Whereas Choate was isolated, high school oriented, and catered to rich conservative parents and students, Columbia was a hot bed of student activism regarding the liberal political causes of the day. Almost from the beginning, Paul found himself as the unwanted center of attention because of the civil war in Spain. When students and professors found out he was Spanish, they were naturally inquisitive about his political leanings.

Naturally, coming from a wealthy family of landowners, Paul was suspected of being an ardent Nationalist. When he tried to explain the nuances of political life in Spain, it conflicted with the set views of his audience. Most American polls showed that 70 percent of the public supported the Republican cause, and at Columbia, the figure was much higher. In the protected, isolated campus environment, students and many professors only saw Fascist Nationalists, supported by the Nazis, fighting democratic, righteous Spanish Republicans. Most of them glossed over the fact that both sides were guilty of abuses and that the principal supporter of the Republican cause was the Stalinist Soviet Union. They conveniently ignored the fact that the western democracies avoided involvement, opening the door for German, Italian, and Soviet intervention. The Nationalist victory the previous April had left many on campus bitter about the outcome.

Paul threw himself into his academic studies with a passion. Like his father, Paul used his work and studies to keep his family's recent tragedy deep in his subconscious. He liked his business and economics courses but most enjoyed the history courses. Because of his background, Paul had already become acquainted with the chair of the history department, who had a more balanced view of the civil war in Spain. The two of them frequently discussed the legacy of the Spanish Civil War and the new European war.

Although Paul tried out for and secured a spot on the Columbia track team, he decided not to participate. Instead, he wanted to spend some time with Ramon planning future business development for the family enterprises.

The letter he had just received from his father outlined how the family's wine trade and other enterprises in Spain proper were still suffering from the effects of the war and that the family's fortunes were still improving slowly only because of the cocoa and coffee exports from Guinea, most of which were now being exported to America.

Just before the fall term started, Paul helped Ramon plan for the next wave of market penetration in America. Paul realized that the family's fortunes now depended on his developing business acumen. Under his plan, he and Ramon would directly contact cocoa and coffee wholesalers throughout the country and work with key chocolate manufacturers to seek more remunerative outlets for their premium cocoa product. Ramon worried about the amount of travel that this would require since these enterprises were spread out everywhere. The American rail network went most places, but it was slow. Travel by airlines was expensive and only connected the larger cities.

Ramon eventually agreed with Paul's solution to this problem. They would travel in their own private aircraft. Paul had learned to fly while at Choate and continued flying at nearby Teterboro Airport to obtain experience in larger single-engine aircraft. The next move would be to acquire one. Paul pondered that bold move as he finished his afternoon walk and entered the classroom.

2.

Alabos, Spain
April 9, 1940

* * *

Pedro Ortega's funeral was a somber yet uplifting affair. He had died several days ago, peacefully, as he slept. Pedro had rallied in January for his eightieth birthday and again in February when he and Maria celebrated their fiftieth wedding anniversary, so his death was a shock. The uplifting part was how widely attended the funeral ceremony was, as dozens of family members, neighbors, business associates, and even government officials came to pay homage to a man they greatly respected.

When Karl heard about Pedro's decline, he returned to Alabos in March, arriving two days before Pedro died, and he and other family members were at his bedside as he slipped away. He now sat quietly in Pedro's study the evening of the funeral, looking at photographs and other memorabilia in the room and realizing that he and Ernesto had some big shoes to fill. The family was still mourning Pilar's death, and Maria, Ana, and Anita were consoling each other even as Karl, Ernesto, and Alfonso made the necessary plans to continue with the family businesses. Karl was grateful that Pedro had the foresight to prepare for this event and ensure a nearly seamless transition of the family's business affairs. He missed Pedro's sage advice and mentoring, but they would go on.

This same transition had occurred the previous month, from afar, as Wilhelm Hoffman similarly divested ownership of his properties to Walter and Karl. Karl had just received the letter and other documents. In the letter, Wilhelm outlined how his lands in West Prussia had been returned to the family after Poland surrendered. Wilhelm chose to liquidate the entire Prussian estate, except for the manor house itself and small adjacent plots. He placed the proceeds in their Swiss accounts and turned ownership of those over to Walter and Karl. The two sons would share ownership of the Mosel estates.

Karl now realized how much life had changed for the Hoffman and Ortega families. Anita had insisted on becoming more involved in the wine business and helping her father, Ernesto. Although it was a very nontraditional role for a woman in Spain to become involved in family business affairs, Ernesto had agreed and was grateful for her support. It was clear that the family was evolving as the world continued to change.

Karl made plans to return to Guinea in about a month. After a lengthy sea journey from Spanish Guinea on one of the family's freighters, Karl already anticipated the scheduled return trip in May. He had booked a flight on Air France, which would take only four days, versus the fifteen- to twenty-one-day sea voyage. This would be the second time Karl would take advantage of improving air transportation to return to Africa.

Considering how to reach America in the future, Karl was intrigued by the news that transatlantic air service had finally begun in mid-1939 when Pan American Airways started serving Marseilles, France, and Southampton, England, from New York with Boeing flying boats. Karl thought the one-way fare of 375 U.S. dollars was reasonable, although it was a small fortune for virtually all but the rich. The war had disrupted service, but another company would soon be serving Lisbon, Portugal, from New York with flying boats.

Karl's musings about transatlantic air travel caused him to think about the other recent aeronautical event in his life. Karl had flown for almost two years and was now a fully licensed pilot. He had followed through on an earlier plan to acquire an aircraft for regional travel in Guinea. After the Civil War, the victorious Nationalist government had disposed of surplus Republican and Nationalist aircraft, and Karl had acquired, at a bargain price, a single-engine Spartan Executive airplane. The Spartan was built in Tulsa, Oklahoma, and this example was the prototype of that design, shipped to Spain earlier in the war. The Republicans had hardly used the aircraft and it was in excellent condition. Karl had it prepared for shipment to Guinea. He mulled over the idea of flying it there himself but decided that his lack of experience was not up to the task of ferrying the aircraft on the six thousand-kilometer flight needed under very hostile weather and terrain conditions. Karl knew that Paul was also about to acquire an aircraft for business travel in America and decided to write him describing the aircraft acquisition. He also wrote to his father, Walter, Hans, and Ernst. He wondered where his two oldest sons were now. He hadn't received a letter in months.

He also needed to think about his return to Guinea, since there would be pressing management issues to deal with when he arrived. He and Alfonso had already discussed this and they agreed that Karl must return to Guinea within a few weeks. Karl began to pen his letters, conscious of the fact that many changes were likely to occur in the family's lives in the next several years and wondering what those changes might entail.

Later that evening, Karl listened to the BBC broadcast from London. The war had suddenly turned less "phony." Germany had invaded Denmark and Norway in the predawn hours. After a few hours of token resistance, Denmark had surrendered, but Norway was resisting with British and French support even though the capital of Oslo had fallen. The broadcast spoke of extensive naval and air battles and large German naval losses. Karl thought of Walter, Hans, and Ernst and their likely role in the battle. He wished that he had been able to contact his sons, but all communications with Germany were disrupted or nonexistent.

Karl was saddened that Europe was now again locked in a struggle that could not possibly have a positive outcome, no matter who won. Spain was still neutral but openly favoring Germany. Civil war had devastated Spain, yet the prevailing Nationalist government policy and even public opinion felt that Germany and Italy had helped rescue the country from communism and anarchy. Yet Spain's export markets in Europe were now severely restricted. In addition, in a move to achieve self-sufficiency, the Franco regime was severely limiting imports, further devastating the economy.

Karl realized how important the family's activities in Guinea were to their continued economic well-being. He also realized that the long-term health of both the country and the family was becoming increasingly tied to markets and politics in America. He was grateful that Ramon and Paul were there and that they realized what was at stake. When he returned to Guinea, it would become harder to coordinate their strategies, but Karl knew he must find a way to do so. But he also realized that the family business was subtly changing as his youngest son began assuming the mantle of leadership.

3.

Tulsa, Oklahoma
April 1940

* * *

Paul and Ramon Ortega were pleased with their latest acquisition. In an interesting irony, they had acquired an example of the same aircraft model that Karl had acquired in Spain. Whereas Karl had acquired the prototype of the Spartan Executive in Spain, Paul and Ramon were picking up one of the last to be built before that model was discontinued. Like the one in Spain, they acquired this aircraft at a bargain price and it came fully equipped with radios and instruments for flying in poor weather. Paul did not yet have the instrument rating on his pilot certificate that he needed to operate the aircraft under such conditions but was planning to take the necessary training soon. It was rare enough for anyone to own a private aircraft in 1940 and rarer still for anyone other than the airlines to fly aircraft in poor weather. The navigation aids of the day were primitive and air traffic control practically nonexistent. It was almost unheard of for anyone actually to use an aircraft for business transportation.

The Spartan was sleek and very art deco in appearance. More importantly, it was capable of cruising at two hundred miles per hour, faster than the airliners of the day. Paul and Ramon weren't wasting any time. They had just taken delivery of the aircraft and would be making several business stops on the return flight to New York. As Paul was preparing the aircraft he contemplated how he and Ramon would develop their business strategy to expand their markets. He realized he must still complete his education and resolved to find a way to accomplish these sometimes conflicting goals.

4.

Dakar, Senegal, French West Africa
MAY 15, 1940

* * *

Bad timing upset Karl's decision to return to Guinea by air. The French airline schedules became a shambles on May 10 when the Germans launched a massive invasion of France and the Low Countries. As a result, Karl was delayed an extra two days in Dakar. The agent assured Karl that the next day he would be able to take the scheduled flight to Abidjan in the Ivory Coast and then the following day to Douala in Cameroon. Karl's instructor pilot in Guinea could fly the newly reassembled Spartan Executive on the short 120-kilometer flight from Santa Isabel to Douala over the Bight of Biafra to pick him up. Santa Isabel did not yet have any airline service, although Karl was working with the colonial government to improve the airport in anticipation of future service.

That evening in his hotel lobby, Karl was stunned as he listened to the evening BBC broadcast. In only six days, the Germans had crushed two French armies and that day had achieved a huge victory at Sedan. Karl was struck by the irony. Seventy years before, the Germans had also defeated the French at Sedan. It was in that battle that Wilhelm Hoffman had distinguished himself. Karl thought of his eighty-eight-year-old father and wondered what he might be thinking now. Karl believed that his father would be disgusted rather than happy, as another generation of young men was thrown away.

5.

In the air, west of Kansas City, Missouri
July 1940

* * *

Paul Hoffman sat contentedly in the left seat of the Spartan Executive, listening to the comforting throb of the 450-horsepower Pratt and Whitney Wasp Junior engine, as he headed between Denver and Kansas City for his next meeting with a coffee company. He was pleased that he had a thirty-mile-per-hour tailwind, making his speed over the ground 215 miles per hour, even at his economical cruising speed of 185 at his altitude of 11,500 feet. The weather was excellent and he would be in Kansas City early. After his meeting with the coffee company, he would remain overnight and was looking forward to going to one of Kansas City's famous jazz clubs. This was his first trip without Ramon Ortega, and Paul already had conducted several successful meetings with various chocolate and coffee distributors across America. Although he had only just turned nineteen, Paul looked as much as ten years older and his deeper voice, facial features, and general maturity commanded respect when he met with potential customers.

When the weather and other flying conditions were undemanding, as they were today, Paul often used his time while flying to think about future meetings. Today, however, he was pondering ideas that were more sweeping. Paul looked around the sky, clear in all directions for hundreds of miles, and then down at the limitless farmland below him. He realized that the abundance in America, its separation from the Old World, and the character of its people spoke to the future like nothing he had ever experienced in Europe, let alone Africa. Everything in America was possible and, with certain exceptions, unbounded by culture, tradition, or boundaries.

As he thought about these attributes, Paul realized that America's isolation in the world would soon end, and when it did, its power to change things in the global arena could be unlimited. Paul thought that the Ortegas did not understand these concepts well, even though they were far more sophisticated than most other Spaniards. Their view of the world was still Euro-centric, even though all three generations of Ortega men understood the importance of the emerging market in the Americas for the family's products from Spanish Guinea. Paul respected all of them, but he thought that Alfonso would be more in touch with future possibilities than his father, Ernesto, who had assumed the mantle of family patriarch when his father, Pedro, died.

Paul thought about his own father and admired what he had done, starting in 1927, to develop markets in America. Yet Paul thought that even Karl Hoffman might not see the opportunities that could unfold in America. Paul realized that his father had a global view but maybe did not yet appreciate the opportunities offered by their American connection.

At that moment, Paul realized what it was that he most wanted. He was now responsible for developing a vision for the future of the Hoffman and Ortega families that capitalized on the coming dramatic changes in the world, especially America's role. Paul thought that he could bridge the gap between the two worlds and not only help the two families prosper but also help Spain to become a part of this world. Paul smiled as he realized how brazen that vision was, given the current situation in Spain and in Europe. Clearly, this called for an extraordinary approach to their business enterprises. Today it was wine, cocoa, coffee, shipping, and export-import activities. What would it be tomorrow?

Paul's reverie was interrupted as the Spartan's engine began coughing and vibrating, commanding his instant attention.

What was it? He quickly scanned the instrument panel and noticed fuel pressure dropping…the fuel gauges…yes, that's it! Paul quickly reached for the fuel selector, realizing he had unintentionally run a tank dry. He switched to the fullest tank and was about to reach for the fuel pump when the engine instantly caught and roared back to life.

Paul decided it was time to get back to the job at hand rather than the next meeting or his family's future. He picked up his sectional chart, looked outside at the land ahead, and then back at his chart, quickly correlating the two to see where he was. Over to the left was Topeka. It was time to begin his slow descent into Kansas City. He would continue developing his vision after he landed.

6.

Governor's Mansion, Santa Isabel, Spanish Guinea
August 1940

* * *

Karl arrived at the governor's office on schedule for a meeting that the governor had requested on some unknown subject. The secretary apologized, saying the governor would be about twenty minutes late. Karl accepted her apology and sat down to await the governor's arrival.

Karl's thoughts quickly turned to the events of the preceding three months. When he had finally reached Guinea, he had many pressing business matters to attend to. Karl had found that their plantations and other properties were in good shape and that planting and harvesting of cocoa, coffee, and timber was proceeding efficiently. However, Karl needed to find solutions to labor and shipping shortages that caused an accumulation of inventory in Guinea rather than shipments to markets. The war was disrupting both areas as the British and French colonies near Guinea tightened up on emigration permits for workers to go to Spanish Guinea and the developing U-boat war caused shipping shortages.

Fortunately, Karl and Ernesto, collaborating with Pedro before his death, had secured lease-purchases on four ocean-going freighters so that they could control the shipping element in their business. So far, this had worked well as the four ships were able to carry much of the Guinea exports to market, mostly to America, and then return to Africa with manufactured and other goods not only for Spanish Guinea but also for the Portuguese African colonies, since they would otherwise be returning empty. Karl needed to develop the trade with the Portuguese in more depth but he had not been able to travel to Lisbon to conduct business development.

Karl worried about the safety of their ships. He ordered that they display large Spanish flags at all times, even in harbor, and that a huge Spanish flag be painted on each side of the ships. German U-boats and surface raiders were extracting a heavy toll on allied shipping and that included some inadvertent attacks on neutral shipping, including Spanish and Portuguese ships. The initial lease term was almost up, and Karl and Ernesto had earlier decided to exercise the purchase option at the earliest opportunity.

Karl decided not to wait until he could visit Lisbon and reflected on the success of his recent flight to the Portuguese island colony of Sao Tome. It was about a 430-kilometer flight over the Gulf of Guinea to Sao Tome. There was, of course, no airline service, but the Spartan had made that flight in only about an hour and a half. Karl flew the Spartan regularly but had engaged his more experienced instructor pilot to accompany him on the flight. That was a good thing, Karl thought, as he reflected on the lessons of that flight. The weather had been unpredictable and they lacked navigation aids. The only landmark was the island of Principe, the other half of the Portuguese island colony and right on their route to Sao Tome, a little over halfway there. His instructor pilot told him that if that little island, about ten by twenty kilometers large, failed to show up at the time they calculated, they would turn back to Santa Isabel. The alternative was to continue and miss Sao Tome altogether and fly into the open ocean.

The Spartan got regular use shuttling Karl and others from the hacienda and plantation on Rio Muni for the short 60-kilometer flight to Bata, which took nearly half a day on land because of the appalling road conditions existing on the mainland. After completing business there and perhaps dropping someone off, Karl continued on to Santa Isabel, a 250-kilometer flight taking only an hour, sometimes less. The alternative was a fifteen-hour one-way trip by boat that only sailed once a week. The cumulative effect of these efficiencies was noticeable on coordination of plantation activities on the mainland and the island. Even without other trips, such as to Sao Tome, the Spartan was paying for itself.

Karl thought about Paul's last letter describing his academic progress at Columbia and updates on the family business from the New York end. Karl realized how indispensible Paul had become to their success, even though he was only nineteen and still in college. Ramon Ortega was now seventy, and Karl knew that Paul would be shouldering an increasing burden of family business activities. Karl wanted to travel to New York as soon as possible to see Paul as well as to personally coordinate family business activities. In the absence of air travel, Karl planned to travel on one of the family's ships. Three of the four ships included comfortable passenger cabins.

Karl looked at his watch and thought of the governor. The incumbent had arrived at his post in early 1937, finally providing some continuity in the colonial government. From 1931 to 1936, the colony had suffered through five separate governors appointed by the Republican government, and all of them had been disruptive and incompetent. Karl thought longingly of the governor that had helped him in 1915 and in the early 1920s to establish their plantations. He had served for fourteen years and had been an invaluable steward for the colony.

At that moment, Karl's thoughts were interrupted as the governor arrived and profusely apologized for his tardiness.

"My dear Karl, I'm so sorry for my lateness, but I had matters to attend to that took much more time than I thought. Please come into my office."

Karl entered the office and sat down. He noticed the governor sweating profusely. He was a short, balding man with a small mustache, slightly portly, with legs longer and out of proportion with the rest of his body. Karl thought he looked very much like Franco.

"May I pour you some sherry, Karl? As you can see, it is a wonderful *amontillado* from your bodega in Jerez."

Karl accepted, and the governor poured them each a glass and sat down. He immediately got down to business.

"Karl, as you know, I just returned from Spain where I had the honor of several private meetings with *El Caudillo* regarding the future of Guinea, economic conditions in Spain, and the general situation in Europe."

Karl immediately thought of the pompous title that Franco gave himself as the governor continued. It was clear that the politician sitting in front of him might be useful somehow in Guinea, but he was clearly a Franco lackey. Karl understood, however, that he must overcome his feelings and find a way to work with the Franco government.

"The information I am about to share with you is very secret, and I must have your assurances that it will be kept in strict confidence. Will you agree to that, Karl?"

Karl replied instantly, anxious to hear more, "Of course, Governor; I understand the need for absolute secrecy in such matters."

"*El Caudillo* believes that Germany's stunning success on the battlefield and France's defeat will change the entire map of Europe and that when

England surrenders it will be too late for Spain to share in the spoils of victory. That is why he believes that we must enter the war soon by Germany's and Italy's sides so that we benefit economically and territorially."

Karl couldn't believe what he heard. Could Franco really be that naïve?

The governor continued, "*El Caudillo* wants me to prepare a position paper which enumerates our resources, military, financial, and territorial requirements in detail so that he can present them to Chancellor Hitler. He is preparing to meet with Hitler in about two months, in occupied France on the Spanish border. I am to return to Spain in about a month with this position paper. This gives me very little time to prepare it."

Karl saw the fix that the governor was in. "Governor, I understand the urgency of this matter and the responsibility you have. How can I be of assistance to you?"

The governor's eyes lit up and he beamed as he replied, "I knew you would understand, and I will be most grateful for your help. First of all, I would like your reaction to what I have said and then some advice on how to proceed. You have listened patiently. What do you think of all this?"

Karl paused before responding, choosing his words carefully. "Governor, I must be frank with you. I believe it's a grave mistake for Spain to enter this war, on either side. We haven't recovered from the effects of the civil war. Our economy in Spain is devastated and the war is already restricting our markets for our exports and the ability to import necessities. Our military is exhausted and has very little, obsolete equipment. If we enter the war on Germany's side, all of these problems will get worse." Karl paused so the governor could react.

"Karl, I am somewhat surprised by your response. You know that Germany and Italy helped us during the civil war. In fact, your brother and two sons were directly involved and now they are fighting for Germany in the war with England. Surely that must affect your thoughts and feelings."

Karl paused again before responding. He didn't want to belittle this man, but he must get through to him. How could he put it in a way that he would understand? Finally, he crafted his response in a way that affected the governor's back yard.

"Governor, please understand. I care very deeply for my sons and my brother, and their safety is very much in my thoughts. However, I must think first of Spain and what is right for my country. I have responsibilities to you and to the colony and…to my other family members. If Spain enters the war with the Axis powers, we will be totally isolated here in Guinea. We will be unable to export our products or import our necessities. Beyond a mere blockade, we will be subject to invasion from British Empire forces in Nigeria and Free French forces in their colonies. We have virtually no military power here in Guinea and no warships or aircraft. I had a similar experience in Kamerun in 1915. We were surrounded and the result was inevitable. Similarly, everything that you created here will be gone. Also, I don't believe that England will surrender or be invaded. Furthermore, they are already receiving aid from the Americans."

Karl paused to let that sink in. He could see from the devastated look on the governor's face that he had made his point. Finally, the governor responded.

"I guess that…you are probably…correct…in your analysis. But what am I to do? Franco wants a position to present to Hitler and I am responsible for preparing it. How would you advise me, knowing this?"

Karl thought about that for a moment. He must come up with a way out, a path that would take the governor off the hook while keeping Spain out of the war. Finally, it dawned on him. He responded, embellishing his answer as he talked.

"Governor, I have an idea. You should prepare the position paper and address all the issues that Franco specified. For example, you can write that Spain must expand its African territories. Let's say that we will enlarge Guinea to include Cameroon and most of French Equatorial Africa, as well as Nigeria. Oh, and since Spanish Sahara and Morocco are divided by French Morocco, we will demand that too, as well as most of Algeria, and of course Gibraltar. We will demand the latest military equipment, supplies, and a large amount of finance aid. We must be brazen and ensure that Spain is compensated for all that it could lose in a war."

The governor was speechless, an incredulous look on his face. He finally responded. "What you propose might be considered outrageous. Are you serious with these proposals?"

"I am very serious. Franco expects you to make bold proposals, or he would not have entrusted you with such responsibility."

The governor sat back in his chair, thought for a moment, took a deep breath, and replied, "Karl, I believe your advice is good. Will you help me prepare this position paper? I have so very little time and I would miss so many details if I completed it myself. I would be forever grateful for your help."

"Governor, rest assured, I will begin drafting it immediately."

* * *

As Karl left the governor's office, he was already thinking about how he would prepare this paper. He now realized that the war was the defining event that would shape the world for years to come. Somehow Spain must craft a way to stay out of the fighting while positioning itself for the postwar world order. It might take another couple of years for that to become apparent. Meanwhile Spain must buy time, and he was well aware of his role in this activity.

Karl completed the draft position paper in only four days, titling it "The Rights of Spain in Equatorial Africa," highlighting that aspect of the requirements, but he included all the other issues he had addressed in the governor's meeting and a number of issues they hadn't discussed. The governor was ecstatic with the paper, gushing that it was just what Franco was looking for. He profusely thanked Karl and soon departed for Spain.

After delivering the paper and leaving the governor's office, Karl contemplated the Trojan horse he had created for Franco and Hitler. Unless he was totally wrong, the content of these proposals would be too much for Hitler to digest and accept. Their potential Spanish ally would be more trouble than it was worth. Karl hoped his creation wouldn't backfire.

Karl also resolved to contact Alberto when he next returned to Spain. Since Alberto was now involved in intelligence work for the Spanish navy, maybe he and Karl could quietly collaborate to protect the position of the country, their family, and their future.

7.

Manhattan, New York
October 1941

* * *

It was Friday evening, and Paul relaxed with Ramon Ortega in Ramon's Fifth Avenue penthouse. They had just finished reviewing financial reports from the prior quarter for their burgeoning American enterprises. The connections between the Ortega-Hoffman enterprises in Spain and Spanish Guinea and Ramon's export-import business had been long established. The family enterprises in America thrived, building on the imports of cocoa, coffee, fine mahogany lumber, and other commodities. As a result, the Spanish Guinea operations were highly profitable. The conditions in Spain itself were still severe because of lingering effects from the civil war and the current European conflict.

Nevertheless, the Ortega bodegas in both Rioja and Jerez exported small amounts of premium wine and sherry to America, almost all of it distributed in New York City itself. As a result of the war, imports of fine wine from France ended, and the American wine trade was still recovering from the disaster of Prohibition. Paul felt that the cheap table wine produced in California was not yet able to compete in quality with the best Spanish wines. He wished he could import more, but economic conditions in Spain couldn't support increased production yet.

Ramon and Paul had made excellent use of the Spartan Executive over the last year and a half. They had visited numerous confectioners, wholesale outlets, and other entities to promote their products, using the Spartan to efficiently visit many more businesses than they could by road, rail, or airline. Their travel was most intense during the summer and college vacation periods when Paul was available full time. Paul even managed to use his time with the business to count for some college credit and thus reduce his academic workload. In addition to promoting their imports from Spain and Guinea, they were fronting now for Spanish, Portuguese, French, and Belgian colonial interests in Africa to help fill the ships returning to Africa after dropping off their commodities in America. These export interests now consumed as much of their time as Spanish imports did.

Paul was in his junior year at Columbia. He had pursued his business coursework intensely in the prior two years and this year concentrated more on history subjects. He had secured a slot in the prestigious current history seminar conducted by the history department chair at Columbia, a lucky break since Paul was only a minor in history and the seminar was usually reserved for history majors. Paul became close to the department chair and was now selected to assist the professor with the seminar for the spring 1942 semester.

The prior month, Ramon had celebrated his seventy-first birthday. He was still going strong but quietly made it clear to Paul that he considered him like a son and the heir to his business and properties. Ramon's wife had died during the 1918 influenza epidemic, they had no children, and Ramon had not remarried. Paul tried to spend time with Ramon outside of their business activities, but the demands on his time were severe. Ramon understood this and urged Paul to continue to give his studies the highest priority, participating in the business as time allowed.

Later in the evening, Paul and Ramon discussed the war over a glass of sherry. They pondered the increasing role that America was playing and the risks that this entailed. Paul summed his thoughts.

"I believe that America will soon be drawn into the war. The navy is already participating in the U-boat war, even though America is technically neutral. A destroyer has been sunk and another one damaged. Combined with the Lend-Lease Act, these conditions will surely provoke Germany." He wondered if Hans was involved with the American attacks. He hadn't heard from either of his brothers in some time.

Ramon continued the conversation. "I'm afraid you're right, Paul. It's already turned into a shooting war. Also, I believe that America's embargo of fuel supplies to Japan will provoke a war in the Far East. In any case, we aren't prepared for a two ocean war militarily. With the European war, and France and Holland occupied by Germany, the French and Dutch colonies in the Far East are isolated and vulnerable to Japanese attack."

Paul summed up their discussion with the possible impact on their own lives. "I think it's likely that America will be in the war within six months. If that happens, it will affect our business. I sent a long letter to my father on the last ship back to Guinea, asking him to accelerate imports over the next few months to increase our inventory here. We have enough warehouse space for some additional product."

Ramon agreed. "Yes, that's a good move from a business sense. Your father in his last communication stated that he still has a surplus in storage that needs to be transported. By exporting that entire surplus here, we will be in the best position to react to the opening of hostilities and the effect that will have on shipping."

Neither Paul nor Ramon needed to comment on the financial arrangements that supported these business activities or the policies that they had followed for some time. Ever since the Spanish Civil War, they had deposited the profits and remittances of the business in secure New York banks, avoiding large-scale conversion to Spanish currency or remitting the funds to their banks and accounts in Switzerland. They were both concerned about the security of their Swiss assets, where most of the family fortunes had previously resided. Switzerland was now surrounded by Axis-occupied or dominated territory, although it did not seem likely that Germany would invade. After all, the Swiss were serving as bankers to the world. The family had quietly transferred funds to the New York banks before the war began.

On the other hand, the Franco government required the family to convert some dollar holdings into pesetas so the Spanish government would have access to precious foreign exchange. The peseta was nearly worthless, so converting dollars generated enormous amounts of pesetas. The family used these funds to purchase the only assets that really mattered in Spain—land. The Ortega family quietly bought up land in the best wine-producing regions of Spain and lately had purchased seafront property in Southern Spain for future development. All of these activities proved to be more instructive to Paul than all of his academic business training at Columbia.

Later, after leaving Ramon's apartment and returning to his apartment near the university, he thought of the impending worldwide conflagration. Germany had attacked the Soviet Union four months ago and now, alone among the major powers, America was barely still neutral. When the inevitable happened, Paul wondered how it would affect the family. He thought of his two brothers fighting for Germany and how he had taken such a different course. *What will the outcome be?* He thought.

8.

North Atlantic Ocean, southwest of the Cape Verde Islands
November 14, 1941

* * *

Karl was in his cabin writing letters to Hans and Ernst that he hoped to post when he arrived in New York in about three weeks. He was aboard one of the family's freighters, en route to the Cape Verde Islands, a Portuguese colony, with cargo. After a quick turn there, the ship would sail for New York. Karl thought it was most likely the letters would arrive in Germany faster from New York than Cape Verde, although wartime mail delivery was proving to be highly unpredictable. Of course, Karl was most looking forward to seeing Paul in New York. The last time he saw his three sons was July 1939.

This particular voyage was a complicated one. After receiving a letter from Paul in October recommending accelerated exports to America before they entered the war, Karl immediately dispatched two of their freighters directly to New York with full loads of cocoa, coffee, and lumber. Karl was following now with another freighter load but took a longer route with stops in Cabinda in Portuguese Angola, Buenos Aires in South America, and soon Cape Verde, to honor contracts for shipments to the Portuguese colonies and Argentina. While in Cabinda, Karl loaded cargo from both the Belgian Congo and the French Congo but, as a precaution, buried that cargo deep in the hold, and it was now under a load of Argentine tinned beef. Both the Free French and the Belgian Congo were belligerent powers and Karl wanted his cargo to appear to represent trade only between neutral powers, such as Spain, Portugal, Argentina, and the United States.

Karl's letter to Ernst was finished, but Karl was having difficulty finishing the letter to Hans. After Pilar died, Walter wrote Karl asking him not to explain the circumstances of Pilar's death, stating it would devastate Hans, even though he was not on the U-boat that sank the *Athenia*. Although Karl did not know the real story, Walter was not being truthful, since Hans had, in fact, been the first watch officer on the U-30. Ignorant of these facts, Karl finally reached an agonizing decision about what to tell Hans and finished the letter.

As Karl sealed the envelope, he noticed that the ship's engines suddenly stopped, without any warning. Karl reached for the interphone, but it rang just as Karl picked it up. Karl quizzed the bridge immediately.

"Captain, why have you stopped the engines?"

"*Señor* Hoffman, please come to the bridge at once. A submarine just surfaced nearby and ordered us to stop for inspection."

"Is it a U-boat?"

"Yes. There is a search party rowing over to us now in a small boat. They've crewed their deck gun but otherwise have not threatened us if we stopped. Of course, I complied immediately because—"

Karl interrupted. "Yes, Captain, you did the right thing. Get the ship's papers ready. Also, alert the wireless operator to prepare to send a message that we're under attack but don't transmit without my explicit instructions. I'll be right there."

Karl leaped out of his chair, but just as he was about to leave the room, he instinctively went back to the desk and picked up both letters and took them with him. He raced up the steps to the bridge level wondering if one of the men in the boat could be Hans.

Within minutes, Karl reached the bridge and joined the captain as they watched the small boat approach their ship. Several minutes later, the U-boat boarding party entered the bridge. The team included four crewmen, and Karl instantly sensed that the U-boat captain himself was leading it. He was tall and handsome with a square face and light-colored hair under his cap. He wore an Iron Cross First Class. He approached Karl and the freighter's captain, saluted, and spoke slowly, in broken Spanish.

"I am *Kapitänleutnant* Clausen and I command the U-129. May I see your ship's papers?"

Karl replied immediately, in German, "Good day, *Herr Kapitänleutnant*. I am Karl Hoffman and my family owns this ship, the *SS Santa Isabel*. My captain will show you the ship's papers. We are en route from Spanish Guinea to Cape Verde with a load of cocoa, coffee, and lumber, Argentine tinned beef, and other cargo. May I ask why you stopped us?"

"*Herr* Hoffman, your German is excellent. I had no idea this ship was owned by a German family."

"It isn't, *Herr Kapitänleutnant*. I and my family are Spanish. I was born in Germany but have been a Spanish citizen for eleven years. Again, may I ask the nature of your inspection?"

Karl sensed that Clausen was sizing him up, as the U-boat officer finally replied, "Yes, of course. As you surely know, we must ensure that this ship is actually registered with a neutral country and is not carrying contraband bound for an enemy of the Reich."

"Very well," Karl replied. "We will cooperate with the inspection and ask that you conduct it quickly so that we may proceed."

"Yes, *Herr* Hoffman, my team will be expeditious. While they are doing that, please tell me as I am curious, how did you come to be a part of this family and enterprise? Is all of your family now in Spain or in Spanish Guinea?"

"I fought in Kamerun with the *Schutztruppe* in 1915 and we were interned in Spain, where my wife and I were married and I joined the Ortega family." Karl paused, deciding to up the ante. "I also earned one of those." Karl pointed to Clausen's Iron Cross.

Clausen's interest was now piqued. "That is quite an interesting background, *Herr* Hoffman. What about the rest of your family?"

"I have three sons, one in New York and two in Germany." Karl paused. "My wife died in 1939…on the *Athenia*."

Karl was pleased when he saw the shock value of his information reflected on Clausen's face as he struggled to respond.

"I am…sorry for your…loss." He paused and then quickly added, "If you have two sons in Germany then perhaps they are—"

Karl interrupted, "Yes, *Herr* Clausen; they are in the *Wehrmacht*. My middle son is a pilot in the *Luftwaffe*. Perhaps you know my oldest son, Hans. He is a U-boat captain like you and, from what I can determine, is based out of Lorient, France."

"Your son…your son is Hans Hoffman?" This time Clausen's surprise was even more noticeable, as if Karl's comment triggered a deeper knowledge of something more tragic, as well it should.

"Yes, *Herr* Clausen, he is my son." He paused. "If you are wondering, I have no need to forgive him for serving on U-boats, maybe even on the one that sank the *Athenia*. He came about his convictions on his own, and every person is entitled to that right. My only regret is that he and his brother will suffer when Germany inevitably faces the consequences of its actions and responsibilities for this war."

The shocked look on Clausen's face turned slowly to one of mild anger as he searched for the right response.

"*Herr* Hoffman, your arrogance and disrespect for the Reich is appalling, given your own service and that of your sons. You know, it would be easy for me to just sink your ship and be done with it." He paused. "But I must account for the fact that the tragic loss of your wife may be responsible for your...bitterness."

"*Herr* Clausen, you mistake my regrets for bitterness. I am only expressing my own opinion about the outcome of this war. As for this ship, we are at your mercy. However, you know that we will at least get our SOS transmitted. Then you would be accountable to U-boat command; my brother, *Vizeadmiral* Walter Hoffman; and *Grossadmiral* Doenitz too, I suppose, for sinking a neutral Spanish ship when the Reich is actively courting Spain to enter the war." Karl paused briefly, noticing some of the arrogance drain from Clausen. "Meanwhile, I have serious responsibilities to my extended family and a business to run on four continents. So, as your team completes its inspection, I will conclude by asking you a favor."

"You...are asking me...a favor?"

Karl was pleased with the incredulous look on Clausen's face as he replied, "Yes; I wonder if you could either deliver these letters to Hans or post them when you return from your patrol. I'm guessing that if you survive this patrol, you will reach Europe long before the letters would otherwise arrive if I posted them."

Karl reached out his hand with the letters and looked Clausen in the eyes. Clausen merely blinked, obviously dumbfounded by Karl's request, before he finally replied in a cool voice.

"I am not a mail boat, *Herr* Hoffman, but I will deliver these letters, as a favor to...Hans." As Clausen took the letters, his boarding team leader walked up to Clausen and spoke quietly to him out of Karl's earshot. Clausen nodded and turned to face Karl.

"Our inspection is concluded. Your cargo does not include contraband, but I see from the cargo manifest that most of it is destined for New York rather than Cape Verde. I also see that you stopped earlier in Cabinda. Even though that is in Angola, we know it to be a transshipment point for cargo from the French and Belgian Congo—representing countries that Germany is at war with."

"Yes, *Herr* Clausen, I understand the politics of this, but Portugal, Argentina, and the United States are neutral so there should be no question as to our right to proceed. Your inspection should have disclosed that our cargo is destined only for neutral countries."

"The United States is neutral in name only. They are already shooting at us, and their provocations carry great risk to them."

"I imagine that they are shooting back because you fired first. The risk is to Germany."

Clausen looked at Karl but apparently decided not to pursue that comment. "We will certainly find out in due course, I suppose. Good day, *Herr* Hoffman." Clausen saluted, turned, and walked briskly off the bridge, followed by his boarding team.

9

Columbia University, New York
December 7, 1941

* * *

Paul relaxed in the student union, enjoying a cup of coffee and doing a final read and edit on the term paper he was preparing for the current history seminar. It was a cold afternoon, and most people in the café were just enjoying the Sunday paper and listening to the Gene Krupa orchestra on the radio. Paul normally could concentrate while working with background music, even swing, but this time Krupa's excellent rendition of "Drum Boogie" and "Jungle Madness" distracted him. Paul paused and smiled as he recalled seeing the movie *Ball of Fire* recently, which had featured Krupa's music.

Paul's reverie was interrupted as the radio broadcast was cut off and an announcer began speaking. Paul was thunderstruck by the news—the Japanese had staged a surprise attack on Pearl Harbor! As everyone in the room stopped their conversations, the announcer continued. Paul caught a few facts as the bad news flowed out. There were many ships sunk…many casualties… attacks throughout the FarEast…Philippines…Netherlands East Indies… Malaya. Soon it all became a blur.

The announcer finally concluded and the radio began playing solemn music. Paul looked around the room. Many people were sobbing, both men and women. All had stunned looks of disbelief and many rushed out of the room to contact loved ones. Paul looked out the window at this campus far removed from the action and thought about the rest of the world. Now everyone would be affected. The world would never be the same.

10.

New York City
December 8, 1941

* * *

Paul Hoffman stared out the window of Ramon Ortega's Fifth Avenue penthouse at the late afternoon, bleak winter landscape in Central Park, balancing emotions of joy and dread. On the one hand, he was expecting his father to arrive any minute. His ship had docked early in the morning and Karl had to deal with immigration, customs, and other issues resulting from the confusion generated by the sudden onset of war. Paul had arrived at Ramon's place after his late morning classes at Columbia. Ramon planned to join Paul and Karl for dinner after completing business associated with the inbound shipment on Karl's freighter at the New York Cocoa Exchange downtown.

Paul's anticipation of seeing his father was tempered by the dread he associated with his visit to the military recruiting office early in the morning before he went to classes. Paul had arrived early but there was already a long line of men. Paul knew what his father's reaction was likely to be when he found out that his son had gone there to volunteer for military service, joining hundreds of thousands of other Americans outraged by the Japanese attacks the previous day.

Paul heard the door to the apartment open behind him. He turned and stood there for a long moment as the two men stared at each other before Paul finally raced to the other side of the room and embraced his father. They held each other close for the longest moment before Karl pulled back, a tear forming in one eye.

"Paul, I'm so happy to see you. I've been waiting for this moment for weeks. The voyage from Guinea was long enough, but it seemed like it would never end, but I'm finally here."

"Father, I've been waiting for months also, anticipating your arrival. It seems you timed it at a most depressing moment for America." Paul paused. "Let me get you a glass of sherry so we can relax and catch up on things."

The two men walked over to the liquor cabinet, and Paul poured them both a glass of *manzanilla* before they sat down. "I trust the voyage went all right and that your visit to Argentina was successful," Paul said.

"Yes, we now have a long-term contract to supply them with cocoa and coffee. I talked to Ramon briefly this morning and he said the price of commodities is shooting through the roof with America's involvement in the war. He expects they will stabilize if America institutes wartime price controls, but we will learn more tonight at dinner about his visit to the cocoa exchange today." Karl paused. "The only adventure on the voyage happened when we were stopped by a U-boat en route to Cape Verde."

"A U-boat! Was it—?"

"No, it was not Hans, but I gave the U-boat captain letters to your brothers. He knows Hans and said he would deliver them." Karl paused. "Meanwhile how are your studies at Columbia? Ramon raved about the importance of your participation in our business enterprises, but I hope it's not at the expense of your academic standing."

"You needn't worry, Father. I'm doing very well and only have three semesters left. I'll be done in a year and a half." Paul carefully considered his next thought before proceeding. "That is, it'll be a year and half if nothing else gets in the way."

"What do you mean?" Karl's smile disappeared.

"This morning I went to the military recruiting office to volunteer. Now that America is at war, it seems everyone must join the cause."

Karl was aghast. "You did what? How could...you do that? Isn't it enough that two of my sons are fighting in this tragic war! I can't bear the thought that you could be potentially taking up arms when your brothers are fighting for Germany. I don't approve of their actions either. This is all so senseless. Surely you can see what war has done to Spain, or maybe you are too isolated here to realize the tragedy that has unfolded. You don't even—"

Paul interrupted. "Father, I know what has happened to Spain. I believe that America will now stand up to tyranny so that future conflicts can be avoided. We need to—"

Karl now interrupted his son, furious with his reply. "You don't have any idea what needs to happen, but I will tell you one thing. If you enter this tragic conflict, I will disown you! You will no longer be my son!"

Paul sensed his father's shock. The two men were silent for a long moment, Karl finally breaking the stony silence to apologize.

"Paul, I'm so sorry. I didn't mean to—"

"That's all right, Father. I realize you're frustrated by your inability to keep your sons out of harm's way, but it seems like there will be no place to hide now and the entire world will be involved. Germany and America will be at war soon." Paul paused briefly. "But before you worry further about me, you might want to know that the military recruiters rejected my application out of hand. It seems that my Spanish citizenship has now made me a leper. The head recruiter said they consider Spain to be a de facto Axis country for our support of Germany and Italy. They wanted nothing to do with me, even now in America's greatest hour of need. I too am frustrated. The only world I have seems to be our family business and my academic life at Columbia. Given what's happening in the world, it all seems so unreal."

"Is that so bad, my son? Isn't it honorable to be protecting our family's business and future in the face of such dire threats? Please consider that your position right now is very important to us and that you are doing the right thing by continuing to do what is best for those interests. I'm very proud of you...even for doing what you did this morning."

Karl reached up to touch his son's arm. Paul smiled.

"Thank you, Father. I know you understand my position. I accept your challenge to lead the family through this. It's clear that the American connection may be the key to our future. Please also realize that I'm looking for ways that we might reconcile our interests with that reality."

Karl looked at his son and replied, "It's true that you may have a better understanding than I do about how this will all play out." He paused. "Come on. Let's get ready so we can join Ramon for dinner. We have a lot more to talk about in order to determine how we will deal with these new realities."

11.

Lorient, France
December 16, 1941

* * *

Walter Hoffman traveled from Berlin to personally deliver the orders to Hans at the submarine base. Walter and other key navy staff in Berlin had quickly recovered from their shock when Hitler impulsively declared war on America on December 11 following the Japanese attack on Pearl Harbor. They realized that the American East Coast was vulnerable and approved a plan, Operation Drumbeat, to immediately send six U-boats to America to attack shipping in coastal waters. Walter had ensured that Hans's boat would be one of those sent.

Walter had personally briefed each boat commander on the mission. Each commander would also receive a briefing from the submarine force commander, Karl Doenitz, at his nearby headquarters the next day. Hans was the last to be briefed, and Walter ensured that they would be in a secure place for their discussion. Hans arrived on time and as they sat down, Walter began the discussion.

"Hans, it's good to see you again. You look well and I congratulate you on the success of your last patrols." Indeed, Hans had been decorated twice for the tonnage of ships that he sank.

"Thank you, Uncle. Our success is pleasing, but the enemy continues to improve their techniques. I'm convinced they are homing on our radio transmissions. It's unforgiveable to require us to report our positions so often to U-boat command and expose not only our location but our direction of movement."

"Yes, Hans. We have received similar feedback from other U-boat commanders. I am working the problem quietly within U-boat command." So far without much success, he thought, before continuing, "Do you have any questions on the written orders?"

"I have only one. The orders are explicit: all Spanish and Portuguese ships are to be exempted from attack, even if we cannot stop them to see if they are carrying contraband. That seems like a departure from our current orders. Of course I understand why you—"

"Hans, do not presume that I have ordered this only because of your father and the operations from Spanish Guinea to America. Of course that is a desirable outcome of this new policy, but the main reason is not to provoke Spain and Portugal and to assist us in wooing Spain to join us in the war. The need for this policy is overwhelming. Only this morning we found out that U-453 sank a Spanish tanker, the *Badalona,* in error, in the Mediterranean three days ago. The Spanish government is incensed. We cannot risk further incidents like this."

"I see. Of course, this will also expose us less to potential attacks from having to surface and force the ships to stop for inspection. That policy resulted in the loss of one of our boats. In my view, it's either all or nothing. Sink them on sight or let them pass. I'm happy that we have chosen the latter approach with the Spanish ships." He paused. "Have you been in contact with Alberto regarding this action?"

"Hans, you know better than to ask that question. For now anyway, it is better that you concentrate on this next mission. When you return, I want you to come to Berlin so I can personally debrief you. I have orders allowing you to fly to Berlin from Lorient in order to save time." He handed the orders to Hans.

"Thank you, Uncle." Hans paused before continuing. "Have you any news from Ernst?" Ernst had been wounded on a mission over Britain the previous month and spent some time in a field hospital.

"Yes, Ernst has recovered from his wounds." This time Walter paused for an even longer period before continuing. "He has volunteered for the Russian front. There is very little activity in the West now and he is needed there, he says. I offered to say a word to *Luftwaffe* command, but he refused."

There was a silence between the two men. Finally, Hans spoke. "I appreciate what you are doing for Ernst and me. I know my father requested that you look after us. But I also know that you appreciate that we must each do our duty."

Walter responded quietly, "Yes, Hans, I understand your attitude, only too well." Walter stopped there, knowing there were things he could never share with his nephew.

12.

Ramon Ortega's office, Manhattan, New York
December 16, 1941

* * *

"I know you are appalled by what you believe was a big risk I took, but in my view the results speak for themselves."

Paul strode to the other side of Ramon's office, placed his hand on the globe, and turned it completely around to emphasize the circumnavigation of the planet that had recently been completed by one of their ships. He was trying to convince his father of the merits of the admittedly risky venture that he had conceived and authorized. More than a year previously, Paul had submitted a term paper for one of his classes at Columbia that outlined a process for maximizing profit based on careful analysis of import and export possibilities for a voyage like the one that was just completed. Indeed, the single voyage with eight port calls had generated a huge profit. Paul waited for his father's rebuttal.

"I can't argue with the numbers, Paul, but it was still a risky bet, given the wartime situation. Why didn't you seek my approval first?"

"With all due respect, Father, you are too remotely located in Guinea to consult with on the details of shipping operations. The nerve center for our operations is here in New York and that is where we must make the strategic decisions and the business decisions. I consulted with Ramon…and he concurred with my decision."

Paul looked over at his uncle sitting at his desk looking very uncomfortable, but Paul expected his support and he got it as Ramon nodded and then turned to Karl.

"Paul's analysis is correct, Karl. Although this venture entailed some risk, it had a huge potential for profit—and our expectations were met and exceeded."

"So how do we replicate it, now that America is at war?" Karl looked to Paul for a further explanation.

"America's entry into the war changes things in the short term, but it doesn't change the principles of what we learned, only the way we carry it out. We built an economic alliance with the Portuguese colonies, an alliance which you pioneered, Father, and on this voyage we exploited it with stops in Sao Tome, Angola, Mozambique, Goa, Macao, and Timor. By including Australia at the end, we obtained a huge markup on our cocoa there and favorable prices for Australian wool, allowing us to make a larger profit here rather than returning to America in ballast, without cargo. Obviously with America and Japan now at war, we might have to suspend further experiments with sailings that circumnavigate the globe, since the Pacific is now a war zone and we could be exposed to more danger."

"What about the U-boats?" Karl replied.

Paul looked at his father, trying to ascertain whether he was probing for weaknesses in his strategy or whether he was merely trying to confirm that Paul had thought of every possibility. Paul sensed it could be both.

"To answer that question," he replied, "we must look at the geopolitical situation and even our own status in that regard. It's obvious that Germany is still trying to get Spain to enter the war on the Axis side, so they are unlikely to deliberately attack our ships, even if we are trading with America. When you were stopped by the U-boat, did you sense that the captain was under orders to spare Spanish ships?"

Paul could see that he was winning his father over as Karl paused before replying, even though he sensed that this was a difficult moment for his father.

"I couldn't be sure, but I thought he might be restraining himself. I certainly gave him enough cause to be angry, and yet his threat became hollow and he pulled back when I mentioned our relationship with Hans and Walter. But we can't count on that; we need to assume that continued trade with America will involve elevated risk. How do you propose to handle that element?"

Paul realized that he had turned a corner. His father was looking to his son for direction, and that realization momentarily shocked Paul. He answered his father's query respectfully but firmly as he laid out his strategy.

"I agree, Father, we need a plan that will mitigate the risk to our shipping interests while maintaining our trading relationships. I propose that we decrease the number of direct sailings from Guinea to America and increase our exports to Argentina and perhaps Chile. From Chile, we can continue shipping to America through their Pacific ports, since the threat from Japanese submarines or other ships is less than the threat from U-boats in the Atlantic. For the ships that sail directly to U.S. Atlantic ports from Guinea, the return trip can still contain manufactured goods for Guinea, the Portuguese colonies, and other possibilities. In any case, we don't yet know what future American exports will be available as they convert to a war economy."

Paul could see from his father's reaction that he was impressed with his analysis. Paul felt a little tinge of pity as he saw his father realize that his son was in command and assuming responsibilities he had once held. Paul erased that thought as he waited for his father's response.

"It seems you've thought this through carefully, Paul. Our decisions this week seemed to have been the correct ones."

Karl was referring to their orders regarding the status of their shipping fleet, which had been expanded from four to six freighters with the lucky acquisition of leases on two Swedish-owned Liberian-flagged vessels. As soon as the lease was executed, Paul had the ships reflagged as Spanish. By coincidence, three of the ships were in New York harbor the day war was declared. Two of the ships were already loaded with manufactured goods, and the family agreed to dispatch them immediately to Africa, before a viable U-boat threat could materialize off America's coast. The ship that Karl arrived on was being loaded now, and Karl would return to Guinea on it the next day. Paul thought of these actions as he replied.

"When you sail tomorrow, Father, we will have in transit an enormous amount of goods that we can reexport from Guinea as you see fit. We'll probably need to defer further sailing from Guinea to America until we size up how bad the U-boat threat will be. It's likely America could face a catastrophe off the coast, since they aren't prepared, and U-boat command will likely take advantage of that."

Paul instantly wished he had answered differently. The shocked look on his father's face told what he was thinking. "U-boat command" to Karl was his brother and first-born son. Paul tried to recover.

"I'm sorry, Father...that was thoughtless of me. I wish we—"

"Paul, please, it's all right, I understand. We both wish the circumstances were different." He looked at Ramon as he touched his son's arm. "Let's go to dinner and celebrate my last night here."

199

Part 2

* * *

Crucible

1942–1944

13.

* * *

Paul poured himself a glass of sherry, walked over to the fire and stoked it, and returned to the couch. It was a clear but very cold day in the city, and although Paul enjoyed the walk back to his apartment from his office, the fire and the sherry were definitely welcome, and he was looking forward to the weekend.

Paul idly looked at the headlines in the *New York Times*, but then tossed the paper back on the coffee table as he took a long sip from his glass of *manzanilla*. The war news was mostly bad, especially in Malaya and the Philippines. At that moment, he felt very remote and isolated from events and his family. *Well, at least classes start next week*, he thought, and between that and the family business, Paul knew he would stay busy.

Yet as Paul stared at the fire, he realized he already missed his father and especially his brothers. He knew he was powerless to restore communication with his brothers as he sat there, frustrated. He realized that the only world he had any control over was his academic life at Columbia and a large amount of responsibility for the family shipping and export-import business. He resolved to work ever harder to excel at both. His dream to expand their business in innovative ways, however, would have to wait until the war and its ramifications were addressed.

Paul thought how fortunate he was to be sitting in his apartment, warm and safe. He wondered how long it would take the war to reach America's shores.

America would not wait long. Five days later, one of the six U-boats of Operation Drumbeat sank its first ship, off Long Island just a few miles from New York City.

14.

The Ortega-Hoffman plantation and hacienda, Rio Muni
January 19, 1942

* * *

Karl landed the Spartan at the plantation to spend the day on paperwork and meetings with the Rio Muni plantation manager. After that all-day meeting, when he finally sat down on the veranda to have a glass of sherry, he pondered the results of his meeting yesterday with the governor. He would make the return flight to Santa Isabel in the morning. It was always better to fly early in the morning in the tropics, as the increasing heat of the day spawned massive thunderstorms.

The new governor had arrived late in 1941 and just four days ago faced his first major crisis, the week after Karl returned from America. In an audacious and surprising move, a large British commando team had arrived in darkness from nearby Nigeria in small boats. They quietly entered Santa Isabel harbor on Fernando Po and seized two German cargo ships and an Italian liner that had been trapped there since the beginning of the war seeking internment rather than capture. Someone on the island had arranged for the ships' officers to attend a party at the governor's mansion while the seizures were taking place. Before the alarm was raised, the three ships raised anchor and sailed away.

Needless to say, the governor was acutely embarrassed by this event, which took place under his nose while he hosted a party for the victims. He could do little; by morning, the three ships were safely in Nigeria. In any case, there were no Spanish warships or aircraft in Guinea to chase them, and the small army garrison had only light infantry weapons with a few machine guns, highlighting the vulnerability of the colony.

The new governor asked for a meeting with Karl to develop a response and to determine how to prevent future such occurrences while strengthening the colony's defenses. Of course the government in Madrid was not pleased, not to mention the German and Italian consuls in Santa Isabel, who were also at the governor's party.

Once again, Karl was in the position of playing senior advisor to the governor. His reputation had preceded him in this capacity. During the meeting, Karl recommended that the governor enumerate the deficiencies in the colony's defenses and specify how to improve them. Karl's recommendations for military hardware included two to three patrol boats and at least one larger warship, some patrol aircraft, more anti-aircraft weapons for Santa Isabel, and heavier armament for the Colonial Guard. When the governor objected to the cost of Karl's list, Karl insisted that the governor needed to dump the problem in Madrid's lap since the governor couldn't be expected to defend the colony without the means to do so. The governor liked Karl's approach. Again, Karl crafted the appropriate memo and supporting paper.

Karl smiled as he sipped his sherry and contemplated all of this. *Why is it,* he thought, *that all politicians are such weasels?* He resolved not to think too harshly of this governor either. Perhaps it was better to be pulling the strings behind the scenes to get the outcome you wanted. *Yes, that's better in the end for Guinea's future.* With that thought, Karl poured himself another glass of sherry and pondered the lack of news from his two oldest sons, his brother, and father in Germany. What could be happening with them? Had Hans received the letters that Karl gave to the U-boat captain?

15

Columbia University, New York
MAY 1, 1942

* * *

It was a beautiful warm spring day on campus. Paul was walking to the office of the history department chair, his mentor and recent professor for two history seminars. Paul had assisted him with the current one, which was nearly over. The professor had asked Paul to come to his office after today's seminar was over. Since it was Friday, Paul was looking forward to the meeting as the last scheduled event of the day, after which he planned to head to the Village to take in the sights and have an adult beverage or two.

As Paul crossed the campus, he thought about the war news. The U-boats had conducted a devastating offensive off the eastern seaboard and they sank many ships, some within sight of the shoreline. He wondered if Hans was among the U-boat skippers who had participated in the attacks. Since the war started, there had been no further letters or other word from either of his brothers. Paul thought often of his brothers now that America was in the war. Would he ever see them again?

Paul erased that thought as he pondered the other recent war news. The surrender of U.S. forces on the Bataan peninsula in the Philippines was depressing, but the recent raid on Tokyo by U.S. bombers provided the first uplifting news since Pearl Harbor. As Paul finished that thought, he finally reached the history department building and he was immediately ushered into the department chair's office. His professor greeted Paul immediately, asked him to sit down, and got right to the point.

"Thanks for coming by, Paul. I know it's Friday afternoon, but I wanted to chat with you before the news is announced."

"What news, Professor?"

"I wanted you to be the first to know. The president has appointed me ambassador to Spain. He signed the appointment today and it will be announced on Monday. He expects an easy Senate confirmation and I expect to leave for Spain in about three weeks."

Paul was stunned but replied immediately. "Professor, this is really a surprise…congratulations! You'll be an excellent ambassador. Your understanding of the European situation is superb, and Spain is fortunate you've been selected for such an honor."

"Thank you, Paul. I do feel it is quite an honor. I've been in the academic world for some time and I'm eager to try something new. I also want to make something clear about you and your future."

He paused before continuing, looking straight at Paul. "You're one of the most exceptional students I've ever met. I've especially appreciated your participation in and assistance with my seminars." He paused one more time, for emphasis.

"I expect that upon your graduation you'll immediately immerse yourself in the family business on both sides of the ocean and will be making more frequent trips to Spain and Spanish Guinea. I know a little bit about your family based on what you've told me, and I know that what they're trying to accomplish will be important for Spain's future. I also expect you to be in the thick of it, perhaps in ways you can't imagine. Your family is unique, what with your brothers' situation and…well, I know you understand what I'm saying. What I really want to say is that, when you're in Spain, or anywhere, please don't hesitate to call on me for assistance. In fact, I want to make it an open invitation. Whenever you're in Madrid you must promise me that you'll stop by the embassy to visit."

Paul smiled. "Professor, I'll be sure to do that. In fact, you can count on it. You've inspired me to excel here and I really appreciate the advice and counsel you've provided. You understand my family's situation, and Spain's. It's my hope that you'll be influential in keeping Spain out of this war."

"That goal will be the highest priority on my agenda, as the president already made clear. I hope to be an honest broker that will help the Spanish government to find a way to turn away from the Axis and toward friendship with the United States."

"Professor, I'm looking for a way to be helpful to both Spain and America. Given the current animosity between our two countries, that may be difficult. When you see me next, in Spain, I may call on you to help me get involved in this effort." Paul paused as he got up and reached his hand across his professor's desk. "In any case, good luck in your assignment."

They shook hands as the professor replied, "All right, Paul, I accept your challenge. I'll look forward to seeing you in Madrid."

16.

Columbia University, New York
October 1942

* * *

Paul sat in the café just outside the campus grounds sipping coffee, idly staring at a textbook, and thinking how his senior year at Columbia had begun. His heavy course load in his first three years and the credit he had received for his participation in family business activities had allowed him to carry a lighter load in his final year. He thought about what he would do after he graduated in the spring. Obviously, he would join Ramon full time in the business, but he also anticipated the need to travel to Guinea and Spain to coordinate activities with his father, Ernesto, and Alfonso. He anticipated seeing his family again—and finding some way to influence larger events.

As he looked around the large café, Paul was struck by the presence of so many women in this regular student haunt, most of them probably Barnard students. After the June graduation, the Columbia campus had emptied of regular students as the majority of Ivy League men headed off to officer school and war. As Paul glanced around the room he continuously caught the admiring stares of many women, who quickly turned to avoid his gaze—all but one, that is. Paul had noticed her sitting about three tables away about a half hour earlier. She was quite stunning, even sitting down, with a pretty face, shoulder-length brunette hair, and expressive eyes, even at this distance. Paul looked at her, smiled, saw her reciprocate, and then returned to his thoughts.

As he propped the book up on his lap again, his mind wandered to his social life. His academics and nearly full participation in family business activities left little time for socializing. He had dated sporadically during his time at Columbia, enjoying women as companions to enhance the pleasure of movies, plays, lectures, and other events that he enjoyed. He always tried to show an equal interest in his companions as they showed in him, but Paul, like his father, was most interested in women as intellectual partners and in the commonality of interests that they might share. Paul had traveled extensively throughout America and realized that the best chance to meet women of that caliber was probably right here, right now. Paul easily attracted women, being tall, handsome, and self-assured, and he realized that he could easily pursue more physical relationships, especially now, with the ratio of women to men on or near campus about ten to one. Paul smiled at that thought as he considered the element of any relationship that his father had once termed "the mindless pursuit."

As that thought persisted, Paul felt someone standing next to him. He looked up and...there she was—the mystery lady! Paul was about to rise, as a courtesy, but the woman put her hand on his shoulder before he could move and spoke first, in a soft, sultry voice.

"Please don't get up, I don't want to interrupt your thoughts; I just have one question, if you don't mind?"

"Yes?" That was the extent of Paul's ability to comply as he gazed at this tall, beautiful woman in front of him. His earlier observations were reinforced as he took in her slender, shapely figure. He couldn't control his gaze from sweeping over her, and he noticed how leggy she must be, even with the unrevealing long skirt. All of this took only a second or two, but to Paul it seemed like an eternity as he contemplated a possible response.

Finally, the woman looked at him and posed her question. "I was just wondering—how did you manage to get through college by reading all of your books upside down?"

Paul stared at her, blinking and uncomprehending, then looked down at his book, still in position on his lap. Indeed, it was upside down, as Paul had merely picked it up as he daydreamed and pondered his future. At this point, he looked up at her, a wry smile forming, which was instantly reciprocated. Finally, he couldn't control himself, and they both broke into laughter.

"Please, sit down and join me. I need to at least thank you for keeping me from looking like a fool."

"Thanks, and I'm glad you don't hold it against me for the question. I'm Elizabeth Kurtz, or Liz, as I would rather be known." She sat down, crossed her legs, and looked intently at Paul.

"I'm Paul Hoffman, or Paul, as I would rather be known." They both laughed again as Paul continued, "I think I've seen you here before, but I guess I must be too preoccupied to remember when."

"I've seen you here also. I guess it's OK to be preoccupied, with everything going on as it has been lately. Are you an undergraduate?"

"Yes, I'm a senior, majoring in business and history and looking forward to getting out in the real world. What about you?"

"I'm a junior at Barnard, majoring in anthropology, with a minor in Spanish. If I were you, I wouldn't be in such a hurry to leave. The real world is pretty ugly right now. I suppose when you graduate you'll end up in officer school, like all the men here seem to have."

Paul noticed her frown and sensed that there was a reason for her sensitivity to the subject. He thought for a moment before responding.

"Actually I'm not likely to end up in the military, at least in America. I'm actually Spanish. I'm here on a multi-year student visa. As a nonresident alien, I'm not eligible for the draft or military service." Paul paused. "I tried to enlist the day after Pearl Harbor, but they rejected me because of my Spanish citizenship. It seems Spain is considered part of the Axis."

"You're Spanish? Your English is so good I hardly would have guessed. Were you born there or migrated there?"

"I was born there; in Spanish Guinea, actually, to a Spanish mother and...a...German father."

Liz's interest was instantly piqued. "Spanish...Guinea? I'm sorry; I guess my geography is rusty."

"Don't feel bad. I haven't found anyone in America who has heard of it, except my history professor. It's a small colony in West Africa, near the equator. My father and my mother's family own coffee and cocoa plantations there on both the mainland and an island called Fernando Po. We also have vineyards and wineries in Spain itself, in Rioja and Jerez , as well as shipping interests. My great-uncle also owns an export-import business here in America that I participate in. He lives here in the city, uptown on Fifth Avenue."

"That's fascinating. Then you are fluent in English and Spanish and... German?"

"Yes, we were raised bilingual, and then I was fortunate that we had an English-speaking servant who took an interest in me and started me on English when I was two. My two older brothers didn't bother to learn much English until they went to school later, but they are still not as fluent."

Liz was clearly intent on learning more. "Were your brothers also born in Spanish Guinea? Did they also come to America for their education and where are they now?"

Paul's momentary pause and frown elicited an instance response from Liz. "I'm sorry, I'm being too nosey and…"

"No, that's all right, I don't mind. They were born in Spain proper. They went to Germany for their education. I started my education in Spain but… just before the Civil War…my parents sent me here. I went to Choate and came to Columbia in 1939. As the youngest, I escaped from Europe before everything fell apart."

"If your brothers were educated in Germany, did they stay there? I mean, did they…"

As her voice trailed off, Paul finished her sentence. "Yes, they stayed, and since they, unlike me, retained German nationality, they are…in the military. Hans is in the navy and Ernst in the *Luftwaffe*. I haven't heard from either of them since before Pearl Harbor." He stopped to let that sink in, finally adding one more item. "My mother died on the *Athenia* in 1939…when it was torpedoed."

Paul saw the shocked look on Liz's face, as she absorbed the impact of his revelation. "I'm sorry that you lost your mother and are now isolated from your brothers and father…it's so impolite of me to be so prying."

"Please don't apologize, I find it comforting to talk about it." He paused before continuing. "But we've just talked about me. What about you? I only know that you're a junior anthropology major. Where are you from and what about your family? Now it's my turn to pry!"

Liz smiled. "I'm from Denver. I was born there and went to school there. My father's a banker. He met my mother in Chicago; they got married and moved back to Colorado. Despite living most of our lives there, my father always believed that the West can be too isolated if a person hasn't had a broader education and seen a little bit of the world. He went to school at Columbia and always thought that the combination of top-quality schooling and the environment in this city was just the ticket. He also traveled to England for his junior year and got to see a lot of the continent. So it was only natural that he would send his two sons, and even his daughter, here also."

Now Paul's interest was piqued. "So you have two brothers. Are they older, still here perhaps?" He paused as he saw the tear quickly form in Liz's eye. "I'm sorry; maybe I shouldn't be prying either."

"No, Paul, that's all right, it's comforting to talk about it." They both smiled. "My oldest brother, Phillip, graduated in 1939. He went in the air corps the next year. After training as a fighter pilot, he was stationed at Pearl Harbor. He was killed on December 7; he managed to get his plane off the ground and got two Jap planes before they got him."

Liz pulled a handkerchief out to dry the tears with her right hand. Without thinking, Paul placed his hand gently on Liz's other hand. She looked up at him. For a moment, time was suspended as they stared deeply into each other's eyes. Finally, she smiled weakly and continued.

"My other brother, Jack, the middle sibling, graduated from here in 1941. He actually went though ROTC, so he was commissioned upon graduation and immediately went to intelligence school. He just finished and was at home on leave when we heard about Phil. My father took it hard, but my mother felt it harder. They're OK now. Jack tried for a combat assignment right afterward, but the military wanted him to stay in intelligence. Needless to say, the foreign travel part of our education has been delayed by the war, except for Jack. Like me, he minored in Spanish, actually, and traveled to Argentina for part of his junior year and part of the summer. He actually speaks the language pretty well." She paused. "Maybe you'll get to meet him."

"Where's Jack now?"

"I'm not really sure. We've gotten several letters and he says he's in a safe place, but we don't know any more than that." At that moment, she looked at her watch, finally realizing the time. 'Oh my, I'll be late for class. I need to leave."

Paul didn't hesitate. "I'll walk with you. This has been so interesting...is it possible...for us...to continue the conversation later? Better yet, how about a movie this weekend. I hear *Woman of the Year* is not to be missed!"

She looked at Paul, smiled, and replied, "That would be absolutely wonderful. I think we both need a break."

17.

Ortega-Hoffman hacienda, Fernando Po, Spanish Guinea
February 1943

* * *

Karl sat on the veranda reading the letters he had received that week. Letters from Wilhelm, Walter, Hans, and Ernst had arrived through diplomatic pouch, routed from Germany through Spain to the German consulate in Fernando Po. Hans's letter was the first he ripped open, since he had not previously received any reply from Hans to his letter that he gave to the captain of U-129 more than a year ago. As Karl opened the letter, he recalled telling Hans that he would always be his son, that he loved him, and that he wanted him to survive the war. Karl had revealed to Hans that his mother had died on the *Athenia*, but Karl emphasized that forgiveness was not an issue and that Pilar was a victim of the war.

Hans said he understood what his father had said and that he would seek redemption in some way, but his duty was still there and his life would go on. Hans revealed that he was engaged to a woman he had met in late 1938, before the war started. Hans and his fiancée planned to hold the wedding in June, in Bernkastel, depending on whether he could obtain leave or not.

Karl read Ernesto's letter, learning that Alfonso was to be married in early May. Alfonso had spent most of the time since 1935 in Guinea but returned to Spain in late 1941, as conditions had stabilized in Guinea and Karl could manage, whereas Ernesto needed help restoring the vineyards. Alfonso had met a woman from Barcelona while there on business, and everything fell into place. Ernesto insisted that Karl should be there for the wedding.

Karl lingered over Paul's letter. Paul's course credits had been reviewed and found to exceed the credits needed for graduation, except for one term paper on economics. He was free for the spring semester and had decided to travel to both Guinea and Spain to coordinate family business activities. He had booked a stateroom on one of the freighters from New York to Guinea. From there he proposed that he and his father take the freighter that was scheduled to depart for Spain from Guinea in early April. After Alfonso's wedding, Paul planned to return to New York by flying boat to turn in his paper for graduation, while Karl could return to Guinea by airline now that the Free French had reopened their system through West Africa.

Karl knew it would be nearly impossible for him to get to Germany for Hans's wedding. In any case, it was unlikely that either Walter or the German security apparatus would look kindly on Karl's presence either.

After reading these letters, and those from his father and Ernst, Karl thought about the results of his recent marathon trip to the Portuguese colony of Angola. He had flown the Spartan, stopping at Brazzaville in the French Congo and Leopoldville in the Belgian Congo while en route and returning. He had succeeded in arranging barter and transportation deals with the colonial authorities at each location. With the war, the mother countries were unable to fully support their colonies, and Karl's skills in brokering deals to pool resources, especially shipping, paid off handsomely. Karl thought about how these deals would be impossible or consume too much travel time if he didn't have the Spartan. He wondered how air travel would change the world once the war ended. The technology was advancing rapidly, and Karl thought he might get a larger aircraft to replace sea travel entirely for the family's business travel needs.

18.

* * *

It was a cold Saturday evening, with snow flurries. Paul added two logs to the fire and brought two glasses of *oloroso* sherry over to the bed, giving one to Liz. He proposed a toast.

"Here's to us and my good fortune in meeting you—to us!"

Liz responded, "Here's to your upcoming trip to Spanish Guinea and Spain. May you have a safe and successful trip—and please return to me soon!"

They took a sip. Paul nuzzled closer to Liz and pulled the covers up over their naked bodies. They had dated for only four months and neither expected to be lying here at this moment. Yet they both felt very secure in this relationship and excited to be together. They found each other fascinating and were mutually stimulated by their respective outlooks on life and their future possibilities as the tumult in the world swirled around them.

Paul downed his sherry, stared at the fire, and pondered how life was unfolding and what the future might hold. Liz interrupted his reverie.

"Here's a penny for your thoughts."

Paul smiled. "I was just thinking how much my life has changed since coming to America and how I might be able to have the best of both the Old World and the New World." He smiled again as he caressed Liz, kissing her gently on the forehead.

"Who says you can't have both? You don't have to give up everything in your prior life just because you are now a part of another world also." Liz replied.

Paul thought for a moment. "Yes, I suppose that's true. But it's difficult to participate in both worlds when you're separated by an ocean, a war, and inconvenient communication and transportation. I'll be glad when this damn war is over, and I'm looking forward to the day when we can routinely fly over the ocean in hours rather than sail across it in days or weeks."

"I understand your impatience, but you can look forward to all of those things happening soon enough. At least your return trip to me will be faster on the flying boat."

Paul smiled again. "Yes, I'll look forward to that experience. It was difficult to arrange." Indeed, it had taken all of his and Ramon's connections to get a scarce seat.

Liz snuggled even closer. "Paul, you'll achieve your dreams—and see more of your family in the process. But let's celebrate the present too." They looked at each other, embraced, and let passion take its course.

19.

Spanish navy ministry, Madrid
February 1943

* * *

Alberto Ortega stood and greeted the man entering his office. Although the person standing before him held the title of commercial attaché in the German embassy, he actually was an agent in Office VI, the foreign intelligence service of the Reich Security Main Office, or RHSA, which was, in turn, a part of the *Schutzstaffel*, or SS. Alberto knew his guest's real job, although he didn't pretend to be able to understand the byzantine organizational structure of the Nazi intelligence agencies. Normally Alberto dealt with intelligence staff of the regular German military, the *Abwehr*, especially naval specialists. Since Spain had such close relations with Germany, it was Alberto's job to exchange information with his German opposite numbers and to occasionally interact on certain issues with German embassy staff in "other" organizations.

Alberto knew this visitor as Peter Schmidt, although he thought that was only a cover name. Schmidt had visited a number of times before, always in the capacity of his cover job. During the last visit, for example, Schmidt came to discuss the supply of naval supplies that Spain had requested from Germany and what Spain would, in return, export back to Germany in payment. Both individuals knew that these meetings were largely intelligence "fishing trips," but they put up with the charade in order to maintain a rational cover story. German espionage was rampant in Spain because of the country's geographic location and neutral status, and the German embassy included hundreds of staff with intelligence duties and thousands of agents throughout the country. Alberto's job was to maintain connectivity with this apparatus.

Schmidt spent time on each visit exchanging small talk and discussing wine, which seemed to be of particular interest to him. Alberto always had a supply of the best wine and sherry from the Ortega bodegas and found that such a commodity was always useful in extracting small favors from "clients."

After sitting down and exchanging some small talk, Alberto got the conversation going. "So, Peter, have you any word on the naval supply request from our last meeting?"

"Yes, but I'm afraid the news is not good. There is such a shortage of these items in Germany that we will be unable to export any, even to our allies and friends."

"I see. I was afraid that might be the case. We need these supplies since without them fewer than half our ships are currently operational. Of course many of them would likely be immobile anyway since we only have sixty percent of our normal fuel supply."

Alberto paused to let that sink in and then opened the liquor cabinet next to his desk. "Forgive me, Peter, for forgetting my hospitality. May I offer you a glass of Pedro Ximenez?" Alberto knew his guest was fond of the sweeter Spanish dessert wines.

"Yes, thank you, Alberto; that would be wonderful. Speaking of hospitality, I was remiss in not asking how your family is. I assume everyone is well. What about Alfonso's wedding? Will all of the family be attending?

"The wedding is in May, in Alabos. Most of the family will be there."

"I assume that will also include someone from the Hoffman side of the family. Of course, I realize that Walter, Hans, and Ernst will be unlikely to be there. With their duties in the *Wehrmacht*, it would be out of the question for them to obtain leave."

"Unfortunately, you are correct. However, their father and brother Paul will be there so that side of the family is well represented."

"It's good they'll be there. It's too bad that the war gets in the way of these events." Schmidt downed the last of his sherry before concluding. "Well, thank you for the sherry. I'm sorry this visit was so brief and without good news on the naval supplies. I need to return to the embassy for a meeting."

They both rose and said their good-byes. As Schmidt left the office, Alberto hoped he would find the information on the lack of naval supplies and fuel useful. Alberto's superiors had asked him to leak that information as a way of urging the Germans to speed up the supply of modern military weaponry to Spain.

As Peter Schulz left the naval ministry, he reflected that he too had gotten what he wanted. It confirmed their suspicion that the partial American oil embargo was affecting Spanish military operations and it could affect Spain's will to resist an allied invasion. More importantly, he had determined that Paul Hoffman would be in Spain soon. Schmidt intended to capitalize on that piece of information.

20.

Alabos, Spain
May 1943

* * *

Alfonso's wedding was a beautiful event despite the wartime atmosphere and lingering effects of the Civil War. Alfonso had married into a well-known, wealthy family from Barcelona with mostly Catalonian roots, but they had managed to thrive and coexist with the Castilian culture that dominated Spanish politics and economics in Madrid. His beautiful new bride, Francesca, studied at the University of Barcelona and typified the emerging generation of Spanish women who quietly sought nontraditional roles in a very traditional society. As a result, she instantly bonded with Anita, who was playing a slowly increasing role in not only the business side of the Ortega family interests but also in the wine making activities.

After a brief honeymoon, Alfonso and Francesca returned to Alabos, although they would split their time in the future between Alabos, Barcelona, and Spanish Guinea. Alfonso returned in time to attend a business strategy meeting with Ernesto, Karl, and Paul. After the meeting, Paul would return to America by way of Madrid and Lisbon.

The four men gathered on the main veranda of the hacienda to taste some barrel samples from the 1942 vintage, which Ernesto had prepared for the start of the meeting. He led the discussion.

"I arranged this tasting as a prelude to our discussion of future strategies. This vintage is absolutely fabulous, the best since 1924, I believe. We'll probably want to age the entire harvest in oak for at least a year or longer. I believe the entire bottling will be *crianza* or higher, with a huge portion that can achieve *reserva* or *gran reserva* classification." Ernesto poured the first samples and raised his glass. "*Salud!*"

As the four of them examined and then tasted the pour, it was clear that Ernesto was not exaggerating. Karl was first to comment.

"This wine has incredible structure with tons of fruit and tannin, but the vanilla is already superb. This wine has real aging potential!"

As Alfonso and Paul chimed in, agreeing, Ernesto continued, "Coupled with the huge harvest and such quality, this will be our largest marketable quantity of top-quality wine in many years. We have an opportunity to reestablish Spain, and certainly our bodegas, as premium producers in the market. It will finally allow us to begin moving beyond the lost decade from the republic and the civil war. What should our strategy be? How do we proceed?"

Paul didn't hesitate. "I believe that America is the best export market for our wine, as it has been for our African commodities. Europe is still at war, but when it ends, the continent will be devastated and economically crippled for some time. We have a real chance to penetrate the American market before their domestic production ramps up."

Alfonso responded, "Shouldn't we diversify more? America could be risky if they increase their tariff barrier, like they did in 1930."

Paul replied, "I believe that America will actually lower its tariffs after the war. They will be the most economically powerful nation on earth, eclipsing Britain. They'll need to export to maintain their prosperity and therefore will drop the tariff barriers. In order for us to consume American manufactured goods, they will allow us to pay for those goods with our own exports, without high tariffs entering the country. In fact, I believe America will end up being Europe's lender, to help rebuild the continent and stimulate demand for their products." He paused. "Of course it's possible that America will not lend to Spain because of our policies regarding the Axis."

They all quietly considered Paul's statement. Finally, Ernesto spoke.

"Karl, how do you see the market for our African commodities unfolding?"

"I believe America will have a pent-up demand for consumer products after the war. The soldiers returning home and their families will want coffee and chocolate and they will need lumber to build new housing. Our products from Guinea serve this market perfectly. For a few more years, we'll still be able to market our cocoa and coffee as premium products, but I believe that eventually these products will become mere commodities on the world market, commanding little or no premium pricing. Therefore, it's important that we keep increasing our capacity."

Alfonso replied, "If I understand Paul and Karl correctly, our overall strategy should be to maximize exports from Guinea over the next few years and plough some of our profits into developing our vineyards and wine making potential. Along those lines, we will eventually need to modernize all of our bodegas and perhaps seek out new vineyards in other parts of Spain."

Paul responded, "Yes. In fact, Alfonso has an excellent idea regarding seeking other wine-producing lands. This will allow us to anticipate future demand and acquire land while it is still cheap in Spain."

Ernesto smiled. "Perhaps we can appeal to Anita's boyfriend to join the cause, since he will soon be part of the family and comes from a wine making family in Penedes."

Ernesto was commenting on Anita's news regarding her engagement. Like Alfonso, she had met her fiancé, Enrique, in Barcelona, while she was representing the family at a meeting of winemakers. Enrique's family had a small vineyard and bodega in Penedes, which was on the Mediterranean south of Barcelona. They planned to marry in October.

Paul continued, "These are excellent ideas about growing our wine business. I believe that the American growth in demand for premium wines will be gradual, starting in New York and gradually expanding. The American cuisine and culture do not yet embrace wine as an everyday beverage as it is in Europe. So we have some time to plan for this expansion, as the demand slowly increases over many years. Meanwhile we should be discreetly traveling to various regions in Spain to find choice land to purchase while it's dirt cheap. We have plenty of cash in our New York accounts to do this. These accounts are U.S. dollar denominated so converting some funds into pesetas will give us a further advantage, because our currency is also cheap right now. To close this thought, however, I suggest we all think about our proposals over the next few months. I plan to return to Spain and Guinea regularly, to help coordinate our operations in consideration of shipping and export-import issues. If we can all convene again around the time of Anita's wedding that would be ideal."

Ernesto summed up. "Paul is right. I know both of our fathers would have urged caution, yet I believe they would approve of the strategy we discussed here today. It would certainly be interesting to hear what Wilhelm would say now, if only we could get him here. Karl, have you any news from Germany?"

"As you know, Hans is to be married in June, in Bernkastel. I would dearly love to be there for the wedding, but that has turned out to be impossible because of the war." Paul noticed the look on his father's face and realized he didn't want to dwell on his missing family members, how much he missed them, and how much the world was changing. Paul felt exactly the same but could only hope that the uncertain future would somehow resolve itself to allow his family to be together again.

21.

Madrid, Spain
May 1943

* * *

The waiter brought the glass of *fino* sherry and the small plate that Paul ordered. He was enjoying the late afternoon break at the small café where he sat outside, alone, before the evening crowd arrived. He had arrived from the American embassy after paying a courtesy call on his friend the ambassador. Paul wanted to maintain close contact with his former history professor, thinking that, as the American ambassador, he could be influential in swaying the thinking of the Franco regime as well as the American government. Paul realized that Spain would likely be very isolated after the war, unless it began to move away from the Axis powers and courted the Allies.

Paul planned to remain overnight in Madrid and take the train to Lisbon in the morning. He was scheduled on the flying boat leaving for New York in three days. Paul realized how much he missed Liz and looked forward to meeting her brother Jack when he returned to New York.

As Paul sat there, lost in thought, he was startled to hear his name called, first in accented Spanish and then German. He turned to see a short stocky man looking at him intently.

"I'm sorry. Do we know each other?"

"No, *Herr* Hoffman, we haven't met before, but I know of your brothers Hans and Ernst and wanted to bring word to you about them."

Paul was momentarily stunned but finally replied with excitement in his voice, "You have word from Hans and Ernst?"

"Yes, but please do not be alarmed. They are both well—now. Ernst was wounded again during a recent operation but has recovered from his wounds. Hans is well and, as you know, will be married next month. He has been granted leave as soon as he finishes with…his current operation. Your uncle, Walter, is also well, as are Erica and Kirsten."

"You are friends with them?" Paul paused, now becoming cautious, and then continued, "Excuse me; you have me at a disadvantage. You know who I am but I don't know you. May I know your name and...capacity?"

"Of course you may. Can I sit down?"

Paul motioned for his guest to be seated.

"I am Peter Schmidt, the commercial attaché at the German embassy. I occasionally work with your cousin, Alberto Ortega, on certain naval economic issues. We have become acquaintances. Since I have access to certain information in Germany, I thought I would return his hospitality by making inquiries about your family. I know it's hard to obtain information about them with the current situation. I hope you don't take offense at my overture."

Paul pondered that for a moment before replying. "I don't take offense, but I am curious how you happened to locate me here. Excuse me, *Herr*... Schmidt...is it? I believe you owe me a better explanation as to how you located me. It seems odd that a 'commercial attaché' would be tracking me in this manner."

"Let's just say for now that I have many other duties that require me to approach you in such a way. In any case, I am also curious as to your own situation. You have two brothers and an uncle fighting for the fatherland, yet you are not serving and are, in fact, living in America, a country with which Germany is at war."

"*Herr* Schmidt, I'm a Spaniard, born on Spanish territory. Spain is not at war with America. In fact, our family owns enterprises that trade with America in civilian goods, not war materials, and as a neutral country, this is our right. I'm concerned for my family in Germany, but I don't consider myself a German citizen, although I am not ashamed of my heritage either. My father is German and served honorably and with distinction in the first war. I'm not, however, either my father or my brothers. You need to respect the fact that I'm different."

"But Germany came to Spain's aid during the Civil War. Don't you feel an obligation to Germany for that assistance?"

"I recognize Germany's assistance to the current government. But I also recognize that many Spanish citizens, on both sides, died during that conflict serving as proxies and cannon fodder for the conflict between Germany and Soviet Russia."

"That is precisely my point. Germans, including your brother Ernst, have shed blood fighting the Bolsheviks on your behalf. Don't you feel an obligation to support and participate in that struggle?"

Paul paused, choosing his words carefully. "I too am concerned about communism. However, I do not believe that Germany's unprovoked attack on Russia is about the battle against communism. Rather I think it was ill-advised naked aggression, and as the recent debacle at Stalingrad demonstrated, I believe Germany will pay the price for that aggression."

Schmidt tensed up, leaned forward, and, pointing his finger at Paul, replied with anger in his voice, "I expected more of you. You could be helping your own family at this point by supporting Germany in some small way, if not as a soldier."

"What 'small way' did you have in mind, *Herr* Schmidt? Do you expect me to become a spy and possibly compromise Spain in the process? America already is suspicious of Spain for supporting the Axis powers."

"*Herr* Hoffman, you can continue to stay on your high horse, above the fray, hiding behind your neutrality and leading a decadent life in America. Or you can reconsider your brash exhortations about Germany's actions and recognize the life and death struggle now taking place, a struggle that involves your own family in Germany. I will leave you with that thought...and my card, so that you may contact me at the embassy if you come to your senses."

Paul stood up, faced Schmidt, and in a low, measured voice, replied, "*Herr* Schmidt, I thank you for your information on my brothers and family in Germany...but I don't expect we have any further business to discuss. If you'll excuse me, I need to complete my meal...alone."

Schmidt rose, placed his card on the table, looked up at Paul, who towered over him, and concluded, "You know how to reach me if you come to your senses. Good day." Schmidt turned and left the café.

Paul stood there for a moment as the anger subsided. As he sat down to finish his meal, he contemplated the brazenness of Schmidt and the Nazi establishment in general. He resolved to contact Alberto tomorrow, before the train to Lisbon departed. He knew that Alberto had probably inadvertently provided Schmidt with too much information. Paul pondered how he might protect himself and his family from further intrusions.

22.

Columbia University, New York
June 1943

* * *

Paul waited eagerly outside the registrar's office for Liz and her brother Jack to arrive to meet him. Paul had just finished the final paperwork relating to the award of his university degree and signed up for a postgraduate summer seminar on predicted postwar economic conditions. Although the seminar would be interesting, the main reason Paul signed up was to obtain a sixty-day extension on his student visa. That would buy him the time needed to find a way to establish residency in America or to obtain a business visa so he could continue to remain in the country to conduct family business.

Paul spotted Liz approaching with a man, obviously her brother. Paul observed them approach, but even at a distance he could see that Jack Kurtz was an impressive presence, standing as tall as Paul, but with perhaps twenty extra well-placed pounds, close-cropped hair, and a chiseled, handsome face. They made eye contact, and Jack broke into an infectious grin as he approached Paul. Paul smiled back, turned to Liz, and as she approached, he leaped forward and embraced her fully with a hug and a peck on the cheek.

"Now that's the way I like to be greeted! I can see you must have finally completed the transition from student. Congratulations!" She turned to her brother. "Jack, I'd like you to meet Paul Hoffman, former student, present entrepreneur, and curious visitor from Spain." She turned to Paul to complete the introduction. "Paul, I'd like you to meet my brother Jack."

The two men shook hands firmly and enthusiastically, and Jack responded, "Paul, this is a pleasure I've been looking forward to for a while. Liz told me all about you, and I can only conclude that you must be the only interesting man on the planet."

"Likewise I've been looking forward to meeting you. Liz was ecstatic when she told me you were going to be stationed in New York and Washington for the next several weeks. You must have an important assignment."

Jack quickly changed the subject. "We can talk about that later. Right now it's late Friday afternoon, I'm thirsty, and Liz tells me you like hanging out with the bohemians down in the Village. What are your favorite watering holes?"

"Right after work, I like to go to the White Horse Tavern, down by the Hudson waterfront. It's sort of a longshoreman's hangout. I discovered it when I met one of our ships from Guinea that had docked near there. Later in the evening, I like the San Remo at the corner of Bleecker and MacDougal. It's the bohemian joint and has lots of great people watching. The food's good too."

"Well, what are we waiting for, let's get going and celebrate!" Jack led the way, followed by Liz and Paul. As they started to walk briskly away, a man in a suit approached Paul.

"Excuse me, are you Paul Hoffman? Could I have a word with you?"

Paul looked at the man, noting his expressionless face and out-of-place attire. Paul looked at Jack and Liz, who had stopped, looking back at the stranger. Paul motioned to them. "Go on ahead; I'll meet you at the corner in a minute."

As they nodded and continued walking, Paul turned to the stranger. "Yes, I'm Paul Hoffman. How may I help you? I don't believe we've met."

"That's correct, we haven't. I'm Agent Frye with the Federal Bureau of Investigation, New York office. As you may know, the FBI is responsible for—"

"I know what the FBI is, Mr. Frye. J. Edgar Hoover, Dillinger; they're household names. Again, how may I help you? My friends are waiting."

Frye was still expressionless as he answered, "We'd like you to come to our office downtown and answer a few questions on your activities."

"What activities are those, Mr. Frye? I'm a graduating college student."

"Yes, a graduating student who comes from a quasi-neutral country, travels to Europe on a flying boat during wartime, and flies his own plane on business while here in America on a student visa. Wouldn't you consider these activities unusual?"

Paul paused, studying Frye and choosing his words carefully. "Mr. Frye, I agree that those may be unusual circumstances, but they are all connected to my family's business and are quite necessary activities; some of them related to my academic work."

"That's fine. Then we should be able to clear the matter up quickly, say Monday morning at nine o'clock in my office?" He handed Paul his card.

Paul looked at the card, looked at Frye, and replied, "Am I under some kind of arrest or something? If it's my visa status, I can explain..."

This time Frye interrupted. "This is not a formal investigation, nor a formal hearing. Of course, if you want your attorney present, we can—"

Paul interjected, "That's all right, Mr. Frye; I'll see you Monday morning."

There was a brief pause. Frye finally nodded, still expressionless, tipped his hat, turned, and walked away.

As Paul raced to catch up to Liz and Jack, he wondered what the FBI was really interested in. Were they watching his activities in New York or Spain? What was their main interest?

23.

F B I office, Manhattan, New York
June 1943

* * *

Paul sat in the waiting room, remarkably unconcerned as he waited to be called into Agent Frye's office. He realized that he was in a completely legal status, had traveled under proper procedures, and had no cause for concern. Finally, he was called in, and Frye introduced him to another agent, Miller. As Paul took his seat, he eagerly anticipated getting this over with.

Frye began the questioning. He got right to the point, speaking in a calm monotone. "All right, Paul, we're interested in knowing why you went to Spain last month, who you met, and anything that would explain the nature of the trip. I'm sure you understand that we are very interested in what happens in Spain because of your country's closeness to the Axis powers."

So that's it. "Well, to begin with, I attended my cousin Alfonso's wedding. Incidental to that, we had several family meetings on our business activities, including those in Spain, Spanish Guinea, and America. I also paid a courtesy call on the American ambassador, who was my former history professor at Columbia, in Madrid."

Frye looked straight at Paul, as if to assess him. "So what family members were at these meetings? Did they include all of your family members? Are all of your relatives, both Hoffmans and Ortegas, involved in these business activities?"

Miller interjected, almost shrilly raising the next point. "What about your brothers, Paul? Are Hans and Ernst involved in these business activities?"

Paul turned to Miller and looked at him coolly. "No, they're not involved. I'll presume you already know that, since you know their names and probably everything else about them." Paul paused. "They are in Germany, in the *Wehrmacht*. I haven't heard from either of them since America entered the war."

Frye then spoke, in the same monotone, with a blank, unrevealing look. "Paul, please realize that we're not accusing you of anything, but we're obviously interested in the role your brothers play in the family business. You answered that."

Miller again interjected, raising his voice accusingly. "What about the airplane that you and your uncle own? It seems unusual that you fly all over America in your own airplane rather than take the train or bus."

Annoyed, Paul turned to Miller. "Agent Miller, our business requires us to meet many people in many places, all over America. The train and bus take too long and the airlines only fly to a few cities. Using our own plane saves us time. That is, it did, until the restrictions on private aircraft were implemented after Pearl Harbor. We've been unable to use the airplane since December 1941, as you know. Also, it's now impossible to get airline or train seats so our business travel is severely restricted."

Miller replied, "Yes, I see. So using the airplane allows you to travel freely and see a great many things from the air, perhaps military installations or—"

Paul interrupted, raising his voice, "Is that an accusation? Perhaps you don't understand that I'm not an enemy of America but a student and businessman from a neutral country, a country that supplies America with essential commodities, and I'm conducting all of this activity within the letter of the law. Perhaps we shouldn't beat around the bush anymore." Paul paused, looking angrily at both agents. "Why don't you tell me what you really want with me? Any competent agent could have discovered these other facts without bringing me in here for questioning."

There was a long pause as Miller glared at Paul and Frye leafed through Paul's file and then casually put it on the desk. He then looked up directly at Paul and spoke, in a low, nonthreatening voice. "Paul, we understand that your activities are completely legal. But it seems to us that you've taken advantage of your neutral status to attend an Ivy League school, operate a business, and travel freely while America sheds blood to rid the world of Nazism and tyranny. Your country openly flirts with the Axis. Don't you think it's time to give something back to America?"

Paul looked at him, collecting his thoughts and controlling his anger. Finally, he spoke. "So what is it that you want me to do, become your spy or something?"

The two agents looked at each other. Frye turned back to Paul.

"We don't like to think of it that way, Paul, but you could be very useful to us. Your cousin Alberto is in the Spanish navy and currently works in the navy ministry in intelligence. You could be useful in obtaining certain information that we need with regard to the naval war in the Atlantic. There are other ways that—"

Paul, now in control of his voice and emotions, interrupted Frye. "Please allow me to be direct, Agent Frye. I will do nothing that would even remotely compromise Spain or use my position to illicitly obtain information contrary to Spanish law. I'm in great sympathy with America and its cause and I believe that Spain must turn to the Allies eventually. You must understand Spain's fears also. We're more fearful of communism, in fact, than of fascism."

Miller interjected, raising his voice. "The Soviet Union is our ally. Germany is the main enemy. Can't you see that?"

Paul replied, "Yes, Russia is your ally now, but why don't we have that conversation again in about five years?" The room became silent for several moments as Paul and Miller glared at each other.

Frye rose. "Paul, I think we're done for now. Let's talk again in a few weeks."

24.

Bernkastel, Germany
June 1943

* * *

Wilhelm von Hoffman carefully explained the vine ripening process to his granddaughter Kirsten. The ninety-one-year-old patriarch of the Hoffman family took eleven-year-old Kirsten under his wing to nurture her building interest in the family vineyards and in wine making. He and Kirsten had earlier climbed the slope of the family's vineyard on the north bank of the Mosel, across from Bernkastel and to the west. He painstakingly described how he had acquired the hillside with its south view many years ago and how today, on the summer solstice, the young grapes were ripening and producing the sugar content that was the Riesling wine maker's raw material for producing a wide range of styles from dry to intensely sweet. Wilhelm concluded his lecture by predicting that the 1943 vintage would be a good one.

Wilhelm later met with his property managers, Eric and Hanna Diehl, to discuss the budding crop. The Diehls had been with the family for many years, and Wilhelm depended on them to manage the cultivation activities when he was absent. Kirsten and her mother, Erica, often stayed with the Diehls when Walter was in Berlin at navy headquarters. Walter's family still had a house in Wilhelmshaven from when Walter was more actively involved in U-boat operations. Both Erica and Kirsten frequently alternated between Wilhelmshaven and Bernkastel, since they both hated Berlin. With the increasing allied bombings, Berlin was becoming less safe, and Walter preferred for his wife and daughter to be out of the city in any case.

Walter was also in Bernkastel today, in Wilhelm's study, waiting for Hans Hoffman to arrive. Walter and Erica had stayed on in Bernkastel after Hans and Freya's wedding, and the newlyweds had just returned from a brief wedding trip to southern Germany. They would return to Wilhelmshaven tomorrow, and from there Hans would return to Lorient. Walter wanted to discuss some things with Hans before he returned to Berlin. Finally, Hans entered the room and greeted his uncle, who began their conversation.

"So the newlywed returns. I trust you and Freya had a memorable time."

"Yes, thank you, Uncle, we only wish it could have been longer." Hans's brief smile quickly gave way to a concerned expression as he sat down and continued. "Last month was a disaster for the U-boat force. I barely got back in one piece from my last patrol. The Allies' technology is now clearly superior to ours. We need boats that can dive deeper and remain submerged longer. We need better sound gear. Above all, we need to recognize that they have broken our code and are homing on our radio transmissions."

Walter paused before answering. Indeed, he was aware that in May the sinking of allied merchant ships had been drastically reduced and forty-one U-boats had been lost, including one with the son of the navy commander, Admiral Doenitz. Walter was acutely aware that the U-boat war had turned against Germany.

"Hans, I recognize that we need new boats to regain our technological advantage. But our codes people assure me that it is mathematically impossible to break the codes generated by our Enigma machines." Indeed, the *Wehrmacht* had almost unlimited faith in the integrity of the coding device used throughout the German military. Unfortunately, this faith was misplaced.

"Uncle, I don't care what the code breakers tell you. There have been too many coincidences where allied ships arrive at the scene when you least expect them. Also, I will no longer make daily position reports since they are reading our radio traffic and homing on our locations." Hans paused. "Tell me about the new Electro boats being built. When will they be available?"

Hans referred to a new, technologically advanced U-boat known formally as the Type 21 that could replace both of the existing Type 7 and Type 9 boats. The new design had great stealth, underwater endurance, and advanced technical features.

Walter replied, "The rumor mill is working too well. This information is highly secret, but the first boats are being built now and will sail early next year. We expect this boat can change the course of the war."

Hans nodded. "That's good to hear. They can't come soon enough. Without some changes in our fortunes, I'm not optimistic about the outcome of the war."

25.

Santander, Spain
July 1943

* * *

Jack Kurtz stood next to his boss, General William "Wild Bill" Donovan, the head of America's central intelligence service, the Office of Strategic Services. They watched Admiral Wilhelm Canaris, the head of German military intelligence, the *Abwehr*, enter the room and walk over to them, accompanied by Alberto Ortega, assigned to the Spanish navy's intelligence branch. Jack had met Alberto two weeks before, when he arrived in Spain to help set this meeting up at the request of Canaris and arranged by the Spanish. A much bigger meeting was to follow, also at Canaris's request, to include Stewart Menzies, the head of British intelligence. Jack knew that Alberto was Paul Hoffman's cousin as a result of his previous vetting of Alberto and their subsequent conversations.

Alberto had arranged to hold this meeting at a Spanish navy villa, on the east side of the Bay of Santander, with a commanding view of both the town across the bay and the ocean on Spain's rocky northern coast. Only two other individuals in Spain knew about the meeting, the navy minister and Captain Luis Carrero Blanco, Alberto's former boss and Franco's current aide.

"I am pleased to meet you. I am Wilhelm Canaris." He spoke in excellent English as he extended his hand to Jack, looking him in the eye and then smiling toward Donovan.

"Likewise, Admiral; I'm Jack Kurtz and I work for General Donovan." Jack looked intently at both Donovan and Canaris and quickly realized they already knew each other.

Alberto ushered the other three men to two ornate sofas in an alcove overlooking the bay. Canaris began, as he turned first to Donovan and then to Alberto, "I would like to thank my Spanish friends for setting this preliminary meeting up, before we meet with our British colleague."

"Yes, of course, but I am in fact uncomfortable meeting with you separately, so would you mind telling me why you wanted this meeting first?" Donovan replied.

"Of course, General Donovan; when we meet with Menzies, my wish is to discuss how we may end this war on honorable terms. But first I wish to talk about Spain and its current position."

"Go ahead; I'm listening."

"My feelings for Spain are nearly as strong as for my homeland, since I've spent so much time here. It's my desire to ensure that Spain does not get drawn into this war, and so far we've been successful. In fact, I want to bring to your attention the fact that there are some individuals that you can rely on to ensure Spain's continued neutrality. Unfortunately, only the navy has advocated that position in the government while the army and most other elements of the Franco cabinet still favor the Nazi regime."

Donovan became impatient. "Look, Admiral, you haven't said anything I don't already know, and as to the Nazi regime, aren't you the head of military intelligence, sworn to uphold that regime?"

"Actually, General Donovan, I and many of my compatriots are no longer loyal to Hitler and the Nazi regime and want to end this war, but that's the subject of our next meeting. May I continue?"

Donovan nodded.

"Of the individuals that I referred to earlier, one stands out in particular. He is Karl Hoffman, a German émigré to Spain and now a plantation owner in Spanish Guinea. In 1940, he prepared a paper at the behest of the governor of Spanish Guinea, who had been tasked with preparing Franco for his meeting with Hitler in October 1940. The paper, as well as Franco's subsequent pitch to Hitler, contained outlandish demands for Spain's entry into the war on the Axis side, engineered by Hoffman to be a 'poison pill' for Hitler. As a result, Spain was not drawn into the war. Individuals such as Hoffman and our Spanish navy friends," Canaris nodded toward Alberto, "hold the key to continued Spanish neutrality."

As Canaris paused, Jack Kurtz could feel tension build in the room as he watched his boss ponder that remark. Finally, Donovan replied.

"So I'm supposed to put my faith in an ex-German in some remote Spanish colony?"

"Actually I will admit that Hoffman can be conflicted regarding his background. His two oldest sons are in the *Wehrmacht*, one of them a U-boat captain. On the other hand, he lost his wife on the *Athenia*, to a U-boat on which his son was first watch officer, and his youngest son is in America. He should have graduated by now from Columbia University. I have known Karl Hoffman for twenty-seven years, but I have never met young Paul Hoffman. I would expect, however, that he is probably much like his father and probably less conflicted about the events I just described."

Jack barely repressed his shock at how much Canaris knew. He noticed a slight smile on Canaris's face as Donovan looked first at Canaris and then at Jack. Donovan picked up on the body language right away.

"Are you plugged into this in some way, Jack?"

"I know Paul Hoffman. We both attended Columbia."

Jack watched as Donovan once more sized up the situation and finally stood and faced Canaris, who also rose. "Thank you, Admiral. I will certainly consider your information and advice. Perhaps we should break away for now and prepare for our meeting with Menzies."

"Yes, of course; I will see you shortly." Canaris shook hands with the two Americans and he and Alberto left the room.

After the door closed, Donovan turned to Jack. "So what was that all about?"

"I think he's trying to clue us in to an inside way that we can control the situation here in Spain."

"All right, Jack, so you know Paul Hoffman. Can he be useful to us here?"

"Yes, General Donovan, he can. You put me in charge of OSS special operations in Spain, so if you'll cut me some slack, I'd like to work this issue my own way."

"All right, that's a deal. I wish I had a boss as permissive as I am with you. I'm probably going to catch hell from the president for holding this next meeting with Canaris, but I wouldn't want to ignore any possibility for ending the war early."

"Do you think Canaris is legit?"

"I'm not sure, but Allen Dulles, our guy in Bern, Switzerland, thinks so. He also thinks Canaris is skating on thin ice with Himmler and the SS, so only time will tell."

26.

* * *

The two FBI agents' conversation with Paul had reached a heated climax. Paul listened impatiently as the agents made their final offer.

Frye summarized. "Paul, we're offering you a fine deal here. We'll extend your visa indefinitely and see that your export-import licenses are taken care of. All we ask is for you to obtain some information for us when you make your periodic trips to Spain."

Agent Miller piled it on. "Yes, and we can see to it that you'll get authorization to fly your aircraft and prevent the military from forcing you to sell it to them."

Paul looked at Miller, disgusted at the man's complete lack of tact and courtesy and condescending attitude. Finally, Paul replied, "As I told you on my previous visit, I will not compromise my country or my integrity to become your stooge. I believe you are abusing my rights as a citizen of a neutral country and I can't believe you would ask me to spy on Spain."

Frye stood up. "All right, Paul, your student visa extension expires in late September. If you don't cooperate, it will not be extended and you'll be deported. Please go think this over, one last time."

27.

Greenwich Village, New York
September 1943

* * *

Paul and Jack Kurtz arrived at the White Horse Tavern midafternoon. Liz had excused herself from this meeting to meet a girlfriend uptown. They had been an inseparable trio all summer. Paul and Jack had become close friends, although their personalities were quite different. Paul was normally reserved, although he could be provoked if the situation demanded, and tended toward the intellectual. Jack, on the other hand, was gregarious and outgoing, athletic, and tended to be the life of the party. Yet they shared a common passion for the broader world and the finer things in life as well as letting their hair down like they were today at their favorite West Village dive.

Several times during the summer, Paul had casually tried to get Jack to talk about his special assignment that kept him in Manhattan in between mysterious absences when there was a world war raging. Jack always dodged the question so Paul eventually dropped the issue.

Paul was a little morose today, internally digesting the results of his last meeting with the FBI agents. Paul saw that Jack sensed this, obviously aware that something was eating at him. They sat at an out-of-the way table, the place almost empty, in advance of the late afternoon after-work crowd. They were momentarily quiet, contemplating their half-empty beer mugs. Finally, Jack spoke, breaking the silence.

"Hey, buddy, you look a little preoccupied today. Was it something I said? Anyway, if you want to talk about it..."

"Oh, I'm sorry, Jack. I was thinking of some decisions I have to make this week."

There was another moment of silence. Finally, Jack continued, "Listen, Paul, listen carefully. Please don't curse me until you hear me out, OK?"

Paul looked at him curiously. "Sure, but what's the big deal?"

"You don't have to agree to Frye's proposal."

Paul blinked and stared at Jack, at first uncomprehending. "What are…
you saying? You know them? You work for them? I don't—"

"Hang on, Paul. Yes, I know them, and no, I definitely do not work for
them. I'm going to take a big risk now and tell you what I really do, so listen
up. I work for the Office of Strategic Services, the OSS, a special organization set up last year to conduct foreign intelligence gathering and…certain
other operations. We're taking over a lot of what was formerly done by the
FBI because…well, frankly, they don't know what they're doing and bozos
like Frye and Miller are the reason America is behind the intelligence eight
ball. Besides, they have no business butting in on operations in Europe." Jack
paused before continuing. "I was recruited early last year from army intelligence. I retain my commission, but I'm on long-term special assignment."

Paul quickly caught on. "So how did you find out about my little alterca-
tion with the G-men?"

"I was in their office about three weeks ago, reviewing their files on European operations so we could take them over, especially the ones that really mattered. I saw yours almost right away…and knew it was one we needed to work."

Paul sighed heavily, shook his head, and looked straight at Jack. "So now
you're going to try to recruit me as a spy, huh? Is that why we've been buddies?"

"Nope, that's not it at all. Paul, I won't insult your intelligence and integrity by asking you to do something you've already refused to do on principle.
I don't need a spy. I need someone I can trust; I need someone I can rely on to
be a trustworthy messenger and someone who wants to help Spain, not hurt it."

"All right, I believe you, but what specifically can I do?"

"I manage OSS operations in Spain. I already have operatives and others,
but I need a well-connected person who can get audiences with the right people and provide them very sensitive information, in confidence."

"Why don't you use normal diplomatic channels?" Paul's interest was
piqued; Jack now had his undivided attention.

"The normal diplomatic channels leak like a sieve, as they usually do, but
even more in Spain, for various reasons. For example, your friend the ambassador, while not too cooperative, is at least discreet, but his staff is way too
talkative and has exposed several of my agents. Also, the Spanish foreign office
and military is riddled with German agents. The British have been buying off
Spanish army generals with Swiss bank accounts for several years, without

much success. The Spanish navy seems to be different. In fact, the navy minister seems to be the only one in Franco's cabinet that sees the big picture. If we can work some of these issues 'back channel' then we can make progress without tipping off the rest of the government or leaking to the Axis."

"That's an incredible situation, Jack, but what do you define as progress?"

"Anything that keeps Spain out of the war, that reduces Spanish economic and military assistance to the Axis, and that increases the chance that Spain will achieve normal relations with the West in the postwar years. I'm afraid that the alternative is Spain's increasing economic isolation from the rest of the world."

Paul leaned toward his friend. "Jack, I'll do anything I can to achieve those outcomes. I'm going to Spain next month for my cousin's wedding. Is there anything I can do on this trip?"

"Yes, but we're going to start with small steps. Touch base with Alberto, your navy cousin, and the ambassador in Madrid. The ambassador doesn't know about your status, but he's generally been against most OSS operations in Spain, for fear of offending the Franco regime. You might be able to sway him that a more activist intervention is needed in Spain. On this trip, I just want you to observe their attitudes. Don't reveal that you have any connection to OSS. We can talk about the next steps when you return."

Paul thought about his meeting with the German economic attaché in Madrid in May but decided against making a complicated situation even more so.

"OK, Jack, I'm convinced this is the right thing to do for Spain, but what do I do about my FBI buddies?"

"You don't have to worry about them anymore. They're permanently off your case and are sworn to forget you ever existed. Oh, and by the way, you will find your new business visa available next week, issued for two years without restrictions. Also, I'll get you a War Department authorization to operate your aircraft throughout America, without restrictions, for the duration of the war." Jack smiled. "After all, we have to keep up appearances and you're a legitimate Spanish businessman who travels a lot."

"OK, let's drink to all this...and our continued friendship, I hope."

"You can count on it, Paul, you can count on it." The two men raised their mugs.

28

U. S. Embassy, Madrid, Spain
October 1943

* * *

Paul was ushered into the ambassador's office, warmly greeted, and offered a seat. Paul thanked him and offered his own greeting.

"Thank you for seeing me, Professor...I mean, Mr. Ambassador. May I present you with some fine wine and sherry from the Hoffman-Ortega bodegas?" Paul presented a bottle of each, a *tempranillo* from the 1924 vintage and an *oloroso* sherry.

"Thank you, Paul, and 'professor' will be just fine and less formal and exalted. I'm sure I'll enjoy these wines. So how has your visit been progressing? I understand that this is your second visit to Spain this year."

"That's right. Both trips have been rewarding, with a chance to see my family and conduct important family business. While I was here, I wanted to stop by and visit." Paul paused. "Professor, you may recall that when we last met at Columbia, I said I may call on you to assist me...in some way that would help Spain stay out of the war."

"Yes, of course, Paul; the offer still stands. How can I help?"

"I'm not exactly sure yet, but at some point I might ask you to provide a cover story for some activity that I might become involved in—activity that would keep Spain out of the war and potentially help the allied cause."

The ambassador's smile diminished and then disappeared as he realized what Paul was suggesting. Then he leaned forward and assumed a serious tone. "Paul, if I heard you right, you're suggesting that you're involved in some undercover activity. Who are you working for?"

"Professor, I wouldn't say I was 'working for' anyone in particular. It's just that I have been asked to provide a conduit for messages and other actions that could achieve these goals."

The ambassador leaned back in his chair, looked at the ceiling, and then shook his head. He then frowned at Paul. "If I were to guess, this has 'OSS' written all over it. It's very difficult for me to do my job here and preserve some kind of relationship with the Franco government when undercover activity is taking place that I'm not aware of. Is that what's going on, Paul?"

"To a certain extent, sir, that's true. But regular diplomatic channels and what you call 'undercover' activity have always coexisted. In this case, I'm trying to make you aware of my role and ask that you be discreetly ready to provide assistance when I need it. Aren't we both trying to achieve the same goals? I apologize if I've gotten in the middle of a turf battle, but I'm trying to be up front with you."

The ambassador shook his head again as he turned to look out his window. Finally, he turned back to Paul. A weak smile had returned.

"You're right, Paul, you needn't worry about the bureaucratic fight going on. I just have one word of caution—remember that this is a serious business and that anything you become involved in carries various risks." He paused. "Just let me know when you need my assistance and I'll do what I can."

29

Two hours later, Madrid
O c t o b e r   1 9 4 3

* * *

Paul took his time strolling back to his hotel after meeting the U.S. ambassador. He planned to freshen up a bit before meeting Alberto, with whom he had taken the precaution of setting up a discreet rendezvous location. The stop at his hotel would allow him to slip out the rear entrance on his way to meet Alberto.

No sooner had that thought gone through Paul's mind than he heard an all too familiar voice calling his name from behind as he walked. He stopped, turned, and saw Peter Schmidt, his "friend" the German economic attaché.

"Good afternoon, *Herr* Hoffman. Did you have a productive meeting at the American embassy?"

"Hello, *Herr* Schmidt. Yes, in fact, I was able to obtain new American import permits for our wine, cocoa, and coffee products. Have you been well?"

"Yes, thank you. I was hoping that you may have considered our conversation in May and may want to talk some more."

Paul thought about his new role as he quickly crafted his reply. "I've thought about it very carefully, but I'm not able to talk about it right now because of other appointments. I can assure you that the points you so carefully made were well taken, but I still need more time to think it over."

"What is there to think over? I believe I made the points very clear regarding the situation your family is in and what your duties and responsibilities are."

"*Herr* Schmidt, you did an excellent job in swaying me on those points, but there are certain practical considerations also. What makes you think I'm the right person to accomplish what you need to have done? How would I be protected from discovery? Who would I report to? When and where would I become involved?"

"Ah, now we are making progress. Those are excellent questions, and I can answer all of them if we can sit down and talk."

"*Herr* Schmidt, please listen to me. I have not made up my mind on your offer. I do not accept or reject it at this time. I assure you that on my next visit I'll give you an answer. You must understand what a big step this would be for me."

"All right, Paul, I understand your concerns now. I will be prepared to work with you when you return to Spain. Remember that the Fatherland and your family need you and that you must take that obligation seriously."

"Thank you, *Herr* Schmidt. I'll contact you when I return. Good day." As Paul walked away, he realized he had kicked this can down the road a little farther, but also may have created some opportunities for the OSS—and some risks for himself.

30.

Several hours later, at a small restaurant, Madrid
October 1943

* * *

Paul and Alberto took a circuitous route to the out-of-the-way restaurant. After they were seated at a quiet, discreet table and had ordered, Paul filled Alberto in on his meeting with Schmidt. After Paul had alerted him in May after his first meeting with Schmidt, Alberto had made sure that his future small talk with Schmidt did not include information on family member movements and activities. Now Alberto elaborated on Schmidt's activities.

"As you guessed, Paul, Schmidt is a member of the SS foreign intelligence service. His real job is to recruit agents in Spain. The war has started to turn, and the SS has increased its efforts to recruit agents, especially those with unique situations like yours."

"So what kind of information are they after?"

"For someone like Schmidt, that could be anything that would make him look good. I'm also sure, because of hints dropped by Schmidt, that a high priority for them is determining when and where the invasion of France will take place."

Paul paused to consider that before replying. "It will help Spain after the war if we are viewed more favorably by the Allies, especially the Americans. If we continue to aid Germany, the more likely it is that the Allies will retaliate economically, either during the war or right after it."

"I agree. In fact, the navy minister advocates that position also and he has tried to support the foreign minister to change the tilt of our neutrality. They are, however, the only ministers who agree with that course of action."

"What do you suppose would change that position?"

"It would have to be pretty serious. An allied invasion isn't likely; perhaps an economic embargo would carry more weight, especially if our fuel supply were threatened."

That instantly gave Paul an idea, but he filed it away and replied, "My friend the American ambassador is sympathetic with Spain's cause, but he can't sway the opinion of allied leaders unless Spain gives some sign that it will change its position on aiding Germany. I believe that a serious event is needed to get the government's attention. This probably needs to be done outside normal diplomatic channels. Otherwise the SS will get wind of it and try to sabotage any allied initiative."

"What are you thinking of, Paul? Do you carry enough weight with the ambassador to accomplish this?"

"I'm not sure, Alberto, but I'll need to contact you when I next return to Madrid."

A quick nod from Alberto signaled his agreement as their food and wine arrived.

31.

Greenwich Village, New York
November 1943

* * *

Paul and Jack again took the opportunity to steal away for the evening to hammer out their plan. Since returning from Spain, Paul had fully briefed Jack on his meetings with Alberto, the U.S. ambassador, and the SS agent, Schmidt. He and Jack were discussing some strategies and options so that Paul could use his next scheduled trip to Spain, in January, as a cover for whatever they planned to do. As the afternoon wore on, Paul finally took the opportunity to sum up what they had discussed and propose a course of action. He outlined his plan to Jack.

"As I see it, Alberto will be a reliable conduit to their navy minister, if he can convince them of my credibility. Jack, you said that Spain must cease its shipments of strategic minerals to Germany, especially tungsten, and stop sheltering U-boats in Spanish ports. You also said that, post war, Spain must not agree to harbor Nazi war criminals, funds, documents, or loot. I think all we need is some teeth to back that up. How about imposing a one hundred percent oil embargo to get their attention?"

Jack whistled incredulously. "Whoa, that's a big step, my friend. That might even get the president's attention, if I kick that idea upstairs. We've already reduced oil exports to Spain to sixty percent of what it was prewar. If we cut them off entirely, it could force Franco's hand and push them right into the Nazis' laps."

"Not if they know the embargo will end before their fuel reserves get really critical."

"How will they know the embargo won't last?"

"As I said, it all hinges on Alberto convincing them that I'm legitimate. The navy minister will have to take that chance—on both Alberto and me." Paul paused. "Also, we need to offer Spain something in return. How about offering them economic aid after the war?"

"I've actually broached that subject up the line. As a result of Spain's past obstinacy, unless they're ready to join the Allies actively, Spain will be relatively isolated for at least a couple years after the war; it's sort of punishment, I guess. The best we can offer is a basic lifeline, such as minimum food and fuel imports, like we're doing now, and maybe eliminate any punishing tariffs on their exports. But there will be no financial aid for rebuilding, like the rest of Europe will get. So we need to get that message to them. They need to join the party soon or they won't get the real goodies after the war."

"What about feeding some misinformation to our SS friend?"

"Paul, we discussed that earlier. I promised you up front that I wouldn't try to turn you into an agent. Working with that creep could be risky for you."

"I'm willing to take that chance, if it will help shorten the war."

Jack looked at him carefully before replying, "Boy, you sure are embracing the cause, for a neutral businessman."

"That's what neutral businessmen do, Jack; they're in the middle of things. Besides, I'm really just following my father's example of how to leverage our influence. We both agree that it's best for the Hoffmans, the Ortegas, Spain, and the rest of the world if we can shorten the war." Paul paused. "So what about planting some misinformation about the invasion of France?"

Jack studied Paul carefully and replied, "All right, listen up. I have a suggestion that's extremely secret and sensitive. Before I cover that, and since you've crossed the line, there is some other information we need. We know that Spain has been funneling intelligence information to Japan. It's probably being gathered by Spanish correspondents, businessmen, and others over here. We'd like to see if you can get the names of those individuals so we can stop that shit."

Paul smiled. "That's a deal. I can work two of these issues through Alberto. That will be the back channel message on reducing help to Germany and the names of the agents providing information through Spain to the Japs. I'll need to use my sniveling little friend Schmidt for the ruse on the invasion location in France."

"All right, Paul, that's a plan, as long as you know the risk you're taking. Now here's the deal on the invasion. You're going to be part of a massive deception effort known as Operation Fortitude." Jack leaned over and explained the operation—and his proposal regarding Paul's role.

32.

Santa Isabel, Spanish Guinea
December 1943

* * *

Karl arrived at the governor's office for the meeting the new governor had requested. Karl understood that the politician occupying that office was not as important as the policies he was responsible for executing. The new appointee was the third one who had served under the Franco regime since the end of the Civil War. Karl had met him twice, briefly, and sensed that he had arrived with a new mandate from Madrid. Again, Karl's reputation as a reliable and discrete advisor was well established and he was eager to see what would transpire. As he processed that thought, he was ushered into the inner office, and the governor immediately rose to greet him.

"Karl, I thank you for taking the time to meet with me! Please have a seat."

"The pleasure is mine, Governor. I'm always eager to help the administration. How may I be of service today?"

"Karl, please call me Juan. I expect we will form a close working and personal relationship and I would prefer that it be less formal. The reason I asked you here was to relate the guidance I received from Madrid regarding Guinea's future and to obtain input and advice from you on how to proceed. I also have two other matters to discuss."

"Of course, Juan, I would be happy to oblige." Karl's interest was definitely piqued.

"As you know, Karl, Spain is still very economically depressed, and there have been less development funds available for Guinea than we would have liked. Yet we have noticed that conditions here are not bad, mainly because of prosperity that has resulted from our exports, largely to America, and largely due to your family's initiatives. I have also noticed that your plantations are more prosperous and successful than those of the other planters. Can you shed some light on how this came to be?"

Karl immediately sensed the opportunity. "Yes, Juan, it's true. My family and I have followed proactive business and export policies, dealing directly with America, and we also follow progressive labor policies that are only slowly being adapted by the other plantations. We believe we will have more success in attracting a stable work force by treating the native workers better. Along those lines, I believe you could support the effort to make operations in Guinea more productive by creating better infrastructure. By that I mean especially better roads in Rio Muni, health care facilities and clinics, and schools for the native population, and especially improved airport facilities in Bata and Santa Isabel, in anticipation of future airline service. All of these improvements will help us to increase production of cocoa, coffee, and timber, to serve the American export market, as well as Spain's internal needs."

The governor looked at Karl, spellbound. "This information is incredibly important. Can you prepare a paper for me summarizing your recommendations?"

Karl smiled. "Of course, Juan, I'll have it ready for you in a couple of days."

"Thank you, Karl. I will be very grateful for your assistance." He paused. "I have two other issues. First, have you met Franz Liesau Zacharias, who is attached to the German consulate here?"

Karl felt a chill in his spine. He had indeed met Zacharias briefly and had an uneasy feeling about his purpose in Guinea.

"I met him briefly several weeks ago when you hosted a reception for the consulate staff, but we haven't interacted since."

"That's fine. He is only here for a short time and will be returning to Germany, through Spain, in several weeks. He has been tasked with obtaining some primates, including monkeys, chimpanzees, and gorillas, to take back to Germany for medical research purposes. They have virtually no access to such animals in Germany. Would you be able to help him gather such animals from Rio Muni? We've agreed to help him in this endeavor and I'd be grateful if you could support me. You know more about the mainland than I do and with your plantation staff would be in the best position to locate and secure these specimens."

Karl thought briefly about this odd request and wondered what kind of research required such animals. Finally, he replied, "I'll be happy to help with this also."

"Thank you, Karl." The governor paused and Karl noticed him squirming in his seat.

"You had one other matter to discuss?"

"Yes; let me begin by saying that the previous governor and his predecessor also were high in their praise of your services to them and to your loyalty, so please keep that in mind as I relate the following information."

"You have my undivided attention."

"Before traveling here, a BPS officer briefed me on...certain files they have on you and your family. These files are largely based on information provided by their counterparts in the German SS—information regarding your previous activities in Germany and lack of loyalty to the current Nazi regime."

Karl realized then that Ernesto had been right when he and Karl discussed the BPS in 1939. It was clear that the SS had tipped off the BPS.

"Juan, let me assure you that my loyalty is to Spain and its future, especially here in Guinea. I worked closely with Franco's first governor here to not only protect that future, but to provide Franco with information that he used in his meeting with Hitler to make such demands on Germany that it would be impossible for us to be drawn into the war on the Axis side."

"I understand completely. I know of your role in that meeting and that is my point. I view your loyalty as unquestionable. My sole purpose in raising this issue is to alert you to the fact that the BPS and the SS are cooperating on intelligence and other issues, notwithstanding Spain's nonbelligerency and neutrality. Use this information as you see fit."

"Thank you, Juan, I will. In fact, I have my suspicions that the SS machinery is active here in Santa Isabel, in the German consulate."

The governor sat back in his chair and looked at Karl. "I'm afraid you're right, Karl...I'm afraid you're right."

33.

Madrid, Spain
January 1944

* * *

Paul and Alberto again discreetly rendezvoused at their customary out-of-the-way restaurant to discuss the information Paul had. They were in an isolated corner of the restaurant in the early evening and were the only patrons as Paul began the conversation.

"Alberto, since I arrived last week, I've met with my friend the American ambassador. I've been asked by the Americans to relay some important information. They believe that the navy ministry is the only reliable conduit for this information because it must be acted on with both discretion and effectiveness. Your position allows you to funnel such information with less danger that it will be revealed to the Germans."

"I'm a little surprised by your evolving role in such intelligence matters, Paul, but you have my undivided attention."

"First of all, in three days America will announce a one hundred percent oil embargo on Spain because of ongoing assistance that it continues to render to Germany." Paul paused as he noticed the desired shock effect of his words, and then continued.

"The Americans do not wish to create economic chaos in Spain and do not intend for the embargo to last long enough to hurt us; they know we have several months of oil reserves. Rather, they want to provide us with cover so we can take certain actions."

Alberto replied, catching on quickly, "I see. So we'll be able to tell the Germans that our options are exhausted and we must do the Americans' bidding. What are the conditions we must satisfy for America to lift the embargo?"

"They want us to cease supplying Germany with strategic materials, especially tungsten, and to cease supplying and sheltering U-boats. They also want us to promise not to shelter Nazi fugitives, money, or other materials after the war ends."

"Those are conditions I would expect. What would we get in return, besides a lifting of the embargo?"

"I believe that's all we can expect from the Allies for now. In the long term, I believe it's in Spain's interest to assist the Allies. If we do not eventually enter the war on the allied side, we can't expect immediate postwar economic assistance." Paul paused and looked straight at Alberto.

"My cousin, I know we haven't been able to talk much about this. I'm now convinced that Germany will face disaster this year or next and we mustn't let that event suck Spain into the vortex of defeat and ruin. It pains me to see my brothers caught up in this, but I believe we must take actions that will curry favor with the Allies, even at the expense of Germany. I hope you don't view me as a traitor for thinking this way. I've given it much thought before acting as I am now."

Alberto sighed. "I've reached the same conclusion, and I know many others in the navy share that view. It will be difficult, even dangerous, for us to act on our convictions, but we must do so. As you said, the only alternative is for Spain to suffer grievously." He looked at Paul. "I'll support you in these efforts. Are there other actions you had in mind?"

"Yes, I'm still playing a little cat and mouse game with our mutual friend Peter Schmidt. I met him two days ago and agreed to work for the SS. I fed him some accurate but strategically unimportant information that the Americans provided so that he might assess my reliability and get the attention of his superiors. In a few months, I'll provide him some less accurate information on some far more important subjects."

Alberto looked up at Paul, an expression of concern etched in his face. "I must tell you that what you are doing is extremely risky. The SS has many agents here, including many that are just butchers disguised as diplomatic or business personnel. You'll be watched to determine your reliability and there will be consequences if they sense that you are betraying them. I can take limited actions to cover you, but you must exercise extreme caution in this little charade. It's not a game."

"Alberto, I know this is risky, but it must be done. There is also one other request I must put before you. In a way, it's something I've agreed to do as a repayment to America for providing what it has to our family's prosperity."

Alberto looked up expectantly, and Paul continued. "The Americans believe that Spanish businessmen and journalists in America are collecting and funneling intelligence information to the Japanese through channels here in Spain. They want the names of those individuals. My guess is that, if we provide those names, we'll be looked upon more favorably by the Americans."

Alberto looked at Paul incredulously. "Yes, it's true. The information comes to our intelligence services who then funnel it to the Japanese embassy. I can gain access to these names, at some risk, but it seems to me the right thing to do. To allow this operation to continue will needlessly provoke the Americans."

"Will it compromise our other intelligence needs?"

"No, we have many more effective ways of obtaining needed intelligence. I'll go ahead and obtain the information. I have a source, another naval officer, who can gain access to those names. I can have them for you in a couple of days."

"Thank you, Alberto. Now you'll be taking some risk also. I'm afraid I don't have the means to provide you with the same cover you offered me."

"That's all right, Paul. We'll be in this together. We have the same objective in mind—to protect the future of Spain and our family."

34.

Berlin, Germany
March 1944

* * *

Walter Hoffman stood behind his desk in the underground bunker below the navy ministry as he waited for his three guests to be shown in by his aide. They had requested a secure room location for a meeting on an undisclosed subject. Walter hoped the meeting wouldn't last long, since he knew Hans would be arriving shortly, having just completed a patrol, and Walter wanted to debrief him. Walter wondered what the three SS officers wanted. The lead officer, *Oberführer* Bruner, was a senior officer in the RHSA, the intelligence section of the SS, and, although known to Walter, he was not a personal acquaintance. Bruner was bringing two aides previously detached from the *Wehrmacht*, Gerhard Hoepner from the army and Claus Hilgemann from the navy. Hilgemann had served previously on Walter's staff and was a reliable and trustworthy staff officer. Walter didn't want him detached to the SS but had little choice in the matter.

Finally, there was a knock on the door and Walter's aide presented the guests. As the aide closed the door behind them, the three officers, all junior to Walter, came to attention and rendered the Nazi salute, which Walter returned.

"Good afternoon, gentlemen. Please be seated."

Bruner got right to the point. "Good afternoon, *Herr Vizeadmiral*. It was kind of you to see us on short notice. We have an urgent matter to discuss with you that is of great importance to the Reich."

"Of course, *Herr Oberführer*; how may I be of assistance?"

"Before we begin, I must emphasize two points. First, what we are about to discuss is of utmost secrecy and may only be revealed to you and one other officer that you will choose based on this operation's requirements. Second, we must emphasize that this discussion is only about a contingency that, in all likelihood, we will never need. Am I clear on these two points?"

"You are perfectly clear, *Herr Oberführer.*"

"Excellent; please sign this to acknowledge your understanding of these two points."

Walter quickly read the one-page document, a standard SS requirement. He signed it. "Since such matters could also affect the *Abwehr's* responsibilities, am I also to assume that they are already privy to this operation?"

"You will assume no such thing. As you may or may not know, the responsibilities of the *Abwehr* have been transferred to the SS."

"What about Admiral Canaris?"

"Canaris has been relieved of his position as head of the *Abwehr.* May I go on?"

"Of course, please continue, *Herr* Oberführer." At least Walter now knew that the rumors were true—the SS had won the power struggle for military intelligence also.

"Very well, *Herr Vizeadmiral,* I will now give you another document which I want you to read in its entirety. Your understanding of this document and ability to comply with its requirements will be crucial to the success of this operation in the unlikely event that it must ever be carried out." Bruner placed the document on the desk in front of Walter.

Walter picked the document up and began reading, curious as to the "contingency" disclaimer mentioned twice already by Bruner.

Case "Valhalla"
MOST SECRET

1. *The purpose of this operation is to enable the securing of highly secret and technical information which has been developed in the last ten years to support the military, scientific, economic, and other advances of the Third Reich. This operation will only be activated as a contingency, in the unlikely event that the territorial integrity of the Third Reich is compromised by enemy forces, and it is necessary to store and secure this information in a location outside current Reich boundaries.*

2. *Case Valhalla may only be activated as Operation Valhalla by my direct order, or by Reichsführer Himmler, acting on my behalf.*

3. *Upon activation of Operation Valhalla, the designated Wehrmacht official responsible for execution will begin the phased implementation of the four phases of this operation. These phases, with timelines and subordinate execution responsibilities, are as follows:*

  a. *PHASE 1 — (to complete 180 days after initiation)*
    i. *Accumulation of technical documents and other materials — SS*
    ii. *Complete preparation of transport vehicle — Wehrmacht*
    iii. *Transport materials to embarkation point — SS*
    iv. *Destruction of remaining physical evidence — SS*
  b. *PHASE 2 — (to complete in 55 days after initiation of Phase 2)*
    i. *Transport materials to secure storage location — Wehrmacht*
    ii. *Elimination of nonsecure information sources — SS*
  c. *PHASE 3 — (to complete 15 days after initiation of Phase 3)*
    i. *Secure disposition of transport vehicle — Wehrmacht*
    ii. *Dispersal of key transport personnel — Wehrmacht*
  d. *PHASE 4 — (to complete upon direction of authorized Reich leadership)*
    i. *Retrieve information as necessary to support Reich reconstitution*

4. *The details supporting this plan summary will be contained in a separate document (one copy only) which also contains a detailed inventory of the information referred to in paragraph 1.*

5. *The transport vehicle referred to in paragraph 3-a-ii must be ready to carry out its mission 180 days following activation of Operation Valhalla, Phase 1. It is the responsibility of the designated Wehrmacht official to ensure that preliminary work is undertaken to select, build, and deploy the transport vehicle in time to execute the operation.*

6. *The SS and Wehrmacht have joint responsibility for determining the location of the secure storage site and ensuring its integrity.*

By order of the Führer,
Adolf Hitler
15 March 1944

Walter read the document again, slowly and carefully, thunderstruck by its potential and acutely aware of its significance. Finally, he looked up.

Bruner spoke first, displaying a barely perceptible, slightly crooked smile. "Does *Herr Vizeadmiral* have any questions regarding this document?"

"Yes, I do, *Herr Oberführer*. First, why am I being briefed on this operation? I assume it has something to do with the 'transport vehicle' that is mentioned."

"That is, of course, correct. We have concluded that a submarine is the only vehicle capable of transporting these materials to a distant location without detection. We did not identify the vehicle as a submarine in order to maintain security and not divulge critical information. We have already ruled out aircraft because they lack sufficient payload to carry this cargo, and by the time it became necessary to activate Valhalla, we assume that an aircraft would not be able to escape undetected."

"I see. May I ask the nature of the cargo?"

Bruner reached into his briefcase and retrieved a thick document, handed it to Walter, and then explained. "I do not expect you to read all of this, but please take a few moments to scan its contents. The inventory of materials is in the appendix. These materials will consist of documents, microfilm, and certain other items."

Walter picked up the document and began leafing through the index and table of contents. He was amazed as he quickly picked up key words that indicated the awesome scope of the cargo...missile technology...atomic physics...virulent biological toxins. Walter paused as the chilling import of these terms registered. He continued to flip through the index, quickly digesting more key words...coal gasification...human organ transplant research...jet aircraft. At this point, Bruner leaned over and reached for the document, and Walter released it to him. Bruner then smiled and spoke.

"I will presume that *Herr Vizeadmiral* is now sufficiently impressed and convinced of the importance of this information and the reason for Valhalla. This document will remain in my custody for now. Do you have any further questions?"

"Yes, I do. Where am I to transport these materials?"

"That is an excellent question. I will initially leave it up to you to determine that, because of your extensive background and knowledge of locations outside the Reich. To save you some time, we have already determined that it will be impossible to transport these materials to neutral territory adjacent to the Reich. Preliminary inquiries have revealed that neither Sweden nor Switzerland is receptive to cooperating with us in this regard. Furthermore, although we have certain connections in Argentina, we have also determined that neither Argentina nor other Latin American locations are viable. Nor do we wish to trust these materials with our Japanese allies."

Walter looked up at Bruner and pondered the import of that last comment. He then replied by stating the obvious. "*Herr Oberführer*, that leaves precious few locations for us to explore."

"That is, unfortunately, correct. However, we believe that Spain and Portugal are good candidates for host locations for Valhalla, and we also believe that your excellent contacts in both locations should portend success in obtaining their cooperation."

"That may have been true two years ago, but it is probably not true today. Portugal would be difficult. They have already ceded bases in the Azores to the Allies and we cannot expect the Salazar regime to cooperate with us. Spain is a unique case. The allied oil embargo that began in January is putting severe pressure on the Franco regime, although they are still sympathetic to our cause."

"That is precisely the case, *Herr Vizeadmiral*. We therefore expect that your considerable connections in Spain will be successful in obtaining a secure location to support Valhalla. Do you have any further questions for us?" Bruner looked at his watch.

"I have just one more. I'll need to disrupt U-boat construction and take other necessary steps to implement Valhalla, and these actions will attract attention. What will be the source of my authority?"

Bruner reached into his briefcase, extracted another document, and handed it to Walter. "This is your copy. Please read it…aloud…if you will."

Walter complied. "*Vizeadmiral* Walter von Hoffman is engaged in a high-priority assignment of utmost importance to the Third Reich. His orders with regard to Operation Valhalla will be complied with instantly and completely and he shall be provided with whatever resources he requires to conduct this operation. For this purpose, he is answerable only to *Reichsführer* Heinrich Himmler and me. It is signed, Adolf Hitler."

"Thank you, *Herr Vizeadmiral*. I assume that you have no further questions?"

"Am I not also accountable to *Grossadmiral* Doenitz for executing this operation?" Karl Doenitz was the navy commander and Walter's superior.

This time Bruner frowned as he replied, "We do not consider this to be a navy operation. The navy is merely providing a vehicle for the operation. The operation is under the total operational control of the SS. *Herr Grossadmiral* has been made aware of the existence of this operation, but not the details, and has been informed as to your role and authority. We wish to shield him from direct involvement. Consequently, you are accountable only to the führer and the SS. We will be in contact with you periodically to assess progress with your preparations regarding the vehicle and the host location." Bruner looked at his watch again.

As Bruner concluded his statement, the overhead light began to shake and Walter could feel the walls and desk vibrate, as highly muffled explosions could be heard, even from their location thirty meters underground. It was probably another thousand-plane American bombing raid. The bombings were the main reason that the navy's operational headquarters had been moved about forty kilometers north of Berlin. Walter could not resist the urge to comment.

"Thank you, *Herr Oberführer*, for answering my questions. Perhaps we have little time to spare for executing Valhalla." Walter looked up at the ceiling to emphasize his point.

Bruner stared at Walter, frowned, and rose, quickly followed by his two aides. "Good day, *Herr Vizeadmiral*. I will be in touch." He saluted, turned, and left the room without waiting for Walter to stand or return his salute.

Walter sighed, looked at the two documents in front of him, and realized that he was now in a dangerous position. At least he knew whom he would select as his "vehicle" commander. Coincidentally, at that moment, his aide knocked on the door, entered, and announced that Hans Hoffman was waiting to see him.

"Please show him in."

The aide complied, and soon Hans entered the office, came to attention, and saluted.

"Sit down, Hans. We have business to discuss, but first…how was your last patrol?"

"It was a disaster. I was leading two other boats in a wolf pack attempting to attack a convoy. The allied escort knew of our presence, or at least of the other two boats, since they were regularly broadcasting their daily position. They were both sunk, and I probably would not be here either if I had broadcast my positions. They evidently thought there were only two boats and I was able to escape by going deep. The Type 7 and Type 9 U-boats are no longer viable for effective combat missions, even with snorkels. We need the new Type 21 boats just to survive."

"Hans, you shall have your wish. I'm detaching you from your operational group to work up a new Type 21 boat for special operations."

Hans leaned forward with a smile. "That's excellent. What special operations are you referring to?"

At that point Walter gave Hans the complete briefing that he had just received from the SS and let him read the two documents provided by Bruner. Walter answered his many questions. Finally, Hans summed up what he had heard.

"I can see that the Type 21 will be the only boat capable of carrying out this mission without being detected. It has more room than the smaller U-boats, but is it sufficient to carry the cargo we will have? Also, it's not clear from your briefing whether we will return to Germany after we have executed the mission."

"We will need to talk to the chief U-boat architect about cargo capacity. But I think we can safely assume that this will be a one-way mission. I actually believe there is a high probability that it will be carried out, and if so, there may not be a Germany left worth returning to."

Both men were silent for several moments contemplating Walter's remark.

Finally, Hans spoke. "What about the destination? Spain may be our only option."

"That's true. We'll need to fly there soon. We will talk to Alberto, as usual, to test the waters and see what's possible. I'll get an aircraft assigned to this project. I plan to have Ernst detached to pilot it. Did you stop to see him at the field hospital?"

Ernst had again been wounded, in the process of scoring his fifty-ninth victory.

"Yes, he's fully recovered. Do you think he will agree to the detachment from his unit?"

"He won't have a choice. Valhalla is a higher priority for the Fatherland."

Hans nodded as Walter went over the details in his mind that would need to be resolved. He would need to act immediately on securing a Type 21 hull for this mission and converting it as required. He needed to call the U-boat architect. But first he needed to call his security chief, to make sure he could finesse the SS and cover his political tracks.

35.

Madrid, Spain
April 1944

* * *

Walter, Hans, and Ernst Hoffman waited for Alberto Ortega in the Spanish navy ministry "safe house" in a small town on the far outskirts of Madrid. Alberto had selected the location to ensure secrecy for their two meetings, beyond the prying eyes of both Spanish and German agents.

The Hoffmans had flown to Spain four days previously in a converted He-111 bomber that was used for regularly scheduled Lufthansa service between Germany and Barcelona and Madrid and had civil markings. The three Hoffmans were the only occupants on this flight. They had arrived two days ago at the safe house for their first meeting with Alberto. In that meeting, Walter had outlined their request to support Valhalla—a secure location in Spain to store the precious cargo that would be transported by the Type 21 U-boat. Alberto had listened to the request and the supporting information and promised to discreetly run it up the chain of command in the navy and beyond if necessary.

Alberto finally arrived midday and quickly summed up his instructions. "I briefed my superiors, who then brought me to meet with the navy minister. Late yesterday I finally received notification that the matter had gone all the way to the top, Franco himself. Although he sympathizes with your request, he made it clear that it was out of the question for Spain to serve as a repository for storing the cargo you described. The Allies are putting enormous pressure on us not to harbor Nazi officials, contraband goods, funds, or other materials from Germany, either during the war or after it is over. The fuel embargo is starting to hurt, and we are in the final stages of negotiations to have it lifted. Therefore, it will not be possible to accommodate your request. I'm sorry."

Walter replied, "I understand, Alberto. Thank you for trying. It's not your fault, and I understand the position Spain is in."

Alberto responded, "Is it really possible that you will need to actually conduct this operation? Surely, it's unlikely that Germany will be occupied. Won't a negotiated peace be an option?"

Walter frowned. "I'm afraid a negotiated peace is out of the question. The Allies have made it clear they will only accept unconditional surrender. As to the operation itself, it will all hinge on whether we can stop the upcoming allied invasion of France and prevent them from invading Germany itself. I know that the SS is actively trying to determine where the invasion will occur. The SS claims they have an agent here in Spain who may be able to access such information. Do you know of such an agent?"

Alberto immediately became uncomfortable but replied without emotion. "I have heard that from your embassy staff, someone who is actually an SS agent, but I don't know the details." Alberto realized that a little white lie was essential to hide the horrible truth—that Paul Hoffman was that agent.

36.

Greenwich Village, New York
April 1944

* * *

Paul arrived early for the meeting with Jack. He chose the San Remo for this meeting because he was becoming conscious of the need to vary their routine to maintain secrecy. He secured an out-of-the-way table. Following his return from Spain in early February, he had provided Jack with the names of agents who were supplying the Japanese with intelligence information through Spain. Jack had requested this meeting to talk about Paul's next trip to Spain. Paul knew that the next trip could be eventful.

Jack finally arrived, bringing two beers from the bar, and sat down. "Hey, buddy, I thought we should celebrate a little. I thought you'd like to know that the list you gave me two months ago really did the trick. We rounded up one hundred percent of them. It turns out that their phony cover as journalists and businessmen didn't do them any good. Also, most of them weren't really Spaniards but were using Spanish passports to betray America and make Spain look bad."

Paul smiled. "That's great. It looks like we scored on that one."

"Absolutely, we did. Also, it looks like our use of the back channel route on the oil embargo succeeded. In a couple of weeks we should have the negotiated agreement finalized on the limits of assistance to Germany and will end the embargo. Paul, your assistance on this, and Alberto's, was the key to our success."

"Alberto and I were in full agreement on what needed to be done. He deserves the credit for following through."

Jack smiled and then spoke, his smile fading away. "This next trip is going to be different, I'm afraid. You'll be going in harm's way this time. That information you fed Schmidt was really of no value, but its accuracy established your credibility in the eyes of the SS. What you're now about to do is different. You'll be feeding them important but false information that will have

275

huge strategic consequences. If they find out you betrayed them, your life will be in danger, and I can't guarantee that my guys in Spain can cover you. Are you sure you won't reconsider?"

"No way; I thought this through long and hard and it's the only thing I can do that might have some impact on shortening the war and put Spain in a more favorable light."

"All right then, here's the deal. Next month you will again travel to Madrid to meet with your ambassador friend and activate his offer to help you. During that meeting, you will 'accidentally' come across a document in the ambassador's office while he leaves to obtain refreshments. You will quickly take 'notes' on the contents of that document and then feed them to your SS buddy Schmidt." Jack then described the contents of the document.

Paul replied, "All right, we have a plan. Let's drink to our success and to the upcoming success of the invasion." Both men raised their glasses and began the night's partying.

37

Navy ministry, Berlin, Germany
May 1944

* * *

Walter and Hans Hoffman were meeting with the U-boat architect to evaluate progress on the conversion of the Type 21 U-boat for Valhalla and afterward to discuss the problem of where to take the Valhalla cargo after hearing Alberto's answer ruling out Spain. Another bombing raid was taking place as the three men were discussing the project, but by now they had learned to tune out the muffled explosions above ground. The architect described construction progress as the walls shook again.

"*Herr Vizeadmiral,* your decision to construct this boat at the Danzig yard was a sound one. The allied bombing raids at the other two yards for the Type 21 boats, Hamburg and Bremen, have greatly reduced output and production."

Walter replied, "Yes, that was a fortunate move. Danzig is at the extreme range for the bombers based in England, and the Russians don't seem to care about strategic bombing. What about construction progress?"

"We have assembled all of the components and the hull is now under construction. Per your instructions in March, we've modified the design to expand the internal space in the hull, with commensurate decreases in the capacity of the saddle fuel tanks. The hull dimensions and profile will be exactly the same, so streamlining and underwater speed will be unaffected. As a result, this boat will have eight times the cargo capacity of a standard Type 21. However, I must point out that range will be greatly decreased because of the reduced tank capacity."

"How much reduced range?"

"I calculate it will only be about fifty-eight percent of a standard Type 21, or about sixteen thousand kilometers, assuming economical cruising techniques and maximum snorkel use."

Walter looked at Hans, who simply shrugged. It would not be possible to determine the impact of the range limitation until they knew where they were going.

"*Herr Vizeadmiral*, if you could give me some idea of the boat's mission, perhaps I could provide information on the impact of the range restriction. The Type 21 was designed for long-range missions to the South Atlantic and return without refueling, but to do that with this boat would require refueling somewhere or the boat would be subject to a one-way mission, and that does not seem—"

"Yes, yes, I believe we understand the situation. Thank you for the update; that will be all. You may return to your office."

The architect looked at Walter but quickly realized that the conversation was over. He got up, came to attention, saluted, and left the office.

Walter and Hans looked at each other and were silent for several minutes. Finally, Walter broke the silence. "We must come up with a secure location to take the Valhalla cargo. I don't think the SS cares where it is as long as it's secure and meets their storage requirements of a cool, dry, dark place."

With that comment, Hans suddenly stood and, without speaking, walked quickly to the other side of the room and back, his expression suddenly changing to indicate that something in Walter's statement had registered with him.

"What is it, Hans? Did I say something that provided you with some insight?"

"Yes, you did! I know a place that will be secure and is cool, dry, and dark. It's not in Spain but is still Spanish."

"That seems like a contradiction," Walter replied.

"No, Uncle, it's not. When my brothers and I were small children, we used to play in a cave on our Rio Muni plantation in Spanish Guinea. Although Guinea is in a tropical climate zone, this cave provides natural refrigeration and dryness. It's large inside, with many alcoves suitable for storing the Valhalla cargo. It's certainly out of the way, and it would be unlikely that anyone would ever think to look there. I also believe that it might provide us with an 'escape' from the strict interpretation of the allied requirements forced on Spain regarding assistance to Germany."

Walter instantly caught on. "I think I see your point. Strictly speaking, it's not in Spain so the government could be more comfortable that they were complying with the allied terms not to harbor Nazi officials or materials in Spain. We'll need to think this through and then travel to Madrid again to propose this to Alberto. Are you sure this cave would work as a storage location? What about your father and Ernesto's family? Wouldn't they need to know about this scheme?"

"One problem at a time; I wonder if the U-boat will now have the range to get there. Do you have chart of the Atlantic?"

Walter nodded, went over to a cabinet, and in a few moments he and Hans were poring over the chart with a compass. Hans announced the results of their calculations.

"It looks to be about ten thousand five hundred kilometers to Guinea, using the safest route. That will work with the sixteen thousand kilometer range but then where could you go afterward with fuel for only fifty-five hundred kilometers? That may or may not be enough to reach a safe place in South America."

"Hans, as you said, one problem at a time. I think I have a solution for that problem." Walter then explained, and the two men spent the rest of the day planning.

38

Madrid, Spain
May 1944

* * *

Paul had arrived in Madrid several days ago. In accordance with the plan that he and Jack Kurtz had devised, Paul met with the American ambassador, who agreed to assist their plan, and Paul generated a page of "notes" based on his fictitious "observations" of a "secret" document left on the ambassador's desk. Paul then contacted Peter Schmidt at the German embassy and arranged a rendezvous. He was now waiting for Schmidt at a private table in the small cantina that Schmidt had selected. As Paul was mulling over these thoughts and the risk he was about to take, Schmidt arrived.

"Ah, Paul, it's good to see you again. Thank you for calling me. Do you have some new information?"

"Yes, I do." Paul paused, looked around, and then continued, "Are you sure we're in a secure place?"

"Yes, of course. This cantina is merely a front. It is owned and operated by us and we will be the only customers for the next half hour. The restaurant is closed until then."

"Very well; I came across some information while I was in the American ambassador's office. He stepped out to obtain some refreshments after we talked about what he called some 'upcoming momentous events' that were about to happen. I quickly went over to his desk and briefly looked at his papers. There was one over to the side entitled 'European Invasion Planning.' I quickly scanned it and memorized some key words and then returned to my seat." Paul paused to let that sink in, but Schmidt quickly seized upon the subject and leaned toward Paul excitedly.

"Yes, yes, that's what we need to know! What did the document say?"

"After my conversation with the ambassador, I left the embassy and immediately jotted down what I had memorized on this paper." Paul waved the paper. "Was that the wrong thing to do? Should I have just taken the document with me?"

"No, no, you did it correctly! If you had taken the document, they would have noticed it was missing and that would compromise our operation. Now show me your notes!" Schmidt reached his hand out, almost frothing at the mouth, as Paul handed him the notes.

Paul started to explain his notations. "From what I read, there will apparently be an invasion in the near future, but the first one will only be a diversion, a feint. The real invasion will take place more than two months later."

Schmidt was now clearly excited. "Where will the two invasions take place and when? We must know that information!"

"The document wasn't clear. It only talked about the diversion taking place in Northwest France, with the real invasion taking place farther to the east. I looked for place names and dates, but the document didn't have that information, as least as far as I could tell. Certainly from the tone of the document it's clear that the feint invasion can't be far away. I thought about looking through more documents to learn more details, but I was afraid the ambassador would return early and I would be caught."

"Paul, you did it correctly. It is better for us that you not be compromised. This information, even without the date and exact place, is crucial to us. It confirms what the high command and the führer have suspected about the invasion. You have done excellent work and my superiors will be very pleased!" Paul envisioned Schmidt trying to score points with his superiors over his discovery.

Paul continued, "I'm scheduled to return to America via Lisbon in three days. I don't really have sources in America itself. My friendship with the ambassador and his trust in me are my best means to obtain information. I'm not due to return to Spain for several months. When I do, I'll be sure to schedule another meeting with the ambassador."

"That will be excellent. We don't wish to overexpose you. The information you have provided today is crucial. When you return, we can discuss new requirements that we may have and what your role might be."

Paul recognized that Schmidt had now taken the bait but that when Paul next returned to Spain, it could be a much riskier affair for him, as Jack Kurtz had warned. Later, after the meeting, Paul went to his favorite café and reflected on the huge step he had just taken into another world. As he sipped his sherry he mused about the metamorphosis of his life from student, to businessman, to emissary, and now as agent in a dangerous game of espionage. He consciously embraced these changes because he knew he must.

War and other random events had originally drawn his family into their current situation. Paul thought of his two brothers and how he had only avoided their fate by being born later, by his father's seemingly minor decision regarding the nationality on Paul's birth certificate, and finally by his parents' decision to send him to America to be educated.

But now Paul was trying to shape events rather than be shaped by them. He knew the risks he was now taking but did so consciously, knowing it might shorten the war, improve Spain's position after the war, allow their families' intercontinental business interests to continue to thrive, and, most importantly, protect his family. Paul hoped that shortening the war, and the small role that he might play in that arena, would actually allow his brothers to survive it.

Paul thought about how his brothers would judge his actions. The gulf separating them was now huge, shaped by their separation, experiences, and completely different reality. He decided that he would be happy just to see them again and to accept their judgment.

39

Greenwich Village, New York
Late June 1944

***

Paul and Jack met at the White Horse Tavern for their usual Friday afternoon beer call and they were discussing the Normandy invasion that had taken place three weeks previously. Jack filled Paul in on some of the details not reported on by the press.

"Paul, the Nazis are really blowing this one. They're holding back their main forces for what they believe is the real invasion farther up the coast. That's allowing us to consolidate the beachhead and prepare for a breakout. What you did was instrumental in convincing them that Normandy is just a feint."

"That's great, Jack, but how long will it take for the breakout to happen?"

"There's still some hard fighting ahead, but it's only a matter of time now. In my view, once we break out and start occupying France, they'll see the handwriting on the wall. That might cause them to take some drastic action of some kind. We'll need to watch for that. It could be some kind of secret weapon or other surprise that they unleash."

"How do you know all this?"

"I wish I could tell you, but for now you'll just have to take it on face value and trust that I'm giving you the straight skinny."

40.

Madrid, Spain
July 27, 1944

* * *

Capitán de Navío Luis Carrero Blanco looked toward his former subordinate as *Capitán de Fragata* Alberto Ortega received his final instructions.

"So, Alberto, you and I have received our instructions from *El Caudillo*. Both Franco and the navy minister emphasize the explicit conditions that our German friends must meet in order for us to support Operation Valhalla, as well as the need for absolute secrecy. You have read them over; do you have any questions?"

"No, sir, they are quite clear. It will allow us to fulfill Franco's commitment without undue risk to our future relationship with the Allies."

"Yes, one would hope so. The agreement with the Americans several months ago to lift the oil blockade was a breakthrough. We must try to adhere to the agreement while satisfying Franco's insistence on continuing to aid Germany. I hope this doesn't backfire on us." Carrero paused. "In any case, Alberto, it has been good to work with you again. You have rendered outstanding service to our intelligence operations, and we will continue to need you in that role for another six to twelve months. I will then intercede to get you a sea command. It will be good for your career and will remove you from some of the turf fights and intrigue."

"Thank you, sir; I'll look forward to the new assignment." Actually, Alberto was more intrigued by what would happen over the next few months, as he left Carrero's office to meet Walter and Hans Hoffman. He would miss his current assignment.

* * *

It took weeks for Walter, Hans, and Ernst Hoffman to return to Spain. The allied invasion of France in June had created problems that Walter needed to deal with, and on July 20, an attempted assassination of Hitler further increased the intrigue in the intelligence community in Berlin. Finally, Walter had secured some time for the trip. The flight from Germany to Spain was sportier this time, since long-range American fighter aircraft were now ranging all over France. The converted bomber they flew in was slow and vulnerable, and twice on the flight, they spotted distant American aircraft that they had to evade. Ernst told Walter that this trip to Spain could be their last, at least in this aircraft. Walter realized that on this trip they needed to secure authorization to use Spanish Guinea for the Valhalla destination...or else.

In a repeat of the sequence of their May meeting, they met Alberto Ortega at the same safe house and outlined their scheme for using Spanish Guinea. Alberto set up the appropriate meetings at the navy ministry. They were meeting again with Alberto as he delivered the news.

"I was successful. Again, the decision was made at the top. You are authorized to transport the documents and other materials to Spanish Guinea for long-term storage. No German officials or military personnel may remain in Guinea after the materials are dropped off and no Germans connected with the operation may visit the site for a minimum of five years. The operation must be conducted clandestinely with a minimum number of people knowing about it. Besides the few in Germany and the crew of the U-boat, only Franco, the navy minister, my superior and I, the governor in Spanish Guinea, certain German personnel in the Santa Isabel consulate, and...Karl Hoffman...may be privy to this operation. The navy minister emphasized that this operation must remain completely secret for the indefinite future."

Walter, Hans, and Ernst looked at each other. Walter finally replied, "Thank you, Alberto. We recognize the key role you played in reaching this agreement and the risk you took." Walter paused before adding one thought. "It would appear that Karl's participation is essential to this mission."

"Yes; based on comments from the last three governors in Guinea, your brother is highly thought of. He has been instrumental in making Guinea prosperous and is considered as a confidential advisor to the office of the governor in Santa Isabel. He is considered trustworthy."

Walter looked at Alberto and paused before replying carefully, "Yes, we believe he will understand the reason why Valhalla is necessary and will support the storage of these materials on the plantation in Rio Muni."

Alberto added, "It will also be good for you to see him again. It would be even better if all of you would be able to travel on this mission." Alberto paused. "How is Admiral Canaris? We understand that the role of the *Abwehr* has changed."

Walter and Hans looked at each other, and Walter replied, "I'm afraid that Admiral Canaris was arrested four days ago. The *Abwehr* has been abolished and the SS has assumed their functions."

"I'm sorry to hear that." Alberto wanted to say more but realized there was nothing he could add.

41.

Navy ministry, Berlin, Germany
late August 1944

* * *

Oberführer Bruner arrived promptly for his meeting with Walter Hoffman to assess progress on Valhalla. Just prior to Bruner's arrival, Walter had received an intelligence update from his staff. The news was not good. The allied armies had broken out of the Normandy beachhead, captured Paris, and were racing across France. It was possible that they would reach the German border in two or three weeks. In addition, the Allies had also invaded the south of France, and it looked likely that in that same period the two allied armies would link up, cutting off access to Spain. These thoughts were obviously weighing on Bruner too as he got quickly to the point after arriving, barely taking time to exchange greetings.

"When will the submarine be ready for operations?"

Walter replied with the details. "The main construction will be complete in about three weeks and it will be launched in October. After fitting out, it should be ready for sea trials in November. As you know, we've had many problems with the initial Type 21 boats because of the prefabricated method of construction and the disrupted delivery of key materials due to allied bombing. In addition, there have been quality control problems and some delays in delivery of new components, such as the underwater detection gear. We're prioritizing the solution of these problems for the Valhalla boat but may still expect further delays."

"You didn't answer my question, *Herr Vizeadmiral.* When will the submarine be ready for operations?"

"I cannot give you an exact date yet. Sometime in the first quarter of 1945 would be my estimate. In any case, Valhalla is still a contingency only, and Phase I has not yet been activated."

"You may expect that situation to change shortly. You must therefore guarantee me that the boat will be ready for operations no later than early March 1945."

Walter was momentarily shocked as he absorbed the meaning of that statement and quickly calculated back 180 days from March before replying, "Are you telling me that Valhalla, Phase I will be activated in early September? Can it be that the situation on the front calls for such action already?"

"I'm telling you no such thing. Phase I is, in any case, intended to accumulate the materials associated with Valhalla, not to actually transport them anywhere. As we speak, there are monumental events taking place to finalize stunning scientific advances that may help Germany win the war. To safeguard these advances, we need to document them and consolidate these documents. Therefore, Valhalla, Phase I is the appropriate tool to accomplish this."

"*Herr Oberführer,* may I inquire as to the nature of these 'stunning scientific advances' that will win the war? We could use some of these right now."

"*Herr Vizeadmiral,* surely you must see that the new Vengeance weapons could change the course of the war. The V-I missile we began using in June is only the beginning. Next month you shall see an even bigger and faster rocket that will terrorize the Allies!" The look on Bruner's face revealed that he wished he hadn't revealed that information, although Walter was already aware of it from his own sources.

"That will be important, I am sure, *Herr Oberführer.* For now I will concentrate on completing the Valhalla boat, anticipating the requirement you specified."

"Thank you for the update, *Herr Vizeadmiral.* Now if you'll excuse me, I must depart for another meeting." Bruner quickly exited Walter's office.

Walter sat there for a long time, contemplating Bruner's revelations. The SS hierarchy was clearly running scared, and Walter thought there was a good reason for that. The course of events was clear. The allied army advancing from the west, and the Russian armies advancing from the east, was ultimately unstoppable. It was only a matter of time. Walter was also concerned about paragraph 3-b-ii in the Valhalla directive, "elimination of nonsecure information sources." He decided he would take some precautions of his own regarding that clause.

42

SS physics research facility, southwest of Breslau, Germany
late August 1944

* * *

Oberführer Bruner arrived for his scheduled inspection of the secret facility after departing from his meeting with Walter Hoffman. The facility was established three years ago and was operated totally under RHSA oversight. Bruner immediately located the chief engineer. The engineer had received SS rank in order to expedite the activities at the research station. Bruner located him and got right to the point.

"When did the reactor go critical?"

"About three weeks ago, *Herr Oberführer.* It has been operating smoothly since then, at about half power."

"That's good. This is a stunning achievement for the SS and Germany. Especially since Heisenberg and the other physicists were unable to accomplish this." Of course Bruner overlooked the fact that Nazi Germany had driven out most of its world-class physicists years ago because of its warped theories about "Jewish physics."

"Yes, *Herr Oberführer.* We must recognize, however, that *Herr* Heisenberg is an excellent theoretical physicist but is not as accomplished in experimentation and engineering. In any case, we have succeeded in creating a working reactor, and I believe we have a viable design for an atomic weapon. The rest of the solution rests with engineering and industrial requirements. We have engineered the bomb design, and the design for systems that can extract weapons-quality nuclear material from this reactor, but we still need many months or more before we will have a deliverable weapon."

Bruner looked at the engineer, aghast. "What do you mean? You promised me a successful result last year!"

"I promised you a working reactor and I have delivered on that promise. We can engineer a bomb design that we think will work, but we need enriched material for that weapon. That will take an industrial process to extract the isotopes we need from the reactor products and that will be expensive, time consuming, and very visible to the outside world. I explained all this in my memo of six months ago."

"Yes, yes, I understand that." Bruner paused. "How much will it cost and how long will it take?"

"It will take billions of marks and at least another year just to get enough enriched material for one bomb, assuming we get the go-ahead right now."

Bruner had seen and heard all he needed to know. He didn't have that much money or time. He thanked the engineer, told him to completely document his work no later than March 1, and then departed the facility for his next stop. If an atomic warhead would not be ready in time, he had an alternative warhead payload in mind.

43.

Kaiser Wilhelm Medical Institute, Berlin, Germany
late August 1944

* * *

Oberführer Bruner reached his next destination, in Berlin, the day after his visit to the reactor facility. He again quickly found the director of the SS research section and asked him for an update on the program. The director did not wear his SS uniform or rank in order to provide cover for his ostensible role as head of the "brain cancer" section of the institute.

"What progress have you made on the research program?"

"We've made excellent progress, *Herr Oberführer*. We completed the program on small mammals about six months ago. We had even better results with the primates that Zacharias obtained for us from Spanish Guinea in Africa."

"What about human test subjects?"

"We are just completing those studies now. The preliminary results are incredible. We have apparently created unbelievably lethal pathogens. We have also achieved some success in our immunology studies. It may be possible to immunize subjects against these pathogens. We are also finding some interesting results with our human subjects. Some of them may have natural immunity to certain pathogens because of their genetic makeup. We need to conduct more research in this area."

"That is excellent *Herr Doktor*. Have you also made progress on a warhead and in designing a capsule that can be used to transport a cargo to a destination without accidental exposure of the pathogens?"

"Yes, we completed the design and have constructed containers and warheads that meet the specifications you provided."

"Excellent. When will you complete production of the first batch of agents? When will you have sufficient quantities available for the first weapons?"

"We can have the specified quantities completed by March, *Herr Oberführer*. Actually, we can synthesize them on relatively short notice. In fact, I must emphasize that it is preferable to wait until just before final assembly and deployment of the weapons before the final synthesis takes place. Although we have taken extreme precautions, an accidental release of pathogens could be catastrophic. We can control our own transport, but we can't control allied bombing and other external events."

"Yes, of course, I understand. I'll be in touch. Make sure you completely document your research and have the documentation and small samples synthesized no later than March 1."

Bruner soon departed the facility. He now had the weapon he needed.

44.

Wehrmacht Rocket Test Facility, Peenemunde, Germany
Early September 1944

* * *

Bruner reached the last stop on his inspection tour and went through the obligatory briefings on the main rocket development program. Germany had just shocked the world by launching ballistic missiles, the V-2 rockets, against Paris and London. The scientists were ecstatic about the success of the A-4, as the V-2 was known internally, but Bruner was not interested in the A-4. After the briefing from the main scientific team, Bruner went to a separate facility that the SS, not the *Wehrmacht*, operated located several kilometers away. When he got there, he quickly found the director, who was also an SS officer but not wearing insignia. Bruner posed the question he needed answered.

"When will the A-9 rocket be ready?"

"We successfully tested the engines and other components but need to do more work on the control and guidance systems. This will take several months. We feel confident we can conduct the first test flight in January."

"Why will it take so long?" Bruner was impatient.

"*Herr Oberführer*, there is a shortage of personnel and resources. You told us not to ask for support from the *Wehrmacht* or to share their resources. I believe we are making excellent progress considering these limitations."

Bruner sighed, realizing he was walking a fine line, running the program half in and half out of the regular *Wehrmacht* rocket program. "Yes, I understand the limitations you are working under. Have you also made any progress on the A-10 booster rocket?"

This time his director was impatient. "We have not. You know the limitations we work under. The A-10 is officially cancelled. We are able to work on the A-9 only because it's called the A-4b and we are able to siphon funding from the A-4 program. We have had excellent support from our colleagues, operating under the noses of the *Wehrmacht*, and I don't want to jeopardize that support, especially if you want an early operational test."

Bruner sighed. He knew the director was right. "Very well. Is it possible that the A-9 can make it to New York without the A-10 booster?"

"It's possible. You saw my paper on that subject."

"Yes, I did. All right, make sure that everything is documented and the final reports are available no later than March 1 and give me an interim report after the January test."

Bruner departed, knowing that he might now also have a weapons delivery vehicle.

45.

Navy Ministry, Berlin, Germany
September 1944

* * *

Walter Hoffman sat at his desk reading the latest intelligence brief and the report from Hans on the progress of the Type 21 U-boat. He focused his attention, however, on the message his staff had intercepted yesterday, activating Operation Valhalla, Phase I. Bruner and the SS had carried through on their intention to activate Valhalla, thereby setting a deadline of March 4, 1945, for achieving operational status on the U-boat. Walter thought it was risky for the SS to activate Valhalla, given that it was a pro forma admission that Germany could be overrun in the next six to eight months. That kind of defeatism could result in the arrest and execution of nearly any German—unless you were at the highest levels of the SS. Walter realized that activation of Valhalla was probably prudent. The American Third Army led by General Patton had achieved a stunning breakthrough in France and was racing for the German border, which they would likely reach in a couple of weeks. Walter was more concerned that Patton's army would soon link up with the allied armies racing up from Southern France, which they had invaded on August 15, thereby cutting off all land access to Spain.

As Walter reviewed these thoughts, he looked at his watch and realized it was his scheduled meeting time with Bruner. As usual, Bruner was on schedule, was promptly shown into Walter's office, and wasted little time on pleasantries.

"*Herr Vizeadmiral,* I presume you saw the message activating Valhalla, Phase I. What is the status of the U-boat construction?"

"Construction is about eighty-five percent complete. We expect to launch the boat in October and begin sea trials in November, as scheduled."

"I expect you to easily meet the March 4 deadline then. A later date is unacceptable."

"We'll do whatever is necessary to meet the date, but I can assure you it will not be easily. The allied bombings, the construction and design problems, and the lack of skilled labor are all having a serious impact on the program."

"Yes, yes, I understand all that. I also have a new issue to bring to your attention. As you recall, the Valhalla directive, Phase 3, holds you responsible for disposition of the submarine and crew following the deposit of your cargo in Spanish Guinea. What progress have you made in selecting a secure site for the disposal and crew dispersal that eliminates the possibility of detection?"

Walter had anticipated this question. "We carefully analyzed this situation and are evaluating every possible method for extending the range of the U-boat, despite the decreased size of the fuel tanks in the modified design required to carry the volume of cargo that you specified. We believe it may be possible to reach an isolated area in central or northern Argentina, or perhaps Brazil or Uruguay, after the boat departs Guinea. We are still working on addressing the detection and security issues."

"You realize this contradicts my earlier information that South American locations are restricted. What are our other options?"

"*Herr* Bruner, with all due respect, I have not concluded that South America is not feasible. In any case, the U-boat will not have the range to reach Japanese bases in the Far East without refueling. The refueling option has a very low possibility of success. The Allies have sunk nearly all of our existing deployed transports and tanker submarines and raiders. It is virtually impossible for a surface tanker to be dispatched from Germany without detection, and even if we could get a submarine rendezvous arranged, which is unlikely, our existing U-boats still cannot transfer enough fuel for this U-boat to reach a Japanese base."

"Well then, when are you going to have an answer for me that will be acceptable? This is your responsibility—or perhaps you would prefer for the SS to deal with this matter!"

Walter thought about paragraph 3-b-ii in the Valhalla directive, "elimination of nonsecure information sources by SS," and realized what Bruner implied. Before replying he paused, looked Bruner straight in the eye, and calmly answered.

"*Herr* Bruner, I can assure you that I am fully aware of my responsibilities and assignments in executing Valhalla. I will meet these deadlines and arrive at acceptable solutions to the problems you pose." He paused. "Is that all for today?"

Bruner scowled but realized that Walter was executing Valhalla as agreed on in their operating plan. Finally, he responded, "Very well. I have one final matter to discuss. Because of the deteriorating situation in France, I have dispatched Hoepner and Hilgemann to Spain as per our operating plan. Hoepner will complete the remaining details with our agents in Spain and with the Spanish navy official, and then make his way to Spanish Guinea at the appropriate time, if and when required. I still don't understand why you insist that Hilgemann continue to Lisbon if you have ruled out Portugal as a source of assistance in Valhalla."

"As we discussed, *Herr* Bruner, I have not ruled out any option yet. In any case, Hilgemann speaks Portuguese and has contacts in the Portuguese navy that may be useful to us for determining allied strength at their new bases in the Azores. He can also obtain intelligence in Lisbon, since we have a well-developed network of agents there."

"I see." Bruner rose. "I believe that concludes our business for today. I will continue to personally monitor progress with Valhalla." Bruner turned and departed Walter's office without saluting.

Walter sighed, aware that he would have to continue anticipating Bruner's future actions. He was at least pleased that Hilgemann would be available to accomplish the other essential groundwork needed that Bruner was completely unaware of.

46.

Ortega hunting lodge, Andorra
September 1944

* * *

Alberto Ortega had met Gerhard Hoepner and Claus Hilgemann at the French-Andorra border several hours ago. They were now sitting by the fireplace in the Ortega family hunting lodge sipping sherry with Alberto about to brief them regarding the process for entering Spain. But first he was interested in finding out whether it would still be possible to maintain any kind of land communication with Germany. He quickly got his answer as Hoepner described their harrowing trip.

"We just barely made it through. We had to dodge numerous allied patrols for the last few days and could barely make any progress at all during the day because of incessant allied aircraft attacks. By now, there will be no chance of getting through as the allied armies from Normandy link up with the forces advancing from Southern France. In fact, by next week, the consolidated allied armies will reach the German border."

Alberto had been expecting that answer. He quickly turned to the business at hand. "You will both wear your civilian clothes and discard your uniforms here. Tomorrow I will go to the Andorra-Spain border just ahead of you to ensure that the arrangements are complete. Here are your Spanish diplomatic visas." Alberto reached into his briefcase and retrieved the documents before continuing.

"You are both certified as economic attachés. Hoepner, you will meet Peter Schmidt in Madrid and receive a further briefing there from him on future activities. Hilgemann, you also have a Portuguese diplomatic visa so that you will be able to travel to Lisbon to coordinate with your counterpart there in the German embassy. It is imperative to maintain secrecy regarding this operation, by mutual agreement of the Spanish navy ministry and the German high command. Are these instructions clear?"

Both German officers nodded their agreement. Hoepner then asked for clarification.

"If Valhalla, Phase 2 is activated, I'll have only fifty-five days to reach Spanish Guinea and complete preparations. Accordingly, *Oberführer* Bruner has modified my orders, granting me discretion to travel to Guinea earlier if I deem it necessary to prepare for the U-boat's arrival. I assume you understand the need for this requirement and will assist with transportation arrangements as necessary. I already have an undated order transferring me to our consulate in Santa Isabel as the economic attaché. I anticipate the need to depart for Guinea as early as November and I am carrying explicit orders to the German consul general in Santa Isabel regarding my assignment. I assume that when I leave I will also be carrying instructions for the Spanish governor and Karl Hoffman."

"That is correct. I will see that these instructions are prepared and ready no later than November." Alberto understood the arrangements but had an uneasy feeling, especially about Peter Schmidt's role. He knew he would have to watch Schmidt closely. Alberto was also concerned about Karl Hoffman, not about his loyalty, but rather about SS intentions regarding his uncle.

47.

Bletchley Park, north of London, England
September 1944

* * *

The two intelligence officers, one American and the other British, were pondering the meaning of the recent Ultra intercept they were charged with evaluating. *Ultra* referred to the top-secret allied operation that successfully broke the German codes imbedded in the Enigma coding machines that the Germans had presumed were unbreakable. However, in a stunning triumph using many mathematical algorithms, scientific talent, and decoding devices, the Allies had broken the Enigma code, and the resulting Ultra intercepts had been highly instrumental in turning the tide of the war. Nevertheless, the meaning of the latest intercept stumped the two officers.

The American officer summed up his assessment first. "I don't get it. This message is much too brief for our convoluted German friends. It says 'Activate Operation Valhalla Phase I, effective September 4, 1944.' With most messages, there's elaborate supporting information, but in this case, we only have nine words. What do you make of it?"

"The Nazis haven't given up their penchant for complexity, you can be sure of that. These chaps obviously have something behind the scenes describing the details of this operation. Since they don't suspect that we've broken their codes, they're probably trying to hide the details of this operation from some of their own blokes. We need to get our hands on these backup documents, since they're not likely to transmit it."

"I'll buy all of that, but what do you make of the code name 'Valhalla'?"

The British officer smiled before replying. "Well, I did a little research, and Valhalla is an Old Norse term that refers to the Viking afterlife where some of the dead come back to life to recreate the previous world. It revolves around a series of events known as 'Ragnarok,' which refers to cataclysmic battles, disasters, and the death of major figures, and from which a new world emerges, the surviving gods meet, and the world is repopulated. The whole concept is highlighted in the fourth opera of Wagner's Ring Cycle, *Götterdäm-merung*, or 'Twilight of the Gods.'"

His American colleague whistled. "Boy, you just about tripled my knowledge of Wagner! Do you think it's just a random name or does it have any meaning?"

"I say the Nazis always have some specific meaning behind these code words."

"You're probably right. I wonder if it has anything to do with that recent intelligence assessment that refers to a last-ditch German defensive fortress in the mountains and forests of Southern Germany."

"It could, but if you take the word Valhalla literally, it means the whole country is 'kaput' and gets resurrected later."

"OK, so let's send it on up to our OSS friends and see what they make of it."

48.

Washington, D.C.
October 1944

* * *

Jack Kurtz and Paul Hoffman met near the Lincoln Memorial for a brief discussion prior to heading for the bars in Georgetown. Jack had picked the spot primarily to avoid any possible tail from the FBI, ever suspicious of the unconventional OSS. Jack had asked Paul to travel to D.C. partly to vary their routine, but also so Paul could discreetly meet a couple of Jack's OSS colleagues. Paul was happy to oblige since it gave him a chance to fire up the Spartan and make the quick one-hour or so flight from Teterboro to the recently built National Airport. Paul also planned to make a quick stop in Hershey, Pennsylvania, on the return flight to talk with the huge chocolate company of the same name about a long-term cocoa contract. This was Paul's first visit to Washington, and he reveled in the entire scene constituting wartime D.C.

"Jack, this city is amazing. It's easy to get caught up in the history and grandeur of the place and what it means to America."

Jack smiled. "You're like any other tourist or first-time visitor. It is impressive, even with all of the wartime crowding and bustle. Just don't look too far below the surface, lest you see the bureaucratic beast that lurks there, ready to stifle innovation and action."

Paul laughed. "You're right, I'm sure. I hope I'm not so naïve as to believe that everything works perfectly here. It's just such an improvement over Europe."

"Yep, that it is." Jack paused. Paul had already sensed that something else was on Jack's mind.

"Hey, Jack, you look a little distracted for someone who's only an hour or so away from the beer call, a nice steak dinner, and some barhopping."

"You got that loud and clear, didn't you? Well, to be truthful, I'm a little worried about your next trip to Spain. You've already earned your keep as far as I'm concerned, and that's the OSS line too. We don't want you going in harm's way anymore."

"Thanks, Jack, for the kudos and the concerns. But you forget that I have a family there and a business to tend to. I'm planning to go over in mid-December and be there for Christmas so I can meet my father and conduct some business with the Ortega side of the clan."

"Are you going to Madrid also?"

"Yes, I'm planning on it. My friend the ambassador will probably be finishing his tour early in the New Year and he wanted me to stop by before he leaves. I want to try to work on a message that he can take back to Washington about relations with Spain in the postwar era. I also want to see Alberto and talk with him about family issues and get his thoughts on Spain's receptivity to working closer with America."

"Boy, you really are serious about these things. Look…I know I won't be able to deter you from this trip, but please do me a personal favor. Be sure to cover your tracks when you're in Madrid. I don't want you bumping into our SS buddy Schmidt. Promise me you'll do that, not only for me but…for Liz."

Paul looked at Jack, surprised, but smiled and quickly recovered. "I can see a conspiracy here, but don't worry, I will be exceedingly conscious. Is there anything else?"

He noticed Jack's discomfort as his friend struggled with another issue. Jack finally turned to Paul, taking a deep breath before answering. "Yes, there is. Since you're going to Madrid and will be seeing Alberto, there is one issue you can raise. We would like to find out if he knows anything about a German operation code named 'Operation Valhalla' and whether he can share that information." Jack proceeded to describe Valhalla and the OSS analysis on it.

"No problem. I'll discreetly raise the issue with Alberto. How did you obtain this information? It seems pretty incredible."

"I can't tell you how we got it. Even raising the matter with Alberto is risky, but we've already made the determination that he's a good guy, just like you. Our hope is that he can pump the Germans for more info."

"Don't worry, Jack. Alberto and I think alike on the need to support America."

"Yeah, I know. Alberto knows the score and I hope you do too. This is now a risky business for both of you."

308

49

F. Schichau Shipyard, Danzig, Germany
November 1944

* * *

Walter Hoffman had traveled to Danzig to meet with Hans on the construction progress of the U-boat. He also wanted to be as far as possible from the prying eyes of the SS although he knew that was nearly impossible in Germany. The U-boat had been launched in late October, and Hans had just returned from the first shakedown cruise in the Baltic. They met in a private shipyard office as Hans described the cruise.

"The damn boat leaks like a sieve. It's the method of construction, not the design."

"Can the discrepancies be rectified in time to make the operational date in March?"

Hans replied confidently, "I'll have no problems with the hull issues; it's all about welding, and if I have the skilled labor we'll get the job done. I'm a little concerned about the machinery, especially the snorkel and the silent running motors, but my engineer has figured out fixes for those also. However, we still don't have the advanced sound gear and some other equipment yet. You may need to wave your magic Hitler memo around some more to get that gear and the other items we'll need to survive this trip."

"Rest assured, Hans, I'll make that a priority. Given all of the items you mentioned, when will the next sea trials be? When I get back to Berlin I know Bruner will demand those answers."

"I estimate we'll go to sea again in mid-December and should finish the shakedown of the machinery issues in January. I will then need about thirty to forty-five days to finish with the electronic and special gear, take the boat over from the shipyard, and start training my crew. We'll be ready by March 1. But then we have some operational problems to contend with."

Walter replied with a concerned look, "What kind of operational problems?"

"The allied bombers have finally started to discover us here. I'm also worried about the Russian advances. It will soon be difficult to work efficiently here, and we need to protect the boat at all costs. I believe that when the initial shakedown issues are fixed, we need to transfer to an operational base for final fitting out, training, and provisioning."

"Where do you propose to do this?"

"All of our normal operational bases in Germany are already allied targets. We have hardened pens in Norway, but that's too far from our special logistical needs for this boat, and we need an accessible and secure location to load the Valhalla cargo. I was thinking that Denmark would be the ideal location."

Walter was mildly surprised. "Denmark seems an unlikely candidate for these activities."

"Actually it isn't. The Allies would never suspect it and there are good land communications with our nearby facilities in Germany. We'll need to attend to security carefully, but the Danes are docile. We could stage out of the islands in Zeeland initially, but near the end I want to base out of Western Jutland, in order to reduce the distance to the Atlantic and get away from the Danish straits. One other thing…regarding security, it's not the Danes I'm really worried about."

Walter knew exactly what Hans was thinking. "Yes, I plan to have our own naval security teams begin moving into place discreetly as we get closer to final operations."

He didn't need to elaborate on the need not to rely on or trust the SS.

Hans had some other questions. "Does Bruner know the location of the cave storage site and where our ultimate destination is after departing Spanish Guinea?"

"He's still pressing me on the storage site location, but I've only told him that it will be a secure location. I'm also putting him off on our ultimate destination, claiming that further analysis and preparation is needed."

Hans nodded before asking his final question. "After all this, do you really think this operation will be carried out?"

"I'm afraid it will be, Hans. The western allies are pressing forward and the Russians are attacking relentlessly. Germany's fate is sealed. It's only a matter of months."

50.

American Embassy, Madrid, Spain
December 1944

***

Paul Hoffman and his friend the ambassador were enjoying a glass of sherry as they continued to discuss Paul's paper supporting American aid to Spain following the war. Now the ambassador summed up the results of his analysis of the political situation.

"Paul, you made your points very dramatically, especially the one regarding keeping communist influence at bay by providing aid. I'm afraid, however, that there will be no loans or other economic assistance for Spain for several years after the war. The best I can see happening is that humanitarian aid and oil supplies will continue and America will maintain low tariffs on imports, including those from Spain. Otherwise I'm afraid that Spain will be on its own and isolated by America and the Allies."

"Thank you, Professor. I appreciate your candid assessment and for trying to change policy in Washington. I know that Spain must ultimately be grateful for the help you've provided over the last two and a half years. What will you do next?"

"The new ambassador has already been appointed. I'll leave my post next month and return to America, probably to academia."

"I wish you the best, Professor. You've been a friend and inspiration to me." The two men soon said their good-byes. Paul knew that the ambassador would be missed and wondered how Spain would replace his advocacy in the American government.

51.

Spanish navy safe house, near Madrid
December 1944

* * *

Paul met Alberto at a discrete rendezvous location and they then traveled to the safe house. They were locked in a discussion about the evolving political situation, including the results of Paul's meeting with the American ambassador.

"So it's clear to me that Spain will be isolated after the war," Alberto said, summing up their discussion. "That means our recovery from the results of the Civil War will be further delayed. Our economic policies are also a shambles. From our two families' point of view, the only good news is that our own financial conservatism, and our business operations in Guinea and America, has left us in a good position. The rest of Spain, however, will continue to suffer, my cousin."

Both men sat there for several moments absorbed in their thoughts. Finally, Paul spoke.

"At least we've helped make the best of a bad situation, since our actions have prevented even worse American retaliation."

"Yes, that's true. I suppose that further back channel communication and cooperation with the Americans may eventually result in a change in their policy. It's clear that Germany will be defeated next year. We should continue to think about how that will affect our policies."

Alberto's comment jogged Paul's memory about the request that Jack had made in Washington. He thought for a moment but finally spoke. "It's clear that Germany will take certain measures as defeat nears. The Americans are worried that Germany will unleash new weapons, try a last ditch stand, or take some other desperate measures. They asked me to run this by you—have you received any intelligence about an 'Operation Valhalla'?"

Alberto instantaneously camouflaged his initial shock as his instincts and training as an intelligence specialist took over. How could Paul have known about Valhalla? These thoughts raced through his mind in a split second as he answered nonchalantly, "Operation Valhalla? No, I'm not familiar with that. I don't know of any intelligence information we've received about such an operation."

He realized that, to protect Paul, he could not say anything further. He paused, and then elaborated, his curiosity raised. "Did your friend the ambassador pose this request to you to ask about this operation?"

It took a few seconds for Paul to craft his response. "All I can say is that it was a request from the Americans."

The two men looked at each other, both realizing that they needed to clear the air. Finally, Alberto broke the awkward silence.

"It's clear we're both caught in the middle by these momentous events and acting in ways we think will be in the best interests of Spain and our families. I believe I understand what you're trying to accomplish and I still support you."

Paul was relieved. Alberto understood. "Yes, Alberto, we're both involved, whether we want to be or not at this point. It would be indiscreet for us to embarrass each other with further revelations about our respective responsibilities."

"I agree. In any case, in a few months hopefully this terrible war will be over and we can work together to help Spain eventually join the international community. Of more immediate interest, we can look forward to more contact between our families. I've been granted leave for the holidays and will be able to join you in Alabos in two weeks."

"That's excellent news, Alberto. I'll look forward to that event."

Both men realized that they would continue to be in an awkward situation but were bound in these circumstances by common goals. Paul hoped that the end of the war would help diffuse the tension but recognized that there would continue to be a veil of secrecy regarding certain issues. When he later left the safe house to return to his hotel he couldn't help but wonder if Alberto knew something about Operation Valhalla, despite his response.

52

Madrid, later that evening
December 1944

* * *

Paul was walking back to his hotel, having stopped for dinner and a glass of sherry along the way. He was still lost in thought about his meeting with Alberto as he turned the corner to take an alley shortcut to his hotel that he often used. Halfway through the alley, a man appeared out of the darkness. Paul immediately stopped, startled as he recognized Peter Schmidt. Schmidt immediately confronted him.

"So, *Herr* Hoffman, we meet again. I was wondering when you would show your face again so I could confront you about your lies regarding the allied invasion site!"

Paul saw that Schmidt was agitated but kept his cool even as his pulse raced. "*Herr* Schmidt, there's no need to make such an accusation. I passed on the information exactly as I saw it. I cannot account for the Allies' use of information."

"I don't believe you! Your duplicity resulted in the withholding of German forces, allowing the Allies to break out of the Normandy beachhead."

"I don't believe that's the case, Schmidt. The forces were withheld because Hitler made a poor judgment…and that action will cost Germany the war." Paul realized he was in a poor position to respond when Schmidt moved against him.

"So on top of your other sins you dare to insult the führer! You must realize that we cannot let your actions go unpunished."

Schmidt was reaching into his coat. Paul realized he might only have seconds to act as Schmidt continued, "It's time now for me to ensure you will not commit further treason."

Schmidt began pulling his weapon. Paul was about to leap forward to try to tackle Schmidt when a muffled shot came from behind him in the darkness. Schmidt's scowling expression instantly turned to one of surprise as he grasped his stomach with both hands and looked up in shock at Paul and then the alley.

The second shot hit Schmidt in the neck. He fell to his knees, dropping his gun, one hand clutching his stomach while the other grabbed his neck. He tried to scream, but only a low, inarticulate gurgling emanated from his throat as blood gushed out of his neck and mouth.

The third shot hit Schmidt in the forehead. He died instantly, keeling over backward and hitting the ground with a thud. The entire episode was over in seconds as Paul looked on in total surprise. Finally, he turned to see the source of the shots.

A man appeared out of the darkness carrying a pistol with a silencer. He walked slowly over, looked at Schmidt's body and then at Paul, who spoke first.

"Who are you?" Paul said in Spanish.

The man replied in English, "I'm a friend, Paul. Jack sent me to watch over you. We need to get out of here fast, but first I need to do something." The man quickly knelt down, pulled Schmidt's ID and wallet out, and grabbed the cash in the wallet, speaking as he did so.

"Our friends in the SS and BPS probably won't believe it's a robbery, but we might as well try to make it look like one."

Jack had previously briefed Paul that Franco's intelligence agency closely cooperated with the SS agents in Spain. Now he asked, "How did you know I was here? Have you been following me the entire time I've been in Madrid?"

"We can talk about all that later. Like I said, right now we've got to scram and I can't be sure it's safe for you to go back to your hotel."

They later went to an OSS safe house until the agent determined that Schmidt had probably acted alone. The following day Paul departed for Alabos.

53.

Ortega hacienda, Alabos, Spain
December 31, 1944

* * *

The entire Ortega clan, joined by Karl and Paul Hoffman, had gathered for a week to celebrate Christmas and the New Year. Tonight, a special feast was being prepared for New Year's Eve. Earlier in the week, the families had held a business meeting, which had included Anita and her husband for the first time. The two families agreed to continue pursuing acquisition of choice land throughout Spain for future vineyard development and to pursue an aggressive strategy to expand their sales of products from Spanish Guinea in America after the war. Paul also revealed his own news—he and Liz Kurtz were engaged.

Before dinner, Paul and Karl Hoffman met on the enclosed veranda, enjoying a glass of *manzanilla* in the waning sunlight of the cold late-December afternoon and discussing details of the wedding plans. The wedding would take place in Denver, where Liz's parents lived. Paul wanted the wedding held after the war so that his brothers could attend, and he wanted Hans to be his best man. Paul and Liz had discussed living arrangements but they knew that, although based out of New York, Paul would be traveling extensively all over the world in the family business. Liz planned to accompany him as much as possible and she would quit her job in New York to be able to do so.

As Paul and Karl concluded their discussion, Alberto Ortega entered the veranda. "Oh, excuse me, I must be interrupting."

Karl quickly replied, "No, no, Alberto, we were just finishing our discussion about Paul's wedding plans. Please come in. I need to talk with your father, so I will excuse myself and let you and Paul visit." Karl rose and left the veranda to find Ernesto Ortega.

Paul motioned for Alberto to sit and poured him a glass of sherry. The two men sat there for several moments in awkward silence. Finally, Paul spoke.

"It's good that we can all be here together, Alberto."

"Yes, and it's especially good to hear your news. I imagine your fiancée is a very special woman. You must be very happy."

"Yes, she is. I hope you'll get a chance to meet her."

Alberto nodded and there was again a silence before Paul continued, anxious to determine what was on Alberto's mind, "Is there a special woman in your life yet?"

Alberto looked up, surprised at the question, but he smiled and replied, "No, there isn't, although I have certainly met many charming women in Madrid." He paused, sighed, and continued. "I'm afraid my responsibilities, especially in the last five years, have kept me from finding the time for deeper relationships. My career has dominated my life."

Indeed, Alberto had just been promoted again, to *capitán de corbeta*, the equivalent of lieutenant commander. He was told that he needed to get back to sea duty to advance his career and he expected to be reassigned in about six months. Alberto enjoyed the work in naval intelligence, especially with the unique circumstances of his assignment and his role in serving the interests of his family as well as his country.

Paul replied, "It's easy to see how your career has consumed your available time. I'm especially grateful that you've supported me in my special circumstances."

"Yes, I'm happy we were able to collaborate." Alberto paused before finally saying what was on his mind. "It may interest you to know that our SS friend Peter Schmidt was murdered in Madrid last week. Although it was made to look like a robbery, the SS and BPS suspect it was for other reasons. They are combing the city for the perpetrator."

Paul almost didn't have to fake the look of surprise, as Alberto had caught him off guard. He quickly replied, "He was murdered? I guess that doesn't surprise me. He seemed so arrogant and confident. It was probably inevitable that it would catch up with him. Who do you think did it?"

"The location and method has the hallmark of an allied hit, probably the American OSS." He paused. "Of course that doesn't explain the why. Schmidt was a fairly low-level agent. There must have been another motive."

Paul realized the charade must continue in order to give them both continued cover. "Well, in any case, I won't have to worry about him anymore." He quickly changed subjects. "I have a feeling 1945 is going to be a momentous year for our families and our country. The world will be changed almost beyond recognition."

Alberto thought about that and replied, "I agree, and although the year may initially begin horribly for Europe and Spain, I hope we will lay the groundwork for a more promising future."

Paul raised his sherry glass. "I know that the future will be better. Here's to our families' fortunes and to the new year."

Part 3

* * *

Reckoning

1945

Götterdämmerung: 1945 – The world transformed

As the year began, Europe groaned under the weight of unparallel destruction and death. Germany buckled under the weight of the allied armies entering from the west as the unstoppable juggernaut of the Red Army pushed from the east. Unlike the First World War, millions of civilians had died and were still dying. In Germany, relentless allied strategic bombing was slowly reducing German cities to rubble. The shabby philosophy of Hitler's Third Reich aided in this destruction as die-hard Nazis sought to fight to the bitter end, regardless of the cost and suffering.

Also unlike the First World War, the social and economic structure was collapsing in all areas that the Red Army "liberated." Old estates and manors were destroyed as their owners fled for their lives before the Russian advances. The old feudal system collapsed and, following the Red Army's rape, plunder, and pillaging, interim governments dominated by the communist victors quickly replaced it.

As civilians and German armies retreated, the Third Reich tried desperately to perpetuate itself, first with the promise of secret weapons that could change the course of the war at the eleventh hour, and when that pipedream proved impossible, the leaders of the Third Reich sought their own desperate escape. As in the final part of Wagner's great opera "Götterdämmerung," the promise of Valhalla was tantalizing as a secret Nazi effort proceeded to try to preserve the legacy of the Third Reich.

Two families, the Hoffmans of Germany and the Ortegas of Spain, were again caught up in the maelstrom of war and economic upheaval. Thirty years previously, bonds of marriage had strengthened their existing relationships, and they prospered over time. This year, they would experience tragedy as well as rebirth. The paths of war and intrigue had caught up to several members of both families as events unfolded. Again, actions by these family members, in support of each other, would involve them in a Valhalla that they never could have imagined.

As the war came to a climax, it was clear that Germany would be devastated while Spain, still reeling from the effects of civil war, would be ostracized and isolated for its passive support of Germany. It would take a new war, a cold war, to change that.

Throughout these swirling events, the steady leadership of family members and their unbreakable bonds proved to be their salvation. The ties to the New World strengthened as the families' fate was increasingly drawn to its American element. A new generation of Hoffmans and Ortegas was beginning to assume leadership of family interests and, in turn, it would spawn the next generation to enter the postwar world.

As these events played out, however, the families' fate would be inextricably linked to the aftermath of the war and the lingering legacy of the German operation code named Valhalla. It would be dormant initially, but how the two families would escape its clutches only time would tell.

54.

Wehrmacht rocket test facility, Peenemunde, Germany
January 24, 1945

* * *

The ground shook as the A-9 rocket's motors ignited, and it stood there for a second as the smoke and flames spread from the bottom of the launch plat-form. Finally, the rocket lifted off smoothly and rapidly accelerated straight up for several more seconds before gradually tilting toward the east as it con-tinued to gain speed rapidly. Within less than a minute, the rocket was out of sight, leaving only the white streak of exhaust marking its trajectory. Within only a few more brief minutes the test was complete, as the rocket impacted several hundred miles east in the Baltic Sea, tracked all the way by both ships and land stations. In the control room, the staff was pleased with the results of the preliminary data. SS *Oberführer* Manfred Bruner, who proclaimed his satisfaction to the lead engineer, witnessed the test.

"That's excellent. You say there was only a partial fuel load on board. Tell me again, what would the range be, assuming a full fuel load and a guided trajectory without power?"

"*Herr Oberführer,* the range could be up to six thousand kilometers, but the key word is 'guided trajectory.' After the powered trajectory ends, the aerody-namic design will allow it to coast and then glide to its target. However, the current internal guidance system is not accurate enough to ensure it will hit its target, and our supplementary guidance strategy assumes a human pilot with midcourse corrections from U-boat radio guidance."

Bruner was impatient. "I understand all that. What I want to know is when you will be able to accommodate the human pilot and implement the U-boat guidance system."

"As you know, a conscious decision was made to keep the A-9 as a semi-covert program. Accordingly we have not coordinated this project with the navy. To accomplish the rest of the program and make the A-9 operational would take at least six to nine months. It will take at least three more months for the next A-9 test article to be ready to test the piloted version. As you

know, Peenemunde is now a target for allied bombers and…the Russians…"
The engineer's voice tailed off.

Bruner said nothing but merely stared into space as he contemplated the significance of the engineer's summary of the situation. He knew that time was his enemy, and unfortunately, time had run out for deploying a weapon of mass destruction, at least in this war. Finally, he replied, "Thank you for your candid assessment, *Herr Doktor*. Given what you said, I need for you to thoroughly document all of your work, data, and test results, and have this documentation completed no later than March 1."

After departing the test site, Bruner resolved to follow through on all the remaining elements in the operations plan, including leaving no trace of any of the key projects covered by Valhalla—or their human creators.

55

The Hoffman manor, west of Bromberg, West Prussia
January 30, 1945

* * *

Wilhelm von Hoffman sat in front of the roaring fire in the manor house, savoring the glass of 1893 *Trockenbeerenauslese,* or TBA, from the Hoffman Mosel estate in Bernkastel, Germany. He was in his full dress uniform as a *Generaloberst* in the German army. Even though he had retired nearly twenty-five years ago, the ninety-three-year-old Hoffman still stood erect, fit, and slim and could pass for someone twenty years younger.

Hoffman had also worn the uniform on the journey to the manor nearly two weeks ago, and it had enabled him to travel when no one other than the military was permitted to travel to areas near the Russian Front. In fact, the mere sight of Hoffman, resplendent with Iron Cross and other medals won during the 1870 Franco-Prussian War, was enough to intimidate any member of the *Wehrmacht.* At the final checkpoint, the *Wehrmacht* officer in charge pleaded with him to return to Bernkastel because of the imminent danger of the advancing Red Army. Hoffman ignored the officer. At his age, he had decided it was more important to be at his ancestral home, the home of generations of Hoffmans.

Wilhelm had sold off the entire estate, except for the manor house and some adjacent plots, years ago. The previous week he had dismissed his last servant and estate manager, urging them to flee west, ahead of the Russians. Wilhelm knew how the Russians, and maybe some Poles, would treat anyone suspected of serving the German aristocracy. The former Hoffman lands were near Bromberg, also known by its Polish name of Bydgoszcz. Poland had reclaimed the land occupied by the estate between the two world wars. Wilhelm knew that they would soon reclaim it again, enabled by both revenge and the advance of the Red Army. In fact, Wilhelm sensed that time was near and he was dressed for the occasion.

Wilhelm took another sip of the TBA, marveling at its silky texture and longevity. He had once predicted that the 1893 could last a century. There were a few more cases left, cellared at the Hoffman Bernkastel estate. He wondered who would be around to taste it in 1993. He hoped that his thirteen-year-old granddaughter, Kirsten, might have that honor. She already showed an interest in viticulture and was likely to play a role in the vineyards' future.

Wilhelm also thought about his two sons and three grandsons. At least Karl and Paul would survive the war. He hoped that Walter, Hans, and Ernst would also but had a premonition that their fate would be more complicated. Wilhelm always tried not to dwell on the past. As to the future, he could only hope that the survivors of this war would learn from their mistakes and prevent it from happening again. Wilhelm had seen Germany fight three wars in his lifetime and knew that the aftermath of this one would change everything.

At that moment, Wilhelm could hear vehicles approaching. He took one last sip of TBA, savored it, and put the glass down. He got up and walked slowly to near the main door of the manor, picked up his favorite high-power hunting rifle, and chambered a round.

The noise outside increased and now included much shouting. Wilhelm moved toward the wall facing the door and raised his rifle.

The door shook as it was slammed from the outside. Finally, it burst open and the Russian soldier rushed in, looked right and then left. He had only a millisecond to contemplate the view down the barrel of the weapon before Wilhelm fired. His aim was dead-on as the shot from only two meters blew the left side of the soldier's head off and he crumpled to the floor, dead. Wilhelm pumped the action on the rifle to chamber the next round as the next Russian soldier entered. He too was careless, and as he raised his assault rifle, Wilhelm again fired, hitting the soldier in the chest and killing him instantly. Wilhelm tried to chamber another round but the next Russian soldier was prepared, jumping into the room in a crouch and firing at once. Though hit, Wilhelm continued to raise his rifle. At that instant the fourth Russian, an officer, who entered behind the soldier, shot him. Wilhelm reeled, keeled over, and died, his last conscious thought being of his two sons.

As he motioned for the firing to stop, the Russian officer slowly approached Wilhelm's body. He looked down at Wilhelm, in full dress uniform, looked up and around at the manor, the fireplace, and the empty bottle of wine. He then looked back down at Wilhelm and shook his head. *What motivates these Prussians and their Nazi heirs?* He thought. *Will we have to exterminate them all to rid Europe of their influence?* He shook his head again, turned, and slowly walked out the door.

56.

Bata, Rio Muni, Spanish Guinea
February 1945

* * *

Karl Hoffman sat outdoors at the small café early in the morning, sipping coffee and enjoying the letter from Paul that arrived yesterday. He missed his two other sons desperately, but neither Hans nor Ernst had written from Germany in nearly three months. Karl thought about his two oldest sons, but just at that moment, he heard a man call his name, in German. He turned, looked at the stranger, surprised to hear German, and finally responded.

"Excuse me, did you call my name?"

"Yes, *Herr* Hoffman. I'm Gerhard Hoepner, the new economic attaché at the German consulate in Fernando Po. I have letters from your sons and brother in Germany."

Karl was stunned. Could he be dreaming? Was this a cruel hoax? "I'm sorry, but please do not joke with me."

"It's not a prank, *Herr* Hoffman. The letters are real. May I sit down and join you?"

Karl motioned for Hoepner to sit down. "I'm sorry, *Herr* Hoepner, but you are taking me completely by surprise."

"I understand that and I'm sorry, but I didn't know how else to do it. I'll give you the two letters from your sons and ask you to read them after our meeting, so that you may have privacy. For now, I would ask you to read Walter's letter while I'm here. In addition, I have another letter from your nephew, Alberto Ortega, and a copy of a directive for the governor. I ask you to read these now, for you will undoubtedly have questions for me afterward."

Completely puzzled by the conversation, Karl nevertheless began reading the letters and documents. As he read them, his expression turned from puzzlement, to shock, to curiosity as he absorbed the content and tried to make sense of it. For several more minutes he continued to read and reread the letters. He focused on key names, terms, and events: Operation Valhalla... storage of documents...a rendezvous with a U-boat. Finally, he finished the letters. It all seemed so fantastic. Karl had spent most of the war in Spanish Guinea, and although he tried to keep informed, his isolation from the events in Europe made all of this unreal. Finally, he looked up.

"You are correct, *Herr* Hoepner, I have many questions. But my main question is whether this far-fetched scheme will ever take place, and when."

"Valhalla was only a contingency plan, but I'm afraid the latest situation in Germany makes it likely that it will be carried out, probably in the next couple of months. As your brother explained, Valhalla is crucial to Germany's future, if the Allies occupy it. You have an important role in securing that future and we need your help."

Karl thought about that for a moment. He was still not sure about this. Perhaps he would need to talk to the governor. He looked at Walter's letter again, hesitated, but finally decided what to do. "All right, *Herr* Hoepner, I will tentatively cooperate with you, pending a discussion with the governor in Fernando Po. Have preparations for the operation been started?"

"Yes, in Germany of course, but they have also begun here. The governor has ordered that some minor improvements be made in the remote landing at the mouth of the River Mbia, as well as to several roads leading from there to your plantation."

Karl thought about this answer, realizing that the colonial government and at least the Spanish navy high command had approved. "All right, *Herr* Hoepner, we will have further discussions after I meet with the governor late tomorrow. For now, you must excuse me since I have two letters from my sons that I must read."

Hoepner stood. "Very well. I'm taking the morning boat to Santa Isabel tomorrow. I'll see you the next day, after your meeting."

* * *

Later that evening, after Karl returned to the Rio Muni plantation, he pondered the meeting with Hoepner, trying to pin down the potential ramifications of the Valhalla operation. Karl knew that he would not be privy to certain elements of the operation and he didn't want to support the dying gasps of the Nazi regime. Yet both Hoepner and Walter, in his letter, had implied that Walter and Hans had completely immersed themselves in the operation. He also said that Guinea was the only place available for the Valhalla cargo, and that Karl's cooperation was essential to enable the discreet storage of the cargo in Rio Muni. Furthermore, the Spanish government and the governor had acquiesced with the plan. Even more importantly, Karl also realized that there was danger lurking inside this operation, danger that he could not precisely pin down. He realized that Walter and Hans were both on the hook now, for better or worse.

As Karl ordered the Spartan to be prepared for his short flight tomorrow to Santa Isabel, he resolved to do a little checking on his own with the governor's staff before his meeting.

57.

Cologne, Germany
March 2, 1945

* * *

Erica Hoffman hurried through the streets of Cologne. She had left her daughter, Kirsten, in the safety of the famous Cologne Cathedral, the Dom, and was racing to reach the residence of Freya Hoffman's mother, a few blocks away. The three women had left Wilhelmshaven two days ago, trying to get to the Hoffman estate in Bernkastel on the Mosel River. Erica's husband, Walter, and Freya's husband, Hans, had both agreed that Wilhelmshaven was no longer safe for them because of the allied bombing. In fact, no city in Germany was safe, although Cologne had not been bombed in several months.

As she walked swiftly through the streets in the waning light, Erica worried about Freya, who was four months pregnant. Erica was also worried that Freya would not leave her mother, who was ill, to accompany Erica and Kirsten to Bernkastel. They had valid travel documents, issued by Walter, whose status as a *Vizeadmiral* in the German navy guaranteed that they would be authorized passage to Bernkastel if they could find transport. The entire Rhine River valley, including its rail lines and roads, was in chaos as German troops and civilians tried to escape the allied armies just a short distance to the west.

Erica finally reached the house where Freya's mother lived. As expected, Freya did not want to leave, even though her mother urged her to do so. As the night wore on, they discussed their plans. Finally, a little before 11:00 p.m., as Erica was preparing to return to the Dom, there was a knock on the door. Both Freya and Erica opened the door, and a uniformed police officer excitedly started talking.

"You must all evacuate the house immediately. There may be another allied air raid tonight. May I see your papers, please?"

Erica quickly produced their identity papers, including the travel authorization from Walter Hoffman. The officer quickly reviewed the documents before speaking.

"Very well, I see that three of you are authorized to travel. You must pack immediately. I will return in thirty minutes to escort you to the train station near the Dom. There will probably not be any rail transport operating, but you may be able to get a ride in a lorry south to Koblenz." With that comment, the officer excused himself and raced to his next stop, carrying a copy of the Hoffmans' travel authorization.

Erica and Freya spent the next ten minutes debating what to do, since Freya's mother was too ill to travel and not authorized to do so. As they continued their discussion, the silence outside was broken as the air raid sirens started. The two women looked at each other. Finally, Freya spoke.

"We must go upstairs to the bedroom and help my mother get down to the basement! We may only have a few minutes!"

The two women raced upstairs and found Freya's mother having a coughing session. Freya raced to find her mother's clothes as Erica consoled the older woman.

In their frenzy, Erica and Freya could not hear the drone of the steadily approaching British bombers over the noise of the air raid sirens. Finally, they got Freya's mother out of bed and started to move her slowly to the stairs.

They were nearly down to the main floor when the lead bomber in the 858 plane raid released its bombs, followed quickly by the other aircraft. The three women barely had time to notice the sound of the progressive explosions when the house received a direct hit from a four thousand-pound "blockbuster" dropped by one of the first aircraft. The bomb had a contact fuse, yet penetrated the thin roof before exploding just a few meters away from the women. As the bomb exploded, the three women were instantly incinerated and the house and adjacent properties exploded into a fireball. Mercifully, there was not even enough time to experience either fear or pain.

Hours later, the officer returned to the location of the house to find only smoldering ruins and a crater. He shook his head. They would not make it to Bernkastel, he thought. He then quickly raced to the next block.

It was the last air raid of the war for Cologne. Throughout the raid, as in previous raids, the magnificent Dom stood, unscathed, spared by the allied bombers.

58.

Navy ministry, Berlin, Germany
March 5, 1945

* * *

Hans Hoffman made his final trip to Berlin, to brief Walter Hoffman on the final training cruise of the Type 21 U-boat, U-3696. Yesterday Walter had notified SS *Oberführer* Bruner that they had achieved their deadline and the U-boat was operational. It was currently at a secret anchorage in Denmark, awaiting Hans's return, with the first watch officer temporarily in command. Walter and Hans were completing the operational planning for the pending Valhalla operation. Hans summarized his recommendations.

"I don't think we should stay long in the current anchorage in Denmark. The risk of discovery is too high. This boat is so quiet underwater, it is actually safer to be out at sea rather than risk being caught by allied bombers. I would like permission to make a short operational cruise, two weeks or so, to check the equipment and fuel consumption one last time and reposition the boat to our final operations base in Western Jutland in Denmark, where we can provision and top off fuel."

Walter thought about that briefly. "All right, that makes sense. I have a hunch that with the deteriorating situation on both fronts, we may receive the order to execute Valhalla, Phase 2 in a matter of days or at most a few weeks. Since we need to get to the operational base, you should do so at once. I'll try to pry some information out of Bruner and let you know if I hear anything."

The two men were about to continue their planning when someone knocked at the door. Walter had left orders for them not to be disturbed. He was about to call his adjutant but instead buzzed the door lock to open it. His adjutant entered, walked over to the desk, and came to attention. Walter looked at him, noticing a look he had never seen before.

"What is it, Sigmund? You look like you've seen a ghost."

The man hesitated, finally getting his voice, and raising his hand, which had an envelope. "*Herr Vizeadmiral,* I have a message from *Grossadmiral* Doenitz. It is marked 'urgent, personal, and confidential.'" The man gingerly put the message down on the desk. "Please excuse me, *Herr Vizeadmiral.*" He quickly saluted, turned, and left the office, closing the door securely behind him.

Walter and Hans looked at each other, puzzled by Sigmund's behavior. Finally, Walter reached for the envelope, slowly opened it, and began reading. Hans watched as his uncle's expression turned to one of horror. He did not speak as he closed his eyes and a tear began to form as he handed the message to Hans. Hans read the message and then dropped it to the floor, placing his hands over his eyes.

For the longest time, neither man spoke, absorbed by the horror of the message and their own private thoughts. Finally, Hans spoke, sobbing.

"Poor Freya, she was terrified by the bombings! Erica and Kirsten too! How can this be? Is there no mercy left in the world?" He continued to sob, lost of further words.

Walter did not reply. He finally opened his eyes, looked at Hans, and realized what it had all come down to. Their family was at the blunt end of a brutal war and their own situation was tragically unfolding. He had not told Hans yet, but two days ago he had received word that his grandfather had traveled to the family estate in West Prussia more than a month ago and had not been heard from since. The Russians had overrun the area a month ago. He could only hope that Ernst was still alive, as he had been transferred to a fighter group operating new jet aircraft.

Walter did not know what to say to Hans, married only two years and expecting to be a father in a few months. *What of my own beloved Erica and Kirsten?* He thought. He closed his eyes again and clenched his fist to fight the pain and tears that he could not control. During all of the years that he and Erica had been together, she had followed him without question, and yet he could not protect her and Kirsten in the end.

Walter forced his eyes open and slowly rose, walking over to Hans, who was still sobbing. He never saw Hans express much emotion, and now it was just overpowering. Walter hardly knew what to do, but knew he must be a rock now. He approached Hans, reached his arms around him, and hugged him. Hans reached his arms around Walter and the two men embraced each other, lost in their sorrow.

59.

Mosel River Valley, east of Bernkastel, Germany
March 13, 1945

* * *

Kirsten Hoffman had slowly made her way toward the Hoffman estate in Bernkastel since leaving Cologne several days ago. By taking refuge in the Cologne Cathedral, she was spared the fate of her mother and Freya. In the mass confusion following the bombing, she had learned of their deaths but also that she was also presumed dead. Nevertheless, she held a copy of the order authorizing her to travel to Bernkastel. Although only thirteen, Kirsten, despite her sorrow, had talked her way onto a ferry to cross the Rhine, since all the bridges had been bombed. From there, she was picked up by a German army column, including many civilians, that was traveling south down the east bank of the Rhine. When she got to Koblenz, she slipped away from the column and began making her way up the Mosel valley toward Bernkastel. Along the way, several families sheltered and fed her.

On this day, Kirsten knew she was close to Bernkastel. While she had seen a few German soldiers the day before, she saw none today as she walked through a small village just northeast of Bernkastel. In fact, the village seemed deserted and very quiet. As she rounded a corner at the end of the street, she froze—there were soldiers there and they were not German.

One of the soldiers spotted her. Corporal Frank Williams, U.S. Army, shouted at his squad leader, Staff Sergeant Ken Sherman. "Hey, Sarge, it looks like we finally found someone." Williams pointed at Kirsten.

Sherman looked up, saw Kirsten, and started walking toward her. Kirsten froze, not knowing whether to run, then realizing it might be safer to stand her ground. Sherman walked over, smiled, leaned over, and spoke. "Hello, where are you going?"

Kirsten shook her head. Sherman turned to speak to Williams. "Go find the guy in the other squad who speaks German, what's his name?"

"Hoffman, I'll go get him." Williams disappeared and returned with Max Hoffman within a couple of minutes.

Sherman gave him direction. "Find out her name and where she's going."

Max Hoffman smiled at Kirsten and spoke in a low, soothing voice in accented German. "Good morning, my name is Max Hoffman. What's your name and where are you going this morning?"

Kirsten's eyes lit up and she smiled weakly. "My name is Hoffman too, Kirsten Hoffman. I'm trying to get back to my home in Bernkastel. My mother was killed last week in a bombing raid in Cologne. My father is in the navy and I can't reach him. Our family owns a vineyard in Bernkastel. I'll be safe there with our housekeepers. Will you please help me get there?"

Hoffman repeated the answer to Sherman and added his own comment. "Let's take her there. Bernkastel is only three clicks away and we already know it's clean."

Sherman mulled that over as Williams added his own two cents. "Yeah, let's take her there, Sarge. We got a jeep; it will only take a few minutes. She looks tired and hungry."

"All right, tell her to come with us." Within twenty minutes they were in the jeep driving down the road and, with directions from Kirsten, arrived at the Hoffman estate. They knocked on the door and soon the door cracked open. Eric Diehl looked at the American soldier, looked down, and shouted out in delight.

"Kirsten, thank God, we've been so worried!" He turned and shouted into the house. "Hannah, come here quickly, it's Kirsten!"

Within seconds Kirsten, Eric, and Hannah were locked in a thankful embrace as they wept for joy.

Sherman spoke to his other two soldiers. "All right, guys, let's get back to business, we need to get back to the unit."

60

Over Munich, Germany
April 2, 1945

* * *

Ernst Hoffman and his wingman ripped through the American fighter formation and then into the bomber formation at the lower altitude. Flying the Me-262 jet fighters, they quickly each dispatched a P-51 fighter and then the two jets' powerful cannons also destroyed two B-17 bombers. They were at least 100 mph faster than the P-51 and under normal conditions could have easily escaped or positioned themselves for another attack. Today, however, Ernst would not be so lucky.

As he pulled out of his dive, the airplane shuddered as the left Jumo 004 engine failed, an all too common occurrence with the new advanced technology. His squadron was only getting ten to fifteen hours of life out of each engine. As he compensated for the asymmetric thrust with his right rudder, the jet quickly slowed. His wingman pulled ahead quickly and was not in a position to protect Ernst. However, the American P-51s, being much faster than the crippled jet with one engine out, quickly closed the distance, out for blood.

Ernst dived, racing for the ground and hoping to outdistance the Americans. A successful bailout from a Me-262 was unlikely and his only hope was to try and evade and quickly land. Unfortunately, it was not to be. The American fighters split into two groups, one to deal with Ernst's wingman. The other group quickly closed to within firing range. Ernst began maneuvering to avoid the Americans, but the P-51 could outmaneuver the Me-262 once the latter lost its speed advantage.

As Ernst desperately tried to avoid the fighters, a P-51 locked onto his tail and began firing, its six .50 caliber machine guns scoring hits on the jet. Ernst tried to maneuver out of the line of fire, but the American quickly compensated while two other fighters blocked any escape route if Ernst attempted to roll off either left or right.

It was now too late to attempt a bailout. Ernst realized what the outcome would be and what he must now do. He rolled off violently to the left one last time and as the American turned to regain the position, Ernst rolled right, back into the American's line of fire. The American fighter saw what might happen and did just the wrong thing by attempting to pull up out of the way. Ernst anticipated the American's move and used his remaining speed to pull up into a zoom right in front of the P-51.

As the Me-262 filled the view in his canopy, the American pulled back hard on the stick in a desperate evasion attempt. Ernst had also anticipated that and turned directly into the American fighter. Its pilot pulled back even harder on the stick, horrified at what was about to happen. The P-51 shuddered under the impending accelerated stall, but a split second before the P-51 would have stalled and flipped over, Ernst's jet slammed into it and both aircraft exploded in a gigantic fireball, instantly killing both pilots.

It was Ernst's eightieth and final victory.

61.

Navy ministry, Berlin, Germany
April 3, 1945

* * *

Walter Hoffman received the order to execute Operation Valhalla, Phase 2, effective on April 6. He quickly made final preparations before departing from Berlin for Flensburg, just south of the Danish border. He and SS *Oberführer* Bruner had agreed to meet there before moving the Valhalla cargo to the secret anchorage in Denmark where U-3696 would be waiting. The cargo was being moved by night in two large trucks, and Bruner was furious that Walter had not disclosed the location of the U-boat anchorage, the storage location for the cargo in Spanish Guinea, or the final destination for U-3696 after leaving the Valhalla cargo in Guinea. Walter had claimed he was merely trying to maintain security and would provide the information to Bruner upon meeting him in Flensburg.

As Walter completed final preparations, his adjutant rang him on the intercom.

"Yes, Sigmund, what is it?"

"*Herr Vizeadmiral*, I have a call from *Generalleutnant* Steiner, *Luftwaffe* Munich operations command."

Walter had known Steiner for some time, since they were both in the intelligence field and had cooperated on a regular basis. Walter felt uneasy as he picked up the phone and had Steiner connected.

"Hello, Steiner, this is Hoffman. How may I help you today? I'm a little busy preparing for an upcoming operation."

"Yes, Hoffman, I understand and I'm sorry to bother you, but I'm afraid I have some news of a personal nature."

Walter momentarily froze. "Yes, Steiner, what is it?"

"I deeply regret to inform you that your nephew, Ernst, was killed yesterday on an operational mission and died a hero's death. The details, including an additional Knight's Cross Award for gallantry, will be forwarded. I'm sorry,

Walter, to bear this news, but I wanted to talk to you personally rather than have it come through normal channels."

Walter covered his eyes, holding back a tear, and composed himself before he replied. "Thank you, Steiner; that was kind of you. I realize you must be under enormous pressure."

"Yes, but we are doing our best. By the way, I could not find a contact for his parents."

"His mother is deceased and his father is…not in Germany…at this time. I will see to that. Thank you." After hanging up, Walter wondered how he would break this news to Hans—and to Karl. It was one more tragedy in the unraveling of their lives.

62.

A cove on the Western Jutland coast, Denmark
April 5, 1945

* * *

It was 4:00 a.m. as Hans and his crew finished fueling and provisioning U-3696 and completed adjustments after its final shakedown. They also tried to camouflage the U-boat, knowing it would be exposed for the rest of the day, until the Valhalla cargo was due to arrive after dark. Fortunately, there was a low overcast that might inhibit allied air reconnaissance. Hans was also worried about discovery from the Danish resistance and wanted to depart the cove the next morning on the high tide for the Valhalla mission.

With preparations complete, Hans departed the cove for the two and a half-hour drive to Flensburg, where he would meet Walter Hoffman and hopefully the Valhalla cargo. He left U-3696 in the care of his trusted first watch officer. Hans selected several key crew members to accompany him and had secretly arranged for a special navy security team at the Flensburg base. Walter and Hans knew what was likely to happen and what they had to prepare for.

During the drive, for the first time, Hans had time to mull over what had happened to him over the last month. His sorrow seemed overwhelming, having lost Freya and their unborn child. He hoped he would see his father in Spanish Guinea but realized that reunion would be all too brief. With the chaos in Germany, he had not received a letter from him in over six months. Hans wondered what other events would affect their lives.

63

Across the cove from U-3696, one hour later
April 5, 1945

* * *

Danish army Captain Oluf Pederson stared intently through his binoculars at the moored U-boat across the small cove. He stayed in a low crouch, partially hidden by the reeds on the opposite shore as he observed the activity on and near the U-boat in the early predawn hours. Pederson had made his way to the cove after another resistance member had spotted the U-boat entering the cove at dusk last night.

Pederson had fought in the brief one-day skirmish in April 1940 when Germany occupied Denmark, and he and several of the men in his company were wounded. Since the initial battle had not been too brutal, Germany allowed a small cadre of the Danish army to remain on duty after the occupation. That changed in 1943, when the Germans forced the de-mobilization of the rest of the Danish military. At that point, Pederson joined the resistance. His major activity that year had been to help the famous Danish physicist Niels Bohr escape to Sweden, to avoid the Nazi dragnet.

Pederson wondered what a U-boat was doing at this location, which the Germans had not used before. It could be that, as the war wound down, the Germans were trying to disperse their vessels to avoid their destruction from allied air raids. His intuition, however, told him that something more important was going on here. He decided to take a chance, stake out the area, and radio the sighting to the Danish resistance contact in London, although that would expose his team to more risk.

64

Flensburg, Germany
April 5, 1945

* * *

Hans had arrived at the temporary base at Flensburg at 7:00 a.m. Now he and Walter Hoffman were discussing the impending arrival of the Valhalla cargo and the accompanying SS escort. The SS convoy was traveling mostly at night and they were due to arrive any minute. Upon Hans's arrival, he and Walter had to take shelter as they suffered an unexpected air attack by American P-47 aircraft. The attack had not killed or wounded any of Walter's naval team but had set a barracks on fire. They should be immune from attack for a while since a heavy fog had rolled in. Walter summarized the situation.

"I believe we're ready for Bruner's arrival. I've deployed forty men, hidden at strategic places in the compound. When Bruner arrives, some of the men will offer to help Bruner's men secure the Valhalla cargo temporarily until we can depart."

"That's good, Uncle. I believe we have anticipated every possibility."

There was a knock at the door and Sigmund Breyer, Walter's adjutant, entered and saluted. "They are here, *Herr Vizeadmiral.* Our men are initiating the process as planned."

"Thank you, Breyer. Hans, you had best get in position yourself." Hans looked back at him. Walter reassured him. "Don't worry, Hans, I know what to do."

Within a few minutes, there was another knock at the door, and without waiting for an answer, *Oberführer* Bruner entered, accompanied by an SS trooper with a slung machine pistol.

Walter rose from his desk, which was covered by various papers. "Good morning, Bruner. I see you're on schedule." Walter noted that Bruner was carrying a large suitcase with him that he carefully sheltered.

Bruner glared at him. "Yes, Hoffman, we are on schedule, and it's now time for you to disclose the location of the U-boat, the storage location in Spanish Guinea, and the final destination you have selected after the Valhalla cargo is deposited there. You must reveal the exact location of the storage site in Guinea. You have only vaguely described it as being 'a secure place.' I demand to know where you will store these vital materials!"

"Of course, *Herr* Bruner; first, as you can see on this top chart, we have located the U-boat in a small cove north of here." Walter pointed to the location as Bruner approached to examine the chart.

Walter continued, bringing up a second map of the South Atlantic Ocean, "Here is where we will sail after departing Guinea. It's a remote location, from which point the crew can continue by land to their ultimate destination."

Bruner glared at him again. "I see. In selecting a dispersal location without consulting me, contrary to my orders, you have exceeded your authority, possibly jeopardizing the entire Valhalla operation!"

At that moment, three additional men entered the room behind the existing guard. Bruner took only a split second to look out of the corner of his eye to note the three additional SS uniforms and then looked back at Walter and continued. "For exceeding your authority, the Gestapo has ordered your arrest! *Gruppenführer* Muller himself signed the warrant. You will pay the penalty for not complying with my orders!"

Walter's agents had already informed him about the warrant and that Heinrich Muller, the Gestapo chief, now had a lead role in overseeing Operation Valhalla. He anticipated this, though, and he waited for his own plan to unfold.

As the front guard started to raise his machine pistol and move toward Walter, two of the men behind the guard jumped him. They caught him by surprise, and quickly tackled and subdued him. Bruner, also taken by surprise, quickly recovered and tried to reach for his pistol. Walter had anticipated that and was faster, retrieving a Walther PPK pistol from beneath a chart, raising the pistol and pointing it at Bruner. "Do not reach for your weapon, Bruner!"

Bruner froze. He finally removed his hands from his holster.

At that moment, Hans entered the office and greeted his three men, who had donned SS uniforms to complete the deception. Walter smiled while continuing to look straight at Bruner. "Hans, your timing was perfect. What about the rest of the group? Did your men suffer any injuries?"

"They are fine. One man suffered a minor injury only. We took them completely by surprise. They were arrogant to believe that with only twenty men they could dominate more than forty of us."

Bruner finally recovered from his shock. "What is the meaning of this outrage? You will all be shot for treason!"

Walter continued pointing his PPK at Bruner. "I think not, *Herr* Bruner. You may safely assume that your personal reign of terror is finally over. You and your SS thugs are finished, although Germany will pay the ultimate price for your crimes."

"You will not get away with this! I will see that—" Bruner stopped in midsentence as the shot from Walter's PPK penetrated Bruner's head right into his open mouth. He instantly collapsed to the floor.

Walter walked around the desk, looked at Bruner's body, and then up at Hans. Placing his PPK back in its holster, he sighed and finally spoke. "Let's see what he has in that suitcase."

Walter quickly found the key to the suitcase in Bruner's pocket and opened it. The contents were quite shocking.

"Hans, look at all this cash." Walter quickly determined that there was at least one hundred thousand dollars in American currency. The other contents were of even more interest.

"Here's the inventory book and extra copies of the Valhalla orders." Walter carefully examined another document as Hans looked over his shoulder. Walter quickly recognized its purpose.

"Hans, these are Swiss bank account numbers and instructions on how to access the accounts." Walter read from the accompanying memo. "It says that anytime a withdrawal is made, a notice will automatically be sent to this address in Asuncion, Paraguay, notifying the recipient of the amount and who withdrew it."

Both men looked at each other. Hans finally spoke. "We can figure this out later. We need to get moving now."

"You're right. Let's get rid of these bodies. You know what to do with them."

"Yes, and we have a better disposal method. We'll place them in the barracks still burning from the air raid. When they are discovered, it will initially look like they were killed in the raid. By the time they find out what really happened, we will be long gone. Those of our men who are not traveling with us on the U-boat already have good alibis for their locations on this day. They won't be able to implicate anyone other than us."

"Yes, it looks like we may be outcasts for a while, but probably not that long. I would be surprised if the regime lasts another month." Both men knew that the Russians were approaching Berlin and that the western front had collapsed as the allied armies penetrated deep into Germany.

Hans replied, "We better finish up what we need to do here and get the trucks moving while we still have the cover from the fog and low overcast. We absolutely need to catch the high tide tomorrow morning at 0400 and get out of that cove."

As Hans was about to join the men taking Bruner's body out and to complete the disposition of the other SS men, Walter stopped him. "Hans, I need to talk to you about Ernst."

"Yes, I was worried about him also. After what we've done, it's possible they'll take reprisals against him. I wish now we had planned to bring him with us."

"Hans, it won't be necessary to worry about that, I'm afraid."

Hans looked at him, and his expression changed, quickly realizing what Walter was saying. He clenched his fist and closed his eyes. "When did it happen?"

"Three days ago." Walter proceeded to relate the details that he knew.

"So it's just you and me now. Our entire family in Germany—Grandfather, Ernst, Erica, Kirsten, Freya, and…" Hans's voice trailed off as he could not bear mentioning his unborn child, lost when Freya died. "To what end were they sacrificed?"

"I can't answer that, Hans. All I know is that all we have left to hope for is outside of Germany…or contained in those trucks."

Hans was silent for a moment. He finally replied, "Do you really think the Valhalla cargo will be important for Germany's future? Will it be important for a Germany that is devastated and about to be occupied?"

"It may be, Hans. We must now try to protect it, in the event that it is important."

Hans finally nodded. "All right, we have nothing to lose. Let's proceed as planned."

65.

A cove on the Western Jutland coast, Denmark
April 6, 1945

* * *

Walter and Hans completed loading and final preparations for getting underway in U-3696 and reviewed their route and other aspects of their plan.

"We'll traverse the North Sea and break out into the North Atlantic between the Shetlands and the Faroes," Hans summarized. "We'll only need to snorkel once in those five days."

Walter replied, "Excellent. We'll soon see how well a Type 21 can evade allied antisubmarine detection." He paused. "What about that resistance fighter?"

"When we spotted him, he made a run for it. We had to fire."

Walter nodded, looked up at the clearing sky to the west, and then turned to Hans. "They will be conducting reconnaissance flights soon."

The first watch officer interrupted them. "We are ready, *Herr Kapitän.*"

Hans looked at Walter; he nodded back. "Let's get moving."

Within an hour, U-3696 departed, reached deeper water, and submerged, just before sunrise. The first allied aircraft flew over the now empty cove about thirty minutes later.

66.

German embassy, Madrid, Spain
April 11, 1945

* * *

The two SS-RHSA agents, one a Gestapo operative, were discussing two messages they had received, one activating Operation Valhalla, Phase 2 and the second containing detailed instructions on a number of subjects from Gestapo Chief Heinrich Muller. They also reviewed the status of their agent network in Spain and the increasing undercover presence of the American OSS, which had deeply penetrated the RHSA agent network and resulted in the sudden killing of several agents in the last four months, including Peter Schmidt. The lead agent expressed his concerns.

"We've lost our ability to function clandestinely, thanks to aggressive action by the Americans. Our Spanish friends in the BPS agree with us that the Americans murdered Schmidt. I strongly suspect it was related to his work with Paul Hoffman."

The other agent agreed. "Yes, that's true. It's certain that Hoffman is a double agent. We must also consider that Walter and Hans Hoffman may be a part of this conspiracy because of hearing about the arrest warrants issued on them. We also have the SS and BPS files on Karl Hoffman. The treasonous acts of this family severely jeopardize the success of Valhalla. We must also conclude that they were assisted by Alberto Ortega."

The lead agent concluded, "Yes, it's clear we must take corrective actions once the Valhalla cargo is deposited in Spanish Guinea. We also need to take action on Paul Hoffman and Ortega. I'll issue the necessary orders right away before we run out of time. We also need to implement the special instructions from *Gruppenführer* Muller."

67.

Greenwich Village, New York
April 13, 1945

* * *

Paul Hoffman and Jack Kurtz sat at their usual out-of-the-way table at the San Remo. Their mood, as well as that of most of America, was subdued. President Franklin Roosevelt had died suddenly the previous day and America was mourning, even as victory in the European war was near and American forces drew ever closer to final victory over Japan. Jack commiserated as he downed another beer.

"Boy, the old man was tight with the president. They went to law school together. It was his connection with Roosevelt that got the OSS going, against all the bureaucratic odds." The "old man" Jack was referring to was his boss, William "Wild Bill" Donovan, a decorated World War I hero and the head of the OSS.

"Does that mean the OSS might be in trouble now?" Paul responded.

"I think it will be when the war ends, regardless of who is president. We can already see the signs that there will be a massive and rapid demobilization. Americans are impatient and they've had more than three years of war and they're ready for it to end, regardless of what it takes."

"I guess I see your point, but in Spain we've been in a state of war, turmoil, and upheaval for fifteen years. It's harder to understand impatience after three years."

"I hear you, buddy. Welcome to America." Jack paused and looked at Paul, seeing that something else was troubling him. "Unless I'm off base, you've got something else on your mind...I think."

"Jack, you have an uncanny way of reading my mind." Paul paused as he too downed the last of his beer. "I'm worried about my entire family in Germany. I haven't heard from them in many months. I'm also concerned that Alberto may be in some danger, after my little incident in December with Schmidt. He was taking a chance by staying in contact with me."

"Alberto had guts to do that, for sure. He's also streetwise though, so he'll probably be OK."

"I'm not so sure. Alberto is in solid with the Spanish navy, but they're arrayed against the SS, the BPS, and even the army, in the espionage game."

Jack realized he had a point. "All right, you've convinced me. I'll make sure we have a little 'guardian angel' look over Alberto's shoulder for the next several months. I'll also see what I can find out about your family."

"Thanks, Jack. I'll be glad when this is over so I can find my brothers."

68.

Madrid, Spain
April 21, 1945

* * *

Alberto Ortega returned home from the office in the Spanish navy ministry, where he had spent Saturday catching up on reports and other paperwork. The office was quiet and he was pleased with what he had accomplished. He now looked forward to a glass of sherry or two and a relaxed evening.

Alberto's apartment was on a peaceful street in a small building with only one other apartment. It was especially quiet today as the other tenant was gone for a couple of weeks. Alberto reached his apartment entrance, which was in the rear of the building, and reached to unlock the door. He turned the key. Strange, he thought, as he noticed the door was unlocked. Could he have forgotten to lock it in the morning?

Alberto's instincts took over. He whipped the door open, ducking as he did so, and reached for the revolver in his briefcase. As he ducked, he was rewarded with the shattered glass from the door's window as the first bullet whizzed by. He quickly rolled out of the door outside and reached for his revolver. He got up, raced several paces, and turned to return fire when another shot came, this one from a different weapon, one with a silencer. As Alberto raised his pistol toward the door, a man staggered out, clutching his chest and gasping for air, having dropped his pistol in the doorway. The man paused, pain etched in his face, looked at Alberto, and then collapsed face forward to the ground.

Alberto held his ground, both hands holding his pistol, still pointing at the man's body, when another man emerged from Alberto's right in the deepening twilight. The man spoke quietly in Spanish as he lowered his pistol and raised his left hand to signify that the event was over.

"That was a good move, ducking as you opened the door. I wasn't sure how I was going to get at him otherwise."

"Thank you, my friend, whoever you are. I owe you my life."

"Actually, with the action you took, I think you would have done all right. In any case, I'm glad I could help. The guy I work for is a good friend of Paul Hoffman, and Paul's the one who insisted we should check in on you."

Alberto smiled. "I see. Are you the one that aided Paul in December?" The man nodded. "I will wager that you work for Jack Kurtz." The man hesitated then nodded again.

"Then Paul and I are both indebted to you—and to Mr. Kurtz." Alberto paused. "I wonder who this man worked for. He could be from the SS, BPS, or even a disgruntled army officer."

"Yes, it seems Spain has become a dangerous place."

Alberto nodded and sighed. "Well, let's figure out what to do with the body."

69.

North Atlantic Ocean, northwest of the Azores, night of
April 21–22, 1945

* * *

Hans had just relieved his first watch officer. The U-boat had been at sea sixteen days since leaving Denmark and had remained submerged the entire time, averaging about six knots. The highly advanced Type 21 U-boat only needed to raise the snorkel above the surface for about five hours every three days to recharge the batteries and refresh the air in the boat. Because of this feature and its much quieter machinery that was harder to detect by sonar, the submarine had remained undetected that entire time. Hans had plotted an extremely conservative route for their voyage, going well out into the mid-Atlantic to avoid allied bases in the Azores but still staying well east of the American coast. Intelligence also indicated that they should avoid other islands, such as the Spanish Canaries, since the Allies were increasing their patrols to try to catch U-boats attempting to reach neutral harbors as the war wound down. Unfortunately, Hans did not also know that the Allies had increased their patrols well to the east of the American coast to catch U-boats making last-ditch desperation attacks, perhaps with secret weapons.

Upon changing the watch, Hans noted that the sound operator was given permission to briefly test his gear and was about to leave the stand-by mode after the ten-minute procedure. Hans and Walter Hoffman were beginning a conversation when the sound operator in the nearby cubicle shouted a warning.

"I have a contact, *Herr Kapitän!*"

Hans replied, noting they were still on their southerly course, "What do you have?"

"Fast-turning screws directly behind us, about five thousand meters and same heading; it's submerged and sounds like one of ours, probably a Type 9." He paused, then resumed with a higher pitch but still carefully controlled voice, "Wait a minute; I now have two additional contacts, on the surface and following the boat about two thousand meters behind it. They just went active with their sound gear! I think they have him localized!"

The men in the control room could now hear the propeller beats of the other cornered U-boat, trying to escape its pursuers, as well as the "pings" of the active sonar on the surface ships. The other U-boat would not succeed in outrunning its pursuers, since the submerged Type 9 might only make nine knots top speed under water while the American destroyer escorts could make twenty-one knots.

At that moment, the first watch officer returned to the control room and quickly alerted Hans regarding their own status. "*Herr Kapitän*, we must switch the electric motors!"

Hans, quickly realizing this, barked a new command. They were cruising on their regular electric motors, not the much quieter special "silent running" electric motors that only the Type 21 had. The regular motors were still quieter than those on the Type 9 boat.

"Switch to silent running motors and silent routine! Turn right to course 270 and submerge to 150 meters!" He had also decided to turn out of the southerly line of attack and go deeper.

The crew listened as the attack unfolded.

* * *

Nearly four miles to the north, the captain of the USS *Carter* spoke through the intercom to his sonar man, supposedly one of the best in the fleet. "What have you got for me, Mac?"

"It's definitely a Type 9, sir, running flat out. Just as you thought, the sonar spooked him and he's squirming, bearing 360 relative, but he's not maneuvering."

The captain barked an order to his executive officer. "Call the *Scott* on the TBS and tell them to close in. Get the *Muir* and the *Sutton* to cut off the escape to east and west." The *Carter's* captain was referring to the three other destroyer escorts in his group.

The sonar man returned. "Captain, I think I have another one. It's much fainter and is ahead of the first contact. It isn't a profile that I'm familiar with. It's not a ghost echo—I'm sure it's another U-boat!"

"What's it doing, Mac, is it maneuvering?"

"I just lost it, Captain. I can't be sure, but as it faded, it might have made a turn to the west. I don't have anything else, like a turn count, but it was definitely screws turning slowly."

Just then, the USS *Neal A. Scott* fired its Hedgehog weapon, unguided projectiles that required a direct hit rather than close proximity, like a regular depth charge. They also had a smaller warhead. The captain of the *Carter* gave his next order.

"We'll follow up with our own Hedgehog attack after the *Scott* pulls away!"

* * *

Hans and Walter listened as the attack on their brethren continued. Hans looked around as his handpicked and well-trained crew intuitively looked up but remained calm. Walter also looked cool, but quite amazed as he watched the technology, so different from the last time he went to sea in a U-boat on a war patrol, nearly thirty years ago.

They then heard a muffled explosion. His sound operator reacted.

"They hit him. The screws are still turning and he's trying to maneuver." A single hit by a Hedgehog wouldn't always immediately sink a U-boat unless it was well placed, but Hans knew the inevitable result. *The fool, why doesn't he blow his tanks and surface!*

The sound operator continued, "The other ship is moving in for the kill." Hans knew what would happen next.

Within seconds, the sound operator announced what everybody could hear through the hull, the sound of more Hedgehogs hitting the water. Within seconds, two nearly simultaneous explosions took place. A second later, the sound operator spoke.

"I hear bulkheads collapsing and rushing water!" It was the sound of a dying U-boat.

Within another few brief minutes, they all heard a horrendous sound as the U-518 exceeded its crush depth and imploded. Hans thought that, if a few crew members had been able to seal off a compartment, they would have lived for another minute or two, just time enough to contemplate their horrific death, nearly instantaneous as the hull gave way. As the sound gradually subsided, they could again hear the screws of the American warships and the active sonar pings.

Walter asked the question everyone in the control room was thinking. "Can they hear us?"

Hans responded, "It's not likely. No German ship could find us during our shakedown cruises, but the Americans have much better equipment. They will keep this up, though, with an active sonar search, trying to spook us and get us to run."

The sound operator spoke. "They're beginning an active search, *Herr Kapitän*, heading toward us. They may've detected our turn west before we switched the electric motors."

Hans quickly gave another order. "Right turn, heading 360; submerge gradually to two hundred meters!" That would be deeper than he had previously dived in this boat.

The American escorts continued their blind sonar search and began dropping regular depth charges, again trying to spook the U-boat. Hans, however, was too experienced to fall into that trap. Within minutes, the contacts faded as the American ships headed west while the U-boat tracked north. Hans planned to resume their southerly track in a few hours. Finally, as it became quiet in the control room, Hans spoke very quietly to Walter.

"If only we had these boats in quantity two years ago, the outcome of this war could be far different."

Walter nodded. "I agree. By themselves, they might not have allowed us to win, but they could have bought Germany more time until our other advances bore fruit."

Both men looked toward the bow of the boat, where most of the Valhalla cargo was carried. Although they knew the general nature of their cargo, in sealed containers, neither man knew the frightening secrets actually contained in them.

70

Berlin, Germany
M a y 1 , 1 9 4 5

* * *

Gruppenführer Heinrich Muller checked his charts and papers one last time as he watched a *Luftwaffe* major perform final checks on the Fieseler Fi-156 "Storch" aircraft. The aircraft was known for its ability to use very short, unimproved runways. High officials had used a similar aircraft to escape Berlin only three days ago. Muller had secured this aircraft six months ago and had it secretly placed in this secret bombproof bunker hangar under a building in the northeast corner of the Reich Chancellery complex, adjacent to the access to the führerbunker.

Muller reviewed his plan one more time. Although he was the dreaded head of the Gestapo in Germany, he had actually been an accomplished pilot in the First World War and had secretly maintained his flying proficiency in small aircraft since then. Tonight he would need every bit of that expertise if he were to succeed—and live.

When Hitler committed suicide the day before, all those remaining in the führerbunker planned their individual escapes. Muller planned his also, intent not only on saving his own skin but also to take actions needed to ensure the survival of the Nazi infrastructure and the accomplishments of the Third Reich after the allied powers occupied Germany. This included ensuring the success of Operation Valhalla. To do that, he needed to get out of Germany and find a way to deal with the Hoffman family, who appeared to have absconded with the precious Valhalla cargo in a U-boat without any SS or Gestapo personnel aboard. When Muller found out about Bruner's team and what Walter and Hans Hoffman had done, he realized he should have issued the arrest warrant much earlier.

Muller planned his escape meticulously. If he could escape the Berlin area, he planned to head for a secret airstrip southeast of Kiel, about three hundred kilometers to the northwest, and then pick up a Messerschmitt Bf-108, another small aircraft that was faster and had more range than the

Storch. From there he would fly to Aalborg, Denmark, and eventually to Oslo, Norway, flying only at night to escape allied aircraft.

Muller watched as the *Luftwaffe* officer opened the hangar door and approached to give his final report.

"*Herr Gruppenführer*, your aircraft is ready. When you taxi clear of the door, you will have 150 meters of clearway before you reach a pile of rubble. My men just finished clearing the last of the debris and they have left. May I provide advice on your flight path, sir?" Muller nodded as the officer pointed to his chart.

"You should stay extremely low and fly at maximum speed. After you clear the chancellery complex and cross Herman Goering Strasse, I suggest flying west, crossing into the Tiergarten, turning northwest to follow Charlottenburger Chausee well west of the Brandenburg Gate. You must stay well away from the Reichstag and the Königsplatz, where there is still fierce fighting. If you turn north to cross over the Kroll Opera House, you may then pick up the River Spree and follow it to and then north across the Humboldt Basin. From there northbound will be your best escape route, according to our intelligence. It is now 2145 local time and almost completely dark, yet you should be able to spot landmarks because of the fires. However, you must leave at once. We just heard that the Russians will begin the final assault momentarily. They are only blocks away."

"Thank you, *Herr* Major. I will take it from here. You must leave at once so that you might join the others in the Mohrenstrasse U-bahn station as they attempt their escape."

The *Luftwaffe* officer nodded, saluted, and walked away. As he did so, Muller pulled out his Walther P-38 and fired twice, watching the man crumple as the rounds hit him in the back. Muller trusted only his closest Gestapo associates and couldn't take a chance that the officer would be captured and reveal his escape.

Muller quickly got in the aircraft, started the engine, taxied clear of the hangar, and took off. He followed the planned route and was surprised at how easy it was. Neither the remaining German defenders nor the Russian attackers were expecting a very low altitude flight in the darkness and by the time they could react the aircraft was gone. Muller's initial zigzag route also confused the Russians, who could not sort out whether it was one of their own aircraft.

A little over two hours later, Muller reached the secret airstrip near Kiel with only a few liters of petrol left. His meticulous planning paid off again as he found the Bf-108 ready and waiting, guarded by a single Gestapo officer. Muller soon took off and reached Aalborg just before daylight. Again a Gestapo officer was waiting and helped Muller fuel and then hide the aircraft. He would need to remain here until the next night before making the flight to Norway.

71.

North Atlantic Ocean, 1,200 kilometers west of Cape Verde Islands
May 5, 1945

* * *

The U-3696 had made steady progress since evading the American destroyer escorts nearly two weeks ago. Hans had decided against surfacing the boat to minimize risk of detection. Instead, prior to raising the snorkel to charge the batteries, he raised his radio detection gear. He detected no allied aircraft or ships within range. It also gave his radioman a chance to listen in on any broadcasts over normal U-boat frequencies, to see how the war was playing out. He soon got his answer.

The radioman handed Hans the decoded message. "*Herr Kapitän*, it is a broadcast to all U-boats to…surface…fly a black flag…and await detection and escort by allied vessels to port."

Hans slowly took the message from his radioman. No one else spoke in the control room.

Walter Hoffman pulled closer to his nephew in the cramped control room and spoke softly so only Hans could hear him. "It's over, Hans. Doenitz is just trying to buy a few extra days so more civilians and *Wehrmacht* forces can escape the Russians."

Hans nodded. "I hope they manage to scuttle all the Type 21 boats."

Walter sighed. "I'm afraid it will be too late for that."

72.

SS physics research facility, south of Breslau, Germany
May 6, 1945

* * *

The station director watched nervously as the SS security team quickly cleared the building of technicians, except for the director and one assistant. The commander of the SS team turned as one of his men entered the room, saluted, and updated his superior.

"*Herr Sturmbannführer*, they are only three kilometers away. We must act now!"

The SS officer realized that the Russians must not capture the reactor intact, but he didn't want to destroy the facility with conventional explosives. He had another plan as he, and other teams, ruthlessly executed paragraph 3-b-ii of the Operation Valhalla directive—eliminating any witnesses with knowledge of the operation.

He turned to the director and spoke calmly. "Pull out all the control rods."

The director stared at the SS officer, aghast at the order. "But *Herr Sturmbannführer*, I cannot do that! The reactor will go critical within minutes. The rods are the only way to prevent an uncontrolled chain reaction."

The SS officer didn't have time for this as he pulled out his pistol and pointed it alternately at the director and his assistant and raised his voice. "You will do as I say if you want to live. Pull the control rods!"

The two reactor station employees quickly complied with the order, and within five minutes, the rods were pulled. Alarms started sounding immediately. The SS officer again calmly looked at the director and asked one final question. "How long before it goes critical?"

"No more than five minutes! We must leave the facility at once!" The man was clearly nervous.

The SS officer coolly replied, "Thank you, *Herr Doktor*." He then raised his pistol and, as the other two men looked on horrified, shot both of them twice, killing them.

The SS officer briefly looked dispassionately at the two bodies and quickly exited the building, noting as he did so that the rest of his team had quickly dispatched the dozen or so other technicians at the station.

He swiftly reached the vehicle with the rest of his team, and they departed the area quickly. He finally relaxed as the vehicle drove away, realizing that he had completed all of his assignments under Operation Valhalla with regard to eliminating anyone in Germany who could reveal Valhalla to the enemy. He and his team would try to flee west and blend into the mass of German troops surrendering on all fronts. He smiled as he contemplated what would happen to the Russian soldiers reaching the reactor as the core melted.

73.

Reichskommissar Headquarters, Oslo, Norway
May 7, 1945

* * *

Heinrich Muller waited impatiently for his second meeting with *Reichskommissar* Josef Terboven, the Nazi political overseer of occupied Norway. Muller had met him briefly on the morning of May 3, with his own local Gestapo chief, Heinz Fehlis, immediately after landing at Fornebu Airport. Terboven, however, had left in a hurry, summoned to Flensburg, Germany, to meet with Karl Doenitz, Germany's new leader. Muller was furious but knew he must wait. Finally, having returned from Flensburg, Terboven walked into the office and sat down at his desk without saluting or shaking hands with Muller. Finally, he looked up, smiled weakly, and greeted his guest.

"So, Muller, I finally returned from my meeting with the new führer. He's quite different from Hitler, I can assure you. He's equally stern and unyielding but very practical." Terboven casually glanced out the window as he finished speaking.

Muller was furious at the lack of respect shown to him by Terboven but realized there was little he could do. He got control of himself and finally answered, "So, *Herr Reichskommissar,* I would assume that you returned with new orders. What about your plan to hold out here in Norway?" It was a reasonable question, Muller thought. There were still four hundred thousand well-supplied German troops in Norway.

"I'm sorry, Muller, but that's out of the question now. Doenitz ordered us to capitulate also, since the general surrender was signed this morning. He relieved me of my duties and transferred power to General Bohme, the military commander. Our capitulation is effective tomorrow. We may expect the Milorg and allied representatives to begin assuming power then."

Muller shuddered. The Milorg was the Norwegian resistance, and he knew they would take a dim view of his presence in their country. He looked at Terboven, who seemed disinterested in the conversation, knowing he couldn't afford to let up on the pressure.

"*Herr Reichskommissar*, I am on an important mission vital to the future of our movement. I demand that you provide me with a submarine so that I may reach my final destination."

Terboven snapped out of his lethargy. "Muller, you are in no position to demand anything. In any case, no further submarines will leave their pens in Norway, per explicit instructions from Doenitz."

Muller sat back and let that sink in. What could he do now? Terboven must have read his concern.

"*Herr* Muller, are your plans that important for you to escape?"

"Yes, I can assure you they are. It's not about me; it's about the need to plan for the future."

Terboven blinked his eyes and sat back in his chair, obviously contemplating his response, Muller thought.

"Muller, there is one chance if you want to take it. Do you know Leon Degrelle?"

"Yes, of course; he's the Belgian who fought on the eastern front and was decorated by Hitler for bravery. He led the Walloon unit of Belgian volunteers." Muller was surprised at the mention of Degrelle.

"Well, he's here in Norway. Like you, he escaped, when his unit was destroyed. He's trying to get to Spain. I offered him my personal aircraft, a Heinkel 111 with a volunteer crew, and he accepted. Actually it's not my aircraft but was provided by Albert Speer for my use. I told Degrelle he must leave tonight or it will be too late. If you want, you can join him. Since you arrived here with the identity of a *Luftwaffe* officer, it will be easy to add you to the crew. In fact, I can see to it that you're assigned to the crew but stay off the manifest. That will increase your chances of being undiscovered, if you survive. I'll warn you now; the flight will be exceedingly risky, even in darkness. You'll be flying more than 1,800 kilometers over territory occupied by the Allies."

Muller didn't hesitate. "*Herr Reichskommissar*, the three flights I made to get here were against the odds. I'll take my chances with Degrelle." He added another thought.

"Aren't you leaving on the flight also?"

Terboven smiled and replied. "No, I think not. Unlike your situation, they know I'm here, and I would be easy to track down. Rest assured, neither I nor your colleague Fehlis will be taken alive. I have it all planned. In fact, this is my last scheduled meeting." He paused. "I will arrange for you to be taken to Fornebu Airport and be on the aircraft's crew and I can ensure that you will not be discovered. Now, if you will excuse me I have these and other final preparations I must attend to."

Beyond Ultra

375

74.

North Atlantic Ocean, south of Cape Verde Islands
May 7, 1945

* * *

The men in the U-3696 control room were silent as they heard the BBC broadcast on their high frequency radio. Hans translated for his men, who quickly passed the word throughout the boat as the broadcast continued. Germany had surrendered.

The crew looked glumly at each other, realizing what this meant. They wondered about their families but then realized it would be a while before they saw them again, if ever. It would be a long time before the crewmembers on U-3696 could surface in society again, at least in Germany.

Walter and Hans spoke quietly at one side of the control room. Hans spoke first.

"Do you think they'll discover that we exist; that we escaped from Germany?"

Walter contemplated that before answering. "We tried everything we could to expunge records of this boat; construction details, crew information, everything. But we can never be sure that the Allies won't find out eventually. That's why we must disappear and not return to Germany for years."

Hans nodded and replied bitterly, "It's just as well. There is nothing there that we treasure anymore."

75.

San Sebastian Bay, Spain
May 8, 1945

* * *

Heinrich Muller was pleasantly surprised as the aircraft came to a stop up on the shoreline, right after dawn. He had been expecting worse, but the second of the three separate impacts was the most violent, and the third was merely a shudder as the aircraft came to a stop. Muller had prepared his little "nest" against the bulkhead, using parachutes, blankets, and other material to provide adequate padding to protect him from the impact. He completed his preparations during the final descent, after the pilot said they would have insufficient fuel to make an airfield and would attempt to land in San Sebastian Bay. He also had enough time to review, and then destroy, one of his documents, after memorizing the contact information for his local Gestapo lead agent in San Sebastian. He should be easy to find, Muller thought, since he was a member of Franco's secret police, the BPS.

Muller quickly exited the aircraft, uninjured, and waded through ankle-deep water to dry land. On the way out of the aircraft, he noticed that Degrelle was severely injured and told the other crew members he would find help.

On the shore, he noticed a uniformed man approach wearing the uniform of the Civil Guard, the national police force. Muller raised his hand as he approached the man and, using his memorized Spanish, made his request.

"I have important information for the *Brigada Politico Social*. Take me to them at once."

76

Paul Hoffman's apartment, New York City
May 8, 1945

* * *

Paul scurried around his apartment trying to simultaneously clean the breakfast table while preparing in advance for dinner that evening. He and Jack had decided to host dinner that night in Paul's place for Liz and Paul's uncle, Ramon Ortega. Today was V-E Day, and the city was wild with excitement. They had quickly realized that every table at every restaurant was spoken for, so they decided to eat at home and then go out on the town to celebrate.

Paul had already "liberated" several bottles of the 1942 vintage Ortega *tempranillo* that just arrived from Spain and managed to secure a nice pork roast with saved ration coupons. He also planned to prepare Lyonnais potatoes and he had just sharpened a knife to cut and peel them before boiling them. The water was on and starting to boil as Paul rushed between the breakfast table, the refrigerator, the stove, and the cutting board.

Paul cursed as the butter fell off the plate and onto the floor as he carelessly picked up the dish. He walked over to the sink to get a rag to clean it up. As he walked to the sink, preoccupied, he did not notice the door to his apartment in the other room open slowly and a man slip in unnoticed. Paul had left the door unlocked when he went out earlier to get the paper. Paul continued to soak the rag and he was preparing to turn when the intruder came to within eight feet of Paul and spoke in perfect Spanish.

"Paul Hoffman—you will turn around slowly, and do not scream, for it will do you no good."

Paul froze in a state of shock. Who could this be? He realized he had to comply. Until he faced the intruder, he didn't know who he was dealing with. He turned slowly.

Before him stood a stocky man, about five-nine, with a scar on his face, a scowl, and a revolver pointing at Paul. The man looked at Paul and his eyes darted briefly to the left and right, checking his surroundings. Paul was silent, but the noise of the boiling water sounded intense as his heart pounded. Finally, he spoke in Spanish.

"Who are you and what do you want? If it's money, I'll get my wallet and you can be on your way." Paul held tight to the wet rag in his hand.

"It's not your money I want, you traitor! You betrayed both Germany and Spain by collaborating with the enemy. Schmidt warned me that you would try to deny it, so I don't want to hear excuses."

Paul held his position as the man slowly inched toward him. Paul knew he might only have a couple of seconds to react—and he was thus caught off guard when the intruder stepped squarely on the stick of butter he had dropped. The man's foot slid, he lost his balance and tumbled backward to the floor, groaning as he did.

Paul reacted instantly. With a rush of adrenaline, he grabbed the handle of the pot of boiling water on the stove with both hands and hurled it at the face of the man lying on the floor not four feet from him.

The intruder was trying to reach for his gun as the mass of boiling water hit his face. He let out an agonizing scream as he put both hands to his face.

Paul did not hesitate. He grabbed the sharpened butcher knife next to the potatoes and lunged forward with it, shoving the knife in the man's chest with all his might. The man let out a muffled scream, then opened his eyes, his skin reddened and peeled from the scalding water. His excruciating pain was short lived, however, as he grasped for breath, tried to reach for Paul, and then finally fell back limp as the fatal wound to his heart silenced him.

Paul pulled back and plopped on the floor, spent from the effort. His quick thinking was instinctive and had saved him, but he now was breathing rapidly as he realized what almost happened.

At that instant, Jack Kurtz raced into the room with his own weapon, a Beretta, in hand. He quickly surveyed the scene, looked at the dead intruder, over at Paul, and then back at the intruder. He quickly overcame his shock.

"Jesus, Paul, what the hell happened! Who is he?"

"I've never seen him before, but he's a buddy of Schmidt's. I didn't know the SS had agents here. But he spoke perfect Spanish." Paul was now breathing normally but still unable to move.

Jack's own instincts took over as he rapidly examined the body, looking for identification. He found a Spanish diplomatic passport identifying the man as a member of Spain's New York consulate. He finally got up and helped Paul stand up.

"Are you all right?" Jack quickly looked around realizing what Paul had done. "Boy, that must have been quick thinking on your part. Jeez, boiling water and a knife; that sure got his attention."

"Who is he, Jack?"

"If I had to guess, I'd say he was a BPS agent who was turned by the SS and then planted here. The SS probably set him up to do you in, after they figured out that you were probably involved in killing Schmidt."

Paul looked at Jack, finally replying, "If that's not it, why would the BPS be out to get me? I'm a solid Spanish citizen who has influence with the Americans."

"It's probably the SS and not the BPS, Paul, but I'll get right on this one and find out. Meanwhile we've got to get rid of this body."

"Shouldn't we call the police?"

"You must be kidding. The NYPD is clueless in these matters and they'll ask too many questions. The FBI is also dangerous in that regard. Nope, let me borrow your phone and make a call."

Paul waited for Jack to make the call, finally recovered from the surge of energy but beginning to realize that he had just killed a man. Finally, Jack hung up. "We're OK; I've got a special 'clean-up squad' on the way."

"What will they do with him?"

"We'll dump him in a Jersey marsh and make it look like a mob hit. Heck, we might even stuff a parakeet in his mouth." The smile on Jack's face was quickly extinguished as the look from Paul indicated he did not appreciate his humor.

Jack continued, "Sorry, I guess that was a lame one. Seriously, we'll make it look like this guy was dealing with the mob in some vice racket. That actually will help us since, unfortunately, we're about to lower the boom on Spain, big time. My agents over there have found out that Franco may be sheltering some Nazis, contrary to last year's agreement, so we'll probably expel some of their diplomatic personnel, including some in the New York consulate."

Paul sighed and was silent for a moment as he considered what Jack had said. Finally, he looked up at Jack. "I guess that all makes sense. By the way, how did you happen by just now?"

Jack smiled. "Liz thought I should come over and help you get ready for dinner. I guess they were worried about you not being able to handle dinner by yourself." Both men laughed. Paul's smile faded as he realized what might have happened.

"Jack, I'm just lucky Liz wasn't here when this happened. I wonder how long I'm going to have to watch my backside."

"It's probably over, now that the war is over in Europe. I wouldn't worry. Besides, you can obviously take care of yourself." Jack shook his head as he looked at the surroundings and then concluded, "I'll tell you one thing—you won't want to have dinner here tonight. I'll call my office and see if we can pull some strings and get a table somewhere else—anywhere else."

77.

Off the Rio Mbia Estuary, Rio Muni, Spanish Guinea
May 29, 1945

* * *

Hans Hoffman and his lookouts searched carefully through their binoculars as he eased the U-boat closer to shore in the waning twilight. He had surfaced the previous three nights, after fifty-two days submerged, in order to take star shots and get an accurate position. He needed to find that estuary without running aground. To help prevent that, he had blown the ballast and the trim tanks so that the boat would ride higher and draw less water to the keel. In any kind of sea this would make the boat unstable, but the Gulf of Guinea was a glassy calm tonight.

Hans looked back west as he observed the diffused but brilliant sky following the sunset and breathed in deeply the humid, fetid air of the tropics. At least it was fresh air, rather than the stale air inside the boat. Since he was already in water too shallow to dive, he had opened several of the hatches so his crew could enjoy the air also.

An abrupt announcement from a lookout interrupted Hans's reverie as the light was spotted on shore, about one thousand meters ahead. Hans stopped the engines to let the boat drift. The light from the shore flashed the agreed upon recognition signal. Within ten minutes, a boat approached with two men in it. Walter now joined Hans on the small bridge of the boat as they eagerly waited for the boat to pull alongside. Both men knew who would be in the boat, if the preparations had gone according to plan. They descended from the bridge to the deck as the two men climbed onto the deck from their small boat.

"Father, it's me...Hans!" Hans could not maintain his normally subdued persona as he recognized his father and quickly went to embrace him.

Karl Hoffman quickly reciprocated, barely recognizing his eldest son with the scruffy beard. He had not seen him in nearly six years. The two men embraced.

"Hans, I barely recognize you but you look…well. Thank God you survived the war!" Karl did not also say that Hans had apparently aged greatly in those six years.

Karl turned toward Walter. "My brother, it's good to see you also. I'm happy you both made it here safely." The two men embraced firmly but with little emotion.

Hans interrupted, "Father, we haven't much time…with the tides and darkness."

Karl nodded. "I understand. I'll direct you through the channel to the dock we built. With the governor's assistance, we dredged the channel and improved the roads from the dock to the plantation. It's about an eighty-kilometer drive and will take us about three hours."

As Karl guided the boat through the channel, the other man in the small boat, Gerhard Hoepner, quietly talked with Walter Hoffman, inquiring as to where the Valhalla cargo was to be stored. None of the documents and plans that Hoepner possessed disclosed where exactly that was. Only Walter and Hans knew that part of the Valhalla plan.

Within thirty minutes, the U-boat was safely tied up to the newly built dock, with barely three meters of water under the keel. That would increase a little as the tide continued to come in, but the boat would need to leave in about four hours or become stranded as the tide went out. All members of the crew, including Walter, Hans, Karl, and Gerhard Hoepner feverishly began the transfer of the Valhalla cargo to the two large trucks that Karl and Hoepner had driven to the dock. Finally, after three hours, the task was completed. Hans issued his final order to his first watch officer.

"Take the boat out to the thirty-fathom curve and submerge. We'll expect you to pick us up tomorrow night." His watch officer nodded. Hans had full faith in him.

The three Hoffmans and Hoepner were joined in the trucks by about half of the crew members from the U-boat, who would help them unload the Valhalla cargo. Karl drove the larger truck, with Walter and Hans sitting alongside, while Hoepner drove the other truck with the rest of the crew.

As the trucks drove slowly down the bumpy but dry road, Hans briefed his father. "We will store the cargo in the caves near the hacienda."

"I was wondering about that. It's the only place I could think of that would be completely isolated and escape discovery. Hoepner has been pressing me for more information, but I told him only you could provide the answers regarding the location for storing the cargo."

The three men were quiet for several minutes as Walter and Hans waited for the inevitable questions. Finally, Karl spoke again. "I cannot wait any longer. I must know about the family. How is Ernst?"

Karl's question was initially met with silence. Finally, Walter answered, "I'm sorry, my brother. Ernst was killed in combat about six weeks ago. He died a hero's death and—"

Karl cut him off. "I don't need to hear how he died! I know his courage was extraordinary. But what did he die for? At that stage of the war and with the Nazis totally discredited, how can I celebrate such a death? I can only mourn his passing!"

There was again a heavy silence as the three men stared ahead into the darkness. Finally, Karl, recovering from his outburst, spoke again. "What about our father?"

Another pause; Walter finally answered. "He went to the family estate in West Prussia in January, just before the area was overrun by the Russians. We did not hear from him afterward and I couldn't get any further information."

"You didn't try to stop him?"

"Karl, you know Father and how stubborn he could be. He was nearly ninety-three and wanted to return to our ancestral home to die. Surely you can understand that. I tried to get him to stay in Bernkastel, but he wouldn't listen."

Karl let out a long sigh, realizing that Walter was right. Again there was silence. Karl had one more question to ask. "What about Erica and Kirsten? Hans, what about Freya? I heard from your last letter that you were to be a father."

This time the silence from Walter and Hans was so overpowering that Karl could feel it bearing down on him. It was Hans who finally replied, turning to face his father.

"Erica, Kirsten, my beloved Freya, our unborn child, they are all dead; killed by a British bomb in Cologne as they tried to reach Bernkastel!" Hans paused as he tried to restrain a sob. "Father, you asked what Ernst died for.

He died for his country. But as to three innocent women, all I know is that they died and now I am empty. There is nothing in Germany for us now. The only hope that Germany may have in the future may be partially contained in these two trucks!" Hans turned his face away.

Karl was shocked by Hans's emotion, never having seen him display it before, yet he was proud that his son could rise to that level. Karl wanted to console the two men but realized that might not be possible. Finally, he turned to face them.

"Hans, Walter, I am so deeply sorry." He paused. "Your loss is my loss too. I don't want to mar this unspeakable tragedy with recriminations. I am sorry for my tone—"

Hans, containing his sob only slightly, interrupted. "Father, about Mother, I want to say that I'm sorry that...that I..."

Karl stopped the truck and looked at his son. "Hans, it wasn't your fault; it was a random act of war, one of thousands that happened. I would forgive you, but there is nothing to forgive. You did your duty and it's not possible to erase this tragic mistake or bring your mother back. You must only look forward. I'm happy you're alive. That's enough for me."

Karl put his hand on his son's shoulder and Hans finally nodded. Karl resumed driving.

The three men were silent as the bumpy journey continued. Finally, at about 1:00 a.m., they arrived at the Ortega-Hoffman plantation. They drove to the hacienda to retrieve a small gasoline generator, portable lights, and flashlights and then drove up a small rise just beyond the airstrip, finally reaching the entrance to the cave. After inspecting the cave, they began the task of again unloading the cargo. Karl by now was curious as to what was contained in the sealed containers but did not want to provoke his son and brother again.

They placed the cargo carefully in the alcoves of the cave, located in a way that obscured their casual viewing by anyone entering the cave that was not looking for anything in particular. The team finally finished and shut down and removed the lights and generator. They returned to the hacienda, where they quickly retired to the sleeping quarters that Karl had prepared. They quickly fell asleep...except for the three Hoffmans. Karl took them to the study and poured them each a glass of sherry. He had one more question to pose.

"Walter, I still don't understand the nature of the contents of those canisters. What is so special about them to require this extraordinary operation?"

Walter looked at his brother with a frown. "You must trust us on this. Everything of importance that was achieved in Germany in the last twelve years is contained in those boxes. I cannot tell you any more right now."

Karl sighed and decided to drop the issue...for now.

78

Ortega-Hoffman hacienda, Rio Muni, Spanish Guinea
May 30, 1945

* * *

Overnight, Karl had lost interest in the Valhalla cargo now stored on his property. He was now more concerned about what Walter and Hans would do next—especially where they planned to sail in the U-boat. The Hoffmans and the rest of the team rested during the day. As they were preparing to depart for the Rio Mbia to rendezvous with the submarine, Karl took his brother and son aside and demanded an answer.

"Walter, Hans, I must know where you plan to sail in the U-boat. I've already lost one son. I don't want to lose another, and a brother too, in the process. Why can't you remain here in Guinea?"

Walter and Hans looked at each other. Walter finally replied, "Our agreement with the Spanish government only extends to safeguarding the cargo in the cave, as long as it remains stored covertly here in Guinea. As a result of pressure from the Americans, the government agreed not to give sanctuary to any Germans anywhere in Spanish territory, not just Nazis but also *Wehrmacht* personnel who...have special status, which includes us."

"Who brokered this arrangement for you?" Karl thought he knew the answer to this.

"From what I already know, I'm sure you know it was Alberto Ortega. He has been of great help to us in this operation and in maintaining secrecy."

Karl looked at Walter with a frown. "I understand now the nature of all of your years of operating in the intelligence and clandestine world. I suppose that after a while this all becomes normal to you." He paused. "But you must still answer my question—where will you go?"

Walter looked at his brother, and Karl realized that he could not give him the answer he wanted. "Karl, it's better for both you and Hans and me that you don't know our next destination. For a while, it will be dangerous for us to surface anywhere with our current identities. After time passes, we may be able to return. It will depend a lot on what happens in Germany—and how vigorously the Allies try to extract vengeance from those of us that escaped."

Karl looked at Walter and Hans, both looking dejected but resigned to their fate. Why must this happen this way? He appealed again—to his son this time.

"Hans, you are not a war criminal or even a high *Wehrmacht* officer. Why can't you stay in Guinea or Spain?"

Hans looked at Walter and then at his father. "I'm sorry, Father, but Uncle is correct—it will be risky for me, and our families, if I were to surface in Spanish territory now."

Karl looked into his son's eyes and knew he could not sway him.

An hour later, the three men said their good-byes as they prepared to drive the two trucks back to the coast. Hans was anxious to get going in order to make the high tide that night. Hans assured his father that they knew the way back to the coast. As they prepared to depart, Gerhard Hoepner came over and spoke to the three Hoffmans.

"I want to round up all the special equipment we've used here and take it back to Bata. Why don't you and your crew members go ahead and return to the boat with the larger truck? I only need the smaller truck for the special gear. Karl can help me with it."

Walter looked at Hans, who nodded. They got the rest of their team, loaded them in the truck, and drove off. As Karl looked at the truck, Hans waved back from the open window. Karl suppressed a tear.

Karl helped Hoepner load the other truck, which took fifteen minutes. Karl told Hoepner he was going to his study to get the trucks' documents. Within a few minutes, as Karl was looking for these papers, he felt someone enter the room. He looked up to see Gerhard Hoepner at the door, pointing a pistol at him. Karl confronted him.

"What's the meaning of this? Whose side are you on, Hoepner, or should it be obvious to me that you are still taking orders from your SS thugs?"

"You shouldn't insult me like that, Karl. It merely proves that you are an unreliable guardian for the information in that cave. Your brother and son have also demonstrated their treachery to the Reich, as my superiors found out. I will need to find another way—and another place—to safeguard those precious documents to secure the Reich's future."

As he aimed the pistol at Karl, Hoepner was startled as someone called out his name from the other room adjoining Karl's study. The instant it took for Hoepner to wheel around gave Karl the opening he needed. He grabbed his P08 Luger sitting under a paper. Quickly raising it, he fired. Hoepner had instinctively ducked and the shot missed. Karl pulled the trigger again but the Luger jammed. Karl cursed. Hoepner raised his right arm to fire, but at that instant, a fusillade of bullets from two weapons struck Hoepner repeatedly. Karl quickly crossed the room after clearing the Luger's jam. Hoepner had collapsed to the floor, having dropped his weapon, severely wounded but conscious. He saw Karl approach and looked in horror as Karl raised his Luger, aimed it at his head, and fired.

Karl stood over the body for a moment, then looked up and saw Walter and Hans approach him from the other room as they holstered their Walther service pistols.

The three men stood there silently for several minutes before Karl finally spoke first, turning to Walter.

"How did you know?"

"I knew almost from the moment that the SS assigned two agents to 'support' us that one or both of them were tasked with spying on us and seeing to it that everyone associated with carrying out Valhalla would be liquidated following the completion of the mission. Fortunately the other agent was formerly on my naval staff and we were able to learn of the SS plans."

"So you and Hans are marked for liquidation too, I suppose."

"Yes, although we plan to make it very hard for them to find us and that's why you can't know our destination. In fact, I'm worried that you will still be in danger here, from other agents." He added a thought, looking at Karl's Luger. "You need to get rid of that antique; you know the Luger is prone to jamming after the first shot." Walter reached into his holster, removed his P-38, and then added a PPK from his back holster, along with his ammunition, handing them to Karl. "Take these, my brother; you may have need for them, unfortunately."

Karl smiled as he took the pistols. "I may have anticipated more than you thought, my brother. The governor and I have closely collaborated to identify SS agents, in and out of the German consulate. Now that Germany has surrendered, he has isolated the consulate and the Colonial Guard has surrounded the building, pending repatriation of the staff to Germany and interrogation by the Americans. Only one may have escaped. His name is Franz Zacharias and he managed to depart from Fernando Po on a Portuguese freighter on May 4, just before the surrender."

"Franz Zacharias—that isn't good!" Walter frowned. "He's a very dangerous SS agent who is probably collaborating with the BPS."

Karl replied, "The freighter was headed for Lisbon, with ports of call at Bissau, in Portuguese Guinea, Villa Cisneros, in Spanish Sahara, Tangier, and Cadiz. He could be planning to exit at any of those ports. The governor would like to follow up on this, but he already has detected that it would be dangerous to pry too deeply."

Walter continued to frown. "The governor is right, Karl. Spain is riddled with SS agents, and it's likely that the BPS, and Franco, will shield at least some of them and may even be collaborating with them. Alberto warned us about this. You may assume that SS sleeper cells or BPS agents that they compromised will continue to be a problem, even with the war ended. Hoepner was the only SS agent that knew about the cave, but sleeper agents may still try to find the location of our cargo through you. You must exercise care."

Karl looked at his brother and nodded. It was beginning to dawn on him that life in Guinea was no longer isolated and that Spain was likely to pay a terrible price for its support of Germany and by continuing to protect Nazis escapees.

Hans spoke to Walter, obviously worried. "I'm sorry, but we must go now in order to catch the tide." He turned to his father. "Please take care of yourself, Father. I'll think of you often and I'll try to contact you when I can."

Both men then hugged and Karl watched his son depart with Walter, suddenly very proud of him.

79

Greenwich Village, New York
June 1, 1945

* * *

Paul and Jack decided to return to their old haunt, the White Horse Tavern in the West Village, for their usual late Friday afternoon meeting. To quench their thirst, they each quickly downed a beer. Paul then bought the next round, brought it to their isolated table, and got right to what was on his mind.

"All right, Jack, what did you find out about my visitor last month?"

"As suspected, he was a BPS agent who was turned by the SS. Schmidt was his controller and had responsibility for a lot of other SS agents in Spain and elsewhere. The goon you met was sent here for the express purpose of getting rid of you, in case Schmidt missed. The agent here was sort of on autopilot when my guy killed Schmidt and he followed his last standing orders—to kill you—if you showed up here. The shit has really hit the fan now. We've surfaced more BPS agents that were collaborating with the SS and will round up many and expel others. Also, the new ambassador in Madrid is raising all kinds of hell and demanding that Franco cooperate—or else."

Paul shook his head and let out a long sigh. "Man, I knew Franco's policies would be bad for Spain, but this is worse than I thought. Since you're in charge of OSS agents in Spain, will you be helping to clean up the mess—clandestinely, of course?"

"I'll be going to Spain next week, in fact, but only to wrap up operations there. With the war in Europe over, there's a huge push starting to wind down the agency. You probably can read the tea leaves as well as I can. Our citizens are sick of war and all it entails—death of loved ones, rationing, sacrifice, everything. Truman is under huge political pressure to wrap up the war with Japan, no matter what it takes."

"That sounds ominous—'no matter what it takes.' Is there some special weapon that can bring that about?"

Paul's offhand remark caused Jack to look directly at Paul. Jack's raised eyebrows gave away his concern about Paul's question.

"I'm sorry, Jack, did I ask the wrong question?"

"Oh, skip it; it's nothing. Listen, I have one other subject to bring up. Your two-year business visa is about to expire. While I still have influence, and while your service to the OSS in Spain is still fresh, I want you to consider applying for permanent residency in the U.S. You would still retain your Spanish citizenship, but as a landed immigrant, you would be eligible for U.S. citizenship. It wouldn't make you a traitor to Spain and it would be an important step, since you're about to marry my sister. Liz thought it would be a good idea too, but she's sensitive to your sense of loyalty to Spain and asked me to bring it up."

Paul smiled. "That's typical of Liz. She always respects other philosophies and viewpoints. Can you really make all that happen?"

"Absolutely; and not only that, I've already tried to 'inoculate' your businesses from retaliation if the U.S. puts more heat on Spain. I saw to it that your import-export licenses were flagged so that the direct trade you have with Spanish Guinea is treated separately from direct trade to and from Spain. For your wine imports from Spain, I created a scheme with customs that will flag them separately, as a 'preferred' importer."

Paul looked at Jack, totally shocked. "I don't know what to say. I'm amazed you have that kind of influence."

"It's the least I can do for my future brother-in-law! In any case, enjoy it while it lasts."

"What's that mean?"

"I've volunteered for service in the Pacific, but I'm not sure how long the war will last. By the time I get back from Spain, it could be over. To hedge my bets, I've applied for law school, both Harvard and Yale. My hitch was for 'four years or the duration,' so I see the next three months as telling the tale. My father wanted me to join him in the banking business in Denver, but neither Liz nor I see myself as a banker working for dear old dad."

Paul smiled. "I agree with both of you; it's not in your nature. But if you go to Harvard, who am I going to drink with every Friday?"

They both laughed and Jack replied, "Well, buddy, I guess you're just going to have to saunter up to Boston in your airplane. I hear they have some great Irish bars and Italian restaurants there."

"I'll look forward to that, although they probably don't hold a candle to the Village." Paul paused, and then suddenly lit up as he realized something. "Hey, Jack, not to change the subject, but I just realized that you and I are going to be in Spain at the same time! Is there any chance you could get up to the family estate in Alabos in Rioja? I would love for you to meet my family."

Jack only thought about it for a second. "Sure, why not; I'm in charge, aren't I?"

"You absolutely are the boss man." Paul paused. "I just thought of one more request. I want my family members to be able to attend the wedding. Not just my dad but the Ortegas too, at least Ernesto, Alberto, Alfonso, and Anita. I'm not sure Pilar's mom will be well enough. They need visas. Also, I think I might ask Alfonso to be my best man since my brothers may not...be able to." Paul's voice trailed off.

"That's all right, Paul, I'll make all that happen, you can count on it."

80

Aboard the U-3696, off a darkened coast, 2,000 meters from shore
June 1945

* * *

Hans and the bridge lookouts anxiously searched the shore for the recognition light. Repeating the procedure he had used before making landfall in Spanish Guinea, Hans had surfaced the boat each of the preceding three nights to obtain a good fix from star shots. He was sure that they had navigated to the right spot. At that moment, Hans spotted the light. It was the proper recognition signal. He stopped the engines, called for the signal light, and flashed the proper response code.

Within twenty minutes, the large fishing boat pulled alongside the U-boat. Walter joined Hans on deck as they welcomed the visitor boarding the boat. Walter recognized his agent and greeted him.

"Claus Hilgemann, it's good to see you again."

"Likewise, *Herr Vizeadmiral;* I see that you are precisely on schedule. I assume that all has gone according to plan. Did everything in Spanish Guinea work as planned with both the cargo and...other issues?"

"Yes, Claus; the 'other issue' you are referring to is settled. The swine Hoepner is dead."

"I see. Then we may assume no one has knowledge that you're here?"

"Yes, we may assume that for now, providing your arrangements are effective."

"I have made every effort to make them so. We're ready to transfer the crew into the fishing boat and complete the operation."

Within twenty minutes, the entire crew and a few supplies and possessions were transferred to the fishing boat. Finally, only Hans and Walter remained aboard the U-boat. Walter looked at Hans who returned his look, nodded, and summarized the next step.

"As agreed, we will go to the control room, open the vents part way, and quickly exit through the conning tower hatch." Walter nodded in acknowledgement.

Within a minute, they were at the vent controls. Hans gave the signal: "Now!"

The two men quickly opened all the diving vents halfway and scurried up the two ladders to the bridge. As they reached the raft, they were pulled away from the rapidly submerging U-boat by the fishing boat. As the water overflowed the deck into the open hatches, the interior of the U-boat quickly flooded. Within seconds, it was gone.

Walter and Hans looked at the effervescent water and then at each other. They realized there was no turning back as they looked to the darkened shore of an alien land and wondered what—and who—awaited them.

81

Ortega Hacienda, Alabos, Spain
June 1945

* * *

Ernesto and Alberto Ortega and Karl Hoffman were awaiting the arrival of Alfonso Ortega, Paul Hoffman, and his friend Jack Kurtz. They were to be joined later by Anita Ortega and her husband, Enrique, who were heading to the village to pick up mail that had just arrived.

The three men had arrived on the patio early in order to have a private discussion. Alberto and Karl had previously both agreed that Ernesto needed to know about what had happened because of the U-boat depositing the Valhalla cargo on their Rio Muni plantation for safekeeping. They quickly brought him up to date, although only Alberto knew about the possible involvement of Paul Hoffman in the Valhalla events. Ernesto reacted to their update.

"While I'm happy you've shared this information with me, and I understand why it was agreed to, I can only wonder how long this information can be concealed. In particular, I wonder what we should tell Alfonso and Paul, since they are rapidly becoming the day-to-day managers of our operations. Since Alfonso will return to Guinea ultimately, shouldn't we tell him? Since he and Paul are so close, that begs the question of what we should tell Paul."

Alberto quickly responded, "Father, although I trust Paul implicitly, he is closer to the Americans than any of us, especially with the former American ambassador and Paul's friend Jack Kurtz, who is an American intelligence agent. This by itself isn't worrisome, but I believe we should shield Paul from the knowledge we have of Valhalla, and therefore Alfonso also."

Ernesto replied, "Won't he discover what's in the cave on the plantation?"

Karl interjected, "That's not likely because of the discreet way we hid the canisters in the cave. I believe we shouldn't tell Alfonso or Paul about Valhalla for now for their own protection."

As the three men agreed on that course of action and completed their conversation, they heard Paul, Alfonso, and Jack Kurtz arrive. The six men quickly interacted as Paul introduced Jack. Jack and Alberto, of course, had previously met, but none of the others knew that. Ernesto and Karl instantly took a liking to their American visitor, soon to be Paul's brother-in-law. Ernesto, as host, continued the conversation.

"So what have you three been up to? I suspect you may have been lingering at the cantina in the village."

Alfonso, Paul, and Jack all laughed as Alfonso replied, "Indeed we have, Father, and we saw Anita and Enrique pass us on their way to receive our mail. They should be here any minute. We tried to entice them to join us, but Anita insisted she retrieve the mail. There may have been a letter—from Germany."

They all instantly took note of that and there was a momentary silence. Jack quickly seized the opportunity.

"I want to thank all of you for your hospitality. I'm happy I was able to come to Alabos after...my business was concluded. In addition to wanting to meet all of you, I wanted to deliver some important papers." He pulled the documents from his briefcase. "I have here American visas so that all of you can attend Paul's wedding in October, in Denver, Colorado. We would be honored by your presence there."

His hosts seemed both surprised and pleased as Ernesto replied, "We would be honored to attend and will make every effort to do so. Thank you so much, Jack. Paul has been very effusive in his praise of you and it's clear why that is so."

The three men continued their conversation as it drifted inevitably toward politics. Ernesto asked his guest for his perspective on the postwar situation. "We are all more than just curious about how America will deal with Spain now that the war in Europe is over. Can you share any insights on how you believe the situation will unfold?"

Jack replied, now in a serious mood, "I must be frank with you. Despite the best efforts of people like the former American ambassador and myself, I'm afraid that America will initially take a very hard line with Spain. With all due respect, America and most of the wartime allies associate the Franco regime with fascism and active cooperation with the Nazis and don't understand the nuances surrounding your civil war. I believe Spain may be the only country in Europe that will not benefit from postwar American aid. This situation could continue for several years."

Ernesto replied, "Do Americans understand anything about the threat of communism and what the Russians have done in Eastern Europe?"

"No, not yet; sometimes we Americans are too trusting, but I believe we will wake up to that threat eventually. For now, I believe you must look to your own resources to sustain Spain and its economy until the situation changes."

Ernesto replied again, "Thank you, Jack, for your candor—and the other actions you have taken on our behalf. Paul has told us about the wonderful steps you took regarding our business interests in your...special business capacity."

At that moment, before Jack could reply, Anita burst into the room followed by her husband, Enrique. She could barely contain her excitement. "Kirsten is alive! She is alive and in Bernkastel! They couldn't get through by phone or telegram and the letter got misrouted but she is alive. This is such a joyous moment! We must get to Bernkastel as soon as possible."

82.

Bernkastel, Germany
July 1945

* * *

Anita Ortega and Kirsten Hoffman hugged each other in a joyful, tearful embrace the moment they saw each other. Karl and Paul followed as the family experienced the relief that at least part of the tragedy they had experienced was reversed. It was especially moving for Anita and Kirsten since they had instantly bonded at their first meeting before the war.

Karl felt the excruciating pain that Kirsten must be feeling. Although he knew that Kirsten's father was probably still alive, he did not know where he was, and in any case could not tell Kirsten. He was in a similar bind regarding his own son Hans. Karl silently cursed as he realized his frustration in not being able to reveal his knowledge to his family.

The emotions of this week were overpowering in so many ways. Karl, Paul, and Anita were horrified by the destruction they witnessed in Germany. Karl's worst fears had been realized. In addition, how could he let Walter know that his daughter was alive when he had no way of contacting him? He put that thought aside as Anita quickly asserted that she would stay with Kirsten for several weeks after Paul left for New York and Karl returned to Guinea.

83

Times Square, New York City
August 14, 1945, V-J Day

* * *

Paul, Jack, and Liz were caught up in the mood and setting as pandemonium reigned in the middle of the square. Japan had surrendered and the war was over. Brought to its knees by American bombers and submarines, the two atomic bombs dropped on Hiroshima and Nagasaki days earlier had swiftly ended the conflict that could easily have cost millions more Americans and Japanese their lives.

At this point, at least for one or two days, work came to a screeching halt as America celebrated its victory and deferred any discussion of what would come next. The celebration was even more significant than the earlier victories over Italy and Germany. This victory meant that the soldiers, sailors, and airmen would return home at last, although nearly three hundred thousand Americans would not return alive. This paled in comparison to the tens of millions of Russians, Germans, and untold millions of civilians in Europe who had died, but that was a matter for another day.

Paul, Jack, and Liz were ecstatic and celebrating in the moment. As with other Americans, they thanked their good fortune and took the moment to celebrate the victory. America, ever optimistic now, had not yet considered the clouds looming on the horizon.

That would change sooner than anyone realized.

84.

Greenwich Village, New York City
August 24, 1945

* * *

Paul and Jack met at the White Horse Tavern for what was likely to be their last Friday afternoon beer call for a while. The giddy celebration of V-J Day had given way to sober realities regarding the transition from a war economy, the chaotic demobilization of the American armed forces, and other doses of reality. Jack began by filling in Paul on the latest news.

"Well, my friend, it's all settled. I'm being discharged from the army on September 30. Also on that day, my hitch with OSS ends because it will go out of business on October I. Before that, I'm headed to Germany for about four weeks, leaving on Monday, for some unfinished business with regard to analysis of...certain intelligence issues."

"What about law school?" Paul knew better than to ask Jack what "certain intelligence issues" meant.

"I just got final confirmation. I've been accepted into Harvard Law School. Like other schools, they delayed the start of the fall term, in this case to October 15, to accommodate returning veterans. It looks like millions of us will be going to college on the new GI Bill, courtesy of Uncle Sam. The good news is that I won't have a schedule issue attending the wedding on October 6. After my return from Germany I'll head to D.C. for a few days of debriefing, be discharged, and then it's on to Denver."

"That's great, Jack. Congratulations on Harvard; that's a real plum. You must be real smart."

"Stop pulling my leg. You and I both know it's a mixture of luck, timing, and connections, with maybe a little gray matter involved too." Jack paused, noticing that Paul seemed preoccupied.

"Hey, Paul, are you all there today? You look a little lost in space."

"Sorry, Jack; when you mentioned Germany, all I could think about was Hans and Uncle Walter. My father tried to find out about their status when he was in Germany two months ago to be with Kirsten, but it looks like Hans and Walter Hoffman just disappeared off the map. He found out that Walter left Berlin for Northern Germany in early April and then disappeared. Hans last surfaced when he was assigned unspecified special duties in mid-1944 and left no trace after that."

Jack looked at Paul, unsure whether to talk worst case or not.

"Look, Paul, I don't want to paint too rosy a picture. The worst case is that they're both dead, caught up in the final collapse of the Third Reich. But I'll bet that's not the case. Your uncle was a savvy politician and survivor, and your brother survived six years in U-boats. That argues pretty well for their survival, especially if your uncle was using his influence to make sure they had an escape plan. There may be a very good reason why they haven't surfaced yet."

"What would that reason be, Jack, especially for Hans? He was just another ordinary sailor doing his job. If he was alive, he shouldn't have any fear about surfacing."

Jack paused before answering, "Paul, I'm afraid I can't answer that."

"I know, and thanks for leveling with me. However, it did occur to me that you will be in Germany. I'm not asking why you're going there, but if you will be in either Berlin or Wilhelmshaven, maybe you could spare a few hours to poke around any records they might have. I know it would mean a lot, not only to me, but my father also."

Jack smiled. "Of course I can spare a little effort to do that." Jack did not mention that the "certain intelligence issues" he was tasked with involved precisely that—the assessment of German submarine technology.

"Paul, let's drink up here and then head uptown to your uncle's place. Let's call Liz and see if we can all cheer each other up."

"That's a great idea, Jack. I need something to take my mind off these things for a while. I've got a wedding to look forward to in a few weeks."

85.

Wilhelmshaven, Germany
September 1945

* * *

Jack Kurtz was at the end of the third week of his four-week assignment in Germany, and it had been anything other than routine. He was part of two enormous undertakings to find and secure all of the scientific and technological knowledge—and talent—of the defunct Third Reich before the Russians got to it. "Operation Paperclip" focused specifically on this task while a sub-element of the effort, "Operation Alsos," focused on the Nazi nuclear weapons effort. Jack had been brought over specifically to help U.S. Navy specialists evaluate German submarine technology.

By this time, most of the German scientists that mattered had already been spirited out of Germany. Those individuals with extreme Nazi backgrounds were supposedly screened out of the process that allowed them to go work in the United States. Unfortunately, the screening process was not always effective and some ardent Nazis ended up in the United States working for the U.S. government.

Jack had spent most of his time tracking down and evaluating the revolutionary Type 21 submarines. He was pleased that he had been tasked with this assignment since he thought it might give him some additional clues as to the whereabouts of Walter and Hans Hoffman. As it turned out, he would find out more than he bargained for—or expected. On this particular day, he and another specialist were trying to reconcile German records on exactly how many Type 21 U-boats were built. As he sat in the windowless office, he looked over at his teammate, puzzled at what he was finding.

"I don't get it, Frank. Most of our sources show that 118 Type 21 hulls were built and launched but the authoritative source, the one listing the final shipyard tallies for the three shipyards that built them, shows that 119 were built. That's not like our meticulous German record keepers to screw up like that."

Commander Frank Evans was Jack's navy liaison and was both an experienced submariner and a thoughtful analyst. "You're right, Jack. It could be that the shipyard tally was erroneous or it could mean that boat 119 was actually launched and the other records were doctored to show that only 118 were launched."

"So if that's the case, and I tend to believe the final shipyard tallies, then what was the reason for trying to conceal the existence of the 119th boat?"

"That's a good question. Did it get a hull number and which yard was it assigned to?"

Jack pulled the folder with the data he was accumulating on the Type 21 boats. "It would have been the U-3696 and it was assigned to the Danzig yard."

"That's great; all we have to do is go to Danzig, check their records, and interview shipyard personnel. What are the chances that the Russians will let us do that?"

"I would say exactly zero, Frank. The Russians have already put a curtain of secrecy around all the territory they've conquered."

"So much for our wartime allies; we can expect no cooperation with them from this point forward. They're looking more like rivals every day." Evans paused. "Say, did you find any additional information on *Vizeadmiral* Hoffman or his nephew U-boat skipper Hans Hoffman? It seems unlikely that the senior Hoffman could just disappear. We're finding out that he was really well connected with intelligence, special operations, and U-boats."

Jack frowned. "I confirmed that Walter disappeared in early April. Hans had previously fallen off the map in late 1944 when he was assigned to unspecified 'special duties.' Yesterday I also found out that the SS issued a warrant for Walter's arrest, and Hans also, on April 5, 1945, right around the time they disappeared."

"Do you think they caught him and bumped him off? Or he could have been killed by any number of last-minute combat actions, as could Hans."

"Either of those options is possible. But I'm thinking of another possibility that would have Walter and Hans working together on some project. According to his brother, Hans was very close to his uncle and spent far more time with him growing up than with his father. Hans was an experienced and very successful U-boat skipper. Walter could have found that very useful—for the right special assignment."

The two men looked at each other. Evans picked up on Jack's inflection right away.

"Do you really think it might have something to do with the 'missing' Type 21 boat?"

"That's a long shot, Frank. I don't have enough data to connect the dots in that direction, but you know that in the intelligence business you sometimes have to follow your intuition to get to the bottom of things. I need several more weeks to try to sniff this out a little more."

"Jack, you don't have that much time. You and I have exactly five days to complete our reports and ship all this stuff back to the warehouse in Maryland. The discharges and staff cuts from demobilization are now so severe that we won't be able to follow up on most of what we already have."

Jack sat back in his chair and let out a long sigh. "I hear you. I sure hope we don't end up missing something really important because we don't have time to complete proper intelligence analysis."

"Yeah, maybe Hitler actually did escape to Argentina in one of those two boats." Evans was referring to the two U-boats that had escaped to Argentina and had been interned.

"Frank, there could be more critical things that a U-boat could smuggle out of Germany."

86

Colorado Springs, Colorado
October 7, 1945

* * *

Paul Hoffman and Liz Kurtz were married on October 6 in a beautiful ceremony conducted outside at the Garden of the Gods. They held their reception at the exclusive Broadmoor Hotel. The wedding venue was changed from Denver to accommodate Liz's grandparents, who lived in Colorado Springs and were in fragile health.

Besides his father, Paul succeeded in enticing some of the Ortega clan to make the long journey from Spain to Colorado. Ramon Ortega, long an American citizen, had traveled from New York. From Spain, Alfonso Ortega traveled to Colorado with his wife, Francesca, and was honored to be the best man. Both Paul and his father deeply felt the loss of Hans and Ernst, and Alfonso did his best to fill Hans's shoes. Ernesto and Ana Ortega also attended, along with their daughter, Anita, and her husband, Enrique. Alberto Ortega could not attend but did obtain leave from the Spanish navy to stay in Alabos with his ailing seventy-five-year-old grandmother, Maria Ortega.

The Ortega clan arrived two weeks early and toured America. They traveled by air to the West Coast, since Ernesto wanted to visit the California wine country, and then by rail back to Colorado Springs. They would begin their journey back to Spain the following week.

Paul and Liz planned to begin their honeymoon the following day, taking their own aerial tour of the West in Paul's Spartan Executive. Paul spent the day with Liz and the wedding guests. Late in the day, however, Liz urged Paul to get together with Jack one last time, since he was leaving the next day for Boston to enter Harvard Law School.

Paul and Jack met at a nearby inn in Manitou Springs and sat out on the deck in the unseasonably warm and crystal-clear air, admiring the view of Pikes Peak and the nearby Rampart Range while enjoying their beers. Paul got the conversation going.

"This place just lifts my spirit so much. New York is great, but I love the West and having the airplane makes me appreciate it even more. Someday I see Liz and me moving out here. Maybe we'll expand the family's wine business to California."

"That's a pretty cool vision, Paul. Just make sure you leave a forwarding address."

They both laughed. "Don't worry, Jack. I'll see to it that my best friend always knows where I am. You just need to buckle down and get through law school."

Both men smiled at each other, and an awkward silence then ensued. Clearly both men had much on their minds on this fine day as the huge transitions in their lives were overtaking them. Paul finally broke the spell with the inevitable question.

"We really haven't had much time to talk since you returned from Germany. You weren't, by any chance, able to find out anything...about...Walter and Hans?"

Jack was expecting the question, but given what he knew, or thought could be possible, he didn't want to say anything that would provide too much hope. In any case, everything that he had learned was classified.

"Paul, I was only able to confirm what you told me before we left. I'm sorry."

"That's OK; that's what I thought. The last months of the war were so tragic. We may not find out what happened to my brother or uncle. That, and Ernst's death, has really affected my father, but Liz and I have told him that we will all press on together. I'm happy that we have our extended family. The Ortegas are great, and now I have Liz and her family. I know that my father will be looking for grandchildren, so it looks like I have to do the deed."

They both laughed, more at ease now, as Jack replied, "That's what I see too, Paul. Your family has stuck together and I know you'll prosper. I can see how you and Alfonso are already inheriting the mantle from your fathers. Your collective family businesses, your lives, and your culture are all interwoven, and so is your destiny. It will be interesting to look back on this time about fifty years from now and reflect on all the events we lived through—and what it all meant."

"That's the truth. I don't think we'll even have to wait that long. I'd like to think we'll now have a long period of peace, prosperity, and stability, but I don't want to be naïve. I'm worried especially about what will happen in Spain and in the rest of Europe. The conditions there are such that it could provide just the right conditions for another communist revolution."

Jack looked at Paul and then replied somberly, "I agree with you, Paul, but I think that the good old USA will come to the rescue, and sooner rather than later. We may have our head in the sand now but it won't last long. We can't afford to let the Russians take over the rest of Europe."

"I hope you're right, Jack. However it plays out, I know I've always been ambiguous about who I really am since coming to America. Am I a Spaniard or am I an American? I know my father has always had to face that dichotomy too. Is he a German or a Spaniard? He really made his choice years ago, as his life evolved, and I'll probably do the same. My father loves Spain, and he's pained by its suffering. He feels the agony of Germany too." He paused. "You know, in the final analysis, I still think it's possible to love your country and still be a world citizen; but what really counts are our families and our emotional roots."

"That's my philosophy too, Paul. Let's drink to that and to our futures. Here's to the best years of our lives."

The two men drank their toast and watched as the brilliant sun set slowly over Pikes Peak—the sunset to be followed by the dawn of their changing lives.

Epilogue

Shattered by the effects of the Second World War, Europe lay in ruins, economically impotent. The old order had been destroyed, and even for the victors, the resulting economic devastation almost constituted a Pyrrhic victory. Upon conquering Eastern Europe and Germany, Soviet Russia threw a cordon around the captured territories creating what Winston Churchill was soon to call the Iron Curtain. With the rapid demobilization of America's conventional military, only its atomic monopoly could prevent further Soviet encroachment. Within three years of the peace, America would be victorious in the first battle of the cold war as it staged the Berlin Airlift.

America itself quickly transitioned to peace, the most powerful nation on earth by far. America was still a net oil exporter and it exported just about everything else and was the world's most powerful creditor, loaning the money to European nations to fight the war. The pent-up economic demand from the Depression and years of rationing, and the college educations for millions of returning GIs, set the stage for the growth that would follow, creating the American Century.

The rest of the world was seething too as decolonization became the dominant international theme. India and Pakistan broke lose from Britain in 1947 and the Dutch lost their futile battle to retain the Netherlands East Indies when Indonesia achieved its independence in 1949.

Other colonial battles dragged out and were bloodier. The French were beaten by the Viet Minh and lost Indochina in 1955, and then began the wholesale granting of independence to its African empire, largely completed by 1960 in sub-Saharan Africa and finishing with Algeria in 1962. Only in Portugal's large African colonies and Spain's much smaller ones did colonialism linger for a few more years after that.

In Europe, Spain, still suffering from the lingering effects of its civil war, was ostracized for several years for its support of Nazi Germany. It sheltered some Nazi refugees and this further enraged the wartime Allies. It took the cold war and the Pact of Madrid in 1953 to finally allow Spain to rejoin the West, as the United States sought bases for its nuclear bombers and provided economic aid in return.

Two families, the Hoffmans of Germany and the Ortegas of Spain, continued to survive and flourish in their bond, although their solidity was marred by the tragic loss—or disappearance—of family members. Paul Hoffman and Alfonso Ortega began to assume the mantle for leading their families and managing their vast landholdings and fortunes. Their fathers, Karl Hoffman and Ernesto Ortega, continued to mentor their sons and guide the families to their destiny. In addition, the strong women in the families were beginning to emerge as *Anita Ortega* and later *Kirsten Hoffman* would become noted wine makers, following in the footsteps of their grandfathers. They would ultimately lay the groundwork for a new economic foundation for the families, replacing the economic importance of their cocoa and coffee plantations in Spanish Guinea.

The deaths of Wilhelm, Ernst, Erica, and Freya Hoffman were tragic and deeply felt by both families, as was Pilar's untimely death on the Athenia. But weighing even more on Karl and Paul Hoffman were the disappearance of Karl's brother, Walter, and Paul's brother, Hans. The weight of the tragedy could be relived only by the solace of the birth of a new generation.

The two families' astute policies and unshakeable bond would propel them to greater achievement, as new members of the extended family provided support. Jack Kurtz would graduate from law school—but would be drawn back to his wartime vocation as his fate unfolded. That would play out in some startling ways.

The initial postwar years were times of transition for the Hoffmans and Ortegas, yet always lingering were the questions they inherited from the war and its aftermath.

How could Spain escape turmoil?

How would the families' future shift among America, Europe, Africa—and elsewhere?

Would they ever learn the fate of Walter and Hans Hoffman?

Most importantly, what were the contents of the mysterious canisters transported to Spanish Guinea by the submarine U-3696—and who would rediscover them?

TO BE CONTINUED

Author's Historical Notes

It would be difficult to imagine a more eventful, and dangerous, time than the period 1915–1945, especially if you came of age in Germany, Spain, or the United States. Our two fictional protagonists, Karl Hoffman and his son Paul, confronted numerous challenges as they clung to their dreams and the ties to their expanded family in Spain. Both world wars were shattering experiences for two generations, but the Spanish Civil War may have been the most tragic experience of all for the fictional Ortega and Hoffman families, as it was for all Spaniards. The wounds from that bitter conflict have not entirely healed but have merely been submerged, still seething below the surface.

I have endeavored to construct a realistic and accurate sequence of events that might have happened to my characters, based on real events that enveloped them and in which they could have participated. These are some of the highlights of the most interesting of such events.

1. In late 1915 and early 1916, the German colonial army in Kamerun, the *Schutztruppe,* was indeed surrounded by allied forces and chose internment in Spanish Guinea and Spain rather than surrender, enabling the fictitious Karl Hoffman to marry and start a family while World War I raged on.

2. Admiral Canaris, the mysterious head of the German *Abwehr* from 1935 to 1944, was a frequent visitor to Spain from 1916 until 1943. It cannot authoritatively be said that he met with the American OSS chief, William Donovan, in Spain in 1943; many sources indicate it was possible or even likely.

3. The OSS operated a large wartime network of agents in Spain, and the OSS frequently clashed with American Ambassador Carlton Hayes regarding the best way to keep Spain out of the war. Hayes was, in fact, a history professor at Columbia University before assuming the ambassador's post in Madrid from 1942 to 1945. Our fictional protagonist Paul Hoffman, as a Columbia student, could easily have had a close relationship with Hayes.

4. One of the most critical secret operations of the war, Operation Fortitude, was conducted by the Allies to deceive the Germans regarding the location of the allied invasion of France in 1944. A key person in this deception was Spanish double agent Juan Pujol, known as agent Garbo to the Allies and agent Arabel to the Germans. My fictional character Paul Hoffman performed this role also, possibly as a means to confirm to the Germans that Arabel was telling them the truth (when in fact, both Garbo and Paul Hoffman fed the Germans incorrect information). Unlike Garbo, who spent most of his time in Portugal, Paul Hoffman exposed himself to danger as a double agent by conducting his operations in Spain.

5. The governor of Spanish Guinea in 1940 did, in fact, prepare a paper for Franco before his only meeting with Hitler in October 1940, outlining Spanish demands from Germany before Spain would enter the war. It would be easy to imagine the fictional Karl Hoffman, as an influential plantation owner, providing support to the colonial governor for this project.

6. There were few places on the planet that escaped the impact of World War II. In fact, British Special Forces did seize three Axis ships interned in the neutral harbor of Santa Isabel, Spanish Guinea, in Operation Postmaster in January 1942.

7. As World War II climaxed, many Nazi officials escaped to Spain, aided and abetted by the Franco government and the Vatican. Leon Degrelle, the famous Belgian Nazi collaborator and SS officer, did make his escape to Spain on the last day of the war, flying in a *Luftwaffe* bomber from Norway.

8. Of all the top Nazi officials, the highest ranking one who disappeared without a trace was Gestapo Chief Heinrich Muller. Perhaps he escaped to Spain on his way to...?

9. On the American home front, the wartime bureaucratic battles between the FBI and the OSS were legendary. This had a severe impact on American "human intelligence" gathering, and it was fortunate indeed that our code breaking efforts, known as Ultra, were so successful. German submarines were notorious for excessive radio chatter, but it's conceivable that some German efforts (i.e. the fic-

tional Operation Valhalla) were conducted under complete radio and communications silence and hence were "Beyond Ultra."

10. The German scientific community was completely harnessed for World War II and introduced futuristic weapons in combat, such as the cruise missile (the V-1), jet aircraft, and short-range ballistic missiles (the V-2). They also tested an early version of an intercontinental ballistic missile (the A-9) that, when perfected, could have reached the United States. It was fortunate that they did not make as much progress with atomic weapons (or did they?). However, if the war had lasted another two years, the results could have been different. Both the United States and the Soviet Union scooped up a lot of this technology when the war ended, as well as many of the German scientists who made it possible. It was no wonder that the United States all too often chose not to look too closely at the Nazi backgrounds of these scientists.

Made in the USA
Charleston, SC
29 May 2011